can work their spells for good or ill when their power is invoked in such fantasy adventures as:

"Geese"—To escape a tyrant's deadly curse she took flight only to find that evil must be fought not fled from. . . .

"Heart's Desires"—Would she be forced to forswear sorcery for marriage and a ruler's throne?

"Song of the Dragon"—Did she dare go beyond magic's bounds to uncover the master sorcerer's secret, a mystery which no student had ever been able to solve?

"East of the Dawn"—Trapped in a human body, could she master her family's shape-changing magic by journeying to a land beyond the Dawn?

SWORD AND SORCERESS VIII

SWORD AND SORCERESS VIII

AN ANTHOLOGY OF HEROIC FANTASY

Edited by
Marion Zimmer Bradley

DAW BOOKS, INC.
DONALD A. WOLLHEIM, FOUNDER
375 Hudson Street, New York, NY 10014

ELIZABETH R. WOLLHEIM
SHEILA E. GILBERT
PUBLISHERS

DAW Book Collectors No. 859.

First Printing, September 1991

1   2   3   4   5   6   7   8   9

TABLE OF CONTENTS

INTRODUCTION

This year, as usual, I received about twice as many good stories as I could use, and I underwent the usual last-minute agonizing reappraisals based more on the inelasticity of the typeface than on the virtues or lack of same of any single individual story.

Part of this is due to the fact that this is now a known market, and we no longer get the perfectly godawful stories. The kiddies who write epics in purple crayon on brown bags—don't laugh, I used to get them, the ones who want to sell me spaceship stories, or the women with more feminist message than story now know me well enough to know they had better go elsewhere; and they have crawled back under their rocks. They know that if they send me single-spaced three page blank-verse epics they won't get anything but a copy of "How to Prepare a Manuscript," and maybe a copy of my "Advice to Young Writers." That's what it is to create a market, for which DAW Books can take at least part of the credit. The conventional wisdom still says short stories don't sell, but all these anthologies are still in print and many of them have been reprinted in England, Germany, and Italy.

So this year, despite many threats to my health—I spent my sixtieth birthday in the hospital, and I chose the final line-up from my hospital bed—I received more good manuscripts than ever. So if your story does not appear in this lineup it means, not that your story wasn't

7

good—on the contrary I received stories which, if they had been sent to me the first year I was doing this, would have been greeted with what my older son would have called "great squeeches of joy," and printed, but are now drowned out by too many others. More and more I am forced to fall back on the inelasticity of typeface as a reason for rejection.

So how do I choose among what has almost become an embarrassment of riches? Among other things I look for old friends; I know that some writers I've used before can be trusted to produce a good story—though one of the temptations to be guarded against in writing of a series heroine, or any series, is to keep writing the same book—or the same story—over and over. When I get discouraged (as any writer/editor frequently does), I wonder if that's what the reading public really wants . . . the same story over and over again.

But I admit it; I am always glad to receive a story which I know will be good from one of "my" writers whom I can trust to produce at least something readable. But one of the major challenges to any editor is to produce new writers. Because writers die—and I've just had a sharp lesson that we're all mortal. They also get new and exciting jobs which leave them little or no time or inclination to write, take up teaching, have new babies, go on honeymoons or round the world cruises, or sell novels, leaving them less time for short story writing; and what's a poor editor to do? So every day's new load of manuscripts is greeted with enthusiasm; I'm still hoping to discover something in it which is so good I can't bear to part with it. My cousin recently brought me a button which said "So many books; so little time." An editor could almost modify this by saying, "So many manuscripts; so few market slots."

But the cry will always be *send me something I can print*. A lot of what I get is still hopelessly bad; but my problem is not how much bad stuff I get, but the embarrassment of riches—at least for this anthology. But if you could be discouraged by the odds, you wouldn't have become a writer. I have a sign over my desk which reads "Nobody told you not to be a plumber." I keep remembering that on bad days; I could always have become a plumber. Sometimes when I'm hopelessly entangled in the flood of repetitive spaceship stories and perfectly run-of-the-mill generic sorceresses, I find myself thinking wistfully of pipe wrenches.

But it never lasts long. And then I'm ready for the next day's mail—which might have *your* story in it.

Maybe it will be something I can print. Maybe it won't. I can only say "try again." But then, if any of us were that easily discouraged we wouldn't be writers, would we?

MASKS
by Deborah Burros

One of the letters I never get tired of is the letter that begins something like this; "When I received your acceptance, I jumped up and down." That's because, though it was a lot longer ago than I like thinking about, I was also one of those wet-behind-the ears would-be writers, celebrating a first acceptance—and I still remember what it felt like.

That, however, does not explain something else. Why it is that when I give my occupation as "Writer" everyone asks "Oh, have you ever been published?" I wonder if they ask a plumber "Oh, have you ever fixed a sink?" Do they ask a doctor if he has ever taken out an appendix? But a writer is always asked if he's been published.

Well, I could be wrong; but to me an unpublished writer isn't a *writer*, but only a would-be writer, and it's publication that separates the would-bes from the actual ones. Anyhow, Deborah Burros has now joined the company of actual (as distinguished from potential) writers; and we hope it's the first of many sales.

This particular story isn't much like what I usually print; but for some unknown reason it reminded me of the classic of fantasy, Robert W. Chambers' "The King in Yellow." Don't ask me why; some random association of ideas, no doubt.

I usually dislike fables; but it seems to me that "Masks" is a fable, and a very subtle one at that.

Deborah Burros is now working on a Master's in library

science and has formerly been a copy editor for a physics journal and a copywriter for a medical publisher; good jobs, both of them, for a writer. And now she can legitimately add "writer" to her resume. She might anyhow; now people can take it seriously. I remember back when I was living in Texas, I gave my occupation once as "writer" to a city official. "Oh, we don't count that," he said, blithely writing down "housewife."

"Oh, goody," I responded. "Does that mean I don't need to pay any income taxes on it?"

"Oh, you're a *published* writer?" he asked.

Well, it got straightened out; but from then on, I gave my occupation as "novelist." They took that a little more seriously.

"**N**o more masks for sale," said the maskmaker to the lady who had just flounced into the shop. The lady tossed back her perfumed curls and scarcely glanced at the empty hooks or at the maskmaker she deigned to address. "I shall have something unique— I saw an early reveler wearing a twin to the mask I was to wear tonight, and that will never do! Then I saw your little shop. . . ."

"Let me reiterate: no more masks for sale." The maskmaker's face and voice were politely bland and, with her ashen hair and gray smock and gloves, she was a drab figure.

The lady smoothed the sanguine lace of her overdress, careful not to snag it on her rings. "Nothing insipid: no rainbow-maned unicorns, no pastel doves."

This time, the maskmaker responded with silence.

The tapping of one of the lady's velvet-shod feet punctuated the silence.

Finally: "Very well, so you have sold all your wares for Midsummer's Fête. How about your *own* mask for tonight? Indeed, a mask from a maskmaker's private collection must be truly dramatic and unique!"

The maskmaker's lips twitched once, but her expression remained otherwise bland along with her voice. "I do not plan to be here for the festival, though I do have a mask intended for my use only and not for sale—"

"—but you shall sell it to me. I insist."

The maskmaker disguised a hiss as a sigh. Then she slipped into a curtained alcove, paused, clicked metal against metal, slid something open and then shut, paused again, and emerged holding a porcelain mask.

The mask was an empress' face of vulpine cheekbones and scimitar eyebrows and a delicately sneering mouth, its porcelain beauty poxed with rubies and blistered with pearls.

The maskmaker spoke. "I give you what you need and send you on your way."

Plucking the mask from the hands of the maskmaker, the lady tried it on. "It will do." She tossed a purse on the floor.

She was about to remove the mask—the maskmaker darted forward and shoved her through the doorway. Out into the city.

But the city's sky had never been so sulfurous, nor had there ever been so many smoking chimneys. In the murk, phosphorescent slime oozed along what should have been clean gutters; it advanced a pseudopod toward the lady's feet, overriding her shock so that she scurried out of reach—almost into a group of coughing pallbearers. And there had never been coffins as clear as glass: clear enough, unfortunately, for her to be able to see the distorted bodies.

She whirled around and ran for the maskmaker's shop. There was no such shop; only a cul-de-sac where a man was peddling ampules of anthrax and ergot.

"No more masks for sale," said the maskmaker to the girl who had just edged into the shop.

"Oh, of course not—I'm sorry—I knew I was too late." Her voice sounded relieved instead of disappointed; also, it was muffled by the iridescent scarf she clutched around her face.

The maskmaker peered at her. "Stop. Why do you *not*

want a mask? Do you not *want* to take part in tonight's fête?"

"Yes'm."

The maskmaker waited.

The girl flushed. "Yes, I do. It's—it's afterward, after I must remove the mask, that I don't want . . ." She hesitated, then pushed back the scarf to reveal a face tracked with birthmarks.

"If only it would not matter when I show my face."

The maskmaker slipped into the curtained alcove again, emerging with another mask.

This mask was a leopard's face made of tawny velvet with rosettes of black spangles, with its eyes outlined in emeralds, and with a medley of beads trailing from it by ribbons of gold.

The maskmaker spoke: "I give you what you need and send you on your way."

The girl reached out a hand to stroke the mask with her fingertips. The maskmaker nodded encouragement; the girl tried it on. Dreamily, she fumbled in her pocket for some coins.

Then, as she was about to remove the mask—the maskmaker darted forward and nudged her through the doorway. Out into the city.

But in the city there had never been leopards sunning themselves on mosaic stoops, nor had there been orchids festooning the avenue and peacocks promenading beneath them. The girl brushed against a spray of these orchids, sending fritillaries into flight.

She turned around to where the maskmaker's shop would be. It was not; instead, there was a courtyard where sculptors carved malachite. They smiled at her. She removed her mask; they smiled more delightedly and began to carve her likeness from the ocellated stone.

In the shop, the maskmaker slipped one last time behind the curtain. She emerged with a valise containing other special masks.

The maskmaker put her hands to her face and tugged, peeling her face away to reveal a steel ovoid with crystalline eyes. She tucked the rubbery mask into the valise, which was bigger on the inside than the outside, and selected from it her next mask.

It was a dragon's face with scales of thick amber and with spikes that were the thin, gold hands from antique clocks.

The maskmaker put on the mask and stepped through the doorway.

WINGS OF FIRE
by Mercedes Lackey

As I've probably said before—I do tend to repeat myself in these introductions, but at least I'm consistent—it's a great pleasure every time to bring back an old friend or friends. Mercedes Lackey was introduced in the third of these volumes, as were her series characters, Tarma and Kethry, swordswoman and sorceress. Every year I read—and reject—a couple of dozen writers who write to me about their "new series." But that isn't how it's done. If I know it's a series, all you'll get is a rejection slip; but if I think the first story is good on its own, I'll buy a second; and maybe a third or fourth, as with Lackey's Tarma and Kethry, or Diana Paxson's Shanna, who has been in all but one of these volumes. But, not contented with that, Mercedes Lackey has written several other books: three novels about Tarma and Kethrey, six "Herald" novels, which I like in spite of their having sentient horses as major characters (the charm of horses somehow escapes me, probably due to my starting out in life by shoveling stables); and contemporary occult novels: BURNING WATER, and her newest one, about a (are you ready for this?) a Japanese vampire.

Mercedes Lackey lives in Tulsa, Oklahoma. Having lived in the desert belt myself, I can only say it's a good place to write—there's not much else to do there, unless you like football. But the locals might get the idea you're a Satanist or something because you write about them. I speak from experience; probably it was because I wasn't much of a churchgoer, though I did teach choir for a while in the Methodist church.

Heat-haze shimmered above the grass stems, and insects droned monotonously, hidden down near the roots or swaying up near the new seed heads. There was a wind, a hot one, full of the scent of baking earth, drying grass, and the river nearby. Kethry held a half-finished basket in her hands, leaned back against a smooth, cool boulder in the shade of her tent, and drowsed. Jadrie was playing with the other youngsters beside the river—Lyan and Laryn were learning to ride, six-month-old Jadrek was with Tarma and Warrl, who were watching him and the other babies of Liha'irden, sensibly sleeping the afternoon heat away. All four of the children were safe, safer than at home, with all of Liha'irden watching out for them.

Kethry felt perfectly justified in stealing a little nap herself. The basket could wait a bit longer.

Then a child's scream shattered the peace of the afternoon.

"Mama!"

Kethry reacted to that cry of fear as quickly as any mother would—though most mothers wouldn't have snatched up a sword and unsheathed it as they jumped to their feet.

Even so, she was a heartbeat behind Tarma, who was already running in the direction of Jadrie's cry, toward the trees lining the river.

"Mama, *hurry!*" Jadrie cried again, and Kethry blessed the Shin'a'in custom of putting women in breeches instead of skirts. She sprinted like a champion across the space that the herds had trampled bare as they went to and from the waterside twice a day.

As she fought through the screening of brush and came out on the bank under the willows, the first thing she saw was Jadrie, standing less than a horse-length away. The girl was as white as the pale river sand, with both hands stuffed in her mouth—she seemed rooted to the riverbank as she stared down at something.

Kethry sheathed her sword and snatched her daughter up with such relief washing over her that her knees were weak. Jadrie buried her face in her mother's shoulder and only *then* burst into tears.

And only then did Kethry look down to the river itself, to see what had frightened her otherwise fearless child half out of her wits.

Tarma was already down there, kneeling beside someone. A body—but a wreck of one. Shin'a'in, by the coloring; a shaman, by what was left of the clothing. Tarma had gotten him turned onto his back, and his chest was a livid network of burn lines, as if someone had beaten him with a whip made of fine, red-hot wires. Kethry had seen her share of tortured bodies, but this made even her nauseous. She could only hope that what Jadrie had seen had been hidden by river water or mud.

Probably not, by the way she's crying and shaking. My poor baby—

The man stirred, moaned. Kethry bit back a gasp; the man was still alive! She couldn't imagine how anyone could have lived through that kind of punishment. Tarma looked up at the bank, and Kethry knew that cold anger, that look of *someone's going to pay*.

And *get the child out of here*.

Kethry didn't need urging; she picked Jadrie up and stumbled back to the camp as fast as she could with the burden of a six-year-old in her arms.

By now the rest of the Shin'a'in were boiling up out of the camp like wasps churning from a broken nest; wasps with stings, for every hand held some kind of weapon. Kethry waved back at the river and gasped out something about the Healer—she wasn't sure what, but it must have made some kind of sense, for Liha'irden's Healer, the man who had nursed Tarma back to reluctant life so many years ago, put on a burst of speed that left the rest trailing in his wake.

Kethry slowed her own pace, as the Clansfolk streamed past her; Jadrie had stopped crying and now only shivered in her arms, despite the heat. Kethry held her closer; Jadrie was both the sunniest and the most sensitive of the children so far. So far she had never seen anything to indicate that the world was not one enormous adventure.

Today—she had just learned that adventures can be dangerous.

Today, she had learned one of life's hardest lessons; that the universe is not a friendly place. And Kethry sat down in the shade of the nearest tent and held her as she cried for the pain of that lesson. She was still crying when angry and frightened voices neared, passed the tent walls, and continued in the direction of the Healer's tent.

When Jadrie had cried herself to exhaustion, Kethry put her to bed in the tent she and Tarma shared with the four children, gathered her courage, and started for the Healer's tent herself.

There was no crowd outside the tent, and the gathered Clansfolk appeared to have dispersed, but the entire encampment was on the alert now. Though there was no outward difference, Kethry could feel the tension, as if a storm sat just below the horizon, out of sight, but not out of sensing range.

She met Tarma coming out of the tent, and the tight lines of anger around her partner's mouth told her everything she needed to know.

"Warrl can guard the children. Do we stay here?" she asked. "Or do we ride?"

Tarma paused for a moment, and in that silence, the keening wail with which the Shin'a'in mourned their dead began. Her eyes narrowed, and Kethry saw her jaw harden.

"We ride," the Shin'a'in said, around clenched teeth.

They followed the river northward all day; then, when it dived beneath the cliff, up the switchback trail at the edge of the Dhorisha Plains. They reached the top at about sunset but pushed on well past dusk, camping after dark in the midst of the pine-redolent Pelagiris Forest. Tarma had been silent the entire trip; Kethry burned to know what had happened but knew she was going to have to wait for her partner to speak.

Being an Adept-class mage meant that Kethry no longer had to be quite so sparing of her magical energies; she could afford to make a pair of witch-lights to give them enough light to gather wood and to light the fire Tarma laid with a little spark of magic. It wasn't a very big fire—in this heat, they only needed it to sear the rabbit they shared—but Tarma sat staring into the last flames after she'd finished eating. Light from the flames revealed the huge trees nearest their campsite, trees so old and so large that Tarma could not encircle them with her arms, and so tall that the first branchings occurred several man-heights above the ground. Most of the time, the place felt a little like a temple; tonight, it felt more like a tomb.

"He didn't tell us much before he died," Tarma said, finally. "By his clothing, what was left of it, he was *For'a'hier*—that's Firefalcon Clan."

"Are they—all gone, do you think?" Kethrny could not help thinking of what had happened to *Tale'sedrin*, but Tarma shook her head.

"They're all right. We sent someone off to them, but he told us he was on his own. Firefalcon has always been—different; the Clan that produces the most shaman, even an occasional mage. They're known to roam quite a bit, sometimes right off the Plains. This one was a *laj'ele'ruvon*, a knowledge-seeker, and he had come seeking up here, in *Tale'edras* territory—the shaman of Firefalcon have a lot more contact with the *Tale'edras* than the rest of us do. Whatever happened to him, happened here in the Forest."

"You don't think the Hawkbrothers—" Somehow that didn't ring true, and Kethry shook her head even as Tarma echoed the gesture.

"No—there's a Hawkbrother mixed up in it somehow, he said that much before he died, but it was no *Tale'edras* that did that. I think he was trying to tell me the Hawkbrother was in trouble, somehow." Tarma rubbed her temple, her expression baffled. "I've been trying to think of a way that a Hawkbrother could possibly get into trouble, and I—"

Something screamed, just above their heads. Kethry nearly jumped out of her own skin, squeaked, and clutched Need's hilt.

The scream came again, and this time Kethry recognized it for what it was; the call of the owl-eagle, a nocturnal predator with the habits and silent flight of an owl, but the general build of an eagle. She might not have recognized it, except that a pair were nesting near the Keep, and her husband Jadrek spent hours every evening in delighted observation of them.

Tarma stood up, stared into the tree canopy, then suddenly kicked earth over the fire, dousing it. When Kethry's eyes had adjusted to the dark, she could hardly believe them. Hovering overhead was an owl-eagle, all right, a much bigger bird than either of the pair she'd seen before—and stark white.

"That's a *Tale'edras* bird," Tarma said grimly. "They say the birds their mages use turn white after a while. I think he's been sent for help."

As if in reply, the owl-eagle screamed once more and flew off to the north and west, landing on a branch and looking back for all the world as if it expected them to follow it. Kethry put her hand on her partner's arm to restrain her for a moment. "What are we going to do about the horses?"

"Damn. Release them, I guess. They'll head straight back to camp in the morning." Tarma didn't look happy about the decision, but there wasn't much else they *could* do; they certainly couldn't leave them, nor could they ride them through dark woods where they couldn't see where to put their feet. And leading them would be just as bad as riding them.

On the other hand, walking back to camp across the Plains in midsummer—

"Let's just leave them unhobbled, and try to get back before morning," Kethry suggested. "They won't stray until then." Tarma grimaced, but pulled the hobbles from her mare's feet and threw them on the pile of tack while Kethry did the same. When she looked up, the owl-eagle was still there, still waiting.

He didn't move until they were within a few arm-lengths of the tree—and then it was only to fly off and land in another tree, farther to the north and west. Kethry had had a little niggling doubt at first as to whether her partner had read the situation correctly, but now she was sure; the bird wanted them to follow.

It continued to lead them in that fashion for what felt like weeks, though by the moon shining directly down through the tree branches, it wasn't much past midnight. Now that they'd left the road, it was impossible to tell where they were; one enormous tree looked like every other enormous tree. For the past several candlemarks, she'd been feeling an increase in ambient mage-energies; her skin prickled so much with it that she felt forced to shield herself, and she wasn't entirely sure that time was passing at its normal rate.

"Where are we?" she whispered finally to her partner.

Tarma stopped for a moment and peered up at the moon. "I don't know," she admitted. "I'm lost. Someplace a lot west and some north of where we started. I don't—I don't think we're in the Pelagiris Forest anymore; I think we're in Pelagir Hills type country. I wish we'd brought the furball with us, now."

"I hate to admit it, but I agree—" Kethry began.

And that was when an enormous, invisible fist closed around them.

The bird shrieked in alarm and shot skyward. Tarma cursed; Kethry was too busy trying to breathe.

It's the paralysis-spell, she thought, even as she struggled to get a little more air into her lungs. But she couldn't breathe in without first breathing *out*, and every time she did that, the hand closed tighter on her chest. *That's—supposed—to—be—*

A darkness that had nothing to do with the hour dimmed the moonlight, and her lungs screamed for air.

—lost—

Blackness swooped in like a stooping hawk, and covered her.

Her chest hurt; that was the first thing she knew when she woke again. She opened her eyes as she felt something cool and damp cross her brow, and gazed with dumb surprise up into a pair of eyes as blue as Tarma's, but in an indisputably male face crowned with frost-white hair.

Indisputably? Not—quite. There was something unusual about him. Not that he was *she'chorne*, that she had no trouble spotting. Something like that, and not even remotely evil, but very, very different.

Beyond the face were bars glinting and shining as only polished metal could; and two light-sources, one that flared intermittently outside of her line-of-sight, and one that could only be a witch-light, hovering just outside the bars.

The stranger smiled wanly when he saw that she was awake and draped the cloth he'd been using to bathe her forehead over the edge of a metal bowl beside him. "Forgive me, lady," he said in oddly-accented Shin'a'in. "I did not intend to lure anyone into captivity when I sent out my bond-bird."

"That owl-eagle was yours?" she said, trying not to breathe too quickly, since every movement made her chest ache the more.

"Aye," he replied, "I sent her for my own kin, but she saw your magic and came to you instead. Now she is frightened past calling back."

"But I didn't—" Kethry started to say, then saw the wary look in the Hawkbrother's eyes. *We're being watched and listened to. For some reason, he doesn't want whoever caught us to know his bird can See passive mage-shields, the way Warrl can.* She struggled to sit up, and the Hawkbrother assisted her unobtrusively.

They were in a cage, one with a perfectly ordinary lock. Beside them was another—with no lock at all—holding Tarma. The Shin'a'in sat cross-legged in the middle of the contraption, with a face as expressionless as a stone.

Only her eyes betrayed that she was in a white-hot

rage; so intense a blue that her glance crackled across the space between them.

Both cages sat in the middle of what looked like a maze; perfectly trimmed, perfectly trained hedges taller than a man on horseback, forming a square "room" with an opening in each "wall." Beyond the opening, Kethry thought she saw yet more hedges.

"As you see," said a new voice, female, with an undertone of petulance, "I plan my prisons well."

The owner of the voice moved into the pallid light cast by the witch-ball; Kethry was not impressed. Face and body attested to overindulgence; the mouth turned down in a perpetual sneer, and the eyes would not look into hers directly. Even allowing for the witch-light, her complexion was doughy, and her hair was an indeterminate no-color between mouse-brown and blonde. Her clothing, however, was rich in a conspicuous, overblown way, as if her gown shouted "See how expensive I am!" It was also totally inappropriate for the middle of a forest, but that didn't seem to bother the wearer.

"For the mages," their captor said, gesturing grandly, "A cage which nullifies magic, with a lock that can only be opened by an ordinary key." She held up the key hanging at her belt. "And since I am as female as you, the spirit-sword won't work against *me*. Even if you could reach it."

Now Kethry saw the blade hanging just outside the cage door, just out of reach.

Of arms. That's her frist mistake.

"For the warrior, a prison that only *magic* can unlock."

She giggled girlishly, without the sneer ever changing. Tarma said nothing; Kethry decided to follow her example. Their jailer posed, waiting, doubtless, for one of them to ask why they were being held. Finally, when she got no response, she scowled and flounced off in the direction of the light that flared and subsided, somewhere beyond the bushes surrounding the clearing where their cages sat.

"When her wits aren't out wandering, who *is* this

woman?" Tarma asked, in a lazy drawl. "And what in the name of the frozen hells does she want with us?"

The Hawkbrother crossed his arms over his chest, leaned back against the bars of the cage, and grimaced. "Her name is Keyjon, and all her magics are stolen," he said, an anger as hot as Tarma's roughening his voice. "As for what she wants—nothing from you, except to be used against me. As my friend was, to his death."

The Firefalcon shaman. He knows the lad died. She tried to read beyond the Hawkbrother's lack of expression and couldn't.

"We're to be used to get what?" Tarma asked.

"Something she cannot steal from me, though she has tried, and blunted her stolen tools on *my* protections." He pointed his chin in the direction of the flaring and dying light. "She has firebirds."

At Kethry's swift intake of breath, he nodded. "I see you know them."

"One of the qualifications for entering the higher levels of a White Winds school used to be the Test of the Firebird." She stared at the light, wishing she could see beyond the bushes. "They're too rare, now. I only saw one once, at a distance."

"They are not rare here, only endangered by such as she." The Hawkbrother's face darkened. "She wishes me to make them her familiars. She *also* wishes *me,* and she is as like to get that as the other, which is to say, when the rivers of hell boil."

At that, Kethry laughed in astonishment. "Windlady— go *ahead!* Give her the birds! The first time she loses her temper with one of them on her shoulder—"

But the young man was shaking his head. "Nay, lady. She knows that as well as you or I. What she means by 'familiar' is 'complete slave.' I would not condemn any living thing to such a fate, even if the dangers of her having such control over something so dangerous were not obvious."

Kethry thought of the things that could be done with a tamed and obedient firebird at one's command and shuddered again. The dangers *were* obvious. There was a history of the mage-wars purportedly written by the wizard-lizard Gervase that hinted the firebirds had been deliberately bred as weapons.

She couldn't imagine a circumstance terrible enough to make *her* breed something like firebirds as a *weapon*. Frighten one, and send it flaming through a village, touching off the thatched roofs, the hay in the stables. . . .

"She was born of mage-talented parents, and given all she desired," the Hawkbrother continued. "But she came to desire more and more, and her own small talent could not compass her ambition, until she discovered her one true gift—that she could steal spells from any, and power from any, and use that power to weave those spells at no cost to herself. Thus she enriched herself at the expense of others, and the more power she had, the more she sought."

To shake the thought from her mind, Kethry stood up slowly and walked the few steps to the bars of the cage, mentally measuring the distance between the bars and Need. And as she studied the blade and how it was hung, another thought occurred to her. *I'm Adept-class. My power is unlimited, for all practical purposes. Could I become like her?*

The Hawkbrother stole silently up beside her, but his eyes were on the light beyond the hedges. "It is not power and wealth that corrupt, my lady, but the lust for power and wealth. When that lust takes precedence over the needs of others, corruption becomes true evil. That you even consider that you could become like Keyjon is a sign that you are not likely to do so. She has never once considered anything but what she wanted."

"Well said," Tarma replied, her expression wary. "I'm Tarma shena Tale'sedrin; this is my *she'enedra*, Kethry."

"Stormwing k'Sheyna," he said, and a little rueful humor crept into his expression. "A use-name chosen when I was young and very full of myself, and now so hardened in place that I dare not change it."

Tarma's expression remained the same. "So how is it that you know this woman?"

"I confess: a dose of the same folly that caused me to name myself for the powerful thundercloud," he replied slowly. "I thought I could help her; I thought that if she had a friend, she could learn other ways. In short, I thought I could change her, redeem her, when others had not been able to." He shrugged. "I thought, at the worst, I was so much stronger than she that there was little she could do to harm me. I thought I could not be tricked; did not even guess that she was planning deeper than I anticipated, that she was using me to come at my charges, the firebirds. Now, not only do I pay for my folly, but others as well."

"What happened to the Firefalcon shaman?" Tarma asked harshly.

A muscle at the edge of his eyelid twitched; nothing else moved. "She caught him, coming to see me, and flung him into the cage holding the birds, making certain to panic them. She knew that if I once used my powers to control them, she could steal that control." His eyes were very bright with tears that he was holding back. "He knew it, too, and even as they lashed him with their flame, he told me to hold fast." He looked from Tarma to Kethry and back. "Will you forgive me when I close my ears to *your* cries?"

"Will you be closing your ears?" Kethry asked quietly, staring into blue eyes that seemed much, much older than the face that held them. "Or will you be heeding instead the cries of those who would suffer if this woman got what she wanted?"

He closed his eyes for a moment, his expression for the first time open and easy to read. Pain—and a relief as agonizing as the pain, if such a thing were possible. Then he opened his eyes again, and took her hand and kissed the back of it, like a courtier. It was in that moment that Kethry identified exactly what it was about him that made him so hard *to* identify. Stormwing was the most uniquely *balanced* human being she'd ever met; so completely accepting of both his own male and female natures that he felt poised, like a bird about to fly—

"But you may not have to worry about it," Tarma said, dryly. "Keth, I don't hear her. You want to try the Thahlkarsh gambit?"

"Why not? It worked before." She kicked off her boots, grabbed the bars and climbed up to the top of the cage; once there (cursing her own laziness, that had let her get so out of shape) she carefully threaded her legs between the bars. As she had thought, her foot just reached the hook Need hung from.

"Get ready," she called down below, grinning a little to see Stormwing's eyes so wide with surprise. "I'm going to unhook the sword-belt and lower it to you."

Stormwing shook his head. "What good will having it do us, if this cage negates all magic?" he asked.

"It won't do *us* any good, but in a warrior's hands she cancels all spells cast against the wearer." Kethry's arms were screaming with pain, and sweat streamed down her face as she inserted her foot in the loop of belt, worked it around to the top of the hook, and lifted, carefully. "Tarma's cage is magicked, remember?"

"I hope that I am as good at throwing as you think me to be," Stormwing replied, straining one long arm through the bars until he caught the tip of the scabbard.

Kethry didn't have the breath to spare to tell him that Need herself would take care of that, once out of the influence of the cage. She simply continued to lower the blade, bit by bit, until Stormwing had it firmly.

Then she dropped to the bottom of the cage and waited for the pain in her arms to stop. *I hate getting old. Why can't we all stay twenty until the end, then fall over?*

When she looked up again, the sword was sailing unerringly across the space between the cages, and Tarma caught it so neatly the movement looked rehearsed.

And no sooner did she have it in her hands, than the entire side of the cage swung open, like a door.

Just as Keyjon appeared in the gap in one of the hedges, accompanied by two enormous creatures, things that looked like nothing so much as walking suits of armor.

"*Sheka!*" Tarma cursed, and threw herself out of the cage, did a shoulder-roll to cushion her impact, and came up running, heading for Kethry. Keyjon was so astonished that she stood there, mouth hanging wide open, while Tarma grabbed Need and shoved her through the bars at Kethry.

Kethry grabbed it just as Keyjon recovered, pointing at the three of them, and shrieked something foreign even to Kethry's ears. Whatever it was, the two suits of armor at her side straightened, drew their weapons, and headed straight for Tarma.

Kethry had seen spells of animation before; this one was better than she had anticipated. The armor moved easily, smoothly—and quickly. Tarma escaped being sliced in half by a two-handed broadsword only because she was a hair faster than they were. She wasn't going to be able to escape two of them for very long, not out there alone.

Hopefully she wouldn't *be* alone much longer.

Kethry pulled out the little lock-pick she kept in the side seam of the scabbard and set to work on the lock of the cage. Keyjon seemed to be concentrating on Tarma and ignoring them; she hoped things would stay that way.

Now, just so Stormwing doesn't decide that since he's a man, he can do this better than I can—

Stormwing pressed in close beside her, and she looked up, ready to brain him if he tried to take the pick, and saw that he was clinging to the bars of the cage with both hands, his body carefully pressed up against the door so that most of what she was doing was hidden from Keyjon.

"Thanks," she whispered, and then set to work on the lock, shutting everything out, including the fact that her partner and blood-bonded sister might die in the next few moments.

When you work on a lock, she heard the voice of her thief-instructor say, *nothing exists for you but that lock. If you let yourself be distracted, that's the end of it.*

Except that he had never had the distraction of two magic suits of armor trying to make his partner into thin slices less than an arm-length away.

She felt the lock give just as Keyjon noticed what they were up to. She shoved the door open as the woman shouted another incomprehensible command, and one of the automata stopped chasing after Tarma, and turned, its blade arcing down over its head—

But not aimed at Kethry.

Aimed at Stormwing.

He couldn't dodge, caught in the doorway as he was. He had no weapon of his own, and no spell Kethry knew could possibly be readied in time to save him.

She watched the blade descend, knowing that *she* would never even be able to get Need up in time—*if only he was a wo—*

CLANG!

When her teeth stopped rattling, her brains stopped vibrating, and her watering eyes cleared, she thought for a moment that she had gone quite entirely mad. For there, with the automaton's blade held a hands' breadth away from his head, was Stormwing, crouched down, one hand raised ineffectually to ward off the blow that hadn't arrived.

For what had interposed itself between him and the broadsword was Need.

They all stood like that for a moment, in a bizarrely frozen tableau—

Then Stormwing dove out from under the arch of sheathed sword and unsheathed, scrambled to his feet as the automaton disengaged and began to turn, and yelled, "Duck!"

Somehow she knew to drop into a ball, and Stormwing dove at the automaton's chest.

The timing couldn't have been any better if they'd

practiced it; the animated suit of armor was very heavy and already off-balance, and when Stormwing shoved it, it went further off-balance, staggered backward, and tripped over her, landing with a hollow clangor inside the cage—

The cage which permitted no magic to function within it.

"Move!" screamed another voice from across the clearing; both Kethry and Stormwing scrambled out of the way as Tarma pelted across the intervening space, the other suit of armor in hot pursuit. She fled right into the cage—it had too much momentum to stop.

Kethry heard a strangled croak, and turned to see Keyjon clutching her throat and turning scarlet with the effort of trying to speak. Stormwing watched her from where he sprawled; his finger traced a little arc, and her arms snapped out in front of her, wrists together, fingers interlaced.

Only then did he rise, with a curious, boneless grace, and pace slowly to where the woman stood, a captive and victim of her own greed.

Kethry got up off the ground, wincing as she felt sore places that would likely turn into a spectacular set of bruises. Tarma climbed down out of the cage, favoring her right leg.

"What happened with the fool sword?" Tarma asked, in a low voice.

Kethry shrugged. "I guess when she couldn't identify him as positively male or female, she decided to act first and figure it out later."

Stormwing looked up as they reached his side, but said nothing. "What are we going to do with her?" Kethry asked.

He ran a hand through his hair. "I do not know," he confessed. "I have a feeling that if I tried to harm her, that blade at your side would turn against me."

"Probably," Tarma said, in disgust. "But she's killed at least one person that we know of. A shaman of the Clans, at that, and sacred. Blood requires payment—"

"Would you accept a punishment that left her alive?" the Hawkbrother asked unexpectedly.

Tarma hesitated a moment, then replied with caution. "Maybe. *If* she couldn't get free to try this again. *If* she couldn't even leave here—and *if* it was a living hell for her. My Lady favors vengeance, my friend."

He nodded. "My thought as well. Lady, would you be content also?"

Kethry only nodded; she felt power building, coming from some source she didn't recognize, but akin to the pool of energy available to all White Winds Adepts. She hadn't realized he was an Adept before—

He raised his hands. "All your life, you have sought to be the power in the center of all, to be the manipulator of the fabric of the world around you," he said to Keyjon, solemnly. "So, I give you that; your greatest desire. Control of all you can see, manipulator of the web—"

He pointed; there was a ripple of the very fabric of the place—and a distortion that made Kethry's stomach roil and eyes water.

Then when she looked again, Keyjon was gone. Instead, hanging from a web that spanned a corner between the hedges, was an enormous gray spider, hanging fat and heavy in the center of the pattern.

"Spiders are notoriously short-sighted," Stormwing said, as if to himself. "Now, I shall have to see to it that nothing comes here but noxious things, that deserve to be eaten—and old or diseased things, that deserve a painless death."

He looked back at Kethry, and in that moment she knew that not only was he enormously more powerful than she had guessed, he was also older. Much, much older.

"Here is a guide," he said, producing another ball of witch-light. "I have much to do here, and this will take you back to your horses before dawn." Now he smiled, and Kethry felt as if all her weariness and aches had been cured. "I could not have been freed without your aid. Thank you, sisters-in-power. Thank you."

"You're—welcome," Kethry said—she wanted to say

more, but the witch-light was sailing off into the darkness, and Tarma was tugging her arm. She followed the Shin'a'in into the maze, quickly losing track of where she was, but torn apart by conflicting emotions. There was so much she wanted to learn from him, so many things he must know—

What have I done with my life? All I have built is one White Winds school. With power like his, I could—

I could make a mess of things, that's what I could do, meddling where I didn't belong. No, I guess that power isn't such a temptation. What would it earn me, anyway, besides envy and suspicion?

If she had Stormwing's kind of power, it would make her a target for those such as Keyjon. Was the knowledge worth the risk?

Risk not only to her, but to Tarma, to the children, to Jadrek?

No, she decided. *And after all, we were the ones who rescued him. Knowledge isn't everything. Sometimes it just takes common sense, good planning—*

A sound of joyful cries arose behind them; she and Tarma turned as one to see the firebirds rising into the air above the hedge, alight with their own flame. They circled, and dove, and sang; everlasting fireworks that made their own music to dance by. She felt her eyes brimming with tears, and beside her, Tarma gasped with surprise.

The firebirds circled a moment longer, then rose into the tree canopy, still calling in ecstasy to each other. They penetrated the branches, making them glow emerald for a moment, as if each tree harbored a tiny sun of its own.

Then they were gone. And in the light from the witch-ball, Tarma's face was wet with tears. So was hers. She understood, now, the other reason why two brave men had been willing to die to save them from enslavement.

She caught Tarma's shoulders, and held her for a moment.

And this *is what's worth having; freedom, and friends,*

and the ability to see a thing of beauty and not want it all for myself, or because of the power it represents.

Then Kethry let her sworn sister go, as Stormwing had set the birds free.

"Come on, partner, let's go home," she said. "We have a tale to tell."

GEESE
by Laurell K. Hamilton

Laurell Hamilton is one of those writers I regard as an MZB "discovery." Her first story appeared in SPELLS OF WONDER, a companion anthology to S&S that I did a few years ago. Her second and third stories appeared in *Marion Zimmer Bradley's Fantasy Magazine*. She has also appeared in MEMORIES AND VISIONS, an anthology of women's fantasy and science fiction, and has a story in SWORD OF SORCERESS VII, as well as a novel called NIGHTSEER. She says she is "happily married" and her hobbies include "reading, jogging, and lifting heavy objects to no apparent purpose." She also collects "dragon figurines and a few select teddy bears." As I always say, it's never too late to have happy childhood. And teddy bears can tell such great ghost stories. (Didn't you KNOW? That's where I get all mine.)

She also has a yellow-naped Amazon parrot, and a canary named Hobbes, after Calvin and Hobbes, and says her "familiar is a cockatiel that just loves to have her head scratched." I'd ask how she knows it's female—the gender of a bird usually being known—or of interest—only to another bird; but I don't think I care to know.

The geese lay in the long shadows of afternoon, gray lumps, with rustling feathers and flapping wings. I dozed, long neck tucked backward, black bill buried in my feathers. I watched the other geese through black button eyes. Soon I closed my eyes and gave myself to the peace of the flock.

Perhaps I had been a goose for too long. Perhaps it was time to become human again, but the desire was hazy. I was no longer sure why I wanted to be human. I could not quite remember the reason I had hidden myself among the geese.

I realized I was losing my human identity, but it had borne so much pain. This was better. There was food, the freedom of wings, the open sky, and the comfort of the flock. I did not remember humanity as being so simple, so peaceful, so restful. I had lost the desire to be human, and that should have frightened me. That it did not was a bad sign.

Beside me, head nearly lost in the feathers of his back, was Gyldan. That was not his real name, but a human name I had given him. One of the last things to leave was this need to name things. It was a very human trait.

In my own mind I still called myself Alatir. As long as you had a name, you were still human.

Gyldan was a young gander but had been with me for two seasons. He was a handsome bird, jet black, cloud grey, buff white, all markings distinct and artificial in their perfectness.

He had chosen me as his mate, but I offered only companionship. I was still human enough not to wish to bear goslings.

He had stayed with me, though there were other females who would have taken him. We had spent long summers on empty lakes, claiming our territory but never going to nest. If I did that, I would never be human again. The thought came that I wanted to be human, someday, but not today.

The children came then, peasant children with their dark hair and eyes. They came from a prosperous household, for they fed us scraps of vegetables and bread. They had almost tamed us, almost.

The oldest was a girl of about fourteen, her black hair in two thick braids around a slender face. The next oldest was a boy of perhaps eleven. The rest were all sizes, with laughing brown eyes and gentle hands.

I had flown over their father's mill many times. I had watched them help their mother in the garden and play tag in front of their house.

They came earlier by human standards, for the days were growing autumn short. By geese standards, the sun was in the same place.

The bread was day old, crisp, and good. I remembered other bread, formed in curves and sculpted for feast days. Gyldan did not press me to share my bits of bread. He sensed my mood and knew my temper was short.

There was a sound of horses riding along the road. All of us craned our necks to hear, to see danger. The oldest girl noticed it and asked us, "What's wrong?"—as if we could speak.

We thundered skyward as the horses rode out beside the lake. The children were still stunned by our beating wings, afraid. The girl recovered and screamed, "Run, hide!"

The children scattered like wild things. The girl was cut off by one prancing horse, and the oldest boy would not leave her.

I circled back, Gyldan beside me. I settled at a safe distance and listened. It took magic for me to hear them, and I found the knowledge to stretch my senses came easily.

The men wore the livery of the Baron Madawc, a white bull on a background of silver, a sword through its heart. I knew Lord Madawc well. Human memories tore through my mind. Blood running between my mother's dead eyes. My father's chest ripped open, so much blood. I had been but newly made a master of sorcery when Madawc slaughtered my family and took over our lands. Five years ago, I had been a child, though a powerful one. Lord Madawc had mocked me when I challenged him to a duel. He had let me live and put a geas on me. A geas to kill him, thinking that it would surely mean my death. Having a geas-ridden child seek the death of a powerful sorcerer amused him.

So I had hidden myself in a form that the geas would not touch. My human mind roared through my animal body. I rmembered. I remembered.

One soldier had placed the girl across his saddlebow. "Our lord will be pleased with this." He slapped her buttocks. She was crying.

The boy said, "Let go of my sister."

Another soldier swooped down on him and carried him, struggling, to the front of his saddle. He said, "There are those at court that like a bit of little boy. You can come along if you like."

I could not let this happen, and I could not stop it as a bird. I hid myself in some reeds. Gyldan felt the magic begin. He hissed but did not leave me.

Human form was cold. I found myself crying. Crying for the family I had forgotten. I huddled in the reeds, in the mud. My skin was pale; my black hair, waist-long. I know my eyes were blue, the pale color of spring skies. I could pass for a lord's bastard daughter just as easily as a true aristocrat. Peasant blood was peasant blood, to some.

Gyldan touched my shivering skin with his firm beak. He croaked softly at me, and I touched his feathered head. "If I live, I will be back to say a proper good-bye, I promise."

I walked up the slopping bank toward the soldiers. He followed me on his thick, webbed feet, but he stopped before I reached the men. He launched skyward in a thrust of feathers and fear.

The soldiers saw only a naked woman walking toward them. I had grown older and was no longer girl, but woman. I doubted Madawc would recognize me. But because of his own magic, I was compelled to find him and slay him, if I could. Fear tightened my stomach, yet there was no time to be afraid. I had to help the children now.

"Let the children go."

"Oh, yes, my lady . . ." They laughed.

I gestured, a bare pass of wrist and hand. The children were set upon the ground, and the soldiers said one to another, "Children—who needs children? We will take a woman to our lord." Freeing the children was their own idea now.

The children were frightened and huddled near me. I whispered to them, "Go home; do not be afraid. I may come there seeking shelter later."

The girl dropped a clumsy curtsey and said, "You are most welcome, my lady. Be careful."

I nodded, and one of the soldiers gave me his cloak as a damp autumn drizzle began to fall. It was his idea to let me ride in front of him, covered, a special gift for Lord Madawc. He was their captain, and the only one I had to control. I had been lucky that none of these soldiers was a spell caster. It would never have gone so smoothly with magic to fight.

It was miles to the castle, and by the time we arrived, the captain believed it was his idea. No magic was required to maintain my safety.

The castle gate was brilliant with torchlight. Our group was one of dozens. Many had brought children, both male and female. One little boy was perhaps six, frightfully young. He clung, crying, to the soldier that held him. The soldier looked decidedly uncomfortable. I marked him for later use, though if I needed help, it would probably be too late. Too late meant dead. I took a deep calming breath. If I panicked I would be useless. Somehow I would kill Madawc. Even if it meant my own death.

We were escorted through the main hall, where there was a party going on. I heard one of the soldiers murmur, "Pigs, all of them."

The captain whispered, "Don't let Madawc hear such talk. He'll skin you alive for entertainment."

Another said, "I'm leaving this foul place when my contract is up." There was a lot of head nodding.

Five years without my father to stand guard against him had not made Madawc popular.

The place smelled of spilled wine, vomit, and sex. Drunken voices, both male and female, called out bawdy suggestions. There was a young man of about fifteen, chained to the center of the room. A line of silk-clad ladies were taking turns with him.

I turned away, and the captain jerked me roughly forward. Fear knotted in my belly, and for the first time I felt naked under the cloak. I had magic, but so did Madawc, and he had beaten me before.

The little boy was given over to an older man. The soldier looked near tears himself as he pried the boy's fingers from him. The old noble offered the child sweetmints and held him softly. He would gain the child's confidence first. I recognized Lord Trahern. He had been thrown out of my father's court for being a child-lover.

The captain led me by the arm through the crowd. Hands pulled at the cape, saying, "A beauty, did you taste her before you brought her here?"

He ignored them and went to the front table. Madawc had not changed, except to grow thicker around the middle. His black hair was dark as any peasant's, but his eyes were the cool blue of autumn skies.

Anger flashed through me warm and whole. Hatred. Memories. My mother's cries for help. Her screams, "Run, Alatir, run!" But there had been no place to run. I needed no geas to want him dead.

The captain went down on one knee and pulled me down as well. We waited, kneeling, faces hidden from the man. Would Madawc recognize me? I was afraid and didn't try to hide it. I was just another victim, a bit of meat. I was supposed to be afraid.

Finally, Madawc said, "Yes, what is it?"

"A special treat for you, Lord Madawc." He pulled my head back, so my face showed.

Madawc said, "Ah, blue eyes. Did you find another one of my own bastards for me?"

"I believe so, my lord."

He smiled and traced my face with his hand. "Lovely. You have done well, captain. I am pleased." He held out a ruby and gold ring. The captain bowed and took it. I was left kneeling.

Madawc pulled aside the cloak. It fell to the floor. I hunched forward using my long hair as a screen. Fear thudded in my throat. He laughed. "Naked, all pleasures bare, as I like my women. And modest, I like that as well." He touched my breast, and I jerked away with a small gasp. I would not let him touch me. I would destroy myself first. No, the geas would not allow that. I had to try and kill him. But I could not perform death-magic here and now. He was not drunk; he would break my concentration long before I completed a spell. I could damage him but not kill him. I needed to get away from him; I needed time.

It came to me then what I needed to do. I had been too long away from the nobility; I had forgotten how silly even the best of them could be.

Even Madawc, tainted as he was, would not refuse challenge, especially from a woman he had defeated before.

I draped the cloak around my shoulders and said, "I am Alatir Geasbreaker, as you named me. Daughter of Garrand and Allsun." I stood, cloaked in deepest blue and the mane of black hair. I was ivory skin and eyes of sapphire. I felt the magic of true-challenge flow through me, born of anger, righteousness, and five years of magic almost untapped. Fear was gone in a rush of magic.

Madawc knocked his chair backwards to scrape along the marble floor. "What trick is this?"

"No trick, Madawc of Roaghnailt. I am Alatir Geasbreaker, and I challenge you to battle."

If it had been another who was trained in sword as well as magic, it would have been a foolish challenge. I knew nothing of weapons, but neither did Madawc. He was of the belief that magic was always enough. Now we would see.

A hush ran through the throng. They turned eyes to their honored lord. He could not refuse, for to do so, even in front of this silken rabble, would be to lose all honor. A lord without honor did not get invited to the king's courts. A lord without honor became the butt of songs by bards known for their comedic talents and biting wit.

I was remembering what it meant to be human and a Meltaanian noble.

"I accept challenge, of course, but you cannot be Alatir daughter of Garrand. I put a geas on you that would have forced you to kill me years ago."

"It was your spell. Test it; see if it still holds me."

I felt a tentative wash of magic, a mere butterfly's wing of power. "You bear my spell, but how have you hidden from it?"

"Shapeshifting, Madawc. Even as a child, shapeshifting was my best spell, and animal cannot answer geas."

"What brought you back?"

"You called me. You might say, I am what you made me: someone who hates you, someone who has to kill you, at risk of her own life if necessary. I am under geas to see you stretched dead before me."

His jaw tightened; the shock and fear were gone. "I defeated you once, easily. I will do so again. This time I will not leave you alive."

"This time," I said, "you will not have the chance."

Meltaanians love spectacle more than anything. In short order, torches were set in a circle outside the castle grounds. You never let sorcerers fight within walls. The walls had a tendency to tumble down. Even that thought did not frighten me. The magic of challenge still held me safe. Fear was a muted thing, for now.

One of the ladies had found me a dress to wear. It was blue silk and matched my eyes. My hair was braided down my back and threaded with silver ribbons. Silver was echoed at bodice, sleeve, and dress front. It was a very simple dress by Meltaanian standards, but the people needed to be impressed, needed to remember what was about to happen.

Madawc faced me in black, run through with silver threads. He glittered like ice in the sun when he moved. He spoke to me as we stood, waiting, "You are Alatir."

"Did you doubt it?"

"I thought you long dead."

"You thought wrongly."

He gave a half bow, a strange self-mocking smile on

his face. "I think, dear lady, that you are some lovely phantom come to haunt me."

"I am flesh and blood and magic."

Magic grew in the circle of torches. Magic ran along my skin and tugged at my hair, like an unseen wind. I called sorcery to me but did not want to commit its shape to any one spell. I wanted to know the measure of the man I fought. In my terror he had been twelve feet tall, an endless fountain of magic. Now he was a man, and I was no longer a child.

Fire exploded around me, orange death. The air was choking, close, heat. The fire died, and I stood safe behind a shield. Lightning flared from his hands. The bolts struck my shield and shattered in an eye-blinding display of light.

I faded inside my shield, willing myself into another shape. I was small, thin, hidden in the grass. A green adder hidden in the uncertain torchlight.

I could feel the vibration as he moved over the earth, but I could hear his puzzled voice asking, "Where is she?"

I felt his magic wash over me, searching, but I was a snake and had no real business with magic. He did not come too near the empty folds of the silk dress, but I slipped out a sleeve hole and began moving cautiously, thin and hidden, toward him.

I was a small snake and could not bite through his boots. As he passed me, put his back to me, I grew. I was an older snake, thick as a man's wrist. There were gasps from the audience. He turned, puzzled, and I struck. He screamed as my fangs tore his flesh, poison pumping home. His struggles flung me away to lie half-stunned in the grass.

I began to shapeshift, slowly. He was yelling, "Get me a healer, now!"

A soldier, the one who had brought in the littlest boy, said, "You cannot be healed until the fight is over, Lord Madawc. That is the rule."

"But I've been poisoned!"

The mercenaries whom he had bullied and made into

whoremongers formed a wall of steel. "You will not leave the circle until the fight is done. Isn't that right, captain?"

The captain, who had brought me in, didn't have a problem with Madawc, but he licked his lips and agreed. He knew better than to go against all his men. "You must wait for healing, Lord Madawc."

"I will see you all flogged for this, no, hanged!"

It was the wrong thing to say. The soldiers faces went grim, dispassionate. They waited for someone to die.

I stood naked and human once more. All I had to do was stay alive until the poison took effect, and that wouldn't be long.

Madawc turned on me with a snarl. "I'll take you with me, bitch!"

He formed a soul-beast, made of magic, hatred, and fear. It was a great wolf that glowed red in the night.

I had never made a soul-beast before. It took great strength, and if it were destroyed, the spell caster died with it. I formed mine of power, vengeance, the memory of five years of unused magic, the quiet stillness of water, and the freedom of skies. It flowed blue and burst into being a moment before the wolf leapt. Mine was a thing of feathers and claws, no known beast.

I felt the power as never before. I rode the winds of it. It lifted me in a dance of death and joy. I was fanged claws and whirling feathers of gold and sapphire. I bit the wolf and raked his sides with claws. I bled under his teeth and staggered under the weight of his body.

The wolf began to fade. As it lost substance, I gained its magic. I drew its power like a hole in Madawc's soul; I drained him until I fell to my knees, power-drunk, stunned.

The soul-beasts were gone. It was effort to turn my head and see Madawc on the grass. His body convulsed, and bloody-foam ran from his lips. The green adder is a deadly thing.

I was stronger than five years ago, but all those years had been without training. Madawc might have killed me without the aid of poison. Then again, he might not.

The geas was gone and I felt pure and empty of it. I had expected triumph, instead I felt relief, and a great empty sadness.

A voice declared the match over and Alatir, the winner.

There were hands, a cloak thrown over my nakedness, the warmth of healing magic, and a warm draught of tea.

Dawn light found me rested, healed, and in the bed chamber that had once belonged to Madawc. By Meltaanian law it was all mine now, both my father's lands which had been stolen and Madawc's. Madawc had never bothered to appoint an heir from his many bastards. No royalty would marry him.

There was a knock on the door, and the captain entered with the mercenary who had brought the little boy in. They both knelt, and the captain said, "My lady, what would you like for us to do? We have weeks left on our contract, and our contract is now yours, if you want it."

I asked, "Have you a guard outside my door?"

The younger man spoke, "Yes, my lady, some of the dead lord's friends are less than pleased at the duel's outcome."

I smiled at that. "Is Lord Trahern still within these walls?"

"No, my lady."

I ignored the captain and asked the other man, "What is your name?"

"I am Kendrick Swordmated."

"You are now Captain Kendrick."

The other captain sputtered, but I interrupted him. "I want you gone from here and never come back. Take the four men who rode with you on search yesterday."

There must have been something in my eyes that told him not to argue. He gave a stiff bow and left the room.

"Now, Captain, how long ago did Trahern leave?"

"Only moments, my lady."

"Then take what men you think you need and find him. Relieve him of the peasant boy he got last night.

The boy is to be healed, then taken back to his home. A gift of gold will be given to his family."

He smiled. "Yes, my lady."

"And free all the others. They are my people now, and no one mistreats my people. No one."

He bowed, grinning. "All will be done as you ask, Alatir Lord-slayer."

"Lord-slayer?" I questioned.

"Yes, my lady, from last night."

"Go then, Kendrick," I stopped him just before he left. "I must attend some business and will be away perhaps until tomorrow. But I will return and expect everything to be done as I asked."

"I will inform the castle staff of your absence and will do as you ask." He bowed and left the room.

I stood at the open window and let the autumn wind shiver over my skin. I changed into a familiar form and took to the sky on gray wings.

I settled on the lake's dark waters and looked for Gyldan. I could not remain with the flock now. I remembered too much, but I had promised him a good-bye.

He called to me from shore, his voice different than any others. I paddled over to him and hopped up on grass. Regardless of what shape I wore, I loved him. We caressed, touching necks and bills. How could I leave him behind? And how could I take him with me?

He stepped back from me, and I saw magic shimmer over him like silver rain. The flock awoke with cries of alarm and took to the safety of the sky. I watched him change, slowly, but his magic was strong and sure.

He lay, a naked man, pale, white hair like moonlight. Eyes sparkled black so they showed no pupil. He blinked up at me with wide uncertain eyes. His voice was deep and song-filled, full of rushing wind and the freedom of wings. "I saw how you changed."

I was human beside him, crying.

He ran hands down the length of his new body. "I could not follow you as a bird, but as a man . . ."

I knelt and kissed his forehead. "You are not a man."

He gripped my hand. "I am your mate. I will follow you, whatever form you take."

We held each other as the sun rose and knew each other as a woman knows a man. Afterward he lay panting beside me with innocent eyes.

How much he had to learn. I could take the memory of my magic, of his magic, away. I could leave him as I found him. I ran a finger tip down the sweat-soaked length of his body. He shivered.

"Your name is Gyldan, and I am Alatir."

He tried the names on his human tongue, "Gyldan, Alatir. Are they nice names?"

"Yes, I think so." I stood. "Come, we can take shelter at the mill for today. They will give us clothing and food."

He nodded, and I helped him stand on his uncertain legs. I led him by the hand along the path that the children took to feed the geese. We shivered in the dim autumn sunlight. It was colder without feathers.

MARAYD'S ESCAPE
by Rima Saret

Rima Saret is one of those writers who believes me when I say that the best possible way to respond to a rejection slip is with another story which pleases the editor—or another editor—better.

This story really belongs in the category "rape and revenge." But I get few enough of them that I'll use one now and then—if it's good enough.

Rima Saret has been professionally published in a couple of Comic book publications, as well as in *Owlflight,* and a variety of amateur publications. She also seems (in her alter ego of Mary Anne Landers) to be a prolific writer for Video publications; which startles me, probably because I followed the advice of a scholar on the subject of television once, to think of three *hard facts* I had learned from television, and I could think only of one—the panda is an endangered species, and I knew that anyway, sort of. What I'm saying here is not "Video writing is all bad"—I've been accused of being intolerant—but "Better her than me." Maybe if my eyes weren't so bad, I, too, could be a video addict. But think of all the good books I'd miss. Personally I have rarely watched a movie that I didn't wonder why I'd wasted the time when I could have been reading a good book. The exceptions are very few and mostly opera. Yes, it's prejudice and I'm stuck with it.

Marayd the Red, warrior of the kingdom of Daizur, crawled through the labyrinthine tunnel leading from the enemy camp. Her sheathed sword trailed behind on a cord; where it usually depended on her belt there now hung a pouch. Inside were the jewels she and her comrades had just stolen from the warlord Helbor's chest, heavily guarded against brute force but not trickery.

The rest of her party were disguised as hired swords; they would escape inconspicuously the following day. However, Marayd had volunteered to carry out the most dangerous phase of getting the jewels out. The only way in which she stood a decent chance of doing so lay in sneaking through this long-abandoned sewer under what was left of an ancient city.

She was not stealing jewels for the usual reason. Marayd would not get a single stone for herself, nor any sort of personal profit other than the respect of her officers and comrades and the thanks of her ruler.

Rather, the objective of this mission was to deprive the warlord of the core of his disposable wealth. Without it, Helbor would not be able to hire mercenaries, buy weapons and supplies, and engage in a drawn-out campaign against her people. Daizur would enjoy another year or two of peace, at least until the warlord again raised enough wealth for an offensive.

The tunnel seemed to go on forever. Her limbs ached; her elbows and knees were raw. She had overestimated the diameter of the passage, and realized she was too large-boned for this job.

Eventually she felt the gradient rising. A little farther and she'd be out of this underworld.

Finally Marayd reached the brush-covered entrance. It was still dark, but the pearl-gray glimmer of a winter dawn lightened the sky. She carefully peered out from the brush, saw to the best of her ability that all was clear in the near-flat treeless terrain, and stepped out.

The dim light outlined her tall, rangy form clad in armor. Framed by the helmet was her square, ruddy face with bold features—large and deep-set green eyes, thick bow-shaped lips, and a prominent nose and cheekbones. Under her helmet was a mass of curly, unruly hair the color of a desert sunset. Hers was a flamboyant beauty, if beauty it was; by the standards of many, her features were too overpowering.

But such hardly mattered to a celibate. In her devotion to her cause of defending her people, Marayd had little time and less interest left over for personal matters.

Right now her sole concern was reaching the lines of the Daizur troops. She would have to make what time she could before the sun rose. After that, there would be no place to hide in this dry grassland; her pursuers would be able to spot her at great distances. She fastened her sword to her belt, checked the pouch to make sure none of the jewels had accidentally dropped out, then headed due north through a clump of brush.

While making her way through the thickest part, a soldier wearing Helbor's colors rose from behind her; he lifted a cudgel, struck her on the head, and sent her sprawling. Her helmet protected her from most of the force of the blow, if not the pain, but the strap broke and it fell off. She automatically drew her sword, but the bushes impeded her. Another blow, this time to her unprotected head, knocked her out cold.

"So you thought that passage was secret, eh?" Helbor grasped his chained but defiant captive by the chin to look into her eyes. "Foolish Daizurite. You tried to relieve me of my treasure, now I'll relieve you of yours."

"I have no wealth, nor do my kinfolk. If you think to hold me for ransom, you'll show no profit for your troubles."

He chuckled; "I'm not talking about that treasure. When my soldiers stripped and checked you for concealed weapons, they found out that you're a virgin."

Marayd panicked, then steadied her nerves and intoned, "I'll kill myself before I'll let you rape me!"

Again he laughed; "Me? I wouldn't even spit on a virago like you. No, I'm going to sell you, to King Gambreol. In three days he's due to pass here on the return leg of a pilgrimage, and he's always on the lookout for virgins to add to his harem. He'll pay me most generously . . . and as you know, I need the money."

As Helbor had threatened, three days later she was dragged to King Gambreol's tent. He had harsh features and tired eyes that spoke of too much easy pleasure and casual cruelty. His manner was arrogant and pompous even for a monarch.

Marayd averted her eyes as he studied her face. He ordered his guards to cut away her clothing, the only way to strip her with manacles on her wrists and ankles.

She cried in shame and anger as Gambreol examined her nude form. He pinched her breasts painfully and had his guards part her thighs so that he could check for himself whether she really was a virgin.

Then he said to a retainer, "She'll do. Take the gold to Helbor. And don't let her out of her chains until we get to the palace, you understand?"

Marayd knew that words would not help her, so she said only in her mind, *You'll never enjoy me, Gambreol. Either you'll be dead, or I will.*

The journey to his palace in the city of Demaforth took eight days. En route, Marayd's virtue was safe; as part of his pilgrimage, Gambreol was sworn to celibacy until it was over. He bought five other virgins on his journey; hopefully he'd be preoccupied with them once he arrived.

She had plenty of time to think. Unless her captor planned to leave her in chains indefinitely, she could always find some way to preserve her honor by the most drastic means. If she were brought a meal, she could break a piece of pottery and use a shard to cut her wrists. If there were sheets on her bed, she could tear them to strips and fashion a noose. If she were near a window or on a rooftop high above the ground, she could jump to her death.

But there was one other option, provided she'd have

the time and the means to pull it off. As part of her training as a warrior, she'd been taught by Meteris, a renowned Daizurite sorceress, a secret mode of teleportation. If Marayd were ever imprisoned, she could construct a framelike apparatus that would instantly transport her one hundred arms' lengths away.

However, she would need twelve rods—six of bronze and six of steel, three hard-to-find types of herbs, and a ruby or sapphire. She would thus create a warp in the natural forces that would allow her to breach any barrier for an instant, long enough to break free. The spell entailed a painstaking process, and it would work for only one person per casting.

She'd memorized the procedure, but had never tried it. How would she obtain the necessary materials? How would she construct the cumbersome apparatus without arousing suspicion?

The huge basalt pile of the fortresslike palace loomed ahead. A guard whispered to her, "No woman has ever escaped the royal harem. Take a good look at the palace on the outside, for you'll never see it again from this view."

Once past the gate to the harem, her chains were struck off and she was conducted by eunuch guards through a series of doors and halls. Her surroundings were luxurious, but their beauties were lost on her. What she really noticed was the heavy contingent of guards, the locks on the doors, and the bars on the outer windows. Never had she seen such heavy security, and Marayd had served as a guard in the women's section of Daizur's largest prison and in the national treasury. Any thoughts she might have had about escaping without the aid of magic were quickly forgotten.

Next to the security measures, what struck her the most were Gambreol's women. One look in their lovely but dead eyes told Marayd more than she'd ever want to know about life in a harem. They had no more spirit in them than the erotic statues of women in obscene poses that some men found arousing.

Once Marayd talked to some of the two hundred wives and concubines, she found that they were equally lacking in individuality. Their souls—and minds, if they'd ever had any—had wasted away through neglect. At least in most of the inmates of the Daizurite prison, their wits had remained keen and their hope for freedom had still burned.

Marayd wondered what these women lived for; but they didn't really live at all, they merely existed. What kind of a man would find such creatures exciting? Any person who thought of a harem as a sensual and pleasurable place should actually visit one.

She was handed over to a hard-mannered matron, a onetime favorite of Gambreol's whose charms had faded, and given a bath. Marayd sat in a veined black marble tub of warm musk-scented water; a handmaid ladled in hot water from a large caldron.

Then a beautiful if affected-looking brunette, bejeweled and clad in elaborate robes of several shades of red, entered and checked over the newcomer. Marayd felt only slightly less disgusted than she had been when Gambreol had done the same.

The lady asked in an imperative tone, "Do you know who I am?"

"Should I?"

"I'm Lady Baytilis, His Majesty's first wife and the mother of the crown prince." She smirked; "I suppose you think that with your youth and looks and virginity, you'll be able to bend him to your will. I'll have you know that only one woman has any influence on him at all, and that's me."

Marayd sighed; "You're welcome to him. I'm a captive here, and I want no part of—" Marayd sneered, "—His Majesty."

"That's what many of them say when they come here, but life in a harem breaks any willfulness in a woman. Pretty soon you'll be like all the rest, servile and fawning and competing with each other for his attention.

"But know this, silly virgin: next to His Majesty, I rule the harem. My word is your law. If you remember this and obey me, we'll have no trouble. If you defy me, I'll make you suffer like you've never suffered before. Do you understand?"

Marayd couldn't help but laugh. "You pompous, absurd bitch! Really, you should hear yourself."

Baytilis shot Marayd a steely glare, then motioned to her four guards. Suddenly they hefted Marayd bodily; as she screamed and struggled, they threw her into the caldron of steaming water.

A week later, Marayd was still recovering from her burns. She was too weak to move, and in no shape for Gambreol to summon to his chamber. He kept busy deflowering his other new acquisitions, not to mention getting reacquainted with the bodies of his favorite wives and concubines.

If Marayd was temporarily safe, she couldn't begin her task of obtaining the materials for her getaway. Would she have time once she was well enough? He might summon her then at any moment, assuming she wasn't menstruating.

During her convalescence, she was cared for by a junior concubine named Verit. She was a doe-eyed blonde barely out of childhood, with a face of piquant delicacy and a softly rounded form under her typically flimsy silks. Her voice was soft and lilting, with an accent Marayd couldn't quite place.

Her manner was servile toward Baytilis and others who outranked her, which was practically everyone in the harem. As with most of the concubines, Verit served as a handmaid to the favorites. In her double bondage of being a slave to slaves, she was at the very bottom of this perverse miniature of society.

However, once Marayd could get her mind off her pain, she noticed that Verit wasn't indistinguishable like the others. She had an air about her . . . just what, Marayd couldn't quite say.

But she decided to find out. One day as Verit was changing her charge's dressings, Marayd said, "Verit, how old are you?"

"Fifteen."

"How long have you been here?"

"Since I was twelve. I was born and raised in the harem of King Zai. He lost a wager at a tournament to King Gambreol, and I was part of the stake."

"Have you never lived outside a harem?"

"No. All I've seen of the world is what I glimpsed from the window of my carriage during the ten-day journey here." Her eyes took on a dreamy look; "But I know what the world is like. I learn about it from the newcomers who weren't raised in harems."

"Like me?"

The blonde head nodded. "That's one of the reasons I asked to take care of you. I usually serve Lady Baytilis; but she has twelve handmaids, and even she can't need us all the time."

"I'm grateful to you, and I can happily repay you by telling you of what I've seen of the world outside. But you said that this is only one of the reasons."

"There's also—how can I say it? You're different from the others. I've seen maybe thirty newcomers during the past three years, but never any with so much spirit."

"And I've noticed that in you. You're not like the other harem women."

Verit whispered in Marayd's ear, "I can read and write."

Marayd blinked; "But I heard that's forbidden in this harem."

"I learned it in King Zai's. It was forbidden there too, but one of the eunuchs befriended me, and taught me letters. He secretly brought me several books."

"You got any here?"

Verit shook her head. "We're searched too carefully. I know places where I can hide little treasures such as jewels or coins, but something as bulky as a book would be easily found. Have you read many books?"

"I can't read. I had plenty of chances to learn, but I didn't. You had hardly any chance, but you did."

Verit was kind and attentive; she showed an interest in Marayd that went beyond caring for an injured stranger. She clearly wanted to be friends with the new-comer—and Marayd would need someone who knew her way around the harem. If Marayd herself were in poor shape to begin her task, maybe someone else would.

Not that Marayd would let on just what her purpose was, of course. Any fellow captive who wouldn't inform on her would demand to escape with her, and then inform on Marayd when she revealed that such would be impossible.

As soon as Marayd had sufficiently recovered, she moved in with Verit. She spent hours regaling the other with tales of her adventures, and those of others. Verit looked impassive as she listened, but Marayd could tell that inside she was longing for the world her stories represented.

During one session Marayd asked, "Verit, what would you do if you were free?"

She sighed; "Everything."

"What would your priorities be?"

"I'd learn all I can. I'd read all the books I could find and attend all the lectures. Once I knew enough, I'd teach others."

"You'd become a scholar, I take it."

"Yes, but I wouldn't just teach other scholars. I'd try to bring learning and wisdom to everyone, especially those who need it most." A pause; "I'd live in dignity and honor, like a human being. Not like I do here."

"How can there be a mind like yours in a place like this?"

"It's happened. My mother, whose name was also Verit—" Her eyes grew misty; "She was the same way. She belonged to a band of outlaws in the western hills— or so I've heard; they were probably just wanderers, and didn't really hurt anyone. But they were all killed or captured. She was taken to King Zai, and he fathered me on her. She hated her imprisonment; she was constantly trying to escape, and getting caught and punished. When I was six years old, she almost made it over the wall—but she was carrying me . . . King Zai decided it'd be the last time, and had her tortured to death. I had to watch."

Verit sobbed; Marayd embraced her. Meanwhile, her mind was working away. Verit was exactly the sort of accomplice she needed.

Once the crying spell was over, Marayd said, "If I were to ask a special favor of you, would you do it? And keep it secret?"

"Why, yes. I swear I would."

Marayd could detect no hesitation, no reservation in her response. Verit had truly become devoted to her.

Marayd said, "I must be certain that you won't tell anyone."

Verit paused, then said, "There's one way to be sure. I'll tell you my secret; that way, if I ever inform on you, you can do so on me."

"I wouldn't, but if you feel a need to unburden yourself, you can tell me."

Verit whispered, "The king has used me twice, and the second time I became pregnant. I aborted the child with a piece of wire."

"Why?"

"Because if it were a girl, she'd spend her whole life in slavery, as I will. She'd never know what it's like to be free. She might not even dream of it, as I do."

"It could've been a boy."

"Then he'd be condemned from birth. According to the custom of this dynasty, whenver a crown prince assumes the throne, he has his brothers and half-brothers killed, lest any of them challenge his rule. But Gambreol wants children, lots of them. Even daughters; once they're old enough, he violates and keeps them like any concubines. And children of either sex are supposed to be proof of his manhood. He has them displayed before important visitors. That's why he has executed any wife or concubine who has an abortion and gets caught. I've seen it happen."

"I didn't know any of the rest were that brave."

"The woman who did it wasn't brave, just desperate. She was in delicate health, and the court physician affirmed that another childbirth would kill her. But the king made her pregnant anyhow. She tried to save her life, and lost it."

"Verit, I can make it so that you'll never be in that sort of danger again."

"How?"

"I learned a little magic, and I know a spell that can help us both. Do you have access to medicinal supplies?"

"Yes. Lady Baytilis is always telling me to go fetch this potion or that powder. And I had to get the ointments and bandages for your burns."

"I'll need three rare herbs, twelve metal rods, and a sapphire or ruby."

Verit glanced at the drapery; "Will curtain rods do?"

"They might. Do you have any jewels like I need?"

"Only paste ones, but I can always . . . Marayd, what exactly is this spell supposed to do?"

Marayd grinned; "It'll guarantee that Gambreol will never summon either of us to his chamber. Can you guess why?"

"No."

"It'll cause us to menstruate without stopping."

Verit clapped her hands and laughed; "Oh, how clever!"

"Are you interested?"

"Am I? Marayd, if I never again feel his clammy hands on me, it'll be too soon!"

During the next few days, Verit secured the three herbs without too much trouble, or so it appeared to Marayd. She wasn't sure what connivances Verit used, but if there were repercussions, Marayd would have felt them as well.

They found in a storage room a couple of old bronze braziers falling apart at the joints, and disassembled them for the six bronze rods. Marayd also came upon a spool of thin wire which she appropriated to fasten the framework together.

Getting the steel rods was a bit more difficult. They had to be of four arms' lengths, but the closest they found in the storage rooms were steel curtain rods just over half as long. They went around checking the larger curtains when nobody seemed to be noticing . . . which, of course, sooner or later someone did. When asked what they were doing, Marayd and Verit concocted stories; the one that they were looking for a bird that had escaped its cage worked best. The guards apparently didn't suspect them of anything worse than eccentricity, and the harem women were too dull-witted or apathetic to think at all. Once alone again, Marayd and Verit would replace a long rod with two short ones lashed together.

Finally, Marayd acquired all the materials except one. She picked as the site for the apparatus a large walk-in linen closet. The door was never locked, but could be bolted from the inside with a chair against the handle. She could temporarily hide the rods beneath little-used piles of bedding, and the room itself was less than a hundred arms' lengths from the outer wall of the palace—and a deserted warehouse she'd spotted on the way in.

Her plans were going smoothly . . . then came the day when the guards announced that all the women were ordered to the harem courtyard to witness a punishment. When Marayd got there, she found to her horror Verit stripped and chained to a post.

Lady Baytilis stepped in front of the assembly and intoned, "You are summoned here to witness the enforcement of justice. This concubine, Verit, stole a ruby earring from me. It was found on her person, and she confesses to the theft. Now see how we deal with thieves."

She motioned to a guard, who picked up a whip and began flogging Verit. She cried out piteously; Marayd averted her eyes. Never had she felt so hurt and angry . . . no, not even when Gambreol had pawed and ogled her.

Now it was Marayd's turn to care for her injured friend. Her wounds were hideous, but Marayd washed and dressed them tenderly.

A day later, when Verit had enough strength to speak, she said, "Marayd, I did my best for you, and. . . ."

Marayd stroked the blonde head. "I know you did, and I wish it'd been me who'd suffered for it instead of you. Oh my poor Verit! I'll kill that bitch!"

"Marayd, don't. Others have tried. She's too well-guarded. And besides . . . listen, is that door shut?"

"Yes."

"Put a chair against the knob."

Marayd complied. "Now what?"

She raised her hand; "See where I'm pointing? There's a loose tile in the floor."

Within heartbeats Marayd had pried it free. There, wrapped in a scrap of silk, lay a glowing red gem.

Marayd gasped, "Is that—"

"Yes. I replaced the ruby in Baytilis' earring with one of my paste gems. Her guards found the earring on me while I was trying to return it. She's more arrogant than smart and hasn't caught on yet. But sooner or later she will, so let's get on with that spell!"

Now Marayd could make her escape at any time, yet she didn't. There was a complication she hadn't counted on: she couldn't bear to leave Verit behind.

Marayd realized that she loved Verit. She cared for her more than she had anyone else, even her kinfolk. Verit was a trusted comrade in a place in which Marayd hadn't expected to trust anybody. They'd forged a bond that had enabled Verit to endure the agony and shame of a public flogging. She'd suffered for Maryd's sake more than anyone else ever had.

And what had Marayd done for Verit in return? She'd lied to her. Tricked her. Claimed she'd protect Verit against being violated by Gambreol. Verit had run great risks and suffered cruel abuse for the sake of a sham promise.

Marayd hated herself. If she'd only known she'd come to love Verit . . . but of course she couldn't have foreseen that. She couldn't have known how painful it'd be to leave her behind.

But if she could take Verit, what a wonderful life she'd lead! With her keen mind and compassionate soul, she'd benefit everyone around her.

Back in Daizur Marayd's onetime tutor Meteris and other leading minds had recently founded a school; it took in a multitude of students whether they could pay or not. All they needed was a willingness to learn. It'd never get a finer student than Verit. Once she got the training she needed, she'd become a shining source of enlightenment. She might even better the position of women, so that harems and other abuses would become things of the past.

But that was not to be. Verit would live out her days inside the basalt walls, hearing tales of the world beyond and dreaming of freedom, but never experiencing it. Her mind would go to waste; perhaps she'd give up trying to think, as had the rest of the harem. Eventually she'd get pregnant again, and knowing her she'd abort the child. This time she might not get away with it.

Seven days later, Marayd noticed with satisfaction that Verit's wounds were healing quickly. "I didn't expect you to recover so rapidly."

"I have a reason to do so, now that I have a friend."

The two embraced; Marayd couldn't help but cry. She felt overcome by both love for Verit, and anger at herself.

Then came a knock on the door. It was a guard, who said, "Marayd, you're to report to the baths at once."

"What?"

"His Majesty has summoned you for this evening. Prepare yourself."

He left; Marayd and Verit stared at each other in shock.

Then Verit said, "It's finally happened. Marayd, you can't put it off any longer. You've got to work that spell!"

Marayd sat down and thought hard for a few minutes. Finally, she realized what she would do—what she had to do.

She pried free the loose tile and grabbed the ruby, then rummaged through her belongings for the three bags of herbs and the spool of wire. She also took out a lamp, a tiny bottle of soporific spirits she'd used to help Verit sleep when her wounds were most painful, and the traveling clothes Marayd had arrived in. She said to Verit, "Come on, let's go to the linen closet."

En route they passed a large double curtain in which they'd replaced the rods. This time, Marayd yanked down the pair of cords and coiled them neatly.

Once in the linen closet, Verit propped a chair against the doorknob. Marayd assembled the rods into a cagelike frame by the faint lamplight. She sprinkled the herbs on the floor within, then fastened the ruby to the highest point in the apparatus.

Once it was finished, Marayd handed Verit the traveling clothes. "Put these on."

"Why?"

"I haven't got time to explain; just do it."

Verit complied; Marayd began reciting the spell. She paused just before the end, then said, "Verit, come here." Marayd embraced her heartily. "I love you."

"And I love you, Marayd."

"I love you so much that I'm going to grant you more than you expected. I'm giving you your freedom."

"What?"

"I lied to you, Verit. This spell, this apparatus is for teleportation outside the palace walls, to a deserted warehouse. It can move only one person; I meant to use it myself, and to make it I took advantage of your kindness. Now I'm sorry; I've got to make it up to you, and there's only one way I can."

Verit stared at the frame, then at Marayd. "But—oh, this is impossible!"

"No it's not! You're finally going to live in the world outside, in freedom and dignity."

"But even if what you say is true, I can't go without you!"

"You can and you must!" Marayd clasped her hand; "Verit, what am I on the outside? Just another warrior.

I live by killing, by waging war. I'm part of the cycle of death and destruction.

"But you, you're different. You can learn, and put your knowledge to good use. You can make a difference in the world. It needs hearts and minds like yours."

"But I need you! You can't stay here and let Gambreol rape you!"

Marayd shook her head; "He won't. For some of us, no price is too high for freedom and honor."

Verit winced; "No! I won't let you throw your life away!"

Marayd grasped Verit's chin; "Then live so that my death won't be a waste. Bring peace to the world, just as I and my kind have brought war. Bring learning and wisdom and compassion. Make it so that women will never again suffer abuse from men as we have, and be forced to make the decision I've made."

"Marayd, I'd never survive on the outside by myself. I don't know how!"

Marayd turned her back to Verit and picked up the soporific spirits and a napkin from a pile on the shelf. "You'll learn. Head for my country, for the New School of Daizur, and ask for Mistress Meteris the sorceress. Tell her Marayd the Red sent you. I promise you'll find a place there."

"But I can't live without you. I love you, Marayd. I—"

Then Marayd sprang upon Verit, pinned her arms behind her back, and pressed against her mouth and nose the spirits-soaked napkin. Verit struggled, but slumped and blacked out within heartbeats.

Marayd dragged and shoved her unconscious friend inside the frame. She kissed her tenderly, then completed the spell.

Suddenly the rods glowed with an amber nimbus. It grew brighter, reaching every corner of the room and bathing Marayd in its warmth. A vortex of energies swirled around the apparatus; the ruby shone as if on fire, then suddenly the glow disappeared.

So, too, had Verit. Marayd sighed and smiled; in a

few minutes the drug would wear off, and Verit would awaken to a new life.

And soon the guards would be looking for Marayd. She calmly disassembled the apparatus, tied the steel rods together in a bundle, and placed it between the upper shelves on opposite walls so that it formed a bar across the room. She uncoiled the cords, tied them together, and fashioned a noose. Marayd threw it over the bar, and made her escape.

SHE WHO SHIELDS
by Gary W. Herring

Gary Herring says that the reputation cats have acquired as writer's familiars is overblown; his cat Cuss "has decided that the word processor is a rival for my affections and spends much of her time trying to distract me when I'm trying to write."

I have now no resident cat; when the kids left home, Kristoph took Mozart, Kat took Pywacket and Isabel (the one we called the plaid kitty, because of her strange coloring), and Beth took Patches, leaving me with no felines in residence but Victoria Regina, to whom, being made of fluff, Lisa is not allergic. I have owned cats since I was four, and the house feels empty without one. However, I swore when Solange died that I'd never get attached to another cat. I don't really know how I acquired the others; but I had to go to considerable trouble to keep Mozart off the keyboard; cat hairs and computers should not be mixed. Or so my field service engineer says (and she's been very nice about it all; she must have replaced my system board at least four times in as many years).

"She Who Shields" was submitted to me as a sequel to Gary's first sale, "Hawk's Hill," which I bought for the last of these anthologies. As you can see, I don't object to series; but amateurs should learn to *write* them first; not talk about them. If there's one thing I can't stand it's the unpublished writer who rambles on about the series he wants to write when not even one story has ever been published. Let him rave about his great unwritten works to his mother, not to a busy editor. Or when an editor invites you to lunch, then (at his or her invitation) you can tell all about your great unwritten works. Until then, keep them for a loving mother—or the equally unsold members of your writer's club. (I go along with Bob Tucker who said the best writer's club was "about eight feet long, with spikes.")

Sharik slung her saddlebags over her shoulder and pounded on the door of the inn. A snow-laden wind whistled through the yard, making the two horses whicker and stamp at the hitching post by the woodpile. Sharik shivered in her winter cloak. Behind her, a baby wailed piercingly, protesting the numbing cold. Swearing under her breath, she knocked again.

"I don't see any lights," Ressa said. She set down her bag and rearranged her thin cloak to shield her baby from the wind. "Maybe this isn't the right inn."

Sharik gestured at the sign over the door. The yellow glow of her oil lantern shone through swirling snow to reveal a red silhouette of a spread-winged bird. "That's my Order's sign," she said. "You don't see any lights because the shutters are closed. The thickwits've all gone to bed." She glanced up at the night sky and added, "Right now I wouldn't care if this was the Winter Lord's palace, long as it's got four walls and a roof." She started hammering steadily on the door.

Whoever's in there has till I count to ten, she vowed silently, *and then, Lord and Lady, I'm breaking this door down.*

The door swung open as Sharik reached "seven." She just missed hitting a handsome fellow of sixteen or so in the face. He ducked and cursed. "What the hell d'you want," he demanded, blinking sleepily and hefting a stick of firewood in one hand.

Sharik snorted and shoved him aside, leading Ressa into the candle-lit taproom. A banked fire glowed in a stone hearth on the far wall and the two women made straight for it. "Stable our horses," Sharik ordered over her shoulder.

"Hell I will," the boy snapped. "You can't just—"

Sharik dropped her saddlebags to the floor, shrugged out of her wet cloak, and faced him; a tall, russet-haired woman of eighteen in the uniform of the Order of the Red Hawk. The emblem on the right breast of her quilt jerkin was the same as that adorning the inn's sign, and for good reason. The Hawks owned this place. The Order held the keep at Atenawa and maintained a small garrison to protect the Grain Lady's temple at Tarzy's Forge. The distance between the two had made a safe haven for couriers necessary. If the inn made a profit from the other travelers on the road, well and good, but the business of the War Lady's fighting order took precedence at all times.

The young man's eyes flicked from Sharik's uniform to the sword at her hip and back again. "Stable the horses," he muttered with a nod. He took a lantern from a peg by the door and lit it from one of the candles, then he put on a jacket and went out into the winter wind.

Ressa had laid her son, Dreyan, on the raised hearth and was blowing on his hands and feet. Brushing snow from her braided hair, Sharik blew out her lantern and set it on the floor by Ressa's bag, then she stirred the coals with a poker until the flames leapt and crackled. Replacing the poker, she sat on the hearth and sighed as the warmth seeped through her clothes.

"Lord and Lady, this feels *good*. Much longer and I'd have frozen to the saddle. How's the kid?"

Ressa had removed her cloak and was letting Dreyan nurse. "He's all right," she said without looking up, "but I think you got us here just in time."

Sharik studied her traveling companion in the firelight. Ressa was no older than she was—maybe a little younger. With hair like light honey and bright blue eyes, she'd have been quite pretty but for the dark, wine-colored birthmark that covered the left side of her face. Since that afternoon, when they'd met on the road, Ressa had held her head so that the mark was out of sight. Now, as she watched her baby nurse, a soft smile melted the sadness of that imperfect face. The difference was striking.

"For a while I thought I'd gotten us lost," Sharik admitted. "I've never been by here before." The wind moaned outside, and she suddenly felt sorry for the man out there with the horses. "Lucky we got here when we did," she said.

"Lucky indeed, with that snow coming down," said a voice that wasn't Ressa's.

Startled, Sharik looked up at a sturdy woman with graying dark hair. Her dress was plain and she wore a gravy-stained apron over it. She smiled at the emblem on Sharik's jerkin and spoke in the Temple Speech, "Greetings to thee in the name of She Who Shields."

Sharik rose to her feet and gave the other half of the ritual greeting, "And to thee in the name of She Who Avenges." Switching back to Hjelmaric, she said, "I'm Trooper Sharik of Eshan. From Atenawa."

"Trin of Gliest," the older woman said, offering her hand. "Welcome to the Hawk's Nest. I'm the innkeeper. How'd you get on Commander Hring's bad side, Trooper Sharik?"

"Huh? How—?"

Trin chuckled and nodded at the saddlebags on the floor. "You're on courier duty," she stated. "To the squad at Tarzy's Forge, right? That old sow, Hring, saves wintertime courier duty for whichever new Trooper-First she likes the least. What was your mortal sin?"

Sharik smiled gloomily. "I was late for morning roll call a few days ago."

Trin hissed with exaggerated sympathy and then laughed. She turned to Ressa, who watched silently from the hearth. "What brings you and your baby here on such a lovely evening, milady?"

"My—my husband died two months ago, Mistress," Ressa answered. She looked away to her left, though Trin had given no sign of having noticed the wine-mark.

"He had no kin, so I'm on my way to Stalo's Heath to be with my family."

"I'm sorry," Trin said gravely. Her smile returned after a moment. "Call me Trin, please. 'Mistress' makes me feel my age. C'mon to the kitchen, Trooper Sharik. Stew's in the pot. You two are the only guests tonight and the servants are all abed, so you'll have to help me fetch your supper."

"I thought we'd be covered up by the snow before that young fellow let us in," Sharik remarked as she followed after the innkeeper.

"Ah well, that's Emry," Trin said with a nod. "He's the ostler's apprentice. A good lad, but set him in front of a fire and he goes right to sleep." She stepped aside to let Sharik go ahead and then pulled the kitchen door shut behind her.

"All right," she asked, the cheerfulness falling away from her like a mask, "who in Winter's Hell is your friend out there, Trooper, and how did you meet her?"

The change from jolly innkeeper to efficient officer was so sudden that it took Sharik a moment to answer. "I—I met her this afternoon. On the road. As for who she is, you heard her yourself."

Trin snorted. "The only Stalo's Heath I've ever heard of is a little place up north—she's heading away from it. A young widow with a new baby could find sanctuary at any temple in return for a few light chores and wait till spring to travel, so what the hell's she doing on the road in a blizzard?"

Sharik felt her face burning. "When I found her, she was almost passed out in her saddle," she said defensively. "I could tell from looking at her that she's only just recovered from birthing, and I could *smell* the Lord-damned snow coming. What was I supposed to do, leave her to freeze? What would you have done?"

Trin glared, then shook her head. "I'd probably have done the same as you," she admitted. "Though it would've served me right if she'd turned out to be a lure in some bandit's trap." She went to a shelf and started setting wooden bowls on the table.

"I'll put her up till it's safe to travel again," she said. "I'll bill it to you. And just in case, we'll arrange it so she doesn't leave till you're well on your way."

"You'd let her travel alone?" Sharik asked coldly. "With a child that young?"

"I've a notion she's used to it. For a woman on courier duty, you collect odd companions." Trin started filling a serving bowl from a large, simmering pot in the kitchen fireplace. The smell was wonderful, and Sharik almost lost Trin's next works in the rumbling of her stomach.

"Besides," the older Hawk said, "whatever she's running from isn't likely to catch up with her in this weather."

Supper was a thick mutton and onion stew, with brown bread and beer. Sharik hadn't realized how hungry she was until she'd started eating. She was already wiping her bowl clean with a scrap of bread when Emry returned from the stables, stamping snow from his boots. Very politely, now that he was wide awake, the ostler's apprentice informed them that their horses were all settled for the night. This done, he sank into an armchair by the hearth and fell asleep.

Sharik regarded him with a speculative smile. Hot food had put her in a much better mood. Emry wasn't so young as he'd seemed at first, and he was rather fine-looking. Maybe. . . .

No, no. She was on duty until she delivered the dispatches in those Lord-damned saddle bags. If Trin found out, and she would, she'd report it to Hring and there'd be hell to pay. Sharik resigned herself to a chilly night and helped herself to another bowl of stew.

Smiling, Trin joined them at their table and began asking about what they'd seen on the road. The questions were bantering in tone, but most were directed at Ressa. Sharik knew that the young mother was being gently pumped for information, and she watched with fascination. Much as the confrontation in the kitchen rankled her, she had to admire Trin's acting skill. Gone was the Hawk with a sword blade for a spine. In her place was a good-humored innkeeper who cared only for hearty food, happy guests, and a bit of harmless gossip.

A brown old man who seemed as hard as a horseshoe, and whom Trin introduced as the ostler, came to look them over and wake his napping apprentice with a kick in the shin. Once he'd left, twin serving girls came to cluck over Dreyan and ask questions of their own. One of them stared openly at Ressa, but Trin cleared her throat dangerously and they both went hurrying back to bed.

Ressa ignored the stares. She spoke only when spoken to, answering all questions with either a "yes," "no," or "I don't know." When Dreyan began crying and Ressa took him to the hearth to change him, Trin finally gave up and started clearing the table. She paused and seemed to listen, then she shouted, "Wake up, Emry!"

The apprentice ostler, who had dozed off again, jerked awake and looked around guiltily. "I think I hear the horses," Trin told him. "Go make sure you've barred the door."

Emry grumbled and rose to fetch his coat and lantern while Trin picked up an armload of dishes. "I'll just leave these by the basin for the girls to clean in the morning," she told Sharik. "I'll be back to show you your rooms in just a blink."

Sharik debated offering Emry a hand, but the wind chose that moment to rattle the shutters and she decided to join Ressa by the fire instead. A blast of cold air blew through the open door when the young man left, and she congratulated herself on her good sense. She yawned and looked over Ressa's shoulder.

"Ugh," she said, making a face. "That's what I remember most about babies. That and the smell."

"You wouldn't mind so much if he were yours," Ressa assured her with a smile.

"Lady spare me," Sharik laughed. "I had my fill of that when I was a girl. Not only did I have to watch my brother when Ma was busy, but every time neighbors came visiting, I wound up minding their brats, too. Never again."

"Here." Ressa handed Dreyan up to her. "Hold him while I put this stuff away."

Sharik hesitated, and then took the boy. She had an awkward moment before she remembered how you held a baby. Dreyan squirmed and waved his fists at her, then he settled down and closed his eyes. She held very still, fearful of the squawk he might make if she woke him.

He looks like a tiny old man, she thought. *All red and wrinkled.*

"Maybe you'll get one of your own someday," Ressa teased.

"Hunh! Not likely." Sharik considered and added, "It happens sometimes. Not very often. After five years, you can petition for inactive status. What you do with it's your business, long as you keep the law and let the Order know where you are if you're needed. Some settle down and raise families."

"Ever had any second thoughts?" Ressa asked. "About being a Hawk, I mean."

"No," Sharik said quickly, which was a lie. There had been doubts. Looking at the child resting in her arms brought some back. *All the girls my age back home are wives by now,* she realized. *Hell, most are probably mothers. This is as close as I'm ever likely to come to a child of my own.*

Trin reappeared with a lantern in hand and a thick wool cloak wrapped about her shoulders. She regarded Sharik and Dreyan with a twitch of her lips and said, "I'll be back soon. We need a little more firewood for breakfast tomorrow."

"Need any help?" Sharik asked.

"No. I'll just fetch an armload in to dry overnight." Trin shut the door quickly, but the momentary chill woke Dreyan. He whimpered, and Sharik held him tighter until Ressa took him back and sat down on the hearth, rocking gently.

"Think we'll be able to travel tomorrow?" she asked.

Sharik shrugged. "Depends on the weather. Might be too much snow on the ground in the morning." Recalling Trin's suspicions, she added, "The Grain Lady's temple in Tarzy's Forge offers sanctuary, and it has a squad of Hawks for guards." Ressa stiffened, but she continued, "If you're in some kind of trouble—"

The front door slammed open and Emry ran in amidst a cloud of snow. "It's got her," he yelled wildly. "A demon's got Trin!"

Sharik's reflexes took over. She was out the door in an instant, sword in hand. The wind cut like a steel blade, and the shifting curtain of snow made vision fuzzy and indistinct, despite the light from the doorway. Up ahead, she saw a smudge of light by the white shape of the woodpile—Trin's lantern. She trudged toward it cautiously, slipping once in the cold, calf-deep blanket that covered the yard.

"Stop."

The voice carried clearly over the wind. Sharik halted and shifted her grip on her sword. A figure stepped from behind the woodpile and into the light of the lantern on the ground. She sucked in her breath at the sight.

Standing naked in the snow, smiling in the freezing wind, was the most beautiful man she'd ever seen. He was lean and well-muscled, with a fine face and dark yellow hair. He stooped gracefully and picked up the lantern, his eyes glimmering red in its light.

"I have the woman," he said in a deep, compelling voice. "Bring me the child, or she dies."

It took a moment for the words to register. Sharik licked her lips. "What child?" she asked, trying to hide her surprise and embarrassment.

The stranger grinned. "Ressa's child," he said. "The son of the woman with the marked face. Tell her that Haldan is here, and that she has till sunrise to give me the boy. Else I'll kill the woman a piece at a time. Now go."

"How do I know she's still alive?" Sharik demanded. "Let me see her."

"Go!"

Sharik shivered and ground her teeth in frustration. He carried no weapon, that was certain. She could rush him here and now. But the damned snow was slippery, and if he could stand there up to his knees in the stuff without a stitch on, who knew what else he could do? There was no telling where he kept Trin, or if he was alone. He had the advantage.

Silently cursing that damned smile, she turned her back on him and marched away. She looked back when she reached the door, but he was gone, lantern and all.

When she returned to the taproom, she found the other servants standing in a circle around Emry. The old ostler looked both worried and skeptical all at once. The twins were wide-eyed with fright—one was crying. They all spoke at once. "What was it?" "What did you see?" "Is she still alive?"

Ressa stood silently by the hearth, holding Dreyan close. She stared at Emry as though he were a viper.

Sharik slammed the door and shouted, "Quiet!" She paused in the silence to collect her thoughts. "Trin's alive," she said with as much conviction she could muster. "Emry, tell me what happened."

The frightened young man swallowed hard and stammered, "I—I was on my way back from looking in on your horses. They'd been spooked and were kicking their stalls, but I got them calmed down. I saw Mistress Trin by the woodpile and called to her. She told me to come over and lend a hand with the firewood." Emry's face twisted. "Something . . . climbed over top of the woodpile and grabbed her."

"And you just ran?" the ostler asked harshly.

"Trin told me to," Emry protested. "It stood there in the light and we both saw it clear. It was on all fours at first, but when it reared up to grab Trin, it looked like a man. Only hairy all over, with jaws like a wolf. Its eyes shone all red."

There was a gasp from the hearth. Ressa's face had gone as white as milk. Her red birthmark stood out like fresh blood.

"Did it speak, Emry?" Sharik asked, keeping her eyes on Ressa. "Did it say anything?"

"Say anything," Emry repeated blankly. "It growled some."

Sharik compared his description to what she'd seen and frowned. She walked up to Ressa, who seemed rooted to the floor, and said, "Haldan."

Right in the heart. Ressa looked around wildly, like a hare in a trap. Seeing no way out, she dropped to her knees before Sharik. "In the name of She Who Shields," she gasped out, "I ask protection for my son."

A sharp tingle went through Sharik, and something seemed to stir at the very back of her mind—something that coolly appraised Ressa and her son. Then her anger rose. Roughly, she took Ressa by the wrist and led her to the kitchen. "We mustn't be disturbed," she told the others.

When they were alone, Sharik ordered Ressa to sit. "Do you understand what you've asked of me?" she asked sharply.

"Y–yes," Ressa said, her eyes on the child in her lap. Sharik doubted her. Protection was one of the Order of the Red Hawk's oldest traditions. It dated from before there had been an Order; when the Hawks had been disorganized bands of women who'd sought sanctuary at the temples of the Lady's other aspects for one reason or another, and repaid that sanctuary by taking up arms to guard those temples from bandits and the like.

"You've asked me to become Dreyan's champion," Sharik told her. "Not just against whatever's out there, but against anyone in here who might try to toss the boy outside.

"What I don't think you know is that protection has a price—the truth. The War Lady won't shield anyone from a fate they deserve. Before I can grant you Her protection, I've got to know from whom and why, and She won't allow Her servants to be deceived." Or so her instructors at the Order's school had told her. She'd never done this before. "Tell me about Haldan," she said. "Who is he and why does he want your son?"

Ressa hesitated for several moments, watching her son. Finally, she said, "Haldan was . . . he is my husband. And Dreyan's father. He's also one of the beastfolk."

"A shapechanger?" Sharik stared in frank astonishment and harked to Emry's description of what he'd seen. It could be, though it was damned hard to believe. The beastfolk were a race apart, occupying remote forests and mountain ranges. They valued their privacy, and about all the rest of Hjelmark knew of them for certain was that they existed. There were stories that they sometimes preyed on humanfolk, but her instructors had dismissed such tales as overblown accounts of starving wolves and bears. "How in Winter's Hell did you come to marry into that tribe?"

"I didn't know what he was," Ressa answered. "I was a servant of the Lord of Pard's Ridge. Haldan was the forester. The new forester—the old one'd been killed by an animal, and Haldan got the job by bringing in a wolf he said had done it. We met at my Lord's house, and he . . . courted me."

Ressa covered her birthmark with one hand. Sharik remembered her own reaction at her first sight of Haldan, wild and magnificent. What had it been like for Ressa, to have someone like that seek her out?

"We married," Ressa continued. "I was happy, though he was away a lot. Many sheep were lost that year, and some shepherds, too. Haldan always came back with a wolf, or a bear, or poachers, but the killings always started again a month or two later.

"It wasn't long before Dreyan was born that he finally told me the truth—that he'd murdered the old forester and the others. He's a renegade among his own kind; exiled because he'd killed men for sport. He wanted to start a tribe of his own, so he'd wed me. All he'd wanted was a child. Once Dreyan was weaned, he meant to leave. Worse, he told me that—that there was chance that Dreyan'd be human instead of a shapechanger. He said he'd be able to tell after a few months, and that if Dreyan *was* human, he'd . . ." Ressa looked down at her son, ". . . he'd be prey."

Horrified, Sharik looked at Dreyan, who yawned and

waved a fist at his mother. *Lord and Lady,* she thought, feeling her stomach lurch, *his own son!* "So you ran," she guessed aloud. "And he followed. Why didn't you just accuse him to your lord?"

Ressa laughed bitterly. "Who'd have believed me if I'd said I hadn't known what he was? I'd been his wife for more than a year."

Ressa fell silent and Sharik leaned back against the wall, ignoring the other woman's eager gaze and waiting for a sign. The story made sense, but something about it felt *wrong,* somehow. The War Lady didn't appear with sword and armor amidst a thunderclap to accuse Ressa of lying, but the sense of someone looking over her shoulder was still there, stronger than before. She felt a growing certainty that could be put into words only by saying, "You have lied."

She wasn't aware of having said the words aloud, but Ressa started and said, "Hawk, I told the truth."

Sharik regarded her coolly, not bothering to reply. Ressa finally bowed her head, defeated.

"I knew from the start," she whispered. "Haldan told me everything before we were married. He didn't think he could keep it secret."

"Why did you agree?" Sharik asked implacably. Was there a hint of someone else's voice within her own?

Angry tears filled Ressa's eyes as she ran her fingers over the wine-colored mark that eclipsed half of her face. "Why should I have cared what he did to the others?" she demanded, half sobbing. "I'd never been any more to them than a night's fun or the butt of jokes. I'd heard stories about the beastfolk. How a man bitten by one becomes one, and how their bodies have no flaws. Haldan was perfect. He swore that when Dreyan was born, he'd make me as he is. Without flaw." She looked away, always to the left, and her voice went dull.

"I believed him. I didn't wonder till later why he needed a child to start his tribe if he could change humanfolk into his kind."

"So you left when you realized that he meant to betray

you?" Sharik's voice was icy, but Ressa looked up and met her eyes.

"I left because he'd have killed my son if I'd stayed."

That, Sharik knew, was the truth. She watched Dreyan, who was looking around crossly. How much of him was human? How much of his father waited behind those blue eyes? It didn't matter. The boy was guiltless, at least so far, and her vows had been specific.

"By She Who Shields," Sharik said, "I will protect your son."

Tension drained from Ressa and she slumped a little. "Thank you, Hawk," she whispered.

Thank your son, Sharik thought sourly as she strode out of the room.

Sharik stepped out into the snow and looked around carefully. There was no sign of Haldan, but she didn't doubt that she was being watched. She walked about four yards from the inn and stopped, waiting.

The storm had died down a little. The wind was merely a breeze now, though it still raised gooseflesh through Ressa's threadbare dress and cloak. Sharik's hair was bound tightly under the hood, and red paint had been daubed on one side of her face. In her arms she held a piece of firewood wrapped in Dreyan's blanket. Hidden by the blanket was a dagger gripped in her right hand.

The dagger's wooden hilt was sweaty despite the cold. She'd have given anything to have her sword right now, but the disguise was chancy enough as it was. She wouldn't fool anyone who got a good look at her, but with some snow still falling, and Ressa's clothes to confuse her scent, Haldan might not realize his danger until she was close enough to use the blade.

That would have to be damned close. She'd spent the last hour quizzing Ressa about her husband, looking for something she could use against him. Fortunately, when Haldan had offered his wife power, he'd mentioned some weaknesses, too. There was silver, of course, but that was no help here. Unless she could stuff a few coins down the bastard's throat. Fire wasn't much better. Steel could do the trick, but not easily. It seemed the beastfolk healed *fast*. Haldan had boasted to Ressa that if a wound made by steel wasn't instantly fatal, he could ignore it. There weren't many places a dagger could reach that would kill a man-sized target at once, and Sharik would have to be standing right next to Haldan to get at them.

It was a pity Ressa hadn't had more nerve. She'd had plenty of chances at her husband. She could've killed him in his sleep any night and spared everyone a lot of—

There was a light up ahead. Sharik tightened her grip on her dagger and watched as two figures walked out of the gloom and stopped about ten yards away. Trin's hands were tied behind her back. She looked frozen, and mad enough to spit nails, but unhurt. Haldan was still smiling and still as bare as the day he was born, but now Sharik found herself regarding him as merely a target.

"Bring him here, Ressa," Haldan called to her.

Sharik didn't trust her voice to fool him. She shook her head and pointed at Trin. Haldan's smile never faltered. He shrugged carelessly and shoved the older Hawk forward. Trin strumbled and nearly fell in the snow, then she staggered toward the inn, stiff from the cold. Haldan beckoned to Sharik, and she began walking toward him.

Through an eye, she thought. *Or an ear. Heart's too risky—too many ribs. Gotta get close, gotta get close. If only we had a bow. Bless me, Lady, this is not how I imagined my first battle!*

She came abreast of Trin and saw her give a little start of recognition. Sharik moved on with a small nod of her head, hoping that the older woman would do the sensible thing and keep walking. Trin couldn't help with her hands bound, and there wouldn't be time to free her. The innkeeper swore softly, and Sharik heard her trudge away through the snow.

She was about three yards from Haldan when his smile vanished. He stared hard at her, then he dropped the lantern, fell to all fours, and *changed*.

Sharik hadn't known what to expect—Ressa had never seen her husband's transformation. She'd hoped that changing shape would be a lengthy process, giving her time to use the dagger, but Haldan's contours flowed like quicksilver in the light of the fallen lantern for no more than a heartbeat. The suddenness of it shocked her into paralysis. Haldan looked up, red-eyed, his straw-colored pelt stiff with rage. He roared a challenge through a wolf's steaming muzzle and lunged over the snow at her.

That roar broke the spell. Sharik hurled the piece of firewood as hard as she could. Haldan ducked under it and slammed into her, knocking her flat on her back. The snow was as cold as death through her clothes, and pain lanced through her side. Haldan was on her in an instant. A taloned hand fastened around her throat and she felt a claw slice through the skin over her jaw. His jaws stretched wide, baring teeth like knives.

Sharik thrust her dagger into his stomach. Haldan grunted at the blow, and then screamed as she cut him across the belly. He twisted off of her and away, blood spraying her arm and chest. She tried to rise and press the attack, but the snow and the pain in her ribs slowed her. By the time she got to her feet, Haldan had recovered. He raked her leg and she fell to her knees with a scream. Haldan wrapped his arms around her, pinning hers to her sides, and bore her down. His breath steamed into her face, hot and rancid. Sharik twisted desperately and his teeth clicked shut next to her ear. His head reared back. Slowly, dreamily, those teeth came for her throat again.

Something hit his back. Sharik felt the blow through his body. Snarling, Haldan leapt up and whirled, releasing her. She climbed painfully to a crouch and saw Ressa standing there, wrapped in a borrowed shift and clumsily lifting a sword as though she were chopping wood. Haldan made a coughing sound that might have been laughter. He backhanded his wife into the snow and turned back to finish Sharik.

Screaming a warcry, Sharik surged to her feet, driving her dagger up through his lower jaw and into the base of his skull. He choked raggedly on the blade and toppled over backward. She landed on top of him, throwing her weight on the dagger, pushing it deeper. She twisted the blood-slick hilt and heard bone crack. Haldan shuddered and lay still.

Sharik looked up at Ressa and grinned fiercely. The other woman shivered where she'd fallen and looked sick. Trin was shouting, and the others were running through the snow toward them. There was blood on the snow, like Ressa's birthmark against her skin. A glint of steel caught Sharik's eye and she noticed the sword lying near Ressa.

"That's *my* sword!" she protested weakly as she was lifted to her feet.

Two days later, four travelers appeared at the door of the Hawk's Nest. Three men and a woman, on foot. Their trail led from the edge of the forest across the road, through snow too deep for a horse. Sharik watched their approach from the little window of her room, and she knew them for beastfolk at once. The way they carried themselves, the way they walked, all reminded her of Haldan's careless, feral grace.

Getting into her clothes was difficult, even after she'd intimidated one of the twins into helping her. Her chest was wrapped to bind her cracked ribs, and the gashes in her leg were stitched up. A spike of pain took her breath whenever she stretched or moved too fast. The collar of her shirt hid the clawmarks on her throat, all but the finger-length cut running along the line of her jaw, from her chin almost to her ear. Sharik studied it for a long time in the tiny mirror the serving girl provided, and then she dismissed it. Scars were something a Hawk got used to, according to her instructors, and this one was mild compared to some she'd already seen.

When she'd finally gotten her sword buckled on, she limped downstairs. Trin met her at the landing. "They came hunting Haldan," the older Hawk said without preamble. "Somehow, his tribe heard about the killings in Pard's Ridge. Two of 'em have gone with Emry to see the body. The others are with Ressa."

"You trust them?" Sharik asked, wobbling a little on her feet.

"Do I have a choice?" Trin said as she took her arm and helped her into the taproom. "You're in no shape to take 'em on. Come sit down before you tear those stitches."

Ressa sat at a table with Dreyan in her lap, talking earnestly to the woman and one of the men. They all looked up when Trin seated Sharik in the armchair by the hearth and took up a post of her own nearby.

The two shapechangers were handsome, though their clothing was ill-fitting wool and plain leather. Both wore necklaces of animal teeth, claws, feathers, and bits of bone on braided leather thongs. They regarded Sharik gravely and spoke to each other in low tones. The language was new to her, though she caught an occasional word of Hjelmaric.

When Emry returned with the others, the woman said something to them and nodded at her. One of the two, a broad man with gray in his brown beard, approached her chair. His necklace was more ornate than the others, with metal trinkets and wire worked in among the rest. Sharik guessed that he was the leader.

"You are Hawk Sharik, who killed Haldan?" he asked in heavily accented Hjelmaric.

"I am," Sharik replied warily. Her hand rested lightly on the hilt of her sword. Behind her, Trin had tensed.

"He was kinless," the shapechanger said. "A rogue who brought us shame. Do what you want with the body." He plucked one of the metal decorations from his necklace and pressed it into her hand. "You have friends in the Gedna Hills, Hawk Sharik," he told her.

Sharik looked at the trinket in her palm. It was a little disk of beaten brass, with a stag's head delicately etched onto its face. "Th–thank you," she said. The shapechanger nodded and rejoined his fellows at the table, leaving her to hope that her friends in Gedna, wherever that was, would forgive her if she never visited.

The beastfolk began talking among themselves. Occasionally the leader or the woman—they seemed to be the only ones who spoke Hjelmaric—would ask Ressa something, and her answer would set them off again.

As best Sharik could tell, Dreyan was the point of the discussion.

Ressa sat calmly and watched the four of them with interest while her son dozed in her arms. She smiled readily, meeting every gaze heedless of the birthmark that was in plain sight. *Might be relief,* Sharik thought, running her thumb along the cut on her jaw, *or it might be something more. Lady, there's still a hell of a lot I don't like about her—she could have prevented all this— but she is changed.*

When the conference broke up, the four visitors trooped outside and headed for the woods. Sharik felt herself relax a little. Trin sighed gustily and made for the kitchen, ordering Emry to fetch the girls to help with dinner. Ressa came over to sit on the hearth near Sharik's chair.

"They'll be back tomorrow," she said, setting her son on her lap. "They want Dreyan to return with them. If he does turn out to be a shapechanger, it's best if he's among his own kind."

Sharik looked down at the child and sought some hint of the otherness that had been so strong in the four who'd just left. She sensed nothing, but he was so young. Even Haldan hadn't been sure. "What if he's human?" she asked quietly.

"Then we'll go someplace else." Ressa replied.

"We? You're going along? They're a clannish bunch, I've heard. Will *you* be welcome?"

"I don't know," Ressa admitted, her eyes on Dreyan. "I don't think these four do either. They didn't try to lie to me; they really don't know if I'll be welcome or not. They offered to foster him, but I can't leave him now." She was silent for a while, and when she spoke again, she almost whispered.

"When Dreyan was born, I—I had no time for a Naming ceremony. You said there's a temple in Tarzy's Forge." She looked up. "Sharik, when you get there, would you ask the priestesses to say a prayer and a Naming for Dreyan of Kelsera? Would you . . . stand in my place for the Naming?"

Sharik blinked in surprise. "You want me to be his godmother?"

Ressa smiled. "I can't think of anyone better."

Sharik looked from mother to child, her head full of objections. She and the boy would likely never set eyes on each other again. She'd never be anything more to him than a story his mother told, and he'd be just a memory to her. What good was such a godmother? The idea was ridiculous.

But someone had to speak for the mother in a Naming, and only rarely did a Hawk raise a family. Given the life she'd chosen, this might be as close as she'd ever come to a child of her own.

"Yes," Sharik said softly. "Yes, I'll do both. May I hold him, please?"

FAIR PLAY
by Jennifer Roberson

Jennifer Roberson has a habit of writing stories which aren't quite what they seem. This is one of the most elaborate—and most subtly feminist—stories I've ever read; though Jennifer—one of my most fascinating and prolific discoveries—has, as I said, a habit of writing stories which aren't quite what the reader expects.

Since making her debut in the first of these volumes she's written eight (seven now in print) of her Cheysuli series—and four of the Sword-Dancer stories which also made their debut here. Under the name Jennifer O'Green she has also written romances; writers have to do the damnedest things to make a living. I used to be becroggled by the lists of weird jobs writers had held; it finally came to me that it's because you dare not, when you're a writer, commit to any job you can't leave at two weeks notice when lightning strikes ... translation; when an editor buys something and gives you a deadline.

Jennifer is married to a former Air Force fighter pilot turned computer game designer; and her household includes a Labrador, a Welsh Corgi, a 160-pound Great Dane/Irish Wolfhound cross—and two cats who "boss around a total of 265 pounds of canine quite competently."

Half-grown, half-starved, and only half a woman; he reckoned her twelve, *possibly*. With the eyes of a desperation more appropriate to the dying.

At the door, resolution wavered. Her hands remained on the rough sacking tacked up to keep out the road dust; wood was too dear for doors. She lingered there, clutching tightly, until a man came in behind her and tore the fabric away, swearing at the impediment. The man wanted ale *immediately*. And a whore, probably sooner.

A second glance, and briefly: then the man was pushing by, muttering of girl-babes just quit of the breast wandering unasked into men's affairs.

The girl bit into her lip, staring blindly after him. Then the tears faded. The small chin firmed. Resolve blazed in dark eyes. She moved stiffly aside from the entrance and stared hard at each man. The room was full of them: ten, twelve, maybe twenty. She looked at every man, weighing each in his turn, until she came to *him*, and saw him staring back. Weighing even as she did.

Color waned, then returned, tinting the dusky skin. He looked back dispassionately, contemplating the girl: disheveled dark hair spilling over narrow shoulders; the curve of brow and cheek, too young yet for coarseness; the fingertip cleft in her chin. Beneath the dust, behind the hair, without the disfiguring bruises, she promised one day to be pretty. *If* she lived that long. For now, no one knew it; it was her only hope.

But in her the hope was extinguished. She knew the world too well.

She came, as he expected. Crossed the room from door to corner, to stand beside his table. Trembling violently, and hating herself for it.

The tapster also came, to shoo away the pest.

"No," he said softly.

The tapster was shooed instead.

The girl stared at him, trying to tame her trembling. Her torn, knee-length tunic matched the door sacking. The stains of it matched the table: drying blood, and spilled wine.

"Well?" he asked quietly.

She reached to the bottom of her tunic and untied the dirty knot. Something glinted briefly. Then she set it down on the table, where he could see the cross-hatching that denoted its worth, and snatched her hand away.

"A three-piece," he observed.

She bit into her lip, then licked it. The words spilled out in a rush. "Is it enough?" she asked. "For that, will you do a thing?"

He smiled without giving offense. "Enough for *some* things, certainly. What one do you want to buy?"

A sheen of tears in her eyes, then a mocking glint of contempt. "A man's death," she declared, and spat onto the floor.

"Ah." Lightly he touched the blood-stained coin with a sensitized fingertip. Metal was not so conductive as fabric or flesh, but neither was he an apprentice. He read the coin easily; he also read the girl. "Ah," he murmured once more.

She was fiercely adamant. "Is it *enough?*"

Idly, he turned the coin over. On the back, the three cross-hatches; on the front, the High King's seal: a hawk stooping on a hare.

"The king's copper," he remarked, "is not easily come by."

"I'm not a *thief!*" she flared. "And I'm not a whore, either . . . but it's what he *wants* me to be." Dusky cheeks burned dark. "That coin bought my mother's death. She hid it, and he killed her. Now he wants me in her place, to earn a living for him." The notched chin rose. "I'm not a thief," she repeated thickly. "And I'm not a whore, either."

"No," he said quietly. "And *I* am not a killer of men."

Swollen lips parted slightly. Nostrils flared, and quivered. Dark eyes lost their passion. "But—you are *here.*"

He understood her. *Here* was a hovel posing as a tavern. The thatching was black and greasy, the packed dirt floors fouled. The common room stank of bad wine, old ale, burned meat, and the stench of unwashed bodies.

"I am *here*," he answered quietly, "because it was the only room I could find. I am only passing through."

A grimy hand darted out and recaptured the coin. He trapped it on the way back and held it in his own.

She tested him once, then went very still. In her fist was the three-piece coin, the High King's own copper. But the fist was in his hand; the dirty, callused hand with bleeding, ravaged nails. And her world in the touching of it.

"*Ah*," he said softly. "Now I understand."

The delicate chin trembled once, then was stilled. "*Do* you?" she challenged thickly. "You are a man. How *could* you?" And then the dark eyes dulled. "Unless you want me to—"

"No." He released her fist. "Take me to him, Safiyah."

She stared. "You *know*—?" But she bit it off. Clutching the coin, she stared. "Just like—so?"

He rose quietly. "Just like so."

"But . . ." Nonplussed, she bit her lip. "I thought it would be in secret. At night. In the dark."

"Would you say it lacks the doing, that it can wait so long?"

"*No!*" she hissed, then gulped. "But—now? And with me there?"

He touched her head gently. "And is it not for you it is done?"

She bared teeth. "For my mother."

"Your mother is dead, Safiyah. This will not bring her back. Therefore it is for *you*."

"Then *yes*," she hissed. "For me."

He smiled very faintly. "Then I think it is worth the doing."

She gripped the coin in her fist. "Do you want payment after?" And then realization flared. "It isn't *enough*, is it? You're only lying to me, to make me go away!"

"Have I not asked you to take me to him?"

Now she was confused. She held out the coin again.

"After," he said quietly.

For the moment, it sufficed.

*   *   *

A hovel, as expected. And the father much the same: foul of clothing and habits, but free with his daughter's body if that body bought him wine.

The father was, at first, overjoyed to see his daughter complying with his wishes: that she take up her mother's trade. The misunderstanding was soon dispelled.

Blood muddied the dirt. But the body was no longer present. "You murdered your wife."

The father's eyes were dark and drugged with wine. He bared rotting teeth. "She stole from me and hid it."

"Coin she earned by whoring. Whoring because she had to; you beat her, otherwise."

Dull dark eyes flickered. "A man does as he will with his woman."

"If nothing else, bad business. A dead whore earns nothing."

The father pointed briefly. "I got *her* for that."

"And if she refuses? Will you beat her, too? Perhaps even kill her, when she does as her mother did in hopes of running away?"

Sluggish belligerence: "A man does as he will with his *daughter,* same as he does with his wife."

"Even to raping her? As you have just raped Safiyah?"

Safiyah's father spat at the stranger's soft-booted feet. "*That* for your words! The woman was mine, as *she* is; I do as I will with them all!"

"Ah," the stranger murmured. Then looked at the girl beside him. "Go outside, Safiyah."

She stared back blankly. Then comprehension flared in her eyes. She fled her father's hovel.

When it was done, he stepped outside into the clean sunlight, deftly straightening one rune-bordered linen cuff just escaping the suede sleeve. As expected, the girl was waiting. In an agony of curiosity and a stricken, sickened anguish.

She stood before the hovel, hugging her hollow belly. "Did you do it? Did you *do* it?"

He squinted slightly against the sun, then lifted a

shielding hand. On the back of it was a mark: a blue crescent moon. "I did what was required."

"He's dead. . . ." she murmured dully.

And then the scream came from the hovel: a keening wail of shocked discovery; of disbelief, comprehension, denial.

"*Not* dead," she blurted, and stared up at the man. "You said he was *dead!*"

"No," he answered gently. "I said I did what was required."

Her father ran out of the hovel. His clothing was torn away to display his despoiled body: full, dark-nippled breasts; slim waist curving into hips; the furred mound beneath.

"A *woman!*" her father screamed. Man's voice. Man's face. But beneath it a woman's body. "*Look what you've done to me!*"

"Mmmm," the stranger answered, then looked down at Safiyah.

"*Look what you've done to me!*"

Safiyah's stare was glazed. The stranger reached down and took her cold hand. He warmed it with a thought, then led her away quietly. Behind them the father sobbed as he fell to his knees: "*Look what he's done to me. . . .*"

He knelt, still holding her hand. Her expression was dulled by disbelief; by the shock of what she had seen.

He still held her other hand. Gently he pressed his thumb against thin skin, feeling the fragile bones. He said a single word. Then, "Be free of it," and took his hand from hers.

Safiyah stared at it. On the back of her hand was a mark: a blue crescent moon. "*What—?*" she began.

"Be free of fear," he told her. "Do you not know the crescent moon?"

Safiyah trembled. "*No. . . .*"

"Ah." He smiled gently. "No more than the High King's mark on the three-piece coin." He displayed the back of his hand. "Do you see? We match."

She stared at the mark. "But—what *is* it? And why did you do it?"

"I did it because you are a woman alone in the world. Honest, decent work is hard for a woman to find when she has no man to tend her . . . and even a man is no guarantee of a safe life, as your mother discovered." He tilted his head toward her father, from whom issued hoarse sobbing. "He will leave here, because he will not be able to bear what he is when others knew what he *was*. You, too, must leave, so you can begin anew. But your way is not his. I have given you safe passage."

Her eyes were huge and wary. "I don't understand."

"Show your hand to a man with bread, and he will give you meat. Show your hand to a cloth merchant, and he will give you silk. Show your hand to a mule-trader, and he will give you a horse." His tone altered subtlely. "It is for survival. Until you can find honest, decent work. But if you attempt to use it for wealth, the mark will disappear."

She stared at the blue crescent moon. "Will I have it forever?"

"Only as long as you need it. But a strong woman such as Safiyah will not be in need for very long; eventually, she will *do*. She will change the world around her. She will remake it to fit her ideals."

"*I* can do that?"

"You must. Women are worth far more than what your father believed. His kind have ruled too long. Now it is for you."

Comprehension brightened her eyes. Then, distracted, she reached out, hesitated, then touched his own crescent moon. "What is it? How did *you* get it?"

"The mark of the High King's mage." He paused. "I was born with it. It was how the priests knew."

She nodded vaguely, uncomprehending; to her it was a word. To her, he was a man. "What about him?" she asked, staring at the woman. "What about my father?"

"Turn-about is fair play." The High King's mage smiled. "He must whore for himself, now."

That, she understood. Safiyah began to laugh.

KAYLI KIDNAPPED
by Paula Helm Murray

Paula Helm Murray has appeared in my anthologies S&S4 and SPELLS OF WONDER, and in *Marion Zimmer Bradley's Fantasy Magazine*—so I can think of her as one of "MY" writers. She has three "mewses" which, as I conjectured, are cats; and has several birds—which I always thought was cruel to either the cats or the birds or at least frustrating to one or the other. She also has a diskette with over a dozen story ideas—probably more useful then my collection of notebooks—but has everything backed up in print, so it's not so bad. She counts surviving her husband's constant stream of bad puns among her greatest achievements. (I hope the parrot doesn't start learning them; she could get them in stereo. . . .)

She's also—who isn't—working on a novel. At this rate she might even get it written. It goes without saying that nobody ever has time to write; what you have to do is *make* time.

Fyl sauntered into the kitchen, ready to digest his recent meal of char-broiled mouse in the peace and quiet of his favorite spot in front of Kayli's hearth. As the small, round dragonet came through the door, a shriek of "DAMNIT!" reverberated in the kitchen, and a plate shattered on the wall over his head.

Goddess! what have I walked into? Fyl thought. He ducked and ran.

"Hugh, what have you done?" Kayli asked, pacing and staring, amazed, at her tall, red-headed husband, arms crossed over her pregnant belly.

"Kay, he ordered . . ." he stammered and looked down at his feet, face flaming scarlet in a blush. He started a gesture with his left hand, then flushed even deeper, as if thinking such a gesture took two hands. An injury the previous spring had cost him the use of his right arm; a leather harness-sling held it against his body now.

"He ordered you to give what was not yours," she finished for him. "Send the messenger back. Troy must speak with me. I want to know what was promised behind my back at our betrothal!" She threw another plate at him. It shattered quite satisfyingly.

She turned, made her way up the steps into their bedroom, as swiftly as she could manage, and barred the door behind her. *Goddess, give me strength!* she thought. *Need to rest, I'm so tired these days.* The baby kicked inside her, distracting her from her black mood. She sat on the edge of the bed.

Why could this not have happened in a month, in a few weeks, for that matter? After you are out! If Hugh promised men for Troy's army—does he have rocks for brains? The distraction didn't last very long. *And me helpless . . . and the weather this spring just as bad as last year's . . . at least my roof doesn't leak anymore . . . Goddess!!!*

"Kay?" Hugh called outside the door, "Kay, please let me in! I've done as you wish!"

"You swear it?" she asked back, "or is this just another of your lies?"

"Kayli, let me in, please. I have sent the messenger back with your words. What Troy does is another matter entirely."

She sighed. He sounded abject. *Never seem to be able to stay angry with him.* She rose and unbarred the door, then stretched out on the bed.

He came and sat beside her on the bed. "Kay, he's

my older brother. I've never been able . . ." He touched her cheek with his left hand, then smoothed her long, white hair.

"Never been able to stand up to him. You've already said that." She sighed and closed her eyes. "Hugh, I doubt I could get these people to defend their own lives, even if the threat were riding over the hill. Some stray priestess left them with an odd religion. They refuse to deliberately spill anyone else's blood."

"But that stranger, last year, when Sylva was kidnapped . . ."

"Apparently he flew at them, in some sort of mad rage. I think his death was an accident of them defending themselves. They're still ashamed of that."

"And you cannot do your magic?"

"Grandmother told me," she reined in her anger, "and I've told you. I want child within to be tall and golden and handsome, just like his father. To use my magic risks him even being born alive."

"You'd not settle for a mage, like yourself?" Hugh asked tenderly. "There's enough of a chance for that, what with my mother's talent and all."

"Oh, aye, I guess." She winced as the baby kicked again. "He's healthy enough." She took his hand and placed it on her belly. "He's been kicking me all day." The baby obliged, much to her discomfort.

"A lively one." He grinned. "And what if it's a girl?"

"I'll take what I get, but I don't want to damage it by using my fire." She flopped back, realizing how tired she felt.

"Ahem?" a small, squeaky voice said, from the doorway. "Are you done fighting, ma?" Fyl peered in around the door. He had been a warm comfort during the cold, wet winter, almost the only bright spot.

"Oh, aye," Kayli replied, "come along, little one."

He readily trotted into the room and climbed lithely up onto the bed, to curl up beside Kayli. Hugh and Kayli both patted him gently.

"What's up?" Hugh asked.

"Messenger left," he replied, turning his long neck so

he could look at them as he talked, with big, amber eyes that matched Kayli's, "Hugh DID tell him off, ma. Said he had to abide by YOUR wishes."

Kayli opened her eyes and looked up at Hugh. "Then I expect we shall have a visit from the king, soon. I'm not pleased, but at least we can talk. What DID you promise him, Hugh?"

"I made no promises to him when we discussed my marryin' you," Hugh said. "He kept saying I'd be lord here and I kept telling him you were the landed liege. Really, Kay, you have to believe me. He just assumed I'd take my right."

Hugh's face always gave him away when he lied; Kayli knew he told her the truth now. "And now he assumes you'll send him men for soldiers." Dealing with her irritable brother-in-law always aggravated Kayli. *That arrogant, cruel man assumes everyone will do his bidding. And after losing Ylgs, my old bridge dragon, last year, I have no wish to risk the life of Thyr, the new bridge dragon, to Troy's archers.*

The weather cleared, as it often did in the spring. A week after they sent the messenger back to Troy, Kayli rested out in the meadow above her castle, watching the sheep and basking in the sun. She could hear Hugh singing as he worked in the stables. She dozed, enjoying the warmth. Fyl sprawled on a rock near her, basking with an equal lack of dignity.

She startled awake at the sound of a horse shaking its bridle, jingling the bits. She sat up and looked up at Troy.

He rode a light horse and wore no royal garments. For a brief moment, she didn't recognize him, he looked so common. He dismounted and stood before her. Fyl woke with a squeak and sat up.

"My lady," he bowed, then extended a hand to help her up as she started to rise.

Kayli pulled back and stared at him a moment. She had read once of wizard-created doppelgängers. The stocky, dark half-brother of her husband usually lacked even the merest manners.

"It is I, really, my lady." He smiled, a small, tight smile. Then his face returned to seriousness. "I'll not harm you."

She extended her hand and he helped her stand.

"I had no idea . . ." he started, looking her over. "I'd wager you didn't even read what I sent Hugh, asking for help."

"No, cousin," Kayli replied, "Hugh told me what it had to do with and I told him to return the reply. Why are you not talking with HIM, my lord?" She looked him over closely.

"I realize that he really meant it, that you ARE liege here." He took off his hat. "I've come to ask a favor, my lady."

"I fear I know the favor. I cannot give you what you want." She realized that the short hairs on the back of her neck suddenly stood straight up. *Wonder what's up.*

He took her hand again, as if to kiss it. "Then, my fine lady, your hand will be forced."

Before Kayli knew what happened, Troy twisted her arm behind her back. "I've got her, men!" he yelled. "She's helpless while she's pregnant. Someone, get the dragonet. Catch him, kill him!"

It never occurred to Kayli to scream; the gag he forced into her mouth was an unnecessary discomfort. She started a panicked spell, one that would make noise and light and didn't need gesturing—the baby gave a twist and a sharp kick inside her. She froze, and stopped the progress of the spell.

She heard Fyl squeak; then he made a sharp, high noise that cut off abruptly. She couldn't see in the melee of men around her. She felt ill.

"I'm certain this will give Hugh the leverage he needs." Troy escorted her to a horse-borne litter. "You gave the man a spine, lass, but let's see how he acts now."

He helped her into the litter. "Do not try to escape," Troy ordered, "my men have orders to kill you." An ugly smile formed on his face. "You are not that quick, and Hugh won't need to know what happened to you until he's already given me what I want." He unbound her hands.

Kayli stared at him a moment. She felt sick at heart. *So much for keeping the wars of the West out,* she thought.

Despite the lurching and jerking, she soon fell asleep; more a reaction to the stress than anything else.

"Hugh!" Fyl fairly screamed as he galloped into the barn.

Hugh bent a nail, pre-set by Wilse, nearly double with one mighty blow at the distraction of the dragonet's entrance.

"DAMNIT! Fyl, what's the matter with you?" Hugh took a deep breath, lay the hammer aside and helped the dragonet up to sit on a stall wall, face-to-face. He realized the dragonet had what looked like a fresh bruise swelling on his side.

"It's . . . it's . . ." Fyl stammered, then curled his long lithe neck to hide his head behind his forepaws and started whimpering piteously.

"What's the matter?" Wilse, Hugh's younger brother, came to them. "He's in quite a state." Wilse had come to Riverwer when Hugh returned, to help his brother rebuild the castle, and stayed on. He married Sylva, daughter of the village headman.

"Little one, WHAT is the matter?" Hugh asked. He had never seen Fyl so abject. The little smart-mouthed beast usually exuded an air of bravado, even when he feared for his life. This was another matter entirely.

Hugh gently cradled the little creature into his sling. Then he started gently stroking him. "Fyl, little fellow. Whatever can be the matter? Come now, you're among friends."

Fyl finally uncovered his face, wide-eyed and trembling. "Kay . . . ma. She's gone, Hugh, taken!" he squeaked.

Wilse's hammer clattered to the floor. "Taken . . . kidnapped?"

"Don't know that word," Fyl replied, after a deep breath. "Some men came, I think the one who grabbed her was your brother, the king . . . I think. Dark, stocky, had your accent. Oh, HUGH!" He wailed and hid his face again.

"Damnit, damnit, damnit!" Hugh kicked the wall, though he still gently stroked the dragonet. "I wondered if he'd pull something like this. Goddess, Wilse, what can I do? I don't want to act rashly . . . this was a rash act on Troy's part." Hugh turned, went down into the castle and carried the little dragon into the bedroom. He pulled Fyl out of his sling onto a nest of blankets and looked around him for a moment. Then he sat backwards on the chair, chin resting on his hand on the back of the chair, staring and thinking.

This cannot be real, he thought, *she seems so close in here!* "Oh, Kay, what am I going to do?" he asked aloud. "I will not send the villagers. That I promised to you and to them. And Thyr would be in great danger if she went; Troy relies heavily on his archers."

Fyl finally unwound. Hugh jumped as the little creature stirred and realized he didn't know how long he'd been here, thinking. The dragonet flowed off the bed and up onto his right shoulder.

"What'cha thinkin', Hugh?" he asked softly.

"On how to get our Kay back," he replied. He laughed.

"What's wrong? What's funny?" Fyl drew back a little.

"A year ago if someone told me I'd be talkin' to a small lizard like yourself . . ."

"I am NOT a lizard," Fyl replied smartly, "I'm a dragonet! BIG difference!"

"Sorry, sorry! That I'd be keeping company with such a fine dragonet," he patted Fyl lightly, then scratched the dragonet's head on the spots where he always seemed to be itchy, "I'd have told him he was mad. Time changes things, doesn't it?"

"Yeah. So what are we going to do to get our Kay back?"

"I've something that just might work, but I must discuss it with Wilse." He rose, then realized he could smell good things coming from the kitchen below. *Later than I thought; can't see the sun in here, but I'd wager it's late afternoon.*

He made his way downstairs, Fyl perched on his right shoulder.

Sylva bustled around the tidy kitchen, fixing a dinner of roast chicken and carrots and potatoes. She looked up briefly at Hugh, then back down at the pot of vegetables. Tear stains marred her pretty face.

Wilse sat at the table, staring glumly into a stein of ale. He looked up when Hugh sat down across from him.

"What've you decided, brother?" Wilse asked quietly. He looked half done-in, as if he had taken his anger out in hard work.

"Troy has violated his word of honor to me. I intend to challenge him to a duel of honor." He felt better once it was said, as if it all were over and done.

Sylva gasped but kept at her work.

"You're mad!" Wilse half stood.

"Sit!" Hugh said firmly. "I've decided and there's no changin' my mind."

"But you're a cripple!" Wilse finished standing. "There's no gettin' around that, Hugh. Honor or no, he'll cut you to shreds!"

"Wilse, I've been practicing with the sword; all I need to work out is a shield. I was more than his match before . . . and I feel I'm to that point again."

Wilse stared, mouth agape. "You are mad!"

"You said that. It's the only way I see, to take him in public, where all can see his stained honor. He promised me, in front of a lot of people, that he wouldn't ask Kayli's villagers to serve in his army. And he promised that my service to him was finished, the price of my arm. I'll have my due in this."

"If he lets you . . ." Wilse started.

"He has no choice," Hugh interrupted, "We are his only kin. He has no heirs, and he has made public vows to respect our rights."

"He holds to no vows. . . ."

"He will hold to my sword," Hugh replied. The grimness he felt weighed on his heart. He had learned a certain new strength of will after living with Kayli, but he missed her sorely. "I am stronger than he."

"I don't like it." Wilse had a certain set to his face.

"You don't have to. You're staying here."

"Hugh . . ."

"Damnit, man, Sylva is pregnant, too. Kayli's in hand. You and Sylva aren't. You are safe as any here."

Wilse stared at him a moment, then looked away. "I cannot naysay you, Hugh, and you make sense in your own way."

"Sylva? Have you anything to add?" Hugh asked.

"Having child within makes me want Wilse here," she replied, after an embarrassed moment.

"Then it is settled," Hugh said. "Wilse, do not follow if I do not return. And, if that happens, TRY to get the men to arm themselves. Let them know that if I fail to return with their lady, Troy will surely come and force them into service."

"I will try, brother."

"I'll go with you, Hugh," Fyl chimed in, after they all stopped talking.

"Little one . . ." Hadn't considered him, Hugh thought silently. Sylva always set out a plate of odds and ends for the little dragon. This night he just pushed his food around a little, without eating at all. "But I'll worry about you every moment," he finished.

"But I can find Kayli, while you fight Troy," Fyl said, "I'll bet I can find her better than you can!"

"You're shy enough of people's feet in the village," Wilse said, "you have no idea what a city is like, Fyl."

"I'd best learn, then." He stared at Hugh solemnly. "You can't make me stay, you know."

"Rather have you with me, knowing you're safe," Hugh said finally, "than knowing you're tagging along somewhere behind, perhaps straying or getting hurt." He sighed. "You may come along."

"Thank you."

They all ate their meal in silence.

Hugh left at dawn the next morning, with Fyl perched on the pommel of Hugh's war saddle. Wilse had helped him figure out a way to strap his shield across his chest with a leather strap the night before. His helmet, shield, sword and mail, along with a bedroll and food for the journey, were strapped on the saddle. He rode his sorrel greathorse stallion.

The day was clear and bright, not too warm, *not a bad day for a ride,* he thought. *But that Kay might be hurt . . . or even killed.* That thought soured it for him. Fyl was in a similar mood, and sat tight, without any chatting or mouthing off.

The villagers gathered and stared as he rode away. He chose not to say a word. *Can't think of how to explain all this to them,* he thought, *not in a way they would understand.*

"Kayli, my lady," Troy bowed to her and kissed her hand. The maidservant announced him, and allowed as the lady would deign to see him, despite her displeasure. "I wish to explain . . ."

"You have a great deal to explain, cousin," Kayli stood and stared at him, lips pursed, arms firmly crossed across her belly, protecting her baby. "Why are you HERE, cousin?" she asked, after a pause. "Why aren't we in the capital?"

"A wizard name of Grimull, and his army, drove us out." Troy pulled up a camp chair and sat. "I won't go into detail, save we need all the men we can get."

"But Troy, the men in my village would be worse than useless," Kayli started pacing, "they are untrained and they are sheep."

"And so they would be with a woman as their leader," he interrupted, "with a man, Hugh or I, they will rise to the task."

"Troy, you are not listening," she took a deep breath, trying to control her temper. "They are sheep under the best of circumstances. And they DO NOT know how to fight."

"Whatever." He shrugged. "I did want you to know I have no intention of harming you or your child."

"Being away from my home harms me, Troy," Kayli said, sitting on her cot. "I grow weaker as the days pass. Please . . ." she crossed her arms again. She realized, as she looked him over, that he told the truth, that his face was as open as Hugh's.

Troy rose. "I will do what I can," he said. "You are stronger than I thought, lady. We will see if I have the luxury of letting you go home." He turned and strode out of the tent.

After three days on the road westward, Hugh started smelling campfire. *What the blazes?* he thought. He hadn't seen a soul, not even a peddler, since he left Riverwer. The weather as he rode westward had turned cold and wet and miserable again. He halted the stallion, dismounted, and pulled on his gambeson and chainmail. *Best be prepared for anything.* Then he remounted and urged his horse on.

He had to pull up as he crested the hill. A great war encampment covered the valley floor beyond. Banners carrying Troy's blazon, and his own, fluttered in the light breeze over the royal pavilion.

"Time for me to go," Fyl said, after looking around. "Think I'll go find my lady."

"She's there? How do you know?"

"Don't know, but she is." He slid off the stallion's back and disappeared into the tall grass without another word.

Hugh took a deep breath, reined up his horse again, and urged him on down to the camp.

"It's Hugh!" He could hear people whisper as he passed. "Come for his lady," someone muttered. A lad ran for the Royal Pavilion.

"Your excellency, your excellency," the boy ran into the pavilion, past Troy's guards. "Your brother rides into camp. He is furious."

"I know." *Wonderful,* Troy thought, *weather turned bad again, I'm cold, it is damp, and I still have that bitch Kayli to deal with . . . hmm.*

Hugh's probably so wrathful . . . if he berserks I can kill him and no one will hold it against me. He grinned to himself. *That still leaves me with the lady . . . I can take her if I kill Hugh.* He rose. The boy had cringed back at the expression on his face, then fled the pavilion.

People gathered behind Hugh as he rode to the pavilion. Troy stepped out of the tent as Hugh pulled his stallion to a halt before the tent.

"So you've come to serve me," Troy said loudly, grinning. "Knew I could have my way." His grin turned to a frown as he looked at Hugh.

"No, brother." Hugh spoke loud enough for all to hear. "I've come for my lady. You've broken your promise, brother. Give her back."

"You know what I want, Hugh. You must give it . . ."

"You broke your oath, Troy. I want my wife back. If you don't give her to me, I'll have your blood."

The crowd gasped. Troy stared at him. "I cannot fight a cripple!"

"Then you would fight me? I demand single combat. As your brother, that is my right."

"But Hugh . . ."

"I am still your better, brother," Hugh interrupted the start of a tirade. "And if you don't fight me, or won't fight me, better I become king than you." And looked at his brother, eyes narrowed, wondering how they came to this pass. *Don't need to wonder,* he thought, *I know. Troy's a hard-headed bastard, hard-hearted as well. Wonder what's going on here, too. That they were not in the city, but three days' ride out . . . don't need to know.*

Hugh could almost feel the soul of the people behind him. *They gather, not to see a cripple whipped, but to see if they would get a better king. Don't want that,* he thought, *want my lady.*

Troy stood and stared for what seemed an eternity to Hugh. Then he took a deep breath. "Someone show him to the practice field. I need to armor and arm myself." He turned and went back into his tent, his squire close on his heels.

The people followed and led Hugh to a stretch of sand to the north of camp. A lad came and led away his stallion as Hugh dismounted. A slender blond youth came to Hugh's side, and bowed deeply to him.

"I'll stand as your second," he said shyly, "I remember seeing you fight before."

Hugh touched the lad's head before he had him help finish putting on his armor. "I thank you. I need someone at my side."

"But all the people are on your side, lord," the lad replied, "Troy is cruel and moody. And, of late, word is that he's turned coward. Surely taking your lady is the act of a coward. When you served at his side, you served to temper his personality."

Hugh looked the youth over more closely before he had him put the great, bear-crested helmet on. He was older than Hugh thought at first. "And who might you be?"

"Folks call me Roger."

"And your father?"

"Don't know, my lord Fitzhugh. Some say you are. My mother died when I was very young. An old lady raised me. She didn't know about my parentage."

Hugh stared at him a little longer, then shook his head and smiled. "No, lad, I lay with no lady before my Kay, though you are as fine and straight and golden as Kay hopes her child to be. My father was certainly not faithful to mother, not that that was a secret to anyone. Perhaps you are a half-brother . . . how old are you?"

"Fifteen."

"Old enough." Hugh extended his left hand. "I'd wager you are a brother," he said, "though there's no provin' it."

"Aye," the lad grinned and awkwardly shook hands with him.

"So tell me, Roger, how did Troy . . . the king, come to this pass?" Hugh asked, as the lad helped him with his helmet.

"Some wizard, name sounds like a snarl," Roger replied, "raised an army and forced us out of the city.

Though I'm only a youth and not trained, I fought along-
side Troy's men. It seems that the king has somehow lost
heart recently—he can't seem to make a wise decision in
battle, even when our city depended on it."

He looked around and gestured. "That these people
are here, and not serving the wizard . . . that is a tribute
to our loyalty to your family, more than to the king."

"Do you know where my lady is?" *Forgot this helm
was so heavy,* Hugh thought, *then again, never wanted to
wear it again.*

"Sorry, no, my lord. But it IS a big camp."

"Ahem." Troy cleared his throat behind him.

Hugh turned to look him over. The stocky, dark man
had changed his helm to that of a raven volant. Troy
stood before him, armed with his own sword, with only
his squire at his back.

Hugh realized that all the encampment stood around
the sand arena. "So, brother, you will do combat with
me." He drew his sword and saluted Troy.

"Aye, Hugh, though it was your men I wanted to fight
FOR me. I never wagered we'd be at this pass."

"You broke your word, brother," Hugh replied, "you
said you'd leave us alone, though now I see the motiva-
tion for summoning them. Why'd you not say you'd lost
the city?" He was beginning to feel very annoyed with
his brother.

Troy drew his sword and saluted Hugh. "Honor,
brother, a matter of shame. Running to your little
brother because your tail is between your legs is a shame-
ful thing. So we fight."

That only made Hugh even angrier.

Troy slashed out at Hugh, stepping past as his blade
missed its mark.

Hugh turned toward him, keeping his shield between
him and Troy. He stepped and slashed out. Troy managed to pull his shield around in time to fend off the
blow. It pleased Hugh that the blow made Troy step
back a stride.

Troy stepped back in after a deep breath, and slashed
at Hugh. The blow bounced harmlessly off Hugh's shield.

Hugh turned and hit at Troy, drawing the blade back high before delivering the blow. Troy staggered back a step, nearly falling on an uneven spot in the sand. Hugh hit again, but the blow swept past Troy. The force of the blow caused him to step on past Troy.

Fyl slipped into the camp at the same time, coming cautiously out of the tall grass. Some children saw him. "Snake!" some yelled, and ran. A tow-headed boy stopped, grinned and started after him. Fyl scampered off through the tents, so quickly that the child soon quit following.

Fyl jogged through the camp, looking and sniffing. He could feel Kayli. *No explaining that to Hugh,* he thought as he looked, *my nature and hers are similar. Getting warm, but so many tents, so many people!* He sent more than one woman running for a stick, to kill "the snake."

Fyl walked and walked. After a time, he thought, *This had better be it, 'cause I'm getting pooped.* He insinuated himself under the hem of a tent, in time to watch a woman hand a small, squalling, blanket-wrapped bundle to Kayli.

"MA!" he yelled, and ran to her.

The woman screamed. "A snake!" she yelled as she ran from the tent.

"I am not a snake!" Fyl called out indignantly to the back of the fleeing woman, tendrils of smoke starting from his nostrils.

"Fyl!" Kayli held the bundle tightly, and looked up at him. "A moment, little one, I must comfort her." She cooed, and jiggled the babe a little, and the squalling dulled and stopped. "There, she'll sleep for a moment. What are you doing here, little one? I thought they'd killed you. Come here!"

He flowed to her and up to sit on her shoulder, nuzzling her face. "Hugh came to fight that man . . . Troy. I knew I could find you, so I left him."

"You . . . what, he came here and you LEFT HIM?" Kayli nearly yelled. The baby stirred and started crying again. "Whatever possessed you to do that?" She realized she could hear the sounds of a fight.

"I left before he came to the camp," Fyl replied truthfully, "I knew where you were."

She stood, almost unseating Fyl. "Then I must go to him. Perhaps I can help. Oh, Fyl, Troy could kill him!"

"But, ma, didn't you just have that . . . thing?" Fyl asked, peering closely at the squalling bundle. She stopped bawling and stared at him, fascinated. Her eyes were like Hugh's, bright, bright blue and she had a full head of red hair.

"No, yesterday," she replied, "the midwife was just making certain we were both all right." She scratched the little dragonet's head, then tried to settle the baby again. "We must go."

Kayli left the tent. The guards started to stop her. She gestured and a small, bright, noisy fireball went off. They fled. *Not good*, Kayli thought, *that took more out of me than it should have.*

Troy recovered his footing and rushed at Hugh, sword raised. "I killed her, you know," he said loudly, "the bitch caused too much trouble."

Hugh parried the blow, and felt a rage start to boil in him. "You should not have said that, brother," he snarled. "That goes beyond breaking your word." He turned and lashed out at Troy.

Troy dodged and hit Hugh. It landed squarely on the shield, causing Hugh to step back a stride. "And when I get done with you," Troy continued, "I shall take those sheep of yours and teach them to fight!"

Hugh's rage boiled over into a berserk. He started pounding on Troy, no skill, just sheer power.

Troy couldn't pick up his blade properly to hit at Hugh after the first few blows because he had to keep parrying them with both shield and sword.

Kayli made her way through the camp to the practice-ground as quickly as possible. She wondered on what she might find. She entered the ground, shouldered her way through the silent, staring people, and stopped at their edge, transfixed by the sight of her husband pounding at his brother mercilessly.

"What's happened?" she asked, to an older woman standing beside her.

"Looks like a berserk," the woman replied, "runs in his family; he'll not stop, not until he's killed the king, and perhaps then some. Hugh's gone off before."

Kayli stared at the woman. *Never even seen him get angry over anything,* she thought, *perhaps now I know why.* "He cannot . . . no. Here, hold her." She gave her baby to the woman. "Fyl, keep an eye out."

"Yes, ma," he said quietly.

Kayli stepped out into the ring of people. "Stop, lady," Roger said, "he'll only kill you, you're not armed!" He rushed to her side.

"I'll not be harmed . . . you're in far more danger," she said. *I feel much less confident than he knows,* she thought.

"Have it your way," he said, and stood aside.

She turned to the fighting men. "Hugh, no, STOP . . . HOLD!" she ordered. "You must stop!"

"Kayli, go away," Troy yelled, "he cannot be controlled." He fell as he spoke, on the uneven spot in the sand.

She made a grand gesture. A loud, bright fireball went off a few feet over Hugh's head, distracting him enough to make his sword bury itself deeply into the sand of the arena, just beside Troy's helmeted head. Then blackness rushed over her. She fainted.

The heat and light broke through the red haze of Hugh's berserk. He looked around in time to see Kayli, laying at his feet on the sand of the sand of the practice field. He shook his head, looked at the sword in his hand, then down at Troy. Then he looked down at Kayli again.

"You may have killed her, Troy, but it was savin' me that she gave her last." He turned, and with a quickness that made Troy gasp stabbed his sword deep in the sand, even closer beside Troy's head. The crowd made a noise that indicated that they thought he'd killed his brother.

That Troy knew exactly what he was doing when he said that he'd killed Kayli ran through Hugh's mind. *He deserves the fright of nearly being beheaded,* Hugh thought, *ought to have done the deed . . . save that would make me king and that would NOT please Kay.*

"Roger, help!," Hugh called, "I cannot get this helm off without your help!" Roger ran to his side and helped him with the helmet, then the shield and his mail and padding. "Cannot come near my lady," he said meekly, "until I get the steel off my body."

He stood, staring down at Kayli. After all the armor was off, he knelt and touched her face. Her eyes fluttered open.

"I'm all right . . . I think. Help me up, love." Her voice quavered.

Hugh helped her to her feet. He felt sheepish, slightly scorched, and, surprisingly, only slightly tired.

"If you can stand," Hugh said, "I must help Troy. Looks as if no one else will."

Troy lay still. Hugh helped his brother sit up, and take his helmet off. Troy just stared at him, silent.

"Are you all right, brother?" Hugh asked.

"Aye," Troy said, after a moment, "feeling a little burned, and worn flat out." Hugh helped him rise.

"And let me take off my armor in the arming pavilion," he added, only loud enough for Roger, Hugh and Kayli to hear, "I think I shamed myself." He left the arena. "Come along, boy." Roger left with Troy.

Hugh turned to Kayli. "Lady . . ." he took a deep breath, "love . . . he told me he killed you. I left myself . . ." He went to her and hugged her, lifting her slightly off the ground. Then he let her down and stared at her. "The babe. . . ?"

"Oh, come along!" she touched his arm and led him to the woman, still holding the baby. Kayli took the infant back into her arms.

Fyl flowed up onto Hugh's right shoulder. "She's beautiful, Hugh!" he said brightly.

"A lass?" Hugh looked, carefully parting the blanket to get a good look at her face. "May I? I'm clumsy one-armed, but if you help . . ."

Kayli helped him get the baby into his arm-sling, and he proudly beamed at his daughter. "A name, my lady?"

"Well, we discussed Eislinn," Kayli said, "For a girl, though I really thought I'd have a lad."

"Then Eislinn it shall be," he replied.

"And your surname," Kayli said, "since your custom deems that. I have none, save the use of my village name."

"Begging your pardon," Roger returned to them after several minutes, "but the king wishes to speak with the two of you." He bowed after he spoke. The people had started dispersing.

"We shall have time for this later," Kayli said, "Troy's situation is far worse than I thought, though I MUST go home." She took Eislinn back into her arms.

Roger led them to the royal pavilion. Troy awaited them, clothes changed and crown on. A large crowd had gathered in and around the pavilion.

"My brother," Troy rose, and bowed to them, "and dear cousin," he nodded to Kayli and sat again. "My apologies for your inconvenience. . . ."

"Inconvenience!" Kayli started a gesture as if for small spell, then paled and leaned heavily against Hugh.

Never seen her this way, he thought. He said nothing, but held her up until she could stand again.

Eislinn startled and started squalling. Kayli turned her attention to quieting her baby.

"Damnit, Troy, I nearly killed you," Hugh said. "What the blazes is all this about? Roger spoke of a war."

"Aye, a wizard who calls himself Grimull," Troy replied, "a friend of yours, mage?"

"Troy, stop it!" Kayli said sharply, "I'm only a fire mage, not a wizard. He ran afoul of me more than a year ago . . . about four months before you brought Hugh to me. I thought he'd leave these lands alone, though three days DOES put you out of my lands."

"I need your help," Troy said, "I need more men."

"My men will not fight; cannot fight," Kayli said, "they'd be more a burden than any help. And I MUST go home, I cannot tarry too much longer here. The birth has weakened me . . . that spell at your fight took more out of me than it should have."

Troy started to speak, then stopped and stared at Kayli. "I remember mention of this before . . . when Hugh wanted you to return home with us."

Kayli nodded her head. "Hugh's mother is much the same."

"That is why she stayed behind, though we feared for her life," Troy said quietly.

"I would wager Grimull will leave her be," Kayli said. "She can do nothing to harm him. And I would have my lord husband at my side at home. You promised him, he gave you enough in his service, Troy."

"Aye." He sighed. "I do not know how this will turn out, Hugh, Kayli. If we fall, the river may become the border to His lands. I cannot promise you will not be left alone."

"Grimull has already sworn to leave Riverwer alone," Kayli replied.

"Then I must allow your return," Troy said, finally, "when you feel up to it."

"Now would be just fine," Kayli said, "I have quite recovered."

"Then bring Hugh's horse and a mount for Kayli," Troy ordered.

Roger flew from the room. The crowd again dispersed.

"I take my leave of you again, brother," Hugh said, "and I thank you for returning my lady."

Kayli realized she had never heard such sarcasm from Hugh before.

"Come along, Kay," Hugh said, "we'll be home before you know it."

They turned and left the room.

YTARRA'S MIRROR
by Diana L. Paxson

Another regular contributor to these anthologies—and one who's made a considerable success both in science fiction and outside it is Diana; who, after marrying my brother—who writes under the name Jon de Cles—evidently found out writing wasn't so hard. She has since published several novels of an imaginary country called Westria, as well as a beautiful historical novel called THE WHITE RAVEN, based on the legendary Tristram and Yseult myth. Her most recent book, THE SERPENT'S TOOTH, is based on the Irish legends from which Shakespeare took his *King Lear,* and is heart-rending. I'm proud to claim her as a protegée, and proud to welcome back the first series character I printed in these anthologies; the female warrior Shanna.

It was the third watch of the night, and below the tarnished mirror of the waning moon, mist was already beginning to blur the sagging shopfronts of the old merchants' quarter of Bindir. Shanna eased through the door and flinched from the caress of the raw air. In the days when she had been a mercenary guarding the caravans, she would have strode without shivering into a storm. But before she had been captured by the slavers, a glimmer of returning humor reminded her, she would

111

have had more sense than to pass up an offer of free food and a blanket by the fire.

Shanna had half-turned to go back in when she heard the thin wail of the newborn child inside. Her belly cramped reflexively, and she let the door close behind her, taking deep breaths of the damp air. The moon had sagged another hand's breadth toward the mist that was rising from the harbor when Tara came out to join her, flushed and triumphant at the successful delivery, the midwife's birthfee jingling in the leather pouch at her side. As they started down the cobbled street, Shanna heard the baby crying again and slid her arm through Tara's, hastening her along.

"I'm sorry to have put you through that," said Tara a little breathlessly, "but we needed the money, and I could not have refused the call." She touched her left breast, where the tattooed crescent of the Moonmothers was hidden beneath her gown. Even as an escaped slave in hiding, Tara could still do some of the work she had been born for, and her oath as a healer forbade her to refuse those who needed her.

And I? thought Shanna. *What oaths still bind me?*

She forced the thought away and her grip tightened. "No—I'm the foolish one, making you walk home in the dark. I thought I could bear it this time. When I listen to the women screaming in labor, I am glad the Dark Mother made me barren, but it's different when I hear the cry of the child."

She felt ashamed. Tara had nursed her through the pain of withdrawal from the drug with which the noble-woman to whom she had been sold had enslaved her spirit, and though she had bitten her lips bloody, she had not screamed. But in the past months she had learned to be a woman again. That must be why it hurt her so.

"Never mind, we'll be in our own bed soon!" Humming softly, Tara pulled off her headwrap and shook out her fair hair.

The mist was curling thickly through the alleys by the time they neared their lodging, close by the harbor where the brackish waters of the Worldriver swirled in to bring the riches of an Empire to Bindir. Shanna squinted into the shadows, relaxing as the movement she had glimpsed proved to be no more than a wharf rat scuttling for its hole. She probed the depth of a puddle with her cane and cursed as her skirts tangled about her ankles once more.

Tara squeezed her arm encouragingly. "Not far now, love—see, there's the Pelican Tavern!"

"I'm not tired!" snapped Shanna. For some time now she had kept the cane not for support but as part of her disguise. "It's these damned skirts you've made me wear!" There was a hurt silence, and Shanna bit her lip in contrition, remembering that Tara had been up all night with the laboring woman while Shanna dozed by the fire.

"Never mind—" she added awkwardly. "I'll have them off soon enough, and yours, as well!"

She was rewarded by a shocked giggle from Tara, not at the thought, but at the fact that Shanna had been able to put it into words. The love between them was still so new a thing. She thought sometimes that Tara's courtship of her body had begun simply as part of the healing. Even now, her own response to it was a terror, and a wonder, that she did not herself understand.

The door of the tavern swung open, releasing a stream of ruddy light across the lane and the sound of men's voices raised drunkenly in a song to Belisama, the belligerent goddess who kept Bindir entertained by keeping the Arena supplied with men.

"Here's t' th' Red Hand," someone shouted from inside. "An' my money t' say another fight an' he'll be free!"

"Never happen—" came another voice. "He was a rebel! Led an army that nearly took Teyn. Why let 'im go?"

"They got to," a new voice replied. "Slave, traitor, whatever he was before, an arena-slave wins the wooden foil an' he's out free an' clear!"

Still arguing, three men pushed through the door, steps steadying as they came out into the cool air. Shanna stopped short, but Tara was still moving; light glinted on her uncovered hair.

"Hey there, pretty— Need a bed? How 'bout sharin' mine?"

Face flaming, Tara pulled her shawl up over her hair, but all three of the men lurched toward them. Sailors, by their clothes, they would be used to rough fighting, with no inhibitions about hitting a female.

"I'm sorry, I'm not—" Tara began, but she could not keep her voice from trembling. The men heard it and laughed.

"Think we've naught t' pay ye? Even the Pelican's prices left us enough coppers to buy a tumble or two!"

"You're mistaken," Shanna said quietly. "We are respectable women. Let us by."

"What respectable woman would walk the streets at this hour?" One of the others grinned skeptically. "No use t' say yer tired—ye've only t' lie on yer backs an' we'll do all the work, eh?" He elbowed his companion in the ribs and they all began to laugh. "I paid for th' last round, boys, so I'll take the fair one. The two of ye can flip for the long lass and the loser take wet decks when we're through!"

Tara gasped and clung to Shanna, and the tone of the men's laughter changed.

"Serve Ytarra of th' Mirror, huh?" the third man growled. "I heard there's whores go that way. Never mind—when I step my mast t' yer keels ye'll learn how t' sail!"

The first man was already reaching for Tara when Shanna's smooth sidestep put the other woman behind her. He shrugged and was opening his arms to her instead when her cane whipped up and poked him just beneath the sternum. The breath whooshed out of him and he went over backward.

"Tara—run!"

Shanna was aware that the other woman's dash had faltered as soon as she reached the shadows, but she could do nothing about that now. The downed man was still gasping, but the other two were coming in together in a move perfected during years of tavern brawls. They might even fight better drunk than sober, when they would have had the wit to worry about Shanna's unexpected skill. But the energy that sparked through her as she settled into a fighter's crouch was like wine.

One man made a clumsy dash and Shanna stepped aside in a move that would have been elegantly efficient if her skirts had not hampered her. She saved herself with a wrench and an elbow to the fellow's gut, sensed the other one leaping toward her and kicked at the same time as the cane slashed round.

The petticoats robbed her kick of force, but the cane scored his face and sent him yowling back toward the tavern. Shanna pivoted and struck downward, and his companion subsided into the mud again. A cobblestone thrown from the shadows where Tara had taken refuge discouraged them, but from inside the inn came shouting, and someone appeared in the door. Fighting the urge to finish off her enemies, Shanna took her own advice and ran.

"Goddess, Shanna, I'm sorry!" Tara breathed as they mounted the curving staircase to the right of the landing and headed for their own door. "The best part of my work is the birthings, but it's not worth it we get raped on the way home!"

"We were careless," said Shanna, letting the door swing open ahead of her as with senses sharpened by the rush of energy from the fight she made sure that no one was inside. "We'll know better another time."

"And I put you in danger, too," Tara went on. "What if they get to wondering where a two-bit whore learned to use a cane like a sword? The Aberaisi have spies everywhere. What if Lady Amniset hears about a fair girl and a woman fighter? She'll give us more than an escaped slave's lashing if we fall into her power!"

Tara had stopped in the middle of the room, trembling. Shanna leaned her cane against the wall and took the basket from her lover's hand, then grasped Tara's shoulders, holding her until she stilled.

"They were drunk, love. Do you think their pride will let them tell the truth? No—they'll say we were bait for a band of muggers. We're safe—the Aberaisi must think we've left the city by now."

Tara's head dropped to her shoulder and Shanna felt the tense muscles of neck and back begin to soften as she kneaded them. But she remembered how Lady Amniset had cursed when Shanna freed Tara from the Dark Mother's altar, and the baleful fire of the ring that she had struck with the finger still within it from the Lady's hand, and knew that she lied.

Tara's skin was smooth as a court lady's; the scent of herbs clung to her hair. Shanna stroked her with the pleasure she had once found only in touching the smooth feathers of her falcon or the satiny coat of her mare, and with a fierce protectiveness that was new, as if only her arms could keep the other woman safe from the world, and Tara clung to her as if it were true.

"Tara, you should leave Bindir . . ." she said finally. "There's no need for you to do your work like a rat in a hole. The Moonmothers can protect you at their shrine."

"And leave you to starve? Do you think I could forget you? You can't even forget that brother you're supposed to be searching for, and you haven't seen him for five years!"

Tara laughed uncertainly and pulled back, fussing with the lamp, sorting through the contents of her basket and putting things away. Frowning, Shanna kicked off her shoes and yanked at the ties at that held her skirts. She had worn gowns and veils in the days when she had been the Royal Daughter of Sharteyn. And then her brother had gone to do homage to the Emperor and never returned, and she had put on the clothes of a warrior and vowed to bring him home again.

She saw the other woman's reflection glimmer in the tarnished mirror as she moved about the room. The building had been part of some shipowner's palace in the days before the noble clans were granted the ambiguous honor of living under the Emperor's eye in the Citadel.

It was built in the old style with balconies and staircases clinging like ivy, and some of the moldings and mirrors and other fragments of vanished splendor remained.

"If you tear off those skirt ties, I'll only have to mend them again. Let me try—" Tara turned to her, her face calm again.

Shanna stood perfectly still as Tara came to her, but suddenly her heart was bounding in her breast. She could feel the warmth of the other woman's body. Tara's head was bent, and the silky fair hair fell away to bare her neck. Then the recalcitrant cloth gave way, and in that moment of release Shanna kissed that tender skin and Tara's arms slipped around her waist and held her fast.

The sagging bed was behind them, but it took them an eternity to reach it, each step marked by another shed garment, until Shanna was conscious of nothing but the sweetness of skin against skin.

"Don't let me go," Tara whispered when they were beneath the covers. Shanna curled her long body around her, but when Tara's touching grew surer, it was she whose spirit floated free on the tide.

When she became aware once more, the first flush of dawn was lending an illusory grace to the room. They had thrown off the covers, and in the old mirror she saw their bodies dimly reflected, an interlace of pale curves gilded by Tara's curls and shadowed by the unraveling strands of Shanna's black hair.

"Ytarra of the Mirror . . ." she said softly. "My body reflects yours, and both are reflected in the mirror. Has any Temple a fairer image of the goddess than these?"

Tara smiled and stretched to face her lover, breast touching breast and thigh laid against thigh.

"I doubt that wretch of a sailor meant it that way— don't you know the story? They say there is an island in the Western Sea where all the women look at each other as Ytarra looks in Her mirror, with delight and desire. . . ."

Shanna laughed. "Do you think one of the ships in the harbor would give us passage? Lady Amniset loves nothing. She could never follow us there."

Tara shook her head. "The way is lost." She rested her head on Shanna's shoulder with a sigh.

Shanna looked back at the mirror, shutting away other images that glimmered in her memory—a hawk and a horse, a woman with a weathered face, a red-haired man, and behind them all, a boy with a face the same as her own. She shut away even the reason why she and Tara were still in Bindir.

"Is it?" She ran her fingers through her lover's silky hair. "I think that is the way that we have found. . . ."

Shanna eased between two merchants and around a knot of women chaffering over fish with a skill that the past months had forced her to learn, and continued toward the herbsellers booths at the other end of the Market Square. Once people had stepped out of *her* way, in the days when she went armed in riveted brigandine of scarlet leather and girt with a sword. Now sword and armor lay wrapped in sacking beneath the bed she and Tara shared. It would have been death, not protection, to wear them now.

In a brightly colored booth near the armorers they were taking bets on the Games. Red Hand's last fight was scheduled for the next holiday in the Arena whose pale walls blazed in the sunlight beyond the Square, and the wagering was heavy. Gladiators had won their freedom from the Arena before, but often enough it was the last fight that killed them, as if the uncertainties of a life in which they were no longer protected from all dangers except the unambiguous challenges of the ring sapped the will to win.

There was a stir in the crowd ahead of her, and she straightened to her full lanky height to see. Then a flare of violet caught her eye, and she recoiled, pulling her shawl up reflexively. *Lord Irenos Aberasi's guards.* The men wouldn't recognize her, for she had spent her time in the women's quarters when she was a slave, but the fat eunuch who rode in the litter they guarded had known her well. She peered past the edge of her shawl as they went by, the eyes of the soldiers flicking over the crowd

with professional alertness, the eunuch staring above the
sea of heads with preoccupied disdain. But she found
herself gripping the handle of her cane as if it were the
hilt of a sword.

Only a woman . . . Shanna tried to blank her mind of
all but those words. *I'm only a woman whom the labor
of a woman's life has aged before her time*. . . . Here in
Bindir she had seen women her age who looked as old
as she was trying to seem. In the days just after the slave-
drug had finally worked its way out of her system she
had been as weak as they, but since the episode with the
sailors she had begun, after Tara went out in the morning, to do the training dances again. She trembled with
the strain of keeping her head bowed to hide the fury in
her eyes.

And then they had passed, and she could take a deep
breath of stinking dust and try to convince herself that
nothing had changed. But she knew that as long as she
and Tara were fugitives, they were both still slaves.

She moved quickly to the herb booth and counted out
the coppers for the cinquefoil and powdered aloe that
Tara had sent her to buy, then began to make her way
back across the Market Square. Sunlight glittered from
swordblades at the armorers' stalls, and Shanna found
herself drifting towards them.

" 'Tis a blade that the Red Hand himself would kill
for, and 'tis often enough he has come here to buy. Only
the best for the lords of the Arena of Bindir!"

Light rippled like lightning as the sword the merchant
was lifting caught the sun. Shanna blinked, then saw it
was all polish. Despite the new gilding on the hilt, she
could see the irregularity in the blade's edge where a
notch had been ground away. Hitting the crest of a helm
might have done that, or the edge of a shield. She smiled
grimly as a young soldier grasped the hilt, hoping he
would fare better than the last owner of the blade.

Beyond the soldier, sunlight glittered from the daggers
laid out on a tray. The merchants' eyes passed over
Shanna as she came toward them, for what interest would
a woman have in fine blades? Most of the smaller weap-

ons were used, like the sword—spoil from battles all over
the Empire. Long dirks from the north were laid along-
side nasty curved daggers from Menibbe; stout seamen's
knives jostled the wicked little stickers that the Dorian
tribesmen liked to conceal in the folds of their robes;
there were even a few weighted Norsith throwing knives.

Off to one side they had arranged a few more noble
weapons. Shanna stopped short as the wine-red glow of
a garnet set in the pommel of a belt dagger caught her
eye. The twisted silver knotwork that surrounded the
jewel was from her home! In the days when she was a
princess of the Royal House Shanna had borne only
the little knives considered suitable for ladies, but the
weapon was oddly familiar. With a trembling finger she
turned it, and saw engraved upon the boss at the hilt the
royal arms of Sharteyn. . . .

"Hey now—what're you doin' there!" One of the
apprentices jerked the tray away.

Shanna straightened. "The dagger!" she said hoarsely.
"Where did it come from?"

"What's it matter to you?" His glance dismissed her.
"This gear's not for the likes o' you!"

"My master lost a dagger very like this—" Shanna said
swiftly. "Let me hold it! Let me see!"

After a moment the boy shrugged, and Shanna's fingers closed around the corded hilt. It was not her master,
but her brother who had worn a dagger like this one.
With a brother's indulgence, he had sometimes let her
practice with the blade. She closed her eyes, inscribing
with supple wrist the defensive patterns in the air. Memories worn thin by the years were vivid again—her brother's teasing smile, his pride, and the death in her father's
face when his son had not come home. But this proved
what a gossiping soldier had once told her—Janos had
been in Bindir. . . .

When she opened her eyes again, the apprentice was
watching her with something very odd in his gaze. Her
first instinct was laughter, followed swiftly by alarm.

"How much?" she rasped, and knew that her tone was

as out of character as the way she held the blade. "He would want it back—how much for the dagger?"

"Have your master send a man for it then, with gold," the young man said suspiciously. "We will put it aside for him—" he reached to take it away. Shanna tried to remember how many coins there were in their little hoard behind the hearthstone. Silver and copper were all that the folk Tara served could give them, when they paid at all. But the gleam of sunlight on garnet reminded her of another red stone.

"He will reward me if I bring it back to him!" she exclaimed, fumbling in her belt pouch with her other hand and bringing out Lady Amniset's ring. The apprentice's gaze brightened as he saw the blaze of ruby and gold.

"Will this be enough?" Shanna saw his glance shift quickly to either side to see if anyone was watching, and knew that she had won.

"Shanna, are you listening to me?" Tara's voice rose, and Shanna reflected that except during her sickness, when Tara had railed at her not to waste all their pain by letting herself die, she had never before seen her lover really angry.

"What do you think will happen when that boy tries to sell the ring? He might not recognize the symbols on it, but be sure that the first jeweler he takes it to will. Mother of Life! The thing had Lady Amniset's sigil inside the band! How long do you think it will take for the Aberaisi to track us down?"

"There must be hundreds of women who look like me in Bindir—" Shanna began weakly, still turning the dagger in her hands.

"Like you?" There was no humor in Tara's laugh. "That apprentice will have seen you as I am seeing you now, as a woman who knows what to do with a sword, and how many of those are there outside the Arena and the Emperor's Valkyr Guard? Right now I wouldn't give a bent copper for your disguise!"

Shanna plunged the dagger quivering into the scarred table where it gleamed redly in the last of the light.

"Tara, I am what I am," she gestured toward the dagger, "a weapon, oath-bound to find or avenge the man to whom this weapon belonged. You're right—even when I'm trying, I don't seem to be able to change!"

"Shanna! Forget it!" Tara reached out to her, but the blade was between them. "Keep the dagger in memory of your brother, but stop trying to find him—can't you see it's hopeless now? Chances are that blade went through a dozen hands before the merchants got it, and even if they know, you don't dare go back to ask."

"I know," said Shanna. "But this dagger never left Janos' side. A seer might be able to read where he was when he lost it . . . tell me if he was alive. . . ."

"You're *not* listening! If you pursue this, *you* will be dead! Bindir was dangerous for us before, but it's going to be impossible now." Tara's skirts swished angrily as she paced across the room. "We'll have to leave, Shanna. We'll find somewhere we can be free!"

Shanna stared at her, remembering that before she and Tara had ever kindled Ytarra's fires, she had sworn an oath at the altar fire of the goddess who was called Yraine.

"You must go," she said softly. "And I must remain. Even on Ytarra's Isle the crescent of the Mother would still burn on your breast, and I would see my brother's face accusing me from the mirror of this blade. What would our freedom be worth if we denied that, Tara? Who would we be?"

"Two women who love each other. . . ."

There was a catch in Tara's voice and Shanna's vision blurred. When she had blinked the tears away, the sun had set and she could see only Tara's face, glimmering in the dusk like a shadowed moon.

On the fourth day after she had traded Lady Amniset's ring for her brother's dagger, Shanna woke from dreams of blood and fire, reaching for her sword.

Tara had gone out already. That had become a pattern

in the past few days. Her lover would probably stay out all day, nursing if someone needed her, or watching for Aberaisi agents in the Market, or feeding breadcrumbs to the seagulls on the shore. And Shanna would stay out of sight in their lodging, patiently striving to recover her old skill with the sword. They had exhausted all the arguments and then covered the wreckage with a fabric of excuses, like a slovenly housewife sweeping dirt under a mat on the floor.

After a time, Shanna rolled out of bed and stripped off her sleeping shift, staring at her body in the mirror. In full daylight it did not look like Tara's at all. In the clear morning light she could see the white ridges of old scars where the mounted fighter gets them, on her arms and thighs, and the puckered dimples of arrow wounds. As she straightened, the balance of her body changed, and the lean length of it glimmered in the mirror like the blade of a sword.

Her gown and skirts and vest lay waiting on the chair, but instead of reaching for them she dragged out the bundle that lay in the darkness under the bed. Tara had washed the blood from the clothing before she hid it away, and though they smelled a little musty with disuse, the black tunic and breeches that Shanna unrolled from the bundle looked almost new; the boots were still polished, the gilded meshmail glinted and against the dark red leather the rivets in the brigandine shone. Her limbs felt curiously vulnerable out of the skirts and shawls that for months had muffled them; the brigandine was rigid and unyielding, or was it only that she had not stood up straight for too long? She took a deep breath, centering her awareness, slipped her brother's dagger into her belt, and drew her sword.

Her first figure was stiff, the second a little less so. By the time she had completed the first sequence of exercises, her body had remembered its balance. By the end of the first hour, it had become an extension of her sword.

Out and back again flared the blade . . . parrying past a high guard or a low one, and around in the singing

stroke that decapitates an enemy. She felt the sweet harmony of muscles working together as she felt the give of
the wooden floor, heard the edge cleave the air as she
heard the wind whisper through the open window, was
aware of her own existence as she felt the deep heartbeat
of the city outside.

She heard the sound of running footsteps without surprise, brought the last figure to a conclusion, and was
standing like the image of Belisama in the Arena when
Tara burst through the door.

"Shanna! Shanna—oh, no—" Tara clung to the door-
post, staring.

"Tara—" she said quietly. "This is who I am. . . ."

"Oh, yes," Tara gasped, weeping, "The Aberaisi will
be delighted—there'll be no doubt they've got the right
girl now!"

"They are coming, then?" asked Shanna. But she
already knew—had known from the moment of waking
what this day would bring.

Tara nodded. "Along the road from the Square! Run,
Shanna! I'll spin them some story to give you time—"

"—Which will hold only until someone rips open your
gown," Shanna interrupted her. "Or had you forgotten
that Lady Amniset hates the Moonmothers, too? We'll
both run, but I will leave first and you will go another
way."

"Meet me at the fountain by the Gate of Wisdom,"
Tara was scrabbling beneath the hearthstone for the
wash-leather bag that held their coins. "We'll split the
money in case one of us is delayed. . . ."

"Take all the money, Tara," said Shanna, listening at
the door. "And do not wait for me." She heard a
bootheel crunch stone and the clink of metal outside. In
one move she was at Tara's side, hand over the other
girl's mouth, whispering.

"Go back to the Moonmothers and be a healer, and
you will love again, because you are made that way. I
will try to live, but I think I was always meant to be
alone."

Tara was weeping soundlessly, and Shanna stole one

more moment to kiss the tears away. Then they heard a mutter of voices below. Tara jerked back and as Shanna's arm swung out for balance the hilt of her sword tapped the mirror. A crack snaked across it and for a moment they stared, seeing themselves reflected separately, then the whole house shuddered to a heavy knock on the downstairs door, and the two pieces of the mirror fell apart and shattered on the floor.

The door below crashed open. Shanna shoved Tara toward the bed and hoped the girl would have the sense to hide beneath it. She could hear her enemies mounting the righthand staircase; for a breath she forced herself to wait, then darted out onto the landing. A dozen men in violet livery were pushing up the stair. In the dim light she could not make out faces, only the gleam of bared teeth and drawn swords. Shanna paused another moment to let them see her, then leapt across the landing and scrambled down the staircase on the other side.

Two of the stragglers had the sense to turn back to cut her off. Her sword took the first in the neck and the other man tripped over his body as she plunged through the open door.

As she trotted down the street she could hear them bursting into full cry behind her. She hoped that all of them were coming—they would have blood as well as duty to spur them now and they could see her clearly—surely they would not delay to search the room. Shanna ventured a quick glance backward and increased her pace. She might have recovered her fighting skills, but it had been a long time since she had done any running, she would have to ration her strength precisely now.

Faster, Shanna—you can lose them in the back streets and get away! Was that her own fear or Tara's yammering in her brain? She shook her head to clear it and took the first obvious turning toward the Temple Square. The Aberaisi men were still following, and now she could see the buff-colored jerkins of City guards. They would be even better witnesses. She dodged around a wagon and ran on.

The Avenue that led toward the temple was crowded,

but its breadth gave her room to run. Folk scattered as she bore down on them, eyes widening as they caught sight of the hunters behind. The white walls of the Citadel soared from their Rock beyond them, but the walls she was looking for were lower. She hoped that they were closer, too, or she would fail after all.

Now the columns of the temples loomed up before her. She dashed past them, saw armed men filing out from the Temple of Toyur ahead of her and swore. She stumbled to a halt and strode forward, trying to appear as if she had no idea who the knot of men unraveling behind her were looking for. She was almost past when one of the priests caught the sense of the yelling and turned.

Shanna batted his spear aside with the flat of her blade. "Sanctuary!" she cried, and launched herself into motion once more. She had a moment of respite as the man tried to figure out which temple she was heading for. Then the Aberaisi men behind her called out a warning, and she realized that they had finally realized where she was bound. At least there was no more danger of losing them. She had only to outrun them now, and past the edge of the Market she could see the Arena's curving walls.

Her lungs were burning as she forced herself the last hundred yards, but she could hear her pursuers' breath sobbing in their chests. A badly thrown knife flickered past her shoulder, and people scattered, screeching. Against the darkness ahead something hung like a fallen moon. There were steps; she stumbled and scrambled upward again, balanced at the top, and swung.

Her pursuers dodged as the sword flared round, but she was not aiming at them. The flat of the blade arced onward, struck, and pain jarred all the way up her arm— no, it was *Sound,* reverberating through her blood and bones, remaking reality.

"Kill her!" cried Lady Amniset's guards. "She's a runaway slave!"

Shanna fought to breathe. She could sense more men crowding in from behind her. Before her the shattered moon still shimmered, but that terrible Sound was dying away.

"No—" she cried. "I belong to Belisama now!"

She forced her eyes to focus. An immense man in a red robe, bald even to his eyebrows, loomed over her.

"The only way out of the Arena is through the Door of Victory or the Door of Death," he rumbled. "Is that your will?"

Lingering where the men made their bets in the Market Square, Shanna had heard how it must be done. Lady Amniset's men were falling back, for they knew that whether their quarry lived or died, she was lost to them, just as Shanna knew that every other warrior who ever stood here had also sworn in his heart to go out by the Door of Victory.

Now her eyes confirmed what she had been told. The moon she had struck was a gong shaped like a great shield, but in its polished surface she saw her own reflection changing shape as it shivered: she saw a dark lady with the wings of a raven in her helm; a white horse-face with velvet eyes; for a moment she even thought she saw Tara's golden beauty there.

"I will fight for the Goddess, forsaking all other obligations and loyalties. . . ." Shanna spoke strongly. "May She grant me victory!"

And in that moment she knew that her words had been true always, and that in giving herself to Belisama she was not rejecting, but fulfilling, the other oaths that she had sworn.

HEART'S DESIRES
by Walter L. Kleine

There are basically two plots; either a good person gets what he—or, more likely in those anthologies, she—wants, or a bad person gets exactly what's coming to her. I couldn't say into exactly which category this story falls; but it's funny. Which may be a category all by itself.

Walter Kleine has returned to fiction writing after a long hiatus; he worked as a newspaper photojournalist for 28 years, but his last fiction sale was published in 1969.

He says that he started writing when he was seven or eight, writing epics in which his stuffed panda bears saved the universe or won the war, via comic strip. "Real" writing started when he read a centerfold story in *Planet Comics* and incautiously said "I can do better than that." After which he found out it wasn't that easy by trying, though after three years he wrote the first of five stories which sold during the 50s. After the University of Iowa, he started a career in photojournalism—five sales in ten years, he said, don't pay the rent—then after a job in classical record reviewing—remember what I said; writers have to do the damnedest things to make a living—came back to science fiction. Welcome back; and may this story be only the first of many.

Princess Yareth grumped, "Shaigiss, did Father tell you he asked me to forswear sorcery?"

In the day-and-a-half since I'd fetched her from the Home of the Sisters of the Hills, those were the first words she'd spoken that she didn't have to. A worrisome change from the child who never shut up before I delivered her to the Sisters, eight years ago.

A bee buzzed under my nose, decided other flowers were better than the ones by my shoulder, and darted off. Something wrong about that. I began to feel uneasy prickles.

"Well," I said, scanning my sentries, "I don't suppose your father thinks it would help the alliance if crockery started flying around Krang's castle after you're Queen of Loth."

She said, "That wasn't me and you know it!"

I saw a problem. "Sereff!" I yelled. "Keep your demonfire-damned eyes on the forest!"

Sereff jumped. So did the other two guards, who were doing their job just fine. The three eating lunch looked a little guilty. Even Yareth blinked, and I've been her favorite guardswoman since she was born. "Sorry, Highness," I said, "the trouble with ten years of peace is that the kids don't understand that our lives depend on guarding as if we were at war. More wine?"

She held out her cup, scowling. "I don't want to get married off to old pig Krang!"

Ah, so that was it. The marriage of the age, and she didn't want it. Figured.

She'd been a willful little bitch from the instant she was born. She always had a mind of her own—not the most desirable trait in a princess, no matter how much I loved her for it. I said, teasing as I used to, "I'd take him. He might even be man enough for me. Queen Shaigiss. How does that sound?"

"But he's *old*, Shaigiss! He's older than *you*! He had gray hair before Father sent me to the Sisters!"

"Well, I suppose I'm *almost* old enough to be your mother—" And then I felt more *wrong* in the air, something far worse than a bee ignoring a perfectly good flower.

I was on my feet, sword drawn, screaming orders, when Cybothi raiders burst from the forest. They were in uniform, not even pretending to be bandits.

Evidently, Cyboth took exception to our alliance.

Politics! It'll kill you faster than sorcery!

There's no way around it. At four or five to one you lose—even if I've trained the men, even if I'm fighting, and even though I'd made the goat-bastards rush their attack.

I kept Yareth behind me, hoping the poor little bitch had sense enough to kill herself before they could take her. The distant part of my mind that heard her muttering assumed she was praying.

The men went down quickly, one after the other. I fought like The Demon in flames, and bodies piled up in front of me.

Then one of the goat-bastards I didn't kill dead enough got his sword into the back of my ankle. The tendon let go, with pain as if every flaming hellpit slid down Demon Mountain into my leg.

I toppled, and couldn't stop myself.

I felt sorcery.

Everything turned stone-white.

Then I was somewhere else.

A blizzard howled, and I was cold.

"Shaigiss! Drink! You've got to drink this!" Yareth's voice, only it couldn't be. I had to be dead and on my way up Demon Mountain and she had to be on her way down to the bosom of the Great Mother Goddess.

Something pressed against my lips and liquid poured into my mouth. My throat was still smart enough to know what to do with water, so I swallowed. It wasn't water. The stuff tasted like stable slime, with muck, and my whole head burned like a choice hellpit.

My eyes cleared, and the pain in my leg blazed. I stared up at a familiar set of sagging rafters. I've been on my back in this abandoned barn before, more times than's worth counting, but the other times were fun.

At least I wasn't on my way to meet The Demon. He wouldn't be caught dead in this wreck. I told the pain to go away, and it went, almost.

I wondered who was left alive. *Somebody* carried me here, and Yareth wasn't big enough. The barn was two miles from the ambush, uphill, across three streams, and through the double row of thorn-hedges surrounding the Summer Palace.

"Highness!" I shouted, and it came out a whisper I could hardly hear. "Take whoever's left and get to the Summer Palace. If three dozen Cybothi attacked us, there have to be thrice that many combing the hills for you!"

"Shaigiss, we're all right," she said, taking my face in her hands like a mother soothing a child, "I wouldn't have minded dying—better than lying under pig Krang— but I couldn't let them kill you, too. You were always my friend, even when no one else was. I remember watching when you brought a dozen warriors before Father for the blood-oath. It was the first time I realized it could be worth something to be a woman! So, when I saw the Cybothi I called a storm. When you fell, I cast a spell of lightness so I could carry you. I've put a spell of avoidance on the barn. Drink the rest of this, and I'll heal your leg."

Slime poured into my mouth again.

Heal my leg? Hamstring wounds don't heal. If I lived through this, that Cybothi goat-bastard had made me a one-legged whore.

"This is a difficult spell," she said, her face close to mine and looking a little funny. "Most of the healing is just surgery. The spell is to make the tendon grow back together. I've never done it without a Sister watching, and I'm very tired from the other spells, but if I don't do it now, you'll never walk again. You have to want me to do it or it won't work. Please say you want me to try."

I hate sorcery. There's always some price you'd rather

not pay that you never know about until the bill comes. But give me a choice between sorcery and one-legged whoredom and I'll take sorcery every demonfire-damned time!

I said, "Do it, Highness!" My whisper seemed a little stronger.

"Thank you, Shaigiss. I'm glad you want me to help you," she said, prim and proper as if she were practicing the tea greeting at the castle. "The spell begins with a dance. Watch me closely. It's a spell of entry, so I'll be inside your body, healing. You may see things through my eyes. Then we'll both have to rest. When we wake, our horses will be here, so we'll have food."

Something didn't make sense, but whatever was in that slimy stuff kept my head too foggy to figure out what.

She'd taken off her riding dress, shift and underskirts, and wore only her corset and leggings. That must be what seemed wrong. But the stupid dances court women do in skirts could hardly weave a sorcerous spell, could they?

I watched her flow across the old barn floor, graceful as clouds and waterfalls and wisps of smoke.

She helped me roll over, enlarged the cut, found the knotted muscle and pulled it down. I saw the cut; felt her fingers as if they were my own. "That's right," I said, "You have it. No, a little to the left. There. That's it."

It all seemed perfectly normal; just routine healing, except that I was awfully tired. Her spell-storm howled like seven deprived demons. Snow sifted through the ancient roof.

I saw myself through her eyes as she sewed the tendon back together, and coated it with herbs and salves and potions. I knew the name of each one and what it did, and that seemed normal, too. She sewed up the cut, wrapped my leg with strips of her underskirt, and splinted it with old barrel staves.

I've never worn a skirt in my life. Now I wore one on my leg. That seemed very funny, but I couldn't laugh.

"I'll dance to complete the spell," she said. "Watch me. Then we'll sleep."

I watched her until my eyes stopped focusing. She covered me with something warm and crawled under, holding me tight and kissing my ear, nuzzling among my rings and dangles. "Oh, Shaigiss," she whispered, her voice aching with fatigue, "I'm so glad you're going to be all right. . . ."

I slept. . . .

And dreamed. . . .

. . . dreamed I brought a dozen fresh-blooded warriors to take the blood-oath from King Lerrig and . . . hid behind a drape while Fat Nurse hunted me, whisper-shouting, "Yareth! Yareth! Where are you? Come out *now!*" Below my window, my father administered the oldest oath in the kingdom to Shaigiss' newly-blooded warriors: *"My Lord, I have tasted the blood of your enemies and found it good."*

I dreamed . . . my life . . . Yareth's life . . . our lives so tangled I couldn't tell one from the other, and it didn't seem strange to dream Yareth's memories until I woke.

I suppose realization only took a second, or less.

It just seemed to go on forever because I knew exactly what had happened and didn't want to face reality.

I was lying under a blanket, wearing a corset and leggings, pressed against blood-caked leather-and-chains armor.

I wasn't just seeing with her eyes.

I was in her body.

And I didn't fit!

I don't panic. If I did, I'd have been dead long since. I never came closer than at that moment.

I just lay there, feeling my body against hers, trying to breath, telling myself she'd wake up and cast a spell and I'd be back in my own body. I told myself she'd said she'd sleep until she recovered from the prices she'd paid for all her spells. All I had to do was wait for her to wake up.

I didn't believe myself.

As I said, I hate sorcery.

And then I remembered something else she'd said. Something about our horses coming when the storm ended, so we'd have food. Summoned by a spell, of course; how else?

Gods and Demons!

Did she think Cybothi would let fine Kertigan horse-flesh wander off by itself? Did she think our horses would come without Cybothi on them?

Well, yes, she probably did.

I pushed the blanket back and looked down at myself. Herself? Hellpits and demonfire! Whose *was* my body when I wasn't in it?

She slept. My armored breasts rose and fell evenly. I looked at my face. Demon's diseased dong, I'm ugly! Never knew how much mirrors flatter me. Square as a stone, two different color eyes, one bigger than the other, a nose the Vanesti ruined, and the long white scar a Cybothi put on my left cheek. My big mouth's the only thing that looks like it might belong to a woman.

It's a good face for a warrior. Scares The Demon out of the enemy.

Well, let her sleep. My body needed to heal, and she needed to rest from casting spells. I cautiously moved one leg, then the other. Strange, to be so small and light, as if I was eight years old again. Why couldn't I breathe?

The corset. The doubly Demon-damned corset! What did a little body like this need a corset for? No wonder I felt like I didn't fit! No wonder I couldn't take an honest breath! I reached behind for the laces, and the tie wasn't at the bottom where it ought to be, but at the top! I tried to get it loose and only seemed to make a tighter knot. I wasn't just trapped in her body, I was trapped in her corset, too!

And I was cold.

I picked up her shift, and dropped it. I've never worn *woman* stuff in my life.

She'd stayed warm, dressed like this.

Abruptly, I was warm. How'd I do *that?* I remembered moving my hands. Didn't say anything. Just wished I was warm and did something with my hands.

Did her body remember trained-muscle spell-patterns, like I learned sword-work until my arms and hands moved without thought? Must be something like that.

I didn't stop to think that some part of me chose sorcery over wearing woman-clothes, but that's what it was. I'd never worried which I hated more.

Body warm, I thought about colder reality. When the storm died—and it was about dead—our horses would come, bearing Cybothi.

I couldn't fight if I was in my own body and wouldn't last long in hers.

Well, I've never been afraid of death. Warriors fight, warriors die. So I'd die stuffed in Yareth's body. So? Death is death.

I found her eating knife and cut the corset laces. I wasn't going to die trapped in that monstrosity! I threw the thing at her pile of clothes. I still felt like I was spilling out of her body.

I went to my sword. It lay where I'd dropped it when Yareth put me down. I picked it up.

Well, I tried. Yareth's body was strong for its size, dancer-trained, but not strong enough to wield my blade.

Maybe speed and surprise would let me take at least one goat-bastard with me. I slid my fighting knife from its sheath. It felt *right* in her hand.

"Shaigiss?" Her voice shook. Her eyes were open—wide—and she looked like she was about to cry. She chewed my lip and my jaw quivered and my eyes blinked rapidly. "Sh–Shaigiss, I–I'm sorry!"

"*Sorry?* God's shriveled balls, Highness, don't be sorry, *do* something!"

"Shaigiss, I can't! Not while I'm in your body! I can't dance!" She started to sit up, grimaced, gasped and lay back. "I must have mis-cast the spell of entry. Even that shouldn't do it. We'd each have to want to be the other. I don't know how many times I've wished I'd been born a warrior like you, free, able to go where I chose, do what I chose, love whom I chose, but I *love* you! I'd *never* wish pig Krang on you! You'd *never* want to be

like me! I don't know what I did wrong! Well, I didn't
really want to be a warrior; I just wanted your freedom!"

She began to cry. My big, ugly, busted-up face crying!
Not hysteria. Not fear. Little choked-off whimpers and
fat tears rolling down my cheeks.

I knelt beside her. I said, as gently as I could, "Highness . . . have you ever thought . . ." And then I didn't
know how to say it. I tried again. "Highness, you only
have to obey your brothers, your mother, and your
father. When you marry Krang, you'll only have to obey
him. I have to obey Hanthor, Odoc, anyone of noble
blood, you, your brothers, mother and father, and anyone they tell me I have to obey. Do you think I've never
dreamed I was some Demon-damned little Queen?"
Speaking those secret desires aloud made me realize the
enormity of my careless wishes.

"Oh . . ." said Yareth, as if she'd never thought of
that in her wildest dreams, and I suppose she hadn't.
"The Sisters will get us back in our right bodies. . . ."
She didn't sound very sure about it.

I prostrated myself on the ground and kissed it, grab-
bing handfuls of dirt. "Oh, Great Mother Goddess," I
implored, "I didn't mean it! I didn't know any better! I
know I haven't paid you much heed, but I haven't taken
your name in vain, either. Well, not often anyway. I
never asked for anything, except to be a warrior and
have lovers, and I already had that! I really never wanted
to be queen of anything! *Really!* It was all talk; just a
warrior bitching! Please, Great Mother Goddess, are you
listening?"

Beside me, Yareth prayed just as fervently.

I stayed stuffed in Yareth's tight little body.

At that moment, I heard Cybothi voices outside,
shouting.

I put my hand on Yareth's shoulder, the same camara-
derie I'd have felt for a fellow warrior. "It doesn't matter, Highness. The Cybothi are here. I'll take as many
as I can." I pulled my sword closer to her hand. "Be
sure you make them kill you."

I don't remember crossing the floor. I was just *there* when four of them slammed through the main door.

I met the leader head-on and whipped my knife through his throat. The one next to him swung his sword. It whistled over my head. I got my knife into his groin as I dropped and rolled, a Yareth-dancer move. He screamed. The other two turned on me, swords raised.

I wished I had my real body and sword.

My sword hurled itself through one of them with such force that it picked him up and slammed into the door frame, leaving him twitching, two feet off the ground. I suppose getting one wish out of two isn't bad, but I'd rather have been granted the other one.

A bale of ancient hay fell from the loft and knocked the other goat-bastard off his feet. I reached him in one long, diving leap and rammed my knife up into his chin.

The one I got in the groin remained standing, weaving, pouring blood, still holding his sword. A barrel, missing half its staves, crashed onto his head. He fell in front of me. I slashed his throat. I rolled to my feet in time to face four more coming in the door.

My sword took the heads off the first pair and hung in the air, glowing, quivering, dripping blood for its entire length.

The other two stared, screamed, and fled.

From outside came the sounds of battle, and the familiar battle-cries of Lerrig, Odoc, Hanthor, and half the guard.

I turned to Yareth. "God without a cock, Highness! Was that you or me?"

"I—don't know! Both of us, I think."

Well, it didn't matter. As long ago as I can remember, Odoc, and his father before him, drilled into me, "Use any weapon you have." If I had a Talent for sorcery, I'd Demon-damned well use it. I grabbed my glowing sword and started out the door.

Too late. Odoc always was too hellfrozen efficient. Not one Cybothi left for me. Then I remembered whose body I was wearing.

They saw me.

I don't think they recognized me, not then. I backed into the barn and ran to Yareth. "Frozen demons, High-ness! What do I do now?"

"Don't swear," she whispered, "A Princess isn't allowed to use such words!"

King Lerrig charged through the door, Odoc on one side and Hanthor on the other. They charged, they stopped, they stared. Except for a tattered remnant of Yareth's leggings, I was wearing blood.

Blessings of the Mother Goddess, none of them had seen Yareth in eight years! I could say anything—almost. I held out my knife and my still-glowing sword—which had no weight at all—and stood as tall as her body could stand, dancer-straight.

I said, letting my voice relax, hoping it sounded like hers, "My Lord Father, I have tasted the blood of your enemies and found it good."

There.

Let him figure out what to do about that!

"Shaigiss!" he bellowed, "Where's my daughter?"

Hellpits! Yareth had to be me, and they all knew me—intimately.

She said, "Your daughter stands before you, Lord, honorably blooded in your service. She is alive, well, safe and virgin, as you charged me." She had my voice and words right, inflection, cadence, everything. She just sounded a little weak and tired.

"Blooded through sorcery?" Lerrig eyed the glowing sword, but moved no closer.

"She killed the first before the Spirits of the Hills, which protect her, came to her aid," said Yareth, a little too primly.

Silence in the old barn. Soft summer breezes blew through the trees outside. Melting snow dripped from the eaves.

Lerrig said, finally, "Daughter, I ordered you to for-swear sorcery."

I said, "Would you rather have us both dead?" I sounded much too much like me. I tried again, quickly, "Father, I can no more forswear sorcery than I could

forswear breathing. Did not Ancient Sister tell you?" I
didn't know if Ancient Sister had, but the line sounded
good.

He looked away from me, frowning, then back. "You
will do your duty, whether as obedient daughter or sworn
warrior."

"As either, Father." I did the acquiescent curtsy I'd
seen Yareth do in his presence, and her body remembered the right moves. "Shaigiss should not be moved
until my healing is completed. Ask the Sisters to send a
healer to assure I have done everything correctly."

He nodded slightly, frowning more deeply.

I realized I still held my glowing sword at arm's-length.
"And I claim the right of a blooded warrior to dress and
arm myself as a warrior!" I did the warrior's raised fist,
with the hand holding the sword.

I saw the demon-fury look I'd always feared in his
eyes, and hoped I hadn't pushed him too far. I put my
sword down and its glow faded.

His thin-lipped stare lasted forever. Then the corners
of his mouth turned up, as if he'd heard some marvelous
joke. He sheathed his sword and strode across the barn
to clap me on the shoulder, as he had many times when
I'd pleased him in battle. "Daughter, I like what the
Sisters have sent me. I never dreamed you'd grow so
strong. Is any of that blood yours?"

"No, Father."

He turned to his men. "Odoc! Water for the Princess'
bath! A robe! Towels! Send for a Sister!" He waved them
out, to worry about where they'd find a tub and water.

"Shaigiss!" He went to my real body and clapped Yareth on the shoulder. "Once more you have served me
well! When you're recovered, pick an honor-guard to
accompany Princess Yareth to Loth. Since she is a sworn
warrior, I charge you with her training. Spare her
nothing!"

Yareth raised her fist, as close to correctly as anyone
could manage from flat on her back. "As you command,
my Lord."

Lerrig put a fatherly finger under my chin. "Will you

tell me why you're good as naked? Or is that a sorcerous secret?''

Mother Goddess, *is it?*

Yareth rescued me. "She couldn't sleep wearing that Demon-damned corset."

Lerrig exited, roaring with laughter, with me staring after him, wondering what was going on that I hadn't figured out yet.

Lerrig seemed delighted to be sending a sorceress to Loth.

Yareth said, in my barracks-whisper, "God without a cock, Shaigiss! We did it! Ancient Sister will send someone who can get us back in our right bodies. I hope."

"Highness to you, Shaigiss," I said. "Or Yareth, in private. And neither of us better slip."

Back in our right bodies—*she hoped?* Seven flaming Hellpits! Was this what I got for all the times I took The Demon's dong in vain? The thought of bearing a child between Yareth's little hips—! How do you go about being a queen, anyway? Great Mother Goddess, I hope you have your reasons!

Then I figured it out. My Lord King Lerrig has not been king for forty years and at peace for ten by being dumb. He understood *exactly* what happened, and couldn't be happier.

Like I said about politics. . . .

All right, my Lord, I'm sworn to your service, whatever you ask. This is too much, but I'll do my best.

Then some deep part of my mind started laughing. I'm thirty-two years old in my real body, and never caught a brat yet. I know things that have never happened in Krang's bed! And *he* hasn't seen Yareth in eight years, either.

I wished the fallen hay-bale would go back up to the loft.

It went.

Queen of Loth, huh?

King Krang, have I got a surprise for you!

A THROW OF THE DICE
by Nancy L. Pine

I never fail to be astonished at the number of people who are fascinated with stories about gambling. I think it was Dion Fortune who commented that the milder a person was in reality, the more bloodthirsty their fiction would be; when you saw a man sun-browned with the look of the ends of the earth, he was probably reading a gardening paper.

True. Nancy Pine works in a library, a kind of person not—to say the least—noted for adventurous lives. She reassures us she is neither a vampire, nor does she have two heads—"One head gets me into quite enough trouble, thank you." She is unmarried, lives in Kingston, and works in the local library; she also sings in the church choir. Sounds just about right for a story about a gambler. She's also working on a novel, which "judging by my current lack of progress (I have to keeping stopping for silly things like going to work), will probably be finished something around the middle of the next century." I'm sure a lot of us are familiar with that feeling.

The smoke of the tavern stung her eyes, causing them to water, and she coughed sharply to clear her throat. Karis peered through the haze as best she could, while she wished the landlord would get his chimney fixed. Some candles would be welcome as well. Perhaps then a person could see something.

Jarale should be in here. But there were so many men, and the room was so dark and smoke-filled, it was difficult to make out one person. She could only see heads bent over tables.

There. She spotted his fair head at a dicing table with a number of strangers and began picking her way across the room, holding her robes away from both the men and the floor. The dicing tables were one reason why Jarale had decided to stay at this low place, rather than a better inn. She had known that from the beginning. The little matter of precarious funds had also come into the decision, of course, but it was the dicing that had been of first importance.

She finally reached him, and by the silence that had grown across the room realized that every man in the place was staring at her. Tall blondes must be rare in these parts.

"Jarale? Is anything wrong?" His face was flushed from too much drink, and his chair was half pushed back as though he were about to leave the table and come upstairs. Perhaps she had interrupted at the wrong time.

He smiled up at her, a thin, wavering smile that did nothing to reassure her. He was so much younger than the other men at the table. What chance did he stand dicing against them?

She could see the expressions on their faces as every man at the table looked at her. Her reflection gleamed in their eyes. Tall, blonde, beautiful, perfect in every feature, with kyraflower eyes that just barely deepened into purple, she stood out in this room like one tall ship among a fleet of fishing smacks.

She avoided their looks and looked down at the table, noticing details. One of the gamblers, a big oily man, had a pile of coins in front of him. He must be the big winner this night.

"Don't worry, Karis, I'm fine." Jarale didn't look fine. He looked worried, and she went over the list of possibilities. If he had lost their traveling money, they would be condemned to sleeping outdoors and hunting for their food. In such a case it would be a long time before he heard the last of it from her. Perhaps it would be better, if, in the future, she held the purse herself.

"You're sure, brother dear?"

"I'm sure." He must have recognized the expression on everyone's face, the same expression that made her so nervous, as though she were being undressed, here in public. "Maybe you'd better wait upstairs. I'll be up before long."

Upstairs, away from this company. An excellent idea. "All right. If you're sure."

"I'll only be a minute." Perhaps, if she left, he would make his excuses and leave. And she didn't like the expressions of some of the men. Karis left, and every eye in the place followed her.

Jarale came upstairs within the half hour and banged on the locked door for admittance. He had someone with him, the big oily man who had been winning so heavily.

"Karis," Jarale said slowly. "I've . . . I've got something to tell you."

There was a thin trickle of fear going down her backbone. What had he done? And why was this stranger gloating over her as though he were examining a new possession?

"I swear," said Jarale. "It must have been something in the wine. I must have been insane to agree."

What had he done?

He motioned toward the stranger. "This is Marant. We've been gambling together, and he's done well. He's won all evening."

She had known that by the pile of money.

"And I don't know what got into me, but I kept wagering more and more money."

The traveling funds. She knew it. What was the penalty in these parts for murdering a brother?

"And finally, I lost everything we had."

Everything? Even the horses?

"And Marant made a suggestion."

She had a few ideas herself.

"And it ended up, I don't understand how I could have agreed, it seems impossible. . . ."

What had he done?

"I ended up wagering you, and . . . and I lost again."

For a moment she only heard the first part of his sentence. Wagered her? Put her up as a stake at a dicing table? Why didn't he just offer her for sale in the public market? Wagered her? *Lost?* The full realization began to sink in.

Marant *was* gloating over her.

"You wagered me? You put me up as a stake?" Her voice wavered and became shrill. He nodded.

"This is a joke. Please, Jarale, tell me this is a joke. I'll forgive you for it." He was shaking his head, sorrowfully. He was serious. Fear and anger swirled together for her.

"What could have possessed you? How could you do such a thing? Jarale, why?" She belonged to this horrible man?

She wanted to throw up. She wanted to weep and storm and throw things. She *belonged* to him?

Never.

"I swear . . . it must have been the wine . . . look, I'm sorry."

Sorry!

"Oh gods, oh Mother." There were tears in her eyes. Lost as a wagering stake to this horrible man whom she couldn't even bear to look at. Hopes, plans, dreams, her whole future wiped in a single cast of the dice. She found it difficult to breathe, and the room began to swim about her.

She cast another glance at Marant, saw the satisfied expression in his eyes, and shivered at what lay in store for her.

A cold, clammy feeling wrapped around her, chilling her to the bone. To her horror, she realized that tears were running down her cheeks.

"How could you do this? Jarale, please, you're my brother. How could you let this happen?" Until she was of age, he was responsible for her, and according to the law could do with her what he liked. But a gambling stake?

He only stammered a few words and stared at the floor. She could see Marant smiling and shrank away from him. This could not be. She would wake in a few minutes and would discover that it was all a dream. Even in these terrible times, when there was trouble everywhere, *how could she belong to this monster?*

"Come, my dear, you will find me most generous to deal with. I am a wealthy man, and have no objections to giving you any trinket you might desire."

He was horrible. Oily, self-satisfied, arrogant. She wanted to rip him apart on the spot. Just the thought of hurting him was pleasant.

"But, oh, please. . . . Jarale, how could you do this?" By this time she was standing with her back against the wall, like a deer at bay, and her fingers were clenching and unclenching rapidly. The initial shock was over, and she was closer to anger than tears. Indeed, anger was growing every minute. She wanted to kill them both.

She *would* kill them both, before she let this man touch her.

"Sister, Karis, I'm sorry. But I'll redeem you soon, I promise. I swear. I'll be back. Trust me."

"Trust you!" After he wagered and lost her in a dicing game, she was supposed to trust him?

"Now, my dear." Marant's oily smile seemed to grow wider at this display of temper. Perhaps she should have remained meek and mild, and accepted it calmly. But who could accept such a thing calmly?

If she could get to his dagger. . . . But even as she was thinking of attacking them both, Marant stepped forward and took her wrist. He stared into her eyes for a long moment, and she began to feel weak. Numb. Her control was slipping, and hazily, from far away, she realized that she would have to do as he bade her.

She could think, though not clearly. But there was no feeling, no sense, left to her. Just numbness, as though her body belonged to someone else.

"Get your cloak, my dear, and we shall be on our way."

Cloak. She reached for her cloak, and Marant helped her fasten it. That brought her partway back from where she had been. She hated his touch, her skin crawled where his fingers brushed against her arm, but she was forced to obey him. She began to have some idea of how he had compelled Jarale to offer her as a stake. He had some of the powers of a wizard, though she had no idea how strong they might be.

As they left, she heard Jarale say, from miles away, "You won't hurt her, will you? You'll be gentle?"

"She will utter no complaint, I assure you."

Utter no complaint. Of course not, not with him controlling her mind. But she knew the expression in his eyes, and knew there would be pain and plenty of it.

He led her home through the darkened streets. His house was far from the tavern, and she wondered, with the corner of her mind that could still think, why he had gone so far to do his gambling. The house was a huge one, and she recalled that he had said he was wealthy.

She watched numbly as he placed warding spells over the front door, and realized that he was trying to prevent Jarale from following him and trying to rescue her.

"Come, my dear." His will was still on her, and she followed him up the stairs obediently. The thick carpets muffled all sound, and she could see other rich furnishings and appointments. Marant must be wealthy indeed. If he had had to go all the way across town in order to win a bed partner. . . .

Of course. A portion of the puzzle fitted into its pattern. He must have seen the two of them, Jarale and Karis, as they rode into town this evening, and had come to the tavern deliberately, seeking her. Or perhaps he had a crony at the tavern who had alerted him to their presence. No doubt the dice were charmed. It began to seem that beauty might be a fatal gift, after all.

His bedroom was enormous, but what took the eye was the bed which was huge. How big a bed did he require? There were things, implements, nearby, which she dared not look at too closely.

Marant placed more warding spells over the door, then turned to her, smiled, and released his will.

She was free. "No! Dear gods, dear Mother, protect me!" Flinging herself away, she fell over the bed, and scrambled to her feet on the other side. His smile only became wider.

"Afraid, lovely Karis?"

Her hood had fallen back, and her hair was lying in loose disarray as she turned to stare at him. Her eyes became wider and wider, and he stared at her with more attention than he had before.

Making a person unconscious isn't that hard if you have the power. Marant collapsed across the bed.

She reached out one light hand and touched him. He would stay asleep for a long time, and she was certain that the servants had been told not to disturb him in the morning. She would have plenty of time.

She took the marked cards and charmed dice from his pockets first, then the money he had won that night. Some was his, some had been hers and Jarale's. Probably some of it belonged to the friends and toadies who had been part of the game, for she had no doubt that the whole thing had been arranged in advance. If he was supposed to return it in the morning, he would have some explaining to do.

She searched the room carefully. One chest stood by itself in a corner, and she had to remove three spells in order to get it open. What it held made her eyes widen, and she whistled softly, under her breath.

This was where Marant must keep most of his winnings. There was money here, money and unset gems, more than enough to keep her and Jarale in funds for months. No more low taverns, only the best of inns, and they would be able to pick and choose their jobs for a while. Excellent. They would celebrate this night's work with a bottle of the best Dermian wine. She picked up a handful of coins and let them trickle back through her fingers. More, much more than they had reckoned on. Her smile glinted in the candlelight.

There was more money than she could carry in her belt pouch, and she searched the room and wardrobe until she found a pair of sacks that could hold it all. Once they were loaded, she could just manage them.

She took nothing that had a spell on it, and nothing that might be identified as having come from here. Marant was only getting what was coming to him, but she had no wish to be named as a thief.

When she was finished searching the room, she stared at him for another minute, seeking the information that she needed. As she turned to leave, a sudden thought occurred to her. She placed one hand on his head (even the touch of his hair sickened her), and then sent a surge through his mind. After a minute or so she stood up and moved away from him, still smiling, though not pleasantly.

When she left the room she replaced the warding spells. She might as well keep the servants out as long as possible. The longer a start they had, the better.

It took a few minutes to figure out the corridors, even with the information she had taken from his mind, but she finally understood where she wanted to go, and trotted up the stairs to a series of smaller rooms. One door had warding spells all over it, and there were waves of pain and despair coming from within.

It took a moment to work out the mechanism for the lock, but then she had it and pulled the door open as quietly as she could. The servants would be up soon, and she had no taste for long, involved conversations. They always ended so unpleasantly.

There was a girl asleep here, a tall, beautiful, blonde who looked much as Karis did, though this one had more red in her hair. The room was shabbier than the room downstairs, though it was still comfortable enough to live in. Was this what she would have had to look forward to when he was finished with her?

She closed the door behind her, lit a pair of candles, then moved toward the figure on the bed. A light touch, and a pair of green eyes opened, startled and wary. For a moment there was fear, then, as the stranger looked at her, fear evaporated, and there was puzzlement.

"Who are you?"

"I'm a friend. I've come to get you out of here. Just do as I say, and you'll be all right. My name's Karis. What's yours?"

"Shelara."

"Fine. Get dressed and come with me, and be as quiet as you can. The servants will be getting up soon, and I want to be out of here before they are about."

Shelara began getting dressed quickly, but she stared at Karis with confusion. "But I don't understand how you came to be here."

"Marant won me in a dice game."

Shelara's expression tightened, and an old sorrow showed in her eyes. "The same thing happened to me. My brother put me up as a stake."

"I wouldn't blame your brother too much. Marant is a minor wizard, and he can overcome minds. Your brother was forced into it."

Shelara looked unconvinced but finished getting dressed and nodded when she was ready. Karis picked up the sacks again and led the way downstairs.

It took her a few minutes to find and remove all the warding spells Marant had placed on the door, and she thought he must be a fearful person indeed. She usually only placed one on any room or campsite she and Jarale used. The bolts she simply ordered to slide back, and they did so as quietly as snow falling on snow.

The door swung open, and Shelara followed her outside. While Karis was relocking the door and putting the spells back on, she heard Shelara draw a deep breath.

"This is the first time I've been outside in months. He kept me so closed up in there, I don't even know how long I've been his prisoner."

"You'd be surprised. Ready to go?"

"Yes, but where are we going?"

"City gates. They'll open in another sandrun, and we can be on our way." Karis looked her over carefully. "Pull your hood up as far as you can."

Shelara did as she was told, and Karis led her through the streets. Jarale had spent months teaching her how to find her way through a strange city, and now she put the lessons to good use.

The streets were nearly deserted, and the only people they saw were too drunk to see them.

When the gates were ahead of them, she looked around, then pulled Shelara into an alley. The girl started to say something, but Karis was concentrating and didn't have time for explanations. "Later," she whispered, and Shelara was silent.

The sound of horses approaching, then a low voice. "Karis?"

"Here."

Jarale came around the corner leading four horses behind him. Three were saddled for riding, the fourth held their packs. The false packs that had been tied on the fourth horse, making him appear to be another pack horse, had been discarded.

Jarale nodded when he saw Shelara. "You got her, good. Any trouble?"

"None. Here are the sacks. With what I've taken from him, we won't have to scrounge for work for months."

Jarale's eyes widened when he felt the weight of what she had brought, and he smiled back at her. "A good night's work. We can celebrate this job."

As opposed to their last two.

While he was placing the sacks on her horse, she began concentrating. There was a glow, and she felt a familiar tingle, then the shape she had been wearing disappeared, and she was herself again, a short, stocky young woman with a mop of dark curls. Only the eyes remained the same, kyraflower blue, deepening into purple.

Wizard's eyes, someone had said.

Now she had to do something about Shelara. The girl was staring at Karis in wonder, and the mage grinned at her. "Let's try this." Karis moved her hands, holding what she saw in her head, and there was a shimmer, and where Shelara had stood there was now a young girl of about fifteen, with light brown hair and a rounded figure.

That should be enough change to confuse pursuit. As she looked down, Karis could see her eyes widen again. "An illusionist," she whispered at last.

Well, Karis was a lot more than an illusionist, but she let it pass. She changed Jarale back into his regular form; tall, dark, and lean, in his mid thirties, with a twisted grin and a cynical eye. No longer a brother, but a distant cousin, chance met on the road.

He sighed with relief when the spell was removed. "Glad to be back as me." He was grumbling, but he had admitted the necessity. No one would have taken him for an easy mark as he stood.

The spell of illusion on the horses was changed, too, returning them to their usual appearance. She and Jarale had been very careful this time.

Karis turned to Shelara. "Ready to ride?"

"Yes, but I still don't understand how you came here."

There was a trumpet call, and a clash as the city gates opened. There were more sounds from the street as people began their day. Jarale and Karis moved toward the horses, helping Shelara to mount. They hoped that after her long imprisonment she would be able to stand the pace they would have to set, but there was nothing they could do about it at the moment. As the two of them mounted, Karis gave her enough explanation to understand who they were and why they were there.

"Your brother hired us to get you back. After he lost you, he swore he wouldn't rest until he got you back. He tried several different methods, and he finally decided that a wizard and a swordsman could do the job better than he could."

They got in line behind some other early travelers, and were waved through the gates. Shelara shivered as she rode out into freedom. "Will Marant try to follow us?"

"He might, but he won't know what to look for. But I'll tell you one thing," she said, chuckling, remembering the final touch she had left in his mind.

"What's that?"

"He won't be able to do much more gambling. From now on, whenever he picks up a deck of cards or a pair of dice, the word 'cheat' will appear on his forehead."

SONG OF THE DRAGON
by Andrea Pelleschi

Usually I don't print any story which begins with some man saying "Women don't . . ." In an anthology like this, it's just a lazy way for a writer to disprove it. Nor, as a general rule, do I care for stories about dragons; by now, they are the biggest cliche in fantasy.

But there are always exceptions to every rule; if the story really holds my attention. This one did. I think it will hold yours, too.

Andrea is a "28-year-old female working full time as a mechanical engineer for an electric utility." I never cease to wonder at the different jobs women can do now; when I was a kid they took it for granted that any woman who wasn't a housewife would be a nurse or a teacher. Times certainly have changed.

Terri ran down the empty hallway of the school, her footsteps echoing on the stone floor. She must not be late—not to Storos' class on magic theory. He was the most powerful sorcerer at the school and she didn't want to see him angry. Breathing hard, she took the steps two at a time and clutched her spell books tighter. As she rounded a corner, she saw Dugan and his gang. They were waiting for her again.

"Did you practice your spells, Terri?" asked one of

them. Terri remained silent and tried to walk past, but they wouldn't let her.

"Oh, she's not talking today," said another as they crowded around. "Maybe she used her Mute Spell on herself."

"Yeah, and maybe she'll use the Cloaking Spell tomorrow and we'll never see her again." They all laughed.

"Hey, Terri, let me see your spell books," said Dugan, the oldest. "I want to see if you did your lesson right." He reached for them.

"No, leave me alone," she cried. There was a tremor in her voice.

"Leave me alone. Leave me alone," they mocked.

"We'll be very happy to leave you alone," Dugan said reasonably. "Just show me your books."

Terri stubbornly shook her head and, suddenly, her books were gone. There was nothing in her arms. She looked around frantically at the boys, but they didn't have them. They were just laughing at her. She looked at Dugan and saw his brows drawn in concentration and his lips moving silently.

"A spell! You've spelled my books. Where are they?" Terri demanded.

"Get them yourself, Terri."

"Yeah, let's see your magical powers."

"Maybe she's afraid. Maybe she doesn't think she knows the right spell."

One of the boys glanced upward and Terri followed his eyes. She saw her books. They were floating in the air, about two feet from the ceiling. She jumped up and made a grab for them, but they glided teasingly away.

"Use your magic. Let's see a spell," they called.

Terri tried to think, but her mind was a blank. All she could hear were the mocking voices of the boys. Tears started to burn in her eyes and she bit her lip. She mustn't cry—not in front of them. The more she tried to concentrate, though, the less she remembered.

Finally, the bell rang and the boys forgot about her and took off down the hall to class. Her books crashed to the floor.

"You'll never be a sorcerer, Terri. Never," yelled Dugan over his shoulder. "Go back home to your cooking and cleaning. Start acting like a girl."

Slowly, the sounds of their voices died away and the hallway became quiet again. Terri stood still and took deep breaths trying to calm her pounding heart. She angrily brushed away the tears that spilled down her face. *It's not fair,* she thought. *Why don't they leave me alone? I have just as much right to be here as they do!*

She looked down at the mess on the floor. Her books lay in a crumpled heap, lesson papers scattered all over. With a gasp, she picked up one of them. It was almost ruined. The binding was broken and the leather cover was hanging on by a couple of threads. Sadly, she tried to smooth its creased pages. This was her first book on magic. Her father had given it to her when she turned twelve.

"You'll be a fine sorcerer some day," he had said. It looked old and worn even then. "This was my first spell book, too. Your grandfather gave it to me when I was your age." His eyes shone with pleasure. "Now it's your turn."

"But I'm just a girl," she protested. "I can't be a sorcerer like you."

"Nonsense. You're my daughter, aren't you. In this family we're sorcerers." Then he looked at her intensely for a moment. "I never got the chance to go to school, because your grandfather needed me too much here. But you're going to get that chance. And I'm going to make sure that you're ready." Then he opened the book and began her first lesson.

For the next two years, Terri's father taught her almost everything he knew about sorcery. He showed her the different herbs and roots and told her about their use in healing. She learned about animals and how to read their tracks. She even assisted him in his work for the villagers and farmers.

The day she had left for school, her father thought she was ready for anything. Neither of them realized that her biggest challenge would be the other students. After being at school for two months, no one took her seriously. No one thought she could ever really be a sorcerer.

Without thinking, Terri muttered the spell that would repair her damaged book. The cracked binding became whole and the cover sewed itself back together. It was almost as good as before. She stared in surprise. The spells seemed to come so easily to her when she was alone. Why couldn't she perform magic like this in front of the boys?

As she stood there, she realized that she was late. As fast as she could, she gathered up the rest of her possessions and ran down the hall. When she got to the door, she hesitated. Storos always frightened her. Maybe it would be better to just skip this class than to show up late. But no, if she did that, the boys would think she was avoiding them.

Resolutely, she pushed open the door and stepped inside. The room immediately became deathly silent. Storos didn't say a word. He simply stared at her. She crept to her chair and sat down.

"Good morning, Terri," said Storos. His voice was mild, but his eyes were like steel. "How nice of you to join us today."

The boys started giggling, but they stopped as soon as Storos turned to them.

"I hope that in the future you'll attend my class at the scheduled time," he said fixing his eyes on her again. "Tardiness is something I won't allow."

"Yes, sir," Terri replied meekly. One of the boys snickered.

Storos turned back to the slate board and contined lecturing. As she listened, Terri remembered all of the rumors she had heard about him during the last two months—rumors that said Storos was not what he seemed. Apparently, no one could remember a time when he had not been at the school. And if that was true, Terri estimated him to be well over two hundred years old. She didn't believe it, of course. Only elves, trolls, and dragons lived that long.

Terri scrutinized him closer. He looked like a man, but the rumors implied he was something else, something not quite human. A chill ran down her spine as she searched his face for a sign of an elf or a troll. His black hair, crooked nose and high, arched brows made him look rather fierce, but human nonetheless. With his customary black robes and sharp eyes that never missed anything, he reminded Terri of a great hunting bird.

"All right, Terri," Storos said jolting her back to the present. "Why don't you tell us how you did your homework. What is the most effective way to kill a troll?"

"Umm, arsenic and silver?" she said uncertainly as she rifled through her papers. She kicked herself for daydreaming.

"Well, is it arsenic and silver, or isn't it?" pressed Storos.

"Yes, umm, well . . ."

"Colin," Storos interrupted. "What do you think?"

"Yes, it's arsenic and silver," Colin said with confidence as he gave Terri a smug look. Terri felt her cheeks redden.

Storos arched one eyebrow at Colin. "That's correct. The best way to kill a troll is with silver arrows dipped in arsenic." Then he rubbed a finger along his long, hooked nose. "Why?"

"Why?" asked Colin puzzled. "What do you mean, 'Why?' "

"I mean, why silver and arsenic? Why not gold and arsenic, or silver and mercury? Why?"

"I guess, well, that's the way it is. That's all. Everyone knows that." Colin looked as though he wanted to be anywhere but in that classroom. His eyes darted back and forth nervously. Terri knew the answer, but she dared not speak now.

Storos' eyes narrowed in displeasure. He turned away from Colin and looked at someone else. "Why?" he repeated.

The boy just looked down at the floor. He didn't even try to answer the question. After a minute, Storos tried another boy and then another, always with the same result. Finally, he slammed his fist down on the table and looked around at everyone in the room. Terri shrank back in her chair trying to become invisible.

"I see that I don't have students in my classroom anymore," he said in a low intense voice. "I have sheep! Sheep who do what they're told without thinking first." He folded his arms and stared at each of them in turn. "Now, why don't we try this again. I'll ask you a question and you'll not only answer me, but you'll give me a reason for your answer."

Like a hawk diving for prey, he fired questions at them. If one student couldn't answer, he asked someone else until he got an answer he liked. No one was spared.

After a while, the bell rang signaling the end of class. Storos raised his hands for everyone to remain seated.

"I won't be here for the next couple of days," he announced. Everyone exchanged surprised glances. "You'll have a substitute, but don't think that you'll be able to relax. The substitute will know what to do." The corner of his mouth twitched. "When I come back, I want to see students of sorcery—not sheep." Then he left the room with a swirl of his cloak.

Everyone relaxed visibly and started talking. Terri felt drained. She closed her book and got ready to leave until she overheard part of a conversation.

"This is it," Dugan addressed some boys. "If anyone wants to follow him, they'll have to leave tonight. Who's going?" Dugan looked around the group and Terri dawdled at her desk. Follow who? she wondered.

"Colin, tell them how it went last year."

"Well," began Colin. "I waited until Storos got out of the school gates and then I just crept after him. A couple of times I tried to use my tracking spells, but it didn't work. Storos had too many of his own counter-spells set up." Then he pulled out a smooth, white stone on a chain from around his neck. A couple of boys whistled. Terri craned her neck to see between them. Apparently, no one remembered that she was still in the room. "I got this amulet from my brother. He wants to see where

Storos goes every year as much as we do. With this on, no one should have any trouble following him."

"I don't get it. Why do we need to follow him at all?" asked one of the boys who had started school the same day as Terri.

"Remember the strange things we told you about Storos?" Dugan asked them. All of the boys nodded. "Well, we think this trip he takes every year has something to do with what he really is. Just look how Colin couldn't follow him last year." Terri had her own ideas about that. "Storos is hiding something. The way I figure it, whatever he's hiding, we could use. Like, if he's an elf, we could get some magic arrows. Or, if he's a dragon, we could get some gold. Who's it going to be?" Dugan pressed.

"And, it can only be one of you," warned Colin. "Because if too many people left, the school might get suspicious."

There was a long silence as everyone considered the plan. All of the boys kept looking at each other, but no one said anything.

"I'll go," Terri said suddenly, surprising herself. Everyone turned around and stared at her in shock. "I mean, I used to help my father track animals all the time and I was pretty good at it. Storos shouldn't be too much harder," she said in a rush. Her heart was racing and her hands were shaking.

Everyone started protesting at once. "A girl can't go. She wouldn't know what to do," they said.

Finally, Colin held up his hand and quieted them down. He gave her a strange look. "I say let her go. Let's see if she can do it." Dugan was about to protest, but he looked around at the relief on the others' faces and just shrugged his shoulders.

Terri breathed again. They were letting her go. Now she could prove to them that she was more than just a girl. She looked around the group and saw some of the boys watching her with respect. At that moment, she knew that whatever else happened, she was glad she had volunteered. For the first time since she'd come to the school, she wasn't being treated like a girl.

Later that afternoon, Terri hid outside the school gates and waited for Storos to appear. She fingered the amulet that was hanging around her neck. Colin had said that the stone would glow if she was on the right path. She hoped fervently that he was right. It would make everything so much easier. Then, for about the tenth time that hour, she checked her backpack. Food, bedroll, and, most importantly, her first spell book were all there.

Finally, Terri saw Storos walk through the school gates. He was carrying a long walking stick and had a bag slung over one shoulder. She remained hidden behind a rock until he went down a path into the woods. When he was out of sight, she followed him. Once she was on the path, she pulled out the amulet. Slowly, she turned in a circle. The amulet glowed when she faced the direction that Storos had gone. It worked. Terri smiled and headed farther into the woods with the amulet as her guide.

For about a mile, it was so easy to follow him that Terri started to get worried. Maybe he's just going to the market; or, maybe he's visiting a sick relative, she thought. Or, maybe the boys played a trick on her. She started to get angry and pictured Dugan and the others laughing at her. She became so caught up in her image that she almost stepped right into a clearing where Storos would have seen her. He was standing in the middle of it as still as a bird.

Terri quickly ducked behind some bushes and watched him. After about fifteen minutes, he moved his hands in some complicated pattern and started chanting in a language Terri had never heard. His voice started out low and then rose to such a level that she had to put her hands over her ears. It was inhuman. She closed her eyes and gritted her teeth in pain. Just when she thought she couldn't take anymore, it stopped.

Slowly, she opened her eyes and lowered her hands. The clearing was empty. Terri frantically looked for him, but without success. Then she ran into the clearing and stood on the spot where Storos had been. With shaking hands, she pulled out the amulet. It was dull. She turned around and around in a circle trying to see if the amulet would glow, but it was no use. Storos had effectively disappeared.

Terri sank to ground in despair. She'd only been gone an hour and had already failed. The boys were right. She could never be a sorcerer. She removed the amulet from around her neck and threw it across the field. It was useless now. Then she sat down on the grass and cried. All of the pent up anger and frustration she had been feeling for the past two months came out. With huge racking sobs she cried for the cruel boys at school and a world that said girls couldn't be sorcerers. Finally, she cried for herself and for wanting to be a sorcerer more than anything.

After a while, she stopped. Surprisingly, she felt better than she ever had for the last two months, tired but peaceful. But, what am I going to do now? she thought. I can't face the boys this soon. She reached into her backpack for some cloth to wipe her eyes and felt her spell book. Suddenly, it dawned on her what she should do. If the amulet wouldn't work, maybe one of her spells would.

Excitedly, Terri opened her book to a tracking spell. This one was supposed to light up the path of the person being followed. Terri stood up and held the book in one hand. She cleared her mind of all distractions and recited the spell. When she was done, she looked around the clearing for a sign that it had worked but saw nothing. Then she tried it again and still nothing. Feeling frustrated, she turned the page and tried another, more complicated spell. It didn't work either. Terri put the book down and remembered what Colin had said earlier about Storos' counter-spells.

"Think," Storos would have told her. She smiled as she pictured him, one eyebrow raised, telling her not to be a sheep. Terri tried to concentrate. She looked back on everything that had happened so far. First, Storos had gone into the woods with his walking stick and shoulder bag. Then, he had stopped in the clearing, recited a spell and disappeared. Finally, she had tried all the magic she knew to find him and none of it had worked.

None of her magic worked, she repeated to herself. Who said she had to use magic? In her mind, Terri saw Storos' walking stick again. He must have walked out of the clearing when he disappeared, she realized. And if he had walked, then he could be tracked on the ground without magic. Terri kicked herself for not thinking of this earlier, but was proud anyway. Maybe her magic wasn't working, but she had just figured out more than Colin or any of the other boys ever had.

Terri put her book away, shouldered her backpack and looked for clues on the ground. It was getting dark, so she created a magical torch that floated nearby and lit the area. There, she spotted a footprint, and then another. They must be Storos'. She followed his track from the field back to the forest, and pretended she was tracking a fox with her father as they had just a few months ago. Following a teacher isn't much different, she thought.

Into the night Terri crept, picking out broken branches and dislodged pebbles, her father gently guiding her all the while.

After walking for hours, Terri came upon a cave in the side of a low hill. She never would have seen it, except that Storos' tracks led straight there. She took a quick break and then ventured forth. As she entered the cave, her magical torch threw shadows that danced eerily on the walls. She walked very slowly and cautiously, afraid that she'd run into him any minute. The only sounds she heard were her own breathing and the steady drip of water nearby. Up ahead, she noticed a light, so she extinguished her torch.

She crept toward the light, feeling her way along the walls and stepping carefully so as not to make a sound. As she rounded a bend, she saw that there really wasn't any light at all. It was the night sky. The cave had ended. Terri left it and hid behind a group of rocks. She was on the narrow ledge of a mountain. In front of her was a

sheer drop down to the valley. On her right, were more
rocks, maybe part of an old landslide. And on her left,
was Storos.

Terri caught her breath, but she hadn't been seen.
Storos had his back to her and was standing near the
edge of the drop-off, his black cape blowing in the wind.
He had something in his hands and was holding it out to
the stars. She heard him chanting in a foreign language
and felt as if she was watching something deeply personal. Just then the moon came out from behind a cloud,
and she saw what he was holding. It was a gold cup.

After he put the cup down, he started chanting louder.
Terri quickly covered her ears and closed her eyes in
anticipation. The chanting did get louder, but not like
before. This time it was musical. It drifted through the
night air and filled her with a sadness like she had never
known. It made her own problems seem petty and child-
ish. She felt a terrible longing. It was a longing for places
and people she could never know or hope to understand.
The song was beautiful and terrible at the same time.
Terri felt tears stream down her face. Her whole body
throbbed with every note.

Suddenly it ended. Terri gasped as the emotions left
her. She wiped her face and tried to get her trembling
under control. For a moment the mountain was silent.
Then, she heard the sound of a thousand birds flying and
felt a strong breeze pick up the dirt and pebbles. She
peered around the rocks and saw nothing but blackness.

Gradually, a few stars appeared around the edge of
the blackness and then some more. Terri realized that
the blackness was a thing. It seemed to be moving away
from her, and as it did, the sound of birds diminished.
She looked over at Storos. He was gone. The thing must
have gotten him. Summoning her courage, Terri ran to
the spot where she had last seen him. The black thing
didn't seem to notice her.

When she got there, she had another shock. In a cache
on the side of the mountain was a fortune in gold. Storos
must have been hoarding it. There were gold cups,
plates, bracelets, rings, everything. Terri picked up one

of the cups and then looked up at the sky. The thing had moved far enough away now, and she could see it clearly. It was a dragon.

He was the most beautiful creature she had ever seen. In awe, she watched him circle next to the mountain. He had black scales that glistened in the moonlight and reflected every color of the rainbow. He had giant wings that moved majestically on the air currents. First he moved slowly and a little awkwardly as if he hadn't flown in a long time. Then he speeded up and became more playful. He dove down toward the valley and then swooped back up at the last moment. He twirled and danced in the air. He even called out to the moon in a loud shriek as if to say, "I'm free. I'm free." Terri laughed out loud and clapped her hands for the sheer joy of it.

The dragon slowed down and drifted nearby. As she continued to watch, his head turned toward her and their eyes met. Terri stepped back in shock. She knew those eyes. They were the eyes of Storos.

In a panic, Terri dropped the gold cup and ran. She ran as fast as she could away from Storos the dragon. She ran through the cave and into the woods without even bothering to make a torch. She ran until her lungs were on fire and her legs were like rubber. He had seen her and she had to keep moving. Who knew how angry he would be now. When she couldn't run anymore, she jogged. And when she couldn't do that, she walked.

Just as the sun was coming up, Terri made it back to the school. She couldn't believe that she had only left it yesterday afternoon. Some of the boys were about and they ran out to the gates to greet her. They pulled her behind one of the buildings, sat her on a barrel and went to get Dugan and Colin.

As Dugan and Colin walked up, Terri realized that she had done it. She had successfully followed Storos and she knew his secret. She had done what no one else at the school had been able to do. Now they would have to accept her as an equal.

"Well, what did you find out?" Dugan asked her with a sneer. Apparently he had already decided she failed.

Terri took a deep breath. After being up all night, she found it difficult to think. Images from the past kept spinning through her mind. She saw Storos holding a gold cup toward the moon. She heard the horribly sad song that still left an ache deep inside her. She felt the wind and the sound of birds. And she saw Storos the dragon, soaring and diving, majestic one moment and playful the next.

Terri scanned the faces of the boys. How could she tell them so they would understand? If she told them that Storos was a dragon, would they listen to her as she explained the beauty and joy of his flight? Or, would they only hear about the gold hidden on the mountain? Terri didn't know why Storos was teaching at their school, but she thought that he must be terribly sad to be land-bound when he could be flying. Did she have a right to interfere? And what would happen to him if she did?

The boys were all waiting anxiously for her to talk. "What happened?" Colin asked.

This was her chance. She could tell the boys everything and win that approval. Or she could keep Storos' secret.

"Nothing happened," she finally said. "The amulet didn't work. I tried a couple of spells, but they didn't work either. Then I headed back here."

"It figures." Dugan said triumphantly. "I told you guys that she couldn't do it! Girls aren't cut out for sorcery!" And with that, he turned and walked back to the school.

The rest of the boys drifted away shaking their heads in disgust. Only Colin gave her a sympathetic glance before he left. Terri didn't care anymore. All she wanted to do was sleep. With legs that could barely carry her, she walked back to her room.

A couple of days later, Terri saw Storos walk in through the school gates, human once again. Summoning up her courage, she went out to meet him. When she was halfway there, he glanced toward her and their eyes met as before. This time, Terri held his gaze. A silent understanding passed between them during that moment. It was an understanding of secrets shared and mutual respect. Then Storos cocked an eyebrow, turned back to the school and walked inside.

BEAUTY AND HIS BEAST
by Vera Nazarian

Rewritten fairy tales are usually not my thing; but I made
an exception for this one, which I found—like all of
Vera's stories—strange, poignant, and exquisite.

In updating her biography, Vera said she's now working for a computer company, and thus has a chance to
test out all kinds of software. She says it's just the kind
of job she likes; where she gets to do about fifty different
things at the same time.

She's also "still chugging away at her novel about a
world without color"—strange, when what she writes is
so colorful. But I guess that's science fiction for you.

She would watch them, sideways out of her cold
clear eyes, the lovers walking with hands and gazes
entwined, among rose-briars and thick verdant
foliage of the gardens. These were her gardens, and they,
the ardent young trespassers, were now and then made
aware of her, when she allowed it to be. It was but a
reminder, lest they forget, that this marvelous idyll, this
wonder of a natural Eden, was but a small place within
her abode, a place she chose to share. And the lovers,
many of whom often came here at a whim, knew in the
back of their minds that upon any random turn of the
meandering path, beyond any thicket revealing a secret

niche, they might come upon her, grimly horrendous and shadowy, the dark queen they all came to know as the Beast.

The gardens—lustrous eyelashes around a glittering eye—sprung forth in abundance to encompass the palace of the queen. This queen, an oddity, was of such an acutely noble ancient lineage that due to an unpredictable genetic quirk she had been born a monster. She was, at the age of twenty-three, and at the time of her coronation, exactly six-and-a-half feet tall, hunchbacked, her muscular and fleshy hominid body covered head to toe by a thick growth of dark bristly hair—including the face—and her head was misshapen and oversized like a boulder. The head grew sable hair which fell in a fearful mane from the scalp to her waist. Her facial features were hardly humanoid, indistinguishable—indeed, no one ever ventured close enough to try—but her eyes, those were bright, coldly intelligent, *human*.

When she spoke, her voice also was frighteningly human, rich and deep and plush as ermine. It carried also tones of remarkable education—faultless really, except for the occasional moments when a hollow wheezing would overcome her—for the queen suffered from a chronic and inborn lung ailment.

The queen inherited her full rank at the moment of her father's death, then proceeded to institute major changes. The now-deceased king had been a grim shadowy man—although physically normal by all means, as human beings go. In his day, the kingdom lay under the miserly clutches of gloom and decay, under a strict control. With his passing, the gloom and decadence suddenly took a different form, emerging as creative energy. A new pulse-beat was given to the land by the beast-queen. But the control remained. For she was strong, strong as a Minotaur, by the sheer force of her will contained in the horrendous body.

Brought up and educated as a normal girl-child of her position, the Beast with the given name Vinnaea (which no one cared to use behind her back), held a fine court in her opulent palace. She was a connoisseur of the Arts and Sciences, patron to those who excelled in such. And she was above all, a subtle lover of beauty.

And that, of all things—some speculated—was the reason for the open gardens and the opulence and the exquisite people surrounding her. They said, the queen wanted the harmony of line and sound and thought to envelop her completely. They said, she wanted to drown in it and lose her *self,* and cease being the Beast—for she knew very well what people thought of her.

When appearing to the court, the Beast wore voluminous robes to cover as much of her grotesque form as possible. And always, the grand chandeliers were raised, and the hall dimmed before she would make her presence.

The bright lights, it seemed, hurt her abnormally sensitive eyes.

In the rich thick darkness of the gardens, the queen would find peace more often than elsewhere. She spent her days here—when the sun burned overhead, she would hide in a grove of maples, or near the weeping willows by the brook, or would lose herself in the artificially sculpted thicket of the Maze. When it rained, she crouched, reading in one of her favorite grottoes, books of philosophy, or else jotted down acutely beautiful thoughts in her leather-bound diary, with her clumsy black-maned hand.

At other times, when the sun spilled itself in an amber sunset, or clouds came to shadow the horizon, the Beast would watch those who strolled in her gardens.

They were beautiful, those young men and women, as perfectly formed to her as any amber sunset, and even more *alive.* The Beast loved to observe them strolling in couples, whispering to each other words of intimacy (which she would guiltily overhear, while a new feeling— one she could not verbalize to herself, but one that appeared persistently—would insinuate into her inhumanly *innocent* heart. It, this feeling, lingered there and occasionally made her soul-sick). But their presence here, no matter that it stirred alien longings in her, made her oddly content.

Until one day, a youth plucked a single bright crimson flower from her most treasured place, and thus there was to be no peace for the Beast.

"Oh, how pretty! How large that one is, I want that one!" cried Aysnera, pointing to the lush exotic flower whose name she did not know, growing larger than the rest on the branches of the tree.

"I'm not sure, lady," said Moere thoughtfully, "I don't know if it would be right to pick the flowers here."

"Why not?" the lady cried, in her petulant, lovely voice. "There are so many here, who would notice? Or care? Or are you afraid of *her?*"

Moere colored lightly. So easy it was to observe the changes on his fair light skin, fine and delicate as porcelain—each blush, each faint blooming of veins under the cheeks, left his face flaming as the dawn, and then, as quickly, pale again. Aysnera was not the only one charmed by his exquisite sensibilities, his curling honeylocks, and his gentle introspective eyes. In their circle of friends, he was affectionately teased with the nickname "Beauty," by both the ladies and the young men.

"Well, then," said lady Aysnera, "I will pluck it myself!" And she proceeded diligently to make the attempt, stretching up her bejeweled hands for some time, and finally gave up, saying: "This stupid bush! It's too tall for me! But oh, how nicely that bright red thing would sit in my hair. If only you were kind to me, Moere! You're tall enough."

The young man gave in, and plucked the blossom. He could not explain it to himself what made him uneasy about doing this—almost, a feeling of being observed.

And the next thing he knew, Aysnera was busy clutching her skirts to sink into a deep reverential curtsy, sudden alarm written on her face, and uttering "Your Majesty," while his own pulse first swooned, then also gained speed (half in fear, half in some other feeling he had no words for). Just before he too lowered himself into the proper courtly bow, his glance froze upon the great dark hunched form suddenly looming before them out of nowhere, and he had a glimpse of coldly burning *human* eyes. The blossom on its stem was still clutched in his trembling hand.

"Rise," said a deep voice of power. Controlled anger was in it also. "Rise, and do not ever do this again. Who taught you manners, lady?" The latter was addressed to Aysnera, who trembled.

"Oh, I am so sorry, Madam! Oh, so sorry—"

As though there existed such an unwritten law, they both stood now, yet neither dared raise their eyes to look at *her*.

"What is your name, girl?" said the Beast.

"A–aysnera, Your Majesty. Lady Aysnera Hild. I am so sorry—"

"When you allow guests into your house, Aysnera Hild, do you also expect them to appropriate the silverware from you dinner table, or the tapestries off the walls? These are my gardens, and you are my guests. This particular flower—although for weeks now beloved by me—has no great value really. It is but the careless attitudes which you carry, lady, that disturbs me. Your *carelessness* in taking it."

"I am the one to blame . . ." the young man blurted suddenly. "I took the flower from the branch." And his eyes rose to meet the Beast. "Moere Deiwall, Your Majesty, at Your service."

"Yes," said the Beast after an instant in which he thought his mind would explode from meeting the gaze out of the hooded darkness. "Only—it was not your intent. I know, for I have been observing the two of you contemplate my favorite flower."

And just as suddenly, the queen addressed Aysnera again: "You are dismissed, lady. And I have forgotten the incident." And then, to Moere: "But not you. I want you to come with me."

Such a cold wave of fear engulfed him then, that the young man, in a chill daze, never heard Aysnera curtsy hurriedly, and go nearly running down the path. She also, never looked back.

Moere stood alone with the Beast.

* * *

The fear accompanied him as he followed the dark hooded form (not knowing what lay underneath the rich heavy brocade of the Beast's cloak, having seen but the *eyes*), as they walked the twisting garden paths, to an unknown destination. He walked as though under a geas, pulled by an intuitive sense of obligation, and some strange new excitement.

"I want to show you things you have never seen before," spoke the Beast, as they walked, "You, unlike these others, I must show."

And it never occurred to him to ask her why.

They passed through groves of maple and oak and birch, and the Beast spoke to him of the perfect sound that leaves make, falling, and the murky breathing of the earth. They glanced into each one of the running streams, and she explained how it is possible to count every single pebble on the stream bed, at a glance. She showed him the patterns of lacework that the sun made through the fine leaves and branches of the weeping willows by the water's edge, and then he realized that, indeed, he'd seen the lacework before, woven into the artful court tapestries.

Next they wandered in the grottoes where he observed the rock formations give off light, eerie and hypnotic, and the occasional streamlined and elegant shapes of the bats evoked in him no longer the customary revulsion and fear, but an odd gentle pity. Indeed, he noticed, that fear which had followed him, was no longer with him, and instead, a lively curiosity had taken hold. Above all else, he wanted to hear the voice of the Beast.

It was at that moment that she stopped, saying: "The sun has almost set, you must now leave, Moere. Keep the flower you have plucked, as my gift. Return here again tomorrow, at the place of our meeting, and I will show you more."

Wordlessly he nodded, knowing that he must.

Moere Deiwall returned the next afternoon as he was told. And then he did so the next day, and the next.

Each time, the beast would take him along with her, and would speak to him, and would *show* him, until it seemed he no longer could keep track of time, and instead began to see the gardens all around him like they were a transparent lacework dream, while the wind seemed to him solid, and the sun was a golden incandescent vapor in the ice of the sky. Each night he would return, before sunset, and friends would greet him, noting his vacant non-presence, and his pallor, and his sightless eyes. "What is it, Beauty, what is it with you?" they strove to know, for his eyes indeed seemed to look elsewhere when he looked at them.

And when they found out that he had been spending time with the beast-queen, odd pitying glances, lacking any comprehension, followed him, and they whispered to each other of madness.

Months had thus passed. The seasons changed, fall replacing summer in the eternal ring dance, replete with its golden decay and ripeness. And in the winter, when the gardens were bare of leaves, and sparkling ice crystallized on the branches, still Moere would go to meet *her*. Breath freezing on his lips, freezing would he stand, as he listened to her words and to her voice.

And slowly, he found himself speaking also, telling her who was forever hooded in velvet darkness, many things he had never told even himself. It was then that she listened gravely, intently, and he was able to catch yet another rare glimpse of her acute clear *human* eyes. And afterward, every time, he would beg to remain with her an instant longer, beyond the moment of sunset, not understanding why it had to be thus. But the Beast insisted, with an urgency he could make no denial to, that he leave.

In the meantime, those he called friends would confront him, question him until he wanted to run and hide and make himself small somewhere. "What is it that you speak with *her* about, Moere? What is it that you *do* with her?" Aysnera, and others of her kind asked.

"Nothing," he would say, "Nothing *real* . . ." And when he saw how unclear his words were, even to himself, and how they provoked even greater suspicion, he would add: "We discuss—philosophy, yes. Her—Her Majesty is very interested in these matters, and in me she has found a good verbal companion."

"Ooh!" Aysnera would cry, "How *can* you? How can you be with the *Beast?*"

And for the first time in months, Moere would flush bright crimson with anger. "Do not call her that. Her name is Vinnaea. And she is our—queen."

"Hah!" Aysnera mocked. "She is, too, the Beast! And what a Beast! You must have gone blind all this while, to have gotten used to the ape-ugliness!"

"I—do not ever—*see* her." And as he said those words, he knew suddenly how odd it was indeed, that he had never even thought to wonder what lay underneath the dark hood, besides the eyes. It came to him then, as though a mental lens had insidiously changed focus, that truly, it was most bizarre, this whole thing. . . . All these days together, and never did he wonder *why*, why all they did was aimlessly wander the grounds, why did she not let him see her, why could he not stay after dark, and finally, hadn't she, the queen, other things to do?

He had been living in a spell, it occurred to Moere, his *vision* had been—due to that spell—forever doubled. Even now, as he looked at the elegant brightly-lit chamber around him, at Aysnera in her lovely jewel-dress, he could see, like a superimposed image hanging in his *other* mind's eye, the semi-transparency of all these things, the dimness (despite the bright chandelier illumination). And almost, he could see *through* Aysnera herself, to the other wall behind her, for she, too, was only half-corporeal and half-shade, and there was, in fact, less and less substance in her, the more he looked. Another instant of this vision, and she would fade. . . .

He tried to blink this away, drowning in a wave of fear—for he was being engulfed by something far greater than he could ever conceive. And for a while it would recede, and things came into focus the *normal* way—that is, the one and only way he had once perceived them. Maybe it was true then, he was losing his mind.

"Do not go to see *her* anymore . . ." Aysnera whispered then, urgently. "Come instead, with us, we shall celebrate tomorrow, riding in the Dragon-sleds! Come with us, this once!"

"But—" he protested, a dark faint soul-sickness entering him.

"There'll be minstrels and song, and tambourines and fools with bell-caps, and we'll ride faster than the wind! And you'll smile and laugh once again, Moere! Come away, and remember how you once had been! So easy to do this!"

"But I promised *her* I will come. As always. . . . She would not know what happened—she will—what if she is hurt by this?"

"Are you *afraid* of her then, Moere?" Again, that taunt. He thought then, intensely.

"Not to see her, only once. Maybe that would not be so bad. She would know I had other things to do. She should guess, by gods! I, too, have my life!"

Only, at that instant, it was as if his inner *vision*, the one that teetered on the edge, doubling constantly, giving him four-dimensional sight, went dim all of a sudden, retreated, and narrowed. And then Moere could only see the normal bleak solid opulence of the room, and Aysnera's attentive eyes.

Somewhere else, placed in the very same glass vase as it had been many months ago, the crimson lush blossom, the Beast's gift—one that oddly went unnoticed by any and all, except for Moere, and one that never lost its bloom—suddenly shuddered faintly, as though kissed by the wind. And the next instant it stood dry and death-brown, charred out of its timelessness into instant decay.

The Beast stood alone on the dreary path of her garden. All about her the winter wind blew, tugging crudely at the nude black branches, and sending snowflakes up in drifts of crystal white. She stood and she listened, and from somewhere far away, carried by the icy gusts, there came to her the sound of laughter, young lovers celebrating the great Ride of Winter. Hoofbeats drummed

against the frozen earth, and the wild wailing of reed
pipes and beating tambourines rose high on the wind.
Wild exuberant joy was upon them, and with her *vision,*
the Beast could see *him,* surrounded by laughing young
maidens and other youths, their cheeks burning scarlet
as dawn from the frost. Young he also was, fresher and
fairer even than any of them, and his golden laughter
rode the winter wind.

The Beast watched the softly inflamed look in his sparkling gentle eyes—so intimate, so dear to her, ever since
the first time when she had seen him, terrified yet stead-
fastly clutching the flower in his chill pale hand. It was
then that she had seen the *kindness* in those eyes, odd
and sympathetic, unlike anything she had ever experi-
enced. And the look of them had pierced the innocence
that walled her in, pierced the invulnerable diamond of
her soul-heart, all the way to her deepest soft core of
rainbow and mother-of-pearl. And it made her bleed
with a feeling that she never fathomed before, and to
which she could give no name.

She watched him who was Beauty, as they had gotten
out of the Dragon-sleds, wreathed with streamers of scarlet and persimmon gold. He was laughing, and then
reached with one gently warm hand to hug a lady's fine
waist, while the lady, Aysnera, trembling with frost and
joy, threw her arms about his marble neck, and lightly
brushed his soft honey-curls.

There was a wetness in the *human* eyes of the Beast;
for a moment her *vision* blurred, and the cold wind froze
the drops that came down her cheek of bristling sable
fur.

She had never once told him that she loved him. She
had never again told him that he must come back, or she
would die.

There was no need for that, for she had taught him to
see.

And again the Beast saw through the blurring mists of
immense distance, and heard the singing on the wind.
And Beauty's head, she saw, was leaned closely to the
maiden's breast. She could see every softly rounded con-

tour of his profile, soft as porcelain, and the rose dawn—
his sweet blushing skin.

And the beast saw the gentle kind look in his eyes,
the same intimate vulnerable look that he had once given
her, and one that now he just as simply and genuinely
gave to another.

It was then that something deep within the Beast, deep
within the furred, muscular, hunchbacked body, broke at
last. No sound she gave, but the strength, the immense
strength of the Beast had left her. She was now only a
crippled thing, wrapped in dark pitiful garments, weight-
less and slowly sinking in a hunched embryonic heap onto
the clear stark-white snow.

Flushed with happiness of the Winter Ride, Moere
returned only to see his secret enchanted thing—the one
that burned like a beacon in his vision—the flower,
standing black and wilted in its vase of glass. And now
he remembered how, all through the Ride, in the back
of his mind, he had felt it, *dying,* flickering out, and
sometimes, oddly, he would see two clear piercing eyes
of the Beast, clear and sharp as day, in his mind's eye.
But never had he seen them thus—they were crying. It
had bothered him then, but he let himself be carried by
the joy-tide of the moment, made himself not care.

And now, in a wave of darkness, he *allowed* himself
to *see* once more, and as his vision once again unfurled,
warped and doubled, expanding as it once had been, he
knew what he had done.

The gardens stood silent and white, and silver-violet
dusk hung in the air. No sound, not even the wind. All
was motionless, hazy.

His pulse raced with soul-sickness, and breath came
short in the icy air, as he ran. Twists and sharp bends of
the garden path, branches striking his face. Another
turn, and with a swooning in his head, he saw *her,* or
what he knew to be her.

The pitiful heap of darkness sprawled on the path
before him, next to the tall familiar flower-bush. A pow-
dery fine sprinkling of snow already had dusted lightly

the black fabric. Somewhere, protruding, he saw a small dark-furred shape resembling a hand—rheumatic and knotted, with longish animal nails. Odd, how he had never noticed her hands before, ghastly and black-haired and sad.

Moere fell on his knees in the snow, next to the Beast. One instant he thought she was only a corpse, but then a faint difficult sound came to him, a light wheezing breath of one dying.

In the next instant, the sun spent its last ray, fell behind the rim of the world, and evening darkness, like a curtain, was about them.

Moere knew a sudden instinctual but unreal fear. He lowered his ear to her chest, to listen for a heartbeat, faint but present.

The Beat's face was, strangely, still hooded. Moere's peculiar unemotional response began to frighten even himself. Again, it was as though a spell engulfed him, only this time he saw and heard everything, but could not *feel*.

He gently removed the hood, and this time, the evening twilight rushed in, black, as though to take its place, and again he could almost see nothing, unless he made his searching gaze burn through the smoke-darkness.

Silent, he at last observed before him the Beast's *face*, like a caricature mask of horror worn at a carnival. And still, he did not feel.

Her eyes, closed before, came abruptly open. And his heart, which was a second ago calm as ice, now swooned in shock.

For, *her* eyes were *different*. Red and burning volcanic pits met him, and after a long moment of recognition, she whispered: "Moere . . . You have come. But oh, not now, no. It is—after dark. And as you see, it is when I lose the last of my humanity. After dark."

She breathed harshly, struggling with effort, and watched with her burning gaze his frozen receptive eyes for any sign of reaction.

"I am—sorry," he whispered. "I had to be away—"

"Yes. How true, away from me. It is only natural,

dear Moere. I—I would be surprised if you—always came here." And the Beast-face attempted to smile.

"I—"

"Say no more." she breathed. And then bared her long teeth in a horrible mockery of a grin. "Well, Beauty. Now that you see me the way I am, my horrible, my ridiculous face and form, what do you think? And don't be afraid to tell me the truth. I'd know if you tried to lie, you realize. I know you—too well. I am the Beast, my dearest Beauty, and as they say, I can tear you *apart*." She spoke fiercely now, with mockery, with a peculiar pride, and waited.

"Don't ever call yourself that!" he exclaimed, bolting into true wakefulness.

"And why not, my fair one? I *am* the Beast indeed. The queen of all Beasts. . . ."

Something began choking him, deep in the throat, and blood rang in his head. He looked at her silently, wordlessly, simply as he always had—looked.

"Well," said the Beast, "What do you *see?*"

And then Moere cried. Silent streaming tears came down his cheeks, freezing and hurting his tender skin, sharper than blades of steel. "I don't—know!" he repeated over and over, "I don't *see!* I don't—"

He never could express himself eloquently, as she could.

And then, as his head was about to explode with the overflow, the pain, of emotion long suppressed, he cried: "Don't *you* yourself understand? Don't you know what I see, you who showed me that other *vision?*"

And then he gulped, choking on his tears, and continued: "When I look at you, Vinnaea, if you must really know, I only see one *thing*, that which I've *always* seen—not this black form that you wear! No! Not this sad shape of darkness that you somehow—long time ago, before you were even born—planned to put on yourself! It is but an incorporeal shadow, like all those other things I see around me! No, you are not *this*—a light! You, my queen, are the most bright glorious form of *light*, more definite to me than the sun, or any of these poor souls that surround me. When I look at them long enough, they fade into nothing before me. And if I pretend to myself not to *see,* then I also, begin to fade, like them. But not you! You are the only one the sight of whom blinds me, you are the most concrete form in the world!

"And yes, my shining one, I was, and still am afraid of you, and to some extent, always will be. For, you are so much brighter than my own being. . . . I can feel how you can burn me away, and yet, I must be, forever be with you—"

And he pulled himself close, underneath her velvet cloak of darkness, and his arms came tightly, inevitably, to embrace the black fur, while his face with its crystallizing tears, buried in the crook of her swarthy neck, and his form shook with weeping.

"Then, my life has not been in vain," said the Beast softly, holding him tight to her. "For, my gentle Beauty, you who are my soul-half, I had indeed been born the Beast only for this—to help you awaken your *vision* of the way things *are.* And that, you have done. . . ."

And at that he wept even harder, and suddenly his constantly wavering sight came into a single great focus, so that he could see *her* fully—bright as day in the middle of night, and more beautiful than he ever suspected. While he also now saw all things to the farthest reaches of the land, and "inside-out," as though they were faceted crystals, and he was looking out from within each one of their glassy rainbow cores.

The cold had gone from the night, as they embraced, two forms of pure energy fused into one.

And somewhere far away, in a cold incorporeal chamber, Moere thought he saw from his unnatural distance, a tiny but brightly glowing form of a lush crimson flower, superimposed in his true *vision* over a dark decayed husk in a vase.

And he thought he could see, next to the great flower on the stem, there had opened a new young fiery bud.

SHARDS OF CRYSTAL
by Stephanie Shaver

Stephanie Shaver was (and probably still is) one of the youngest writers ever to sell to me; my usual form requesting information, instead of dry statistics, produced a splendid chatty letter which she blamed on a surfeit (during school vacation) of "Teenage Mutant Ninja Turtles." Don't let that bother you, Stephanie—most people can't tell the difference between us and horror films.

She complains that she's never been to a con, a book-signing, or a filksinging. She recently went to a Renaissance Faire and bought "an annoying but neat little instrument known as the ocarina or medieval kazoo, a wooden longsword (it's hanging on my wall), and a dragon-claw holding a crystal (it's hanging around my neck). Also a large amount of cherry cider, bread and sausage." She tried the dark ale but didn't like it. Oh, to be fifteen again . . . or to go to the Renfaire for the first time. Or to make one's first sale again.

But then, I'd have to be back in Texas with my first husband and a three-year-old kid again. I guess I'll stick to being sixty. Notice how colorful this story is . . . which just goes to show that age isn't everything.

Stephanie has asked me to say that this story is dedicated "To Judith Louvis and Leslie Crawford, who both know why."

S hadows lifted and wavered as she entered, her steps resounding from the iron-shod boots she wore.

Magelight danced and flickered as she passed the glowing spheres. It seemed as if a cold wind followed her, making the lights throw crazy shadows toward the figure that sat on the Throne of Umbra; shadows that added to those of the Throne.

Greasy orange light gleamed on the unwrapped metal hilts of the two swords that crossed her back. The naked daggers fixed in the sash glittered, as did the bracers on her wrists. The only sound in the room was the steady *click click* of her boots on the marble-and-gold-veined floor. She wore nothing but black, and her sable hair was pulled back tightly, two streaks of silver shooting through from the temples. Lines of age and pain etched her face; she was not a young woman.

Her cold eyes sparkled like green ice as she approached the Throne of Umbra.

She stopped.

Silence.

And then. . . .

"You, my enemy?"

The hissing voice issued forth not from the shadows of the Throne but from the air above it.

She did not smile, just nodded. "Yes, Imadrail, it is I."

A long pause followed. She waited.

Slowly, unnaturally, the shadows that gave the chair its name lifted. Beginning at the two sandaled, skeletal feet and moving up along the multi-silver colored robes that shifted and changed and gave the fabric the quality of motion. Over the handrests upon which a pair of bony hands sat, the shadows went. Up to the osseous neck, over the jutting face still graced with a few tufts of once-blond hair, the shrunken and hollow cheeks sticking out as if no skin remained on the body, and all that did was a hide stretched over bone. The only things that showed life were the two vibrant blue eyes that seemed to glow with an unnatural life, and the circular, hazy blood red stone that was inset in the high brow—pulsing with a livid power.

"You have returned?" The voice that did not come from the mouth said. The warrior nodded again.

"I have." She paused, and held out empty hands. "The Guild of Dei is as dead as their Goddess. You have no one to back you now, Imadrail."

Imadrail's eyes flickered with something vaguely human, and then was snuffed out as the cold, *in*human light returned.

"You have come to kill me." The words were final. There was no question in the voice, but she answered anyway.

"Yes. I must kill you. I vowed that many years ago, as well you know." She drew one of the daggers from the sash that crossed her right breast. "But I have honor. *You* may still kill yourself."

The eyes stared down at the sharp edge. The knife lifted into the air, and one shaking hand took it. The man contemplated the steel knife for a moment, and then shook his head minutely. The dagger crumbled to dust as if had been nothing more than a dried dirt clod.

"You are an old fool, my nemesis, and now you are one who is without hope." The woman bowed her head. "I will—I *must*—kill you."

A fickle smile flashed on the face and then was gone. The voice answered, "How do you propose to do that? I am immortal, even without the Guild."

"You were human once."

The head nodded a fraction of an inch. "Perhaps. But now that I have this—" the inset stone burst with light "—I need not worry of the threat of death. I was a man once, within the boundaries of Death, but not anymore. Not with the Stone of Life to sustain me."

She spat at his feet. "The Stone of Death."

"The Stone of Life, of Tetkiris Herself, that gives me a reign over my people for eternity."

"The Stone of Death, of Dei, that gives you a living death and chains your soul to a body of dust. Look at yourself! Too weak to lift a hand, imprisoned forever on this chair. Already you have lived thirty years beyond your life span!" She shook her head, and touched one of the silver streaks that marked her hair. "*I* am even old!" She pointed at him. "And even if *I* fail today, my daughter might not."

His eyes flickered again. "You have a daughter?" the bodiless voice asked.

She nodded. "Her name is Ysanne. After her grandmother."

The quiet that followed seemed to permeate the room.

And then the voice that was not quite Imadrail's snarled:

"Just try and kill me!"

The warrior drew her shining swords and prepared to attack.

Slowly, she circled the skeletal creature on the Throne. The eyes followed her, and, quick as lightning, she struck.

The swords bounced off an invisible magical barrier and shattered. The woman smashed against it and fell back on her rump. Her ribs ached, and she was sure at least one was cracked.

Imadrail's laughter filled the room, and her face burned hot as she prepared her second attack.

Next, she drew the daggers and began to throw them at the figure. They met a fate similar to that of the swords, except the daggers exploded instead, sending bits of metal at her. When all but one were used up, she was forced to use her final, hidden weapon.

The strange giggles continued, and her face flushed heatedly.

From within a concealed pocket on her body, she drew a shard of clear crystal that pulsed in time with the one that was fixed in the King's forehead. She saw the blue eyes widen at the sight of one of the sacred weapons of Tetkiris in her hand. The crimson stone throbbed angrily, the laughter abruptly ceased, and then she threw it, like a dagger.

The shard flew forward, cut the invisible wall—

—and shattered, inches from the man's face.

"You see!" the voice screamed. "Even the mightiest of weapons are *nothing* opposed to me! Nothing! I *am* Power, I *am* immortality! *I AM A GOD!*"

And the woman lifted her voice against that of the Stone of Death, and cried, "You were my father!"

She leapt forward, her final dagger poised high, and the eyes of the King glowed when he heard her last words. They were a color of blue so brilliant, those glorious orbs, she thought she would be blinded. But they knew, oh, yes, those *human eyes* knew what she was doing as she slipped through the barrier. The dagger flew on silver wings down, down, so far down, cutting the air, shearing through the shadows, while the stone pulsed brighter and brighter—

The dagger caught on something, and she heard a gasp of breath leave the chest of the old man. And finally that dreadful, awful silence, once again.

The body of Imadrail slipped into her arms.

She heard his breath, labored, but human, as the once preternatural glow faded and left behind the milky eyes of an old man again.

She felt the tears despite her thirty years hatred toward him, and she watched through a glittering layer as the tears dropped, one by one, on the hollow cheeks.

He spoke then, through his lips, in a voice that cracked with age.

"Ysanne . . . you say?"

She nodded and blinked away the tears as she lowered herself and the bleeding form of her father to the floor, away from the Throne.

"Does . . . does she have . . . your eyes?" The light of life was receding rapidly from the sad face.

"Yes, yes she does."

He nodded gently, and drew one final breath.

"She has your mother's eyes . . . Kalyra."

And Imadrail, father of Kalyra, died.

The body crumbled to dust in her arms, the empty robes sank to the marble floor, becoming no more than tattered rags.

The stone remained.

Gently, Kalyra lifted the pulsing crystal from her lap into her hand. It burned with a cold power as she stared into its depths. The temptation was there, powerful and strong, just as it had been thirty years ago when her father had been given it as a gift from the Guild of Dei, the Guild she had fought and destroyed after thirty years. Many questions ran over in her mind, one prominent.

Had those eyes really known, and—dare she think?— *welcomed* what she did?

Or was it all a lie.

She would never know. He could not answer now.

Kalyra still stared at the stone, and now she lifted it high, the many facets dancing angrily—

—and shattered it into a thousand pieces on the floor.

Shards of crystal glittered as the magelight faded. The daughter of Imadrail stood and did not bother to brush the dust off herself. In the hall, a cold wind seemed to follow her as the hissing magelights extinguished, one by one, wherever she passed down the hall, heading toward the doors.

The Throne of Umbra stood, an obsidian memorial that now stood empty after a score and ten years. At its feet, a small, scattered pile of dust remained, along with the faded gray scraps of a threadbare robe.

And as the door closed, the light died on shards of crystal both clear and crimson.

SPELLBINDER
by Eluki bes Shahar

Eluki bes Shahar came to us by way of DAW BOOKS and her editor Sheila Gilbert.

She is a Public Information Officer for the Greater Poughkeepsie (New York) Library District. It makes me think of *Basingstoke*; I grew up in upstate New York, and when I was in grade schook, Poughkeepsie was nothing but the location of an enormous state mental hospital. Now it's a city with a population of 80,000. Things do change.

Be that as it may, she is also the author of three Regency Romances (under the name of Rosemary Edghill), and under the name of Eluki bes Shahar, the author of a science fiction novel called HELLFLOWER. I read a book by that name by somebody else—George O. Smith I think—when I was a young fan . . . 1953 or so. Time, as somebody or other must have said before, certainly flies.

Her name was Coelli Lightfoot, and she wore two pieces of green turquoise in her left ear and a dangly gold moon in her right. Her eyes were blue, her hair was brown, and her chin was stubborn.

She had been given to the Order in Harkady when she was born, and spent the first twelve uneventful years of her life cooking and cleaning and running errands for the masters there. The Order had once been servants of a god whose name had since been lost. Now it welcomed women over men for their deftness in its delicate profession, and as Coelli grew her one hope became that she would be asked to stay.

Not all the Order's fosterlings were given a choice. The Order was offered many babies every year because it would feed them, and every year it sent children who were found useless to it away. Some who were offered the chance to stay declined it, for the Order's rules were hard.

But each year the masters in Harkady found some merit in Coelli Lightfoot. She grew tall in a world of silent busy men and women, and when she first began to bleed like a woman the Chief Illuminator called her to his study and asked her if she had a will to join their number. He told her what she knew already—that she must teach no one the secrets she would be taught, and that there would be no children for her save those she would learn to make.

But Coelli wanted no other life than this, and so they fed her the drug that would stop her woman's bleeding forever and began to train her in their arts.

The preparation of vellum. The mixing of pigments. The annealing of gold, the distillation of ink, the shaping of quill and brush and all the other minutiae of the bookmaker's craft.

And when she had learned all they could teach her, she began to do.

Coelli Lightfoot made books. Books copied fair from wax or clay tablets, books copied new from tattered and ancient originals, books multiplied so that two or three or five copies stood where only one had been before— all the same, and each as different as the hand that made it. And when her work was done, holographed and illuminated, the vellum sheets sewn to the leather backing, the covers made and ornamented according to the degree and wealth of the client, and the locks and buckles clasped firmly in place, she could say: this would not have existed without me.

In that sense, she did not lack for children.

In five years Coelli had a Clerk's tortoiseshell pencase of her own to dangle at her hip, and stayed on. In five more it was ornamented with the lacquer and silver fittings of a Scribe, and still she was invited to remain. In yet another five years of practice at her art the red silk tassels of a Master Illuminator, fat with amber beads, dangled from her pencase, and it was time for her to leave.

The Charterhouse had room for only so many, and the young and the strong and the gifted must leave to earn the Order's wealth and their own. In the spring of her twenty-seventh year Coelli Lightfoot took her masterwork to the Hiring Fair outside the town and waited there to see who would come to claim the services of a Master Illuminator of the Charterhouse in Harkady.

Chief Steward Meule was a cold-eyed man who looked from her book to her and back again until Coelli was sure he would wear away the color on the pages. Hiring Fair gossip told that he came from a Great House called Windwalls that lay over the desert and high in the mountains beyond, and the list of questions that he asked about her skills made Coelli certain he was measuring her for mastership of a great scriptorium filled with clerks.

Meule had a mouth that would not shape yea or nay, but he paid good red gold enough to the Order to take her away with him without a single scrap of paper being signed. He promised fair copies of indentures sent as soon as his lord had set hand to them, and Coelli had no doubt that the hand that shaped each careful letter would be her own.

It was two weeks across the desert and then a racking handful of days ascending what surely were less than goat tracks. Giant trees pressed in all around—the source of the oak gall and mistletoe and powdered willow that made ink for the Order's use. At last they arrived at the white stone roundkeep, and Coelli learned just what sort of Great House desired her services.

". . . but the term of service, Master Meule. It is not here."

Coelli tapped the vellum with one calloused pale finger and Meule frowned. Bornless fool; if he'd hired her to write surely he knew she could read as well.

"Look again, girl."

Meule set a withe-basket down on the table where the indentures were spread. Three copies: one for the House and one for her and one for her masters at Harkady.

"Oh, come, Meule, will it crack your face to give me my title? You hired a Master Illuminator of the Charterhouse at Harkady—call me Master Coelli and display the wealth of your House."

"We've hired nothing till you've signed, Master Coelli. And if you didn't mean to sign, you've wasted everyone's time coming here."

"I'd waste it further signing indentures that have no force in law," Coelli muttered. She turned back to the contract that had so far eaten all of her first morning here.

The sun slanting in through the high narrow windows illuminated script as fine as any she could do, but Meule had told her there were no others of her Order here. Perhaps Meule had been telling the truth after all, and the lord of the house could read and write.

In that case, why make such fuss over the possession of her expensive self? She looked at the documents again, and a phrase she somehow hadn't read before jumped out at her.

" 'For the life of the cat'? What cat?"

"This cat," said Meule, and plucked a gingery ball of fluff from his willow basket. Automatically Coelli cupped her hands to receive it, and it gazed up at her in owlish independence from eyes that were still kitten-blue.

"Meule, you are mad," Coelli said, amused. "Give me the pen, or shall I use mine?"

But the pen he gave her to use was fine silver, with

the nib edged razor-sharp, so that when he pressed her
fingers around it her blood welled to make the ink. And
she swore, a bit, because it hurt, but no Master from
Harkady was likely to have any more objection to sorcery
than to wealth, and so she signed the papers all three,
in the bright scarlet ink that endures as long as any other.

Then Meule took the ginger tom in one hand and
Coelli's fingers in the other, and squeezed open the kitten's jaws to let her blood drip freely over its tongue.
And then Meule said a word that leached all the light
from the sun and made the pen Coelli had held smoke
and fizzle away. The kitten sat and washed its face with
miffed economy, and now when it was late and beyond
too late to do anything at all about matters Coelli wished
she had been more frightened.

"Meule, what have you done?" she asked, and for the
first time since she had known him, Meule smiled.

At the end of the first year she tried to buy her way
free.

At the end of the third year she tried to escape.

This was her seventh year in Windwalls.

Cheyne was sunning himself on the window ledge of
the scriptorium as usual when she arrived to begin work.
The big ginger tom flicked an idle ear as she passed him.

How long could a cat live, anyway?

She opened her desk and laid out pens and inks for
her work. On the windowsill, Cheyne shifted in his sleep.

In after years memory failed her. She could recall no
face, no voice, no idle moment's pleasance from the time
she spent in the white stone roundkeep. There was the
work, and on unpleasant occasion there was Meule, and
there was nothing more. Of the lord who must have set
her tasks, the servants who brought her food and ink and
linens, of nights and meals and idle hours she had no
memory.

But she remembered Cheyne. Cheyne to hold warm
against the winter darkness, Cheyne who once had

chased butterflies in the spring and later made a
motionless ginger mound on her windowsill. Cheyne, the
only living thing in Windwalls who gave her what all
living things need.

Cheyne, her jailer.

The sun was setting as she tidied away brushes and
pens. A good day's work, just as every other these last
seven years had been. Her employers would be pleased.
Solid, workmanlike . . .

Maddening.

It was not the work she had dreamed of doing when
she was a student—not the art her masters at Harkady
had encouraged her to, knowing she was capable. The
unbound pages spread beneath her hand might have been
done by any clerk—page after page of letters becoming
words becoming an ocean of pages with no farther shore.
She did not jewel the covers of the books she made here,
nor write any of the letters large and red, nor draw fair
borders to soothe the eye. All was small and round and
neat—safe, gray, and dependable.

And unworthy of her skill, or the love that had been
spent in training it.

Why, if this was what Windwalls wanted, had they
hired a Master Illuminator? And why wouldn't they let
her go?

Coelli sighed. She had talked and reasoned and per-
suaded—they could hire an army of scribes for what her
bond had cost—but Windwalls had hired her, and to her
tears and threats and pleas Meule returned soft words of
joy at her utter suitability, and reminded her of the terms
of her indenture.

For the life of the cat.

The days grew shorter, and Coelli was forced to
acknowledge that another summer had gone and left her
here. Soon it would be winter, and she would spend her
hours making safe gray books by lamplight and dreaming
of spring to come when she might hope for her release.
Her skills, unchallenged, withered, until it seemed that

every morning she could chart each small relinquishment
of power and grace, and each day a new book that might
have been added its stillborn wailing to the wind.

They were crippling her. Each day, with each assur-
ance that they only wanted her mediocrity, Windwalls
stole her greatness. With each loss her desperation grew,
but where her will had been was only the smooth surgery
of Windwalls' sorcery.

Were they cruel? Did they hate? She had nothing left
with which to judge or measure. The house was a house
that liked to be more than sure in its dealings, and so at
the Master Illuminator's indentures they had taken her
soul and placed it into the body of the tabby cat. And
now Coelli Lightfoot could not run, nor even dream of
running for as long as Cheyne might live.

The branches whipped across her face. Sobbing, terrified, sick with what she had done, Coelli Lightfoot blun-
dered through the darkening forest. The blood crawled
sticky over her hands until she wished her skin had eyes
to weep.

Was it worth it to preserve the spark of her art that
she had felt so glorious? Shivering in the damp twilight
of the wildlands, she saw her gifts for the paltry common-
places they were, and certainly not worth her juvenile
theatrics.

She had forfeited seven years pay, and when word was
sent to the Charterhouse she would be stricken from their
rolls, so that she had forfeited the livelode that a Master
Illuminator could claim as well.

And she had killed Cheyne.

Coelli moaned aloud and stumbled on through the
dark, crying out against the tiny inward voice that told
her she had been right to do what she had done in
defense of that self which must not be sacrificed. At
length she was sick with running: throat burning and
chest constrained, grey skirts torn and sodden and thin
boots pierced to uselessness. Now, she thought, she
would stop, and see what there might be in her Master's

pencase with which to celebrate her dearly-purchased freedom.

As she realized what it was that she meant to do the ground gave way beneath her, and she fell through mud and sharp tangle and landed hard enough to take the last of the hysterics out of her. Though the light was fully gone when she began to move again, her nose told her plainly where she was. So she straightened her skirts, set her back to the sheer mud cliff that edged the swamp, and waited for the moon to rise.

There were no footsteps to be heard in last autumn's leaves, and before her only an occasional splash in the water. Coelli had no idea how far from the edge of the swamp she was, and had no desire to find out.

She waited. Perhaps there was some penance she could do to make her forget that Cheyne was dead for her convenience. But she had done seven years' penance already; payment in advance for her crime. When the moon rose, she would go on and see if she had bought a life she cared to live.

Would the never-seen Master of Windwalls follow her just as if she were any runaway bondservant to be hailed back for a branding and beating? But the term of her bond was served, even though she'd hastened its end. They would send no one, she decided finally, and be satisfied with an octade's work unpaid-for.

The darkness began to lighten enough for her to see cut-out shapes in the canopy of trees. The nightsounds that had returned after her fall came si'ent once again, until Coelli's slow breathing was the only sound she could hear and she wondered what she listened for. Then the moon topped the trees, and the dun-colored beast slid toward her over the glassy water of the swamp.

Its small flat head jutted low between burly shoulders, and the spread clawed paws made no mark on the moon-silver surface of the swamp. Coelli could clearly see the roached fur along the spine that spoke of stalking, and the white whiskers bristling from the muzzle as the beast sang low hunting songs of prey and enticement.

It was Cheyne.

There was no recognition in the fearful yellow eyes; not even the sleepy indifference with which he had used to regard her. By black sorcery he was reanimated and enlarged a thousandfold, and in that mad lamp gaze there was no lingering spark of soul.

Cheyne's soul was elsewhere. Bound to hers and untimely unhoused, it had fled with hers as well. Before she could stop herself, Coelli bared her soft puny teeth and caterwauled wild defiance at her stalker.

It paused as if it had just now heard something that could interest it as much as murder. Then it came onward as before; directly toward her and faster.

Whatever death it would give her was more than she had earned. Fighting back the alien impulse to stand and fight, Coelli ran along the edge of the water for precious squandered seconds while her death advanced, then scrambled up the roots embedded in the clayey bank.

The risen moon flattened detail and made the trees resemble the pillars of a vast temple of which they alone remained. There was no help there; the thing that followed could climb them better than she could. Coelli began again to run, knowing it was futile. Having loosed that against her, Windwalls would not take her back.

The rattle of amber beads commanded her attention, making her look down as she ran. She suppressed a despairing giggle at the impulse that led her to cling to her badge of rank as if a Master's pencase could impress what followed.

Her stumbling run slowed to a stop, and she turned. Her second wind was done, and now she must fight. If she could. Coelli was neither priest nor soldier; she was "armed," could you but dignify it so, with a laquered pencase containing the tools of her art: quills, brushes, ink stick and block, and a tiny silver-handled penknife. She held her pencase before her as if it were a holy amulet and tried to summon the scrap of faulty memory that made her think she had a chance to live. Too short a distance away the shadowcat clawed its way up the bank.

It was the need to hold a weapon, any weapon, that

made her rummage for the tiny knife now. The bright scrap of metal bloomed in the moonlight, and struck an answering spark from the hellbeast's eyes in the instant before it charged.

She never expected it to be so solid. It knocked her down; there was a moment's slip-slide of wet leaves over decay beneath her back and the hot wind of its breath, foul beyond reality, as it lowered its head to bite. Drunk with terror she slammed her fist against the side of its head, and felt the penknife turn in her hand to cut her. The cat's hind talons ripped great weeping furrows down her legs as it scrabbled for the purchase to disembowel her, and the massive demon head swung toward her again, jaws open wide. And Coelli remembered at last why she thought the penknife would serve her. She clutched up all her courage against pain-to-come and thrust her arm down the shadow's throat. Within her the spirit of Cheyne howled approval, drowning fear.

The beast was so surprised it forgot, for an instant, to bite. Vised by the convulsing slickness, Coelli opened her hand and freed the knife. She felt the cat's jaws begin to close, and knew in that instant that she had been wrong.

Then the nightmare vanished in a soundless howling, burned by iron and silver. It left behind only the deep tracks on her legs and an armlet-circle just below her shoulder where the blood welled like rubies.

A Master Illuminator is necessarily also a scholar. To properly ornament and bind a work, one must be able to understand as well as simply read its text.

Iron breaks the sorceries of the Moon.

Silver breaks the sorceries of the Sun.

And the little knife had both.

After a long time Coelli curled on her side and began to cry. Now she was truly free.

The sun replaced the moon in the sky and she washed her wounds clean at the place where the brook ran clear on its way to the swamp. She bandaged them with moss and strips torn from her shift and chewed a certain bark until her head was clear. Her pencase she left where it lay. And then she started back to Windwalls.

The forest had always been the storehouse of her art. Now she made it feed her and keep her alive until she finished her task. She was three days covering the distance she had come in half a night's run, and when the bark she had gathered was gone it began to seem to her that she wasn't alone. Cheyne stropped about her ankles sometimes, making her fall, but Meule or others she did not know hovered anxiously, urging her to rise and come to where they could help her. When she walked they spoke to her, approving once again, though she couldn't afterward remember what they said.

On the third day her fever broke, and she knew that she would live to make scars.

She passed the boundary-stones of Windwalls a little after midday. Meule was waiting just outside the gate, wearing white instead of his green castellan's robes, and behind him stood the others Coelli knew only from dreams. She came forward slowly, determined not to stumble.

"Welcome," said Meule. "Welcome home, Master Coelli."

Then there was a whispering like the wind running through the trees, and though she needed no more proof Coelli knew what had shaped and sent the cat.

/Welcome,/ the gathered lords of Windwalls said to her. /Welcome . . . Welcome . . . Welcome . . ./

"I've come for my manumission, Meule." Her voice was harsh; her throat parched and unused to speech. But it was what she had meant to say.

At first Meule could not believe what he heard. His face shaped itself to emit soothing platitudes and Coelli felt a flare of sudden panic, fear that she would believe him once more.

But Cheyne spoke first. The cat-self that was part of her and now would never leave her sang disgust and contempt of this magic-place and its madness. Coelli-Cheyne wailed and took a step backward.

"The cat," said Meule in disbelief. "You have the cat."

"Cheyne's dead. And by your own words you have to free me now."

The wind-sound came from the watchers again, and Coelli looked beyond Meule. The roundkeep no longer looked strong and fine. It looked soft, as though it had been a living thing from which the animating spark had been withdrawn.

"Free you? To what? There is no home for you but this. Your Order was told that you betrayed it. No papers ever reached Harkady. You are dead to them.

"We chose you with care, Master Illuminator. A gifted one who would fight her destruction, and never know what use you were to us, or why. You hated us. And you burned—oh, so brightly. You would have burned for years—to warm us."

/Warm us,/ sighed the ghosts.

Meule started toward her, looking suddenly less like a man than like something that had once tricked her into thinking it was a man.

"And now we will have to take what we can, all at once."

The ghostly chorus wailed assent, and in their disharmonies Coelli thought she saw Windwalls grow slowly more real, dragging her back into the dream from which she would not awaken twice.

/Join us

—burn for us—

firechild

—queen—

—stay with us—save us—/

Queen out of time, to rule Windwalls forever and lord it over a race out of legend. In the glory of Windwalls she could already see her coronation robes.

"No," Coelli said. Part of her was Cheyne. Cheyne had no interest in legend, only in hunter and prey. And she would not be prey.

"You cannot wish to go on as you are," Meule said, just as she hefted the weight in her hand and threw.

Her eye measured its arc as it flashed through the sunlight, and heard it ring down on the white rock.

Then the wind was silent and the air did not dazzle. Coelli stood on a situation of land that might once have held a keep called Windwalls and watched a small silver and iron penknife glitter in the sun on the rocks below.

"The cat is dead, as I told you. And in Harkady, Master Meule, we only sign bonds with human men."

If you go to a certain shop on a certain street in Choirdip, you will see a woman with two pieces of green turquoise in her left eat and a dangly gold moon in her right. Her eyes are blue, her hair is brown, and her chin is stubborn.

She is a dealer in antiquities and curiosa, so she says, and the magistrates of Choirdip know that what is stolen will one day find its way to the shop of Coelli Cheyne. It is said that she was once a scribe who fled her chapterhouse with her lover; that she takes the form of a cat when the moon is full; that she is a sorceress and communes with the creatures of the upper air.

Many things are said. But of where she goes, or what she does, or how she came by the books that line the walls of her shop, nothing is known for sure. She pays Choirdip well for that ignorance, and Coelli Cheyne is neither a poor thief nor an honest one.

But she is very kind to cats. And she is free.

THE PRICE OF THE WIND
by *Josepha Sherman*

Josepha Sherman has appeared before this in these pages; each time with a subtly crafted tale. Usually I'm not terribly interested in the story of "rape and revenge"; but I didn't identify this one as such until I had finished it—and by then I was hooked, as I predict the reader will be.

Josepha Sherman has two novels which should be out by the time this anthology is published: THE HORSE OF FLAME (for Avon) and CHILD OF FAERIE, CHILD OF EARTH (for Walker). She is the winner of the 1989 Crompton Crook Award for THE SHINING FALCON, a fantasy based on Slavic folklore, and (in addition to having appeared in S&S IV and V), she has sold over 45 other short stories. In today's tight fiction market, that's quite an accomplishment; I'll bet they're all as much fun to read as this subtle little tale which drew me in at once.

I had passed beyond the border of despair into the numbness of exhaustion by the time I fell across the threshold of that mountain hut with the cold wind all about it. Hut? Hovel, rather, ruin, bare planks held together haphazardly. A poor shelter, I thought vaguely, but enough to let me catch my breath and try to guess where else I might hide. That they were still close on my trail, I had no doubt.

The broken door fell in on itself. I nearly cried aloud in shock as a hand closed on my shoulder, and glanced wildly up. Ieran's men—No, no, this was a woman, an old, gray, ragged wren of a woman. The wind blew her wild, long hair stingingly about us both as she stared down at me, the steady, steady gaze of an ancient predator. Her eyes were pale as the wind, oddly pale in that land where most eyes were dark, and I stared back as bewildered as any bird before a snake for what seemed a long, frozen while.

The woman released me. "Yes," she murmured, and then, in an almost courtly voice, "Poor youngling. Come within, out of the wind."

"Lady—Old Mother—I—I dare not, they will—"

"They will not catch up with you so very swiftly."

"How do you—"

"I know." The pale eyes glittered. "Come. I mean you no harm. Inside."

A witch? A madwoman? At any rate, the heat of my run had left me, and I was fairly shuddering with cold and weariness. The thought of getting out of that wild wind, even for a short time . . . Ai, what harm from a poor old thing so fragile I towered over her when I stood?

There was, as I had expected, little of comfort within the hovel: some broken bits of furnishings, some scraps of fur. Something of my distaste must have shown on my face, because the old woman gave me a wry smile.

"I no longer feel the cold."

"Pardon, I meant no rudeness."

"Here is bread. And this." She held up an earthen jug. "Wine. It will warm you."

Poison? Some arcane potion? I was past the point of caring. I drank, and it was wine, and I was warmed, at least a bit.

"Sit, youngling. Now, who are you? A rich lord's son?"

"Oh, hardly! Old Mother, I am only a student, come up from the university at Berin-Lar. This is—was—my season for travel."

"So now? What went wrong?"

I couldn't meet the fierce gaze, staring instead at the jug still in my hands. Yet the laws of hospitality demanded I give my hostess the truth. "I . . . slew a man."

"Did you?" She hardly sounded surprised. "How?"

Ahh, how, indeed? I had been trying to avoid the lands of Lord Ieran, thinking that even if half the tales I'd been hearing about that cruelty-loving man were true, I didn't want to meet him or any of his folk. But . . .

"There was a hunting party stopped near the road," I began reluctantly, "all rich pavilions and banners. But farther on, in the darkness of the forest, one of the party had caught a girl, some poor little peasant girl, and he was laughing while he— I—I come from Tailan, where we worship the Mother, where no man would ever, ever . . . I was a fool. He was a trained warrior, and I was unarmed. He simply struck me aside, leaving me stunned. I heard the girl's screams, and then . . . I don't know what happened then."

"Eh?"

"It . . . was as though the wind was all about me, within me, the cold, chill, raging wind, making me more than human, more than mortal—" I broke off abruptly, shivering. But the unblinking gaze of the old woman was still upon me, and I sighed and continued softly, "When I came to myself, the power was gone from me. The man was dead before me, and in my hands was my student's staff, its end all bloody. And before me stood the very one I had been trying to avoid: Lord Ieran, no mistaking the noble crest he wore, Lord Ieran himself, with the heat of anger in his eyes. I had slain his man, the captain of his guard. And the punishment for that was to be slow, slow death."

"So you ran, poor youngling, ran and ran, the human hounds behind you. They never yield, those hounds, not while their master drives them."

"How would you know—"

"Hush. I know. But now there's an end to running for a time."

"No! They'll be—"

"Not yet, not yet. Rest, youngling. Rest for now."

Her hand was chill but gentle in my hair. Her voice was soft and soothing. The wine warmed and weakened me. And I— Oh, a soul can hold only so much fear and strain. *Madness*, I told myself, *this is madness*! But for all that, my weariness overcame me. For all my struggles, I slept.

And in my sleep, I saw . . . a man, a woman, young, beautiful, in terror for their lives, running even with the panic I had known, running with their small son held tight in the man's arms. There! There! The horsemen were coming up quickly behind them, trapping them against a wall of rock, laughing at their fear. The leader—Ieran! Lord Ieran!

Then came horror. I saw the hunted man thrust wife and child behind him—ah, useless! I saw him die, harsh, bloody death. I saw the child torn shrieking from his mother's arms, heard his screams ended by Lord Ieran's spear. I saw the woman—

But Ieran never touched her. No, no, far crueler than any death to leave her there, unharmed, there amid the wreckage of her life. As the slayers rode away, still laughing at their sport, she knelt, bent double with the weight of grief, long hair spread in the dust, and I thought in anguished pity, *Let me wake! Oh, let me wake!*

But then at last the woman raised her head, pale, drawn with strain. And in her eyes, terrible eyes, I saw the death of love, death of hope, death of mercy. She climbed the mountain slope, she stood at last on the utter peak, the cold winds all about her no colder than her eyes. And she called out in a voice as pure and sharp and hard as ice:

"Ai-Chan! Ai-Chan! Ai-Chan!"

She called upon the lord of all the Winds. She called on that Great One—and Ai-Chan came. There was a swirling, dazzling shimmer, there was a whisper like the wind's own voice:

"What would you?"

No pity in that voice, no human softness. And no softness was there in her answer:

"Vengeance. Grant me the wind's strength, Ai-Chan.
Grant me vengeance!"

"There is a price," whispered the wind-voice. "For
such power, a powerful price. Will you pay it?"

"Yes!" she cried out. "Yes!"

"Then know what—"

But a coldness was upon me. The old woman's chill
hand was on my arm and shaking me awake.

"Hurry, youngling! The hounds have come."

Gasping, I struggled to my feet, glancing wildly this
way and that, fighting off the mists of sleep. The cold
hand closed on mine.

"This way, youngling! Up this way! I will show you
how to hide."

She moved with uncanny ease, out into a mountain
world gone gray with fog. I stumbled in her wake, unable
to see clearly, knowing only that we were climbing up
and ever up.

"This—this can't be the way to escape!"

"Yes, yes! Hurry!"

The fog grew thicker still, chill and damp and smoth-
ering. Choking, I tried to slow my pace, and felt the old
woman's hand slip from mine. "Wait!"

She was gone, gray woman into gray fog, but I heard
her sharp laughter echoing back: "Follow, youngling!
Follow!"

But I was frozen, stunned by terror, listening to the
rough sounds of pursuit, so near! Ieran's men— No, from
the sound of it, one man only. Ieran? Of course, of
course, even if his men were lost in gray confusion, he
would come ahead, he would never risk the losing of his
prey, not he! Panicked anew by that relentlessness, I
turned and fled, hearing his panting breath behind me
as I slipped and stumbled on fog-wet rocks, blinded by
grayness, struggling on like someone in the foulest
dream.

"Fool!" I heard him gasp, almost in my ear. "I have
you!"

But for all and all, he couldn't see me clearly, and I—I couldn't see the ground before me! It was gone from beneath my feet, and I was falling—

Not far. A cold, strong hand closed on my arm, pulling me roughly down, even as the panting Ieran, sensing me if not seeing me, made a savage lunge at where I'd been a scant instant before. I heard his sudden startled shout of terror, and wondered, *What*—

—even as the wind swept down to tear the fog asunder. Dear Mother! We were on the very edge of the mountain, the safe world far below us!

And Ieran, in that savage, mindless lunge, had gone beyond the point of balance. There he hung, clinging to the crumbling rock with frantic hands. But when I, even knowing what he was, couldn't help but reach an arm out to him, the old woman slapped my arm aside. And the eyes that blazed into mine were now truly the eyes of a predator. While I watched, dazed, she slipped lithely to her feet. Small and terrible, she stood over the desperate man, watching his struggles with neither pleasure nor the slightest trace of pity.

"Ieran."

"Help me up, woman!"

"Think, Ieran."

"Are you mad? Help me—"

"Remember, Ieran. Remember Tierel. Young Tierel, whose only crime was that he couldn't be as cold as you. He couldn't slay the ones you wanted secretly, shamefully, dead. Tierel and Sarai-ye, his wife. Tierel and Sarai-ye and their son, their little son. Husband and wife and babe, one in their love, one in their joy. Do you remember, Ieran?"

"Madwoman!"

"Ah, you remember! You might have spared them. They were no threat to you, you had Tierel's heart-pledge never to speak your secrets. You might have turned aside and honored their joy. But Ieran does not show mercy. Ieran never turns empty-handed from a hunt. You do remember that hunt, those ugly, ugly deaths. You do remember."

"Damn you, woman, who are you?"

"Death, Ieran. Your death."

She raised a thin arm, and the wind came. She pointed, and the wind swept down and plucked Ieran from his shaky hold. For an instant I saw his eyes, wild and disbelieving. Then Ieran fell, and from the edge of my glance, I watched the woman watch his fall, all the long way down. And still there was no sign of grief or pleasure, nothing but . . . relief.

"Vengeance," she breathed after a time. "Ah, sweet."

She remembered me. She looked at me, and I flinched from the wide eyes and stammered, "The wind—the fog— They were yours!"

"Yes."

"Then . . . Dear Mother. What of the wind that seized me, that made me slay? Was that yours, too? Was it?"

"Yes."

"You—you—you used me! But why? What had I done to you?"

"Nothing, youngling." Now, at last, there was the faintest hint of pity in her voice. "There are limits on me. I cannot leave this mountain, not and keep the power of the wind. Ieran's men have minds like winter ice, as slick, as chill. I could not touch them from afar. But you . . . your mind was young, and open, and hot with outraged justice. Don't you see? I needed someone who would lure my enemy away from his safe, warm lowlands, here to this spot where the wind could take him. Here, where I could watch him fall."

"Who are you? What?"

"The dream, now, think of the dream I sent you."

"I—I don't understand. You are . . . Tierel's mother?"

"Youngling, I am Tierel's wife."

"Sarai-ye! But that c–can't be! Her eyes were dark—"

"The wind bleached their color away."

"And she was young, so young, and you're so . . ."

My voice faded. For, as I stared, I thought I saw in that face of age the hint of youth, the same shape of eye, the same sweep of bone. . . .

"So old?" the woman finished gently. "Oh, youngling,

power must have its price. And so I gave Ai-Chan my youth. I gave him all the years of Might Have Been, and watched my time be torn apart and lost upon the wind."

I must have made some small sound, of shock, of pity, for the woman stirred in sudden impatience. "Enough. Ieran's human hounds won't find their way up here. You can safely elude them down that path, there by the mountain's north face." Her voice softened slightly. "Hush, now, listen. You were my tool, yes, no more to blame than ax or sword. Be free of blood-guilt. Go to priest or priestess if you must, and bare your soul. Then live out all your years in peace."

I had to say it. "But . . . to give up your youth. . . ."

"Why, with my dear ones dead, I no longer had a use for it! Don't you see? I have no need to live beyond this point."

Her eyes were peaceful. And, as I stared in disbelief, the old woman who'd been young Sarai-ye stepped lightly out into space, and I was left alone on that chill mountain peak.

STAINED GLASS
by Linda Gordon

I keep telling my writing students—I'm an undiscouragable lecturer—that there are basically two plots; a good person gets what she wants, or a bad one gets just what's coming to her. This story definitely falls into the second category.

Linda Gordon has sold to us before; but, perhaps due to being suddenly evicted from her last address, failed to update her biography this time around; so I can only suggest that the reader is free to imagine her as an ivory-tower lady-professor type or a harried housewife trying to write while simultaneously raising five kids. (It's been done.)

Actually I think she's a truck driver who writes while she and her husband are on the road. Or was that someone else? She's had stories in SWORD AND SORCERESS V and VI, so her bio must be around here somewhere, if I could only find it in the clutter. Never a dull moment in this business.

Cathon tried to duck the queen's leather-wrapped stick as it swung toward her cheek, but she was not fast enough. Just missing her dark brown eye, the stick cut a line through her flesh, leaving a wet red streak.

Instantly, Cathon's anger flared, and she raised a hand to throw a fireball toward the queen.

"Not so fast, witch," Queen Isra said. The older woman held up a small bottle, its contents glowing with an iridescent lavender fire. "This would doubtless shatter should it slip from my grasp."

Cathon froze. While staring at the container, she sucked in a deep breath and forced her anger into hiding. Then, reluctantly, she lowered her hand.

Queen Isra smiled. "You make the special glass for me, in time for the king's damnable birthday celebration, and I will return this to you." She gestured with the container.

"Why do you want the stained glass?" Cathon's eyes were fixed on the queen, yet her attention was on the container Isra clutched.

Isra's smile faded then burst tight-lipped across her face. "Why, it is a gift for His Majesty."

Cathon sighed. "Isra, the special glass is not a gift for this king."

Isra's smile faded, and she gritted teeth. "Queen Isra to you, witch. I am the queen!" She worked the small vial in her hand, rolling it about, the gesture not lost on Cathon.

". . . Queen . . . Isra," Cathon said hesitantly. *You may be queen to some but not to me*, you hellspawn, she thought.

The queen briefly smiled. "I know you to prefer a life of privacy where you can work your glass." She paused and leaned toward Cathon. "Where you think to hide your secret, where you think no one will be the wiser that you do more than those beautiful stained glass pieces of yours." Isra grunted. "But your secret is out, witch, and I intend to take full advantage."

"Who told you about me?"

Isra's eyes narrowed. "Do not fear, witch, nor think of vengeance."

"What do you mean?"

Isra shrugged. "Some people think to hide their thoughts and knowledge from me, but I can work wonders with a white-hot poker and a sharp knife." She smiled, her gaze settling on Cathon's shocked countenance. "Do not fear. Your secret is still safe for now it rests only with me."

Cathon knew no one in the land who knew of her special ability, and those she had helped before had been sworn to secrecy. But perhaps the person Isra forced answers from *was* from her past. Or, perhaps it was someone who only knew things in passing. Even though that person told of secrets better left unspoken, her heart felt heavy. It must have been difficult—

"I doubt you know much of our yearly custom, so I will explain this once. Each year the king has this damnable birthday feast, and all his subjects are invited." Isra's face screwed up in annoyance. "Not just those with wealth and jeweled treasure, but also the lowly villagers and peasants, who have nothing. He puts out food enough for everyone and does not even require nor ask for gifts." Isra snorted. "I would be so much richer should he require a gift of gold or perhaps jewels in exchange for the feast." She paced, anger making her gait abrupt. "He is daft, my husband. He does not believe in war if matters can be solved through discussion, forgives the taxes I talked him into from those who he says truly cannot pay." She snorted again. "His perpetual kindness just kills me."

Cathon grunted mentally. Would that the Gods of Fate smile upon us.

Isra slipped the small container into a velvet pocket then leaned toward Cathon. "I was told all he must do is touch the special glass, just hold it, then his very fiber will be gone forever. He will remain a shell of the man he once was, but a man whom I will then control with a mere whisper." Isra cackled. "Then the whole kingdom will be mine, as it should be, and no one will be the wiser." She paused for several moments then smiled. "He will be trapped forever."

Cathon eyed the queen then her gaze dropped briefly to the pocket that held the bottle. Did Isra know how fast she would waste away without her inner fire?

Already a slight chill replaced her waning strength. "The glass is what you truly want?"

Isra's gaze darkened. "Yes! It is I, a woman of strength, who should command here. A ruler should not be weak like my husband." Amusement danced behind her gaze. "And should I make some small error in judgment, it will be His Majesty who pays, not I!"

Cathon gritted her teeth as Isra removed the iridescent vial from pocket and held it within view.

"You will make the special glass for me, witch, and make the piece flowers or something I will enjoy looking at for the rest of my life. Then, just before the feast, I will privately present it to him as a gift." Isra arched an eyebrow. "A yearly feast that will end this year, I might add."

"Stained glass takes time to make, Queen Isra."

Isra shrugged. "Take all the time you need." She glared at Cathon. "As long as it is ready by celebration."

Cathon wrapped the dark worn cloak around her shoulders tighter as she leaned over her project. Cold tantalized her insides, her skin was paling, and weakness washed over her.

She arranged the glass pieces over the hawk pattern she had prepared and smiled. "Since it will be for the king, it will be a picture of something I think he will like."

The glass pieces were void of color, some crystal clear, others opaque, and others rippled as if water had been spilled over them. The area surrounding the hawk was made of frosted glass.

Cathon carefully worked the grinding stone over the edges of the glass a piece at a time, then laid each piece over the pattern to check the fit.

As each section satisfactorily took shape to the pattern, Cathon said the proper incantations over the special glass. Then, satisfied each piece was ready for joining, she wrapped the glass edges with a special cloth-thin metal.

Suddenly weakness again washed over her. Soon she

would no longer be able to heat the metals that bound the glass together, and then the hawk would not be finished. Knowing there was no time to waste, she struggled to stand.

Again, she laid the pieces on the pattern to check the fit, and satisfied, began to melt the metal together where it joined, using a firestick heated by her waning powers.

Evening turned into darkness, and darkness moved on into the witching hours. The witching hours drew to a close and dawn entered, bringing a life of new light to Cathon's world. Finally, the stained glass was complete.

Cathon held the rectangular piece up to the morning light that now streamed into her workshop. The hawk's wings spread out in splendor as it soared above the frosted clouds. She smiled wanly. It would be even prettier when the colors came to life.

The celebration would not be for yet another day, so now Cathon could rest. Her bones ached, her eyes burned, and all color had drained from her complexion. She pulled the wrap closer to her body to ward off the inner chill, but it did no good. She needed that firelike substance the queen had managed to take from her. She needed her essence.

Making it to her cot, Cathon flopped onto the straw mattress and pulled the blankets up over shoulders. Cold. She was getting so cold. A burning sensation flared to life on her cheek as rough blanket touched raw skin, and finger tip went to the red streak there. Struggling against the weakness that again washed over her, brown eyes closed then popped open. She wondered if she would last long enough to give the hawk to the queen, and as her cheek burned again, determination and anger flared, answering her question.

Thoughts drifted and disjointed memories filled her mind. Memories of lands long ago forgotten, of people never again seen, of things pleasant and not so pleasant. Brown eyes closed again, and a sense of warmth swept over Cathon.

Suddenly, someone pounded on the workshop door.

The noise disturbed Cathon, and she struggled to ignore it, while it drug her up from the warmth of sleep.

The pounding sounded again, louder, impatient.

Cathon reluctantly opened eyes and raised from the cot. Wrapped in blankets, she worked her way to the door and pulled it open, thinking it to have gained considerable weight since she last touched it.

"Have you finished the glass?" Queen Isra shouldered passed Cathon on into the room.

"Yes, it is ready." Pulling blankets tighter around shoulders, Cathon shoved the door to. "Did you bring the vial?"

"The piece first, witch." Isra's gaze darted from Cathon, to table, to hawk, to other pieces Cathon had made at various times, then back to Cathon. "I see no glass flowers."

"How do I know you would keep your word and return my inner fire?"

The Queen smiled, dug into her pocket, then held up the small container. "I thought you would hide the needed piece until the return of the bottle. Remember. If I have to, I can again obtain that which I return." She seemed reluctant to hand over the vial, but did so. "Now, my glass?"

Cathon quickly held the bottle to her chest, magically examining it for any spells the queen might have had put upon it. "It is the hawk on the table." She uncorked the vial and the substance inside suddenly drifted out and upward, then disappeared into her chest. Warmth began to spread over Cathon's body. Strength returned.

"What is this? I told you to make something I would not mind looking at for the next the Gods know how many years. I do not like hawks!" Isra's gaze narrowed in anger.

"But the king probably does, and it is a gift for him." Cathon went to the table and picked up the finished glass piece. "Would you want to give him a thing he did not like?" She held the glass work toward the queen.

"Give me that!" Isra jerked the piece from Cathon's hands and suddenly realized she had made a mistake.

"As I told you, Isra, this is not a gift for this king."

Isra heard Cathon's voice, but her concentration was on the sense that thin strands of something were being pulled from every little hiding place inside her body. Her strength went with that thin something, and an emptiness filled the spaces. Isra's thoughts were fleeting and puzzled, her eyes blurred, and Cathon's voice echoed inside her head. She tried to move away from the witch, tried to drop the hawk. She wanted to run, go anywhere, go as far away as possible. Then suddenly; she could no longer grasp any desires, and her will dissolved. The woman in front of her was saying something. The words sounded so distant, so strange, and she could not quite understand them. Isra managed a frown.

"Stained glass, Isra, my special stained glass, is only for those who have hearts such as yours. It is not for the likes of my king." Cathon took the glass hawk from Isra's grasp and held it up to the light.

Dark browns, rich tans, brilliant golds, and a slight lavender swirled into the appropriate pieces of glass, bringing a life of color to the hawk.

"You now have a stained glass gift for His Majesty's birthday." Cathon turned back toward Isra and held the piece out to her.

Isra's eyes widened, and she moved back. "Stained . . . glass?" Her frown deepened. There was something about glass, something she was supposed to do—

"As I said, it is intended for those with evilness within. Surely you understand that is why it is called stained glass?"

Word of the queen's sudden sickness quickly spread throughout the kingdom. She had suffered from a fever so intense, it had burned her mind away. Nothing could be done for her. Now, those around her described her as being there yet not being there, and many wondered at the pleasant ways she had about her.

The king declared the feast be held as usual, saying the queen would want it that way, and insisted everyone have a joyous time.

The day of feast arrived. Villagers, lords and ladies, musicians, artists, magicians, and many others from far and wide attended. The sound of musical instruments and singing mixed with laughter and idle chatter. The smell of roasted meats and vegetables and baked pies wafted on the warm breeze. Games for knights, farmers, wives, and children alike were being played all around. People meandered about, stopping to chat or refill tankards and plates.

Even though he asked for none, as usual, a multitude of people had gifts for the king. Holding their carefully selected parcels, they lined up along the specially cordoned off area to await their turn at presentation.

Cathon held her stained glass hawk wrapped in worn cotton, the best cloth she had, moving forward slowly as the line moved.

She watched as gifts of fine silver and gold were given by the lords of surrounding lands. She saw quilts, coverlets, pottery, leather works, herbs and spices, baked goods, and other gifts being given by those less rich. She watched as the king gratefully and sincerely accepted each gift offered.

Clutching her stained glass, Cathon moved forward until finally, she was next to make her presentation.

Cathon looked at the king who was seated on a large chair brought from the great room. A table was next to him where servants carefully laid each gift. The queen sat at the king's side, quietly, casually watching the festivities about her.

Cathon curtsied as the king's warm gray gaze settled on her, a smile parting his lips. "Your Majesty, please accept this gift, made with care for you." She extended the cloth-wrapped stained glass.

"Thank you." The king took the piece, unwrapped it carefully, then held it up to the sunlight. Gray gaze moved over the artwork, and his smile broadened. "A hawk. It is beautiful." He turned toward Isra, extending the stained glass. "Look, dear, is it not lovely?"

Isra's gaze was drawn by her husband's voice. She looked at the piece he held out to her and her gaze briefly widened. She drew away from the glass hawk, saying nothing.

The king turned back to Cathon. "My wife has not been herself, please forgive her." He again held the piece up to the sunlight. "I will have this hung in our chamber window." He nodded. "I thank you for your kindness."

"You are most welcome, Your Highness." Cathon smiled and dipped her head then stepped back and moved away.

Satisfied her gift was truly liked, Cathon's attention turned toward the delicious smells of food. As her stomach rumbled its desires, she briefly wondered just who had guided the queen into believing she could use the special stained glass against a king with a heart such as his.

It was obviously someone who did not know what he was doing.

Suddenly she smiled.

Or was it?

EAST OF THE DAWN
by Jere Dunham

Werewolf stories, as a category, are quite literally a drug on the market; it seems that I read a couple of dozen of them every season. As a result it seems I've become hyper-critical; a werewolf story, for me, must have something very special, or it's "just another werewolf." But when I get one that's not just another rip-off of the latest horror movie, like this one, it commands attention.

This is another writer making her first fiction sale. She has a husband, a nine-year-old daughter, and as she puts it, "three pit bulls who, fortunately for us and our neighbors, were born in Chihuahua bodies." (Ah, another dog person.)

She also tells me that "the women of Sauromatia, as you probably know considering your line of work, may or may not be the historical Amazons." Well, no, I didn't; I thought, if there ever were any Amazons historically, which I doubt, they'd have been found among the Etruscans. Your guess is as good as mine, which is what fiction is all about and why we write fantasy.

Sofyia awoke on the far bank of the river, her mouth and eyes full of grating sand. Her bare feet were still in the water. A cold wind chilled her heavy, sodden clothing. She raised her head and struggled to her hands and knees, dragging herself a few more paces

216

up the bank before collapsing. Weeks of eating the bloodless unnourishing food of humans, roots and berries and tasteless leaves, had taken away all her strength. She longed for meat, but there was no one to hunt for her.

She closed her eyes and pictured each brother and sister in wereform, in summer coat, sleek and shining every glorious shade of gray. She heard their howls at her leaving, the short, sharp barks of their farewell. The barking was so real; she could hear it again, right now, like laughter, only was it sad, or mocking laughter?

East of the dawn, the tribe's witchwife had promised. *Moon Woman told me you will go on all fours.* So East and East Sofyia traveled, hoping every morning to see the sun rise behind her. But it never had, and now it seemed that she would die in the hairless weak body she had hated all her life.

Good. Sixteen years of changeless sorrow was enough. The sand pillowed her head. The water lapped steadily, like a heartbeat. It was not so bad a place to die.

The barking began again, so real, louder and closer, becoming friendly whines. Cold snuffling noses pushed at her. For a moment Sofyia thought she was home, or that she had died under the ugly gray sky, and the wolves of Heaven were welcoming her.

If only she could rise up from the bank to greet them! But the crossing had taken every last drop of her strength. She heard a heavy hollow clop-clop-clop-clopping, like melons dropping one after another. The sounds stopped. Human feet, shod, squished across the sand and stopped behind her head.

"Ho, girls, what's this? What's this you've found?" The cold noses withdrew. "Good girls." Fingers went to the base of her neck, then away. The fingers were hot as fire against her cold skin. Sofyia smelled human, and something else, a large grass eater; its smell faded as it retreated, *clop-clop-clop-clop.* A hand grasped her shoulder and pulled her over onto her back.

Sofyia stared up unblinking into the weathered face of a blue-eyed woman with light hair braided into a crown. How lovely her fur must be when she changed! Flanking the woman, their heads on the same level as hers, sat two huge bitches, twitching the cold noses that had nudged Sofyia awake. They were nothing like her people; they had narrow heads and arched backs. Under their long, fine, particolored fur the prominent bones of their spines and ribs could be seen. "Thank you, heavenly sisters," she said in wolf-speech, addressing them first as was proper. They smiled but said nothing. Were angels so stupid?

The woman dropped forward onto her knees and helped Sofyia to sit up. She unclasped her cloak, blue like the night sky during moonface, and draped it over Sofyia. She held a skin of wine to Sofyia's lips, and Sofyia drank. It was strong wine, and she felt a little warmer.

"I am Sofyia," she said in human speech. "I thank you."

"My name is Nitra. I lead the Sauromatian huntresses." Nitra wore a white tunic covered with little blue horse heads. Sofyia wondered why anyone would decorate clothing with the shape of a prey animal. The Sauromatian's trousers were of the same design, coarse but close-woven. Her boots, dyed the exact shade of blue as the little horse heads, laced over many tiny hooks up the front.

"Where am I?" Sofyia croaked.

The woman smiled kindly. "Just east of the Dawn."

Sofyia gasped and reached out joyously for the woman's forearms. "Then you can help me?"

"Of course!" the woman exclaimed. "Did you think I would leave you here?" She scooped Sofyia up as though she weighed no more than a newborn pup, frowned, and whistled. "Turek! Where have you gone, mare?"

A beast trotted up, and Sofyia recognized the grass-eater she had smelled earlier. A horse. She was embarrassed at not having identified it. Now its closeness filled her with excitement and she realized how hungry she was for meat. "Put me down! You can change and slay it," she whispered helpfully to Nitra.

"Change?" The woman looked down at her in disbelief. "Slay my mare?"

The horse came closer. It was a kind Sofyia had never seen before, bigger, not tan but white as the Death Wolf. It was wearing scraps of leather and bone on its head. Her heart began to pound wildly. The old witchwoman had lied! Here was no rescue. East of the Dawn was the realm of the dead.

The horse came closer and stood quietly. Its eyes were soft and brown, with a split pupil, like a goat's. When Nitra placed her sideways on its broad back, Sofyia whimpered in terror.

"Can't you ride?" said the woman. "Just swing your leg over. Here, let me help you get those skirts out of the way." Her pale hands came closer. Her blue eyes leered like a demon's. Sofyia feared Nitra would change right there, and devour her.

She fainted.

"If you let me cook it, you would find it easier to chew," Nitra said for the third time.

Sofyia shook her head violently and spat. If Nitra would not wait politely until she finished her meat, that was all the answer she would get. She tore another chunk off the raw haunch, feeling the eyes of Nitra's hunting companions, all female, upon her. She felt she was being watched by phantoms. Their eyes did not reflect the firelight. Only their smell told her they were real. And the smell of their tasteless food, burnt to nothing.

"Ungrateful bitch," someone muttered.

Nitra turned on her companion. "Hush! She's half-drowned and frightened out of her wits. She fainted when I put her on my horse."

"Out of shock you wouldn't allow her to eat it." The woman's eyes narrowed into rods of darkness. "I still say she's an ungrateful bitch."

That was twice now. Sofyia put down the haunch. "Why do you insult and praise me at the same time?" she demanded.

Nitra reached out and touched her arm. "What do you mean?"

"I suppose I am ungrateful." Sofyia looked at the

golden hairs on the back of Nitra's hand. They glimmered a little in the firelight. "You save me from the water and give me your own cloak; I recoil from the prey animal you make serve you. You share your kill; I eat it greedily and without thanks. So I am bewildered when your companion gives me a title I have long coveted among my people."

Nitra tried to hide a laugh behind her hand but it bubbled out. "In your country 'bitch' is a compliment?"

Sofyia put down the fresh haunch and started to cry. "The witch-woman mocked me. She said you would help me. Instead, you mock me, too."

"What did this witchwoman promise you?" Nitra was not laughing now. "Where are you from, little one?" Her eyes had turned hard and suspicous. The eyes of the other huntresses were shadowed holes.

Suddenly she feared to tell them. But no one could do more to her than had happened already. Weren't these women her saviors? Sofyia wiped tears and lingering river-sand from her eyes, and the pain that flared when she took her hands away made her wish she had not touched them. "I am of the Neuri."

"The Neuri!" Nitra exclaimed. "The wolf-people?"

Sofyia nodded. "But I cannot change like the rest of my people. It's not so bad when we make the village, and everyone is human. When the tribe abandons the village and moves to new hunting, they change into were-form to travel and I fall behind. I must share my parents' kill when it is I who should hunt for them, since they are getting old and toothless. I am not allowed to seek a mate, though I came of age this very year. So I begged our witchwife to ask Moon Woman to heal me. Tonight, I will take my wereform." As she said the words, Sofyia's heart sang with hope.

"The wolf-people," one of the huntresses said thoughtfully. "So the Neuri still exist."

Nitra knelt in front of Sofyia and took her by the arms. "What did your witchwoman tell you? Her exact words."

The Sauromatian huntresses leaned forward with interest.

"The witchwife promised that East of the Dawn, I would go on all fours."

"She didn't lie." The woman who had called her bitch laughed, not unkindly. "Nitra said you crawled out of the Dawn on all fours."

"I didn't crawl out of the Dawn," Sofyia pointed out. "I crawled out of a river."

"The river Dawn." Nitra said quietly.

"What?" The languages were very similar, but Sofyia was not certain she'd heard properly.

"You are not East of the Sunrise. You are East of the river Dawn."

Sofyia could not speak for a moment. Then, at last, she whispered, "Do you mean the witchwoman tricked me? But she is a priestess of Moon Woman. She would not lie."

"I, too, am a priestess of Moon Woman, and I say no one can walk beyond the sunrise."

"No," Sofyia insisted. Her voice trembled. "The whole tribe bade me farewell. My mother and father, my brothers and sisters—can I believe they meant for me to walk until I died!"

Nitra only shook her head.

"When Moon Woman climbs into the sky, I will gain the strength to change," Sofyia said firmly. "I will run back to my people on four legs! You'll see."

"You have been tricked. You have been mocked," said the blunt huntress who had named her bitch. "Even if you could cross all the rivers and get back to where you started, your people will be gone."

"I don't believe you," Sofyia said stoutly. "I will wait by the fire until I feel the change approaching."

"Leave us," Nitra commanded. The Sauromatians, even the one who had mocked her, moved in and patted Sofyia awkwardly before leaving the fire. At last only Nitra remained with her. The moon broke over the mountains, and still Nitra sat staring thoughtfully into the fire.

Sofyia's family had described the feeling just before the change as an involuntary shudder of joy. The moon rose a hand, then another hand, then another. It was a good strong full moon, and it should have given her the strength. But nothing happened, and at last Sofyia realized nothing would. The deep despair she had felt on the riverbank returned, seizing her heart like a powerful fist, draining her of everything but sorrow.

She threw back her head and howled from her soul. But it did not satisfy her; it was only an imitation, coming from a throat forever human. She was East of the Dawn, and the change would never come. Drawing up her knees, she buried her face in them and sat that way for a long time. At last she remembered Nitra was still there, watching her. "Please go away," Sofyia whispered. "I know you have to change now, and I can't bear to watch."

"I have no magic!" Nitra replied.

"You are not a werebitch?" Sofyia raised her head and peered shyly at her friend. "But you had fresh meat tonight. Did your males kill it for you? I have seen none."

"Ha!" Nitra drew herself up. "In Sauromatia women and men live separately. We only come together to make children; we do our own hunting and fight our own battles."

"What?" Sofyia was too shocked to say more. "You have no wereform at all?"

Nitra shook her head emphatically.

"Oh. I am so sorry."

"Don't be." The blue eyes studied her. "I think your tribe has forgotten the old tales which say Neuri, Sauromatian, Sycthian, indeed all people arose from the beasts. Long ago, when the Moon Woman showed us all, both women and men, how much more we could do with our hands and our minds than with our claws and our teeth, the Sauromatians made their choice. But the Neuri refused to renounce their animal natures."

"Of course. Why would anyone who could run as a wolf decide to stay all human?" Sofyia asked wistfully.

"I wonder just how human the Neuri really are." Nitra rose swiftly, decisively and brushed off the seat of her decorated trousers. "I must consult the Moon Woman on the knoll." She vanished into the forest that topped the riverbank.

Sofyia had not known a human could go so quietly. In a little while Nitra returned, just as silently, grinning such a hungry grin that Sofyia doubted she was not a were-bitch. She looked up at her fearfully.

"Why are you frightened?" Nitra asked. The firelight gleamed off her teeth.

Sofyia said nervously. "You kill your meat without changing."

"Tomorrow, at first light, I will show you how to do the same," Nitra pledged. "And the witchwoman's promise will be fulfilled in a way she did not expect."

Winter was coming. The Neuri would abandon their village and their human forms and move south. Sofyia rode a course to intercept them. She wore a cloth tunic and trousers patterned with the heads of deer, her favorite meat, and her boots were dyed the color of fresh blood. Her stallion, full brother to Nitra's mare Turek, covered the ground with eager strides. His mate Vacha kept pace beside them on a leading rein. Whenever Sofyia made a kill with her bow the mare would carry the meat until Sofyia and the mated deerhounds Nitra had given her finished eating it.

She crossed all the rivers she had crossed before, but this time her weak body was no hindrance; the horse swam for her. The peoples she had once hidden from fled from her in terror. Horses they had seen in plenty, but never a horse with a woman growing out of its back. Sofyia rode with forgiveness in her heart. She no longer felt angry at the old witchwoman. Had not her prophecy been fulfilled? Now she was no longer a burden. Her people would fawn over her when they saw what she could do. They would call her grown, and she would choose a mate.

Sooner than she expected she found spoor larger and deeper than those of ordinary wolves. Joyously she killed a deer and tracked her people all night, by moonlight and scent, too excited to halt for sleep. She found the Neuri stopping-place on a branch of the Maris river that the Sauromatians called the Tiarantos. No village had been set up yet; the tracks were all wolf, no bare human footprints. Sofyia barked and whined a greeting in the language of the wolf, as much as she had mastered.

They came, slowly, and sat in a wary ring around her and the horses. In a few short months from Midsummer to Autumn her parents had grayed sadly around the muzzle, and they were probably more toothless than ever. "I brought meat for you," Sofyia called, expecting them to change and accept her gift. They only looked at each other and coughed, and others of the tribe growled. The deerhounds raised their hackles. "Down," she said softly. They obeyed, but the Neuri wolves drew no closer.

Sofyia forced herself to stretch her lips and smile. "Witchwoman!" she called. "I thank you for your magic. East of the Dawn river, I learned how to go upon four legs, Moon Woman be praised. And look at this!" She patted the stallion's shoulder. "I have brought a mare also. They will breed. Soon we will have enough horses for everyone. I'll care for them, and during lean times we can range far on them, hunting what we like without tiring ourselves."

The witchwoman peered at her from slitted eyes and whimpered.

"Answer me!" Sofyia begged. No reply. Her anger grew. "I am a huntress now!" she cried, challenging the witchwoman with direct eye contact. "I have earned the right to breed! Let me hear acceptance from the lips of your human form." She strung her bow. The string trembled against her cheek as she drew it back. She aimed the arrow at the witchwoman's heart. "Change, damn you," she snarled.

The witchwoman turned her belly to the sky and whined for mercy.

Sofyia's father stepped forward. He spoke the wolf tongue, slowly so Sofyia could understand his coughs and barks.

"Do not torment her. For the witchwoman's deed, the Moon Woman took away our power to change," he explained. "Moon Woman will not be mocked."

"What deed?" she demanded, still not willing to believe.

"You have always been a little stupid." Her father yawned, curling his long pink tongue. "The witchwoman sent you East of the Dawn, when there is no such place."

"But there is," Sofyia cried. "Look, I can ride, I can hunt. I brought you meat."

Her father sniffed. "The deer smells good. But you stink of human. You are all human now." He looked at her with sad yellow eyes. Then he turned his back and slunk toward the woods. Her mother followed without a backward glance. One by one the tribe melted away into the trees.

A light snow began to fall. Sofyia reached over and undid the strap that bound the dead deer to Vacha's back. It slipped off and fell to the ground.

Tears slipped down her cheeks. Human tears. Sofyia reined her horse around, toward the East, toward the Dawn.

TRADING SWORDS
by Dave Smeds

Dave Smeds is not a new writer—he has written three novels, and with this story Dave returns to the pages of S&S, after having taken a "three-year, near-total layoff from writing." His wife has just completed her R.N. degree and started working, so he's back at the word processor full-time—which probably means there's another fantasy novel in the offing—news which will probably be greeted with cries of pleasure by editors everywhere. I hope he continues to turn out short stuff, too.

The raiders caught up with them on the open heath. The Islanders made their stand on an ancient Dyrie barrow—little more than a bump on the broad expanse of moor grass and wildflowers, but at least it was high ground. Above them clouds gathered into a dark, oppressive mass.

The bond-warriors and other fighting men formed a human wall around the barrow. Reila joined the bond-witches at the summit. There was no time to erect the ritual tent. The women would be unshielded from the screams of their husbands; they would smell the blood as it spilled. Reila forced the prospect from her mind, seeking the concentration essential to her magic.

The Hrogi closed in with characteristic ferocity, as if

to decimate the party of Islanders as rapidly and thoroughly as they had obliterated a dozen Islander villages. The invaders outnumbered the natives four to one.

"Fight to the end," High Witch Maer called, both to the warriors and to her sisters. "If we make good account of ourselves, there will be too few of them left to endanger the heartland."

Reila spared one last glance at Kelf. Her spouse already had his back to her. Sword high, he braced to meet the coming charge.

Reila closed her eyes, folded her hands in her lap, and cleared her mind. To her great relief, the earth did not resist as she tapped its essence. The high witch had guessed well. The barrow must have been an ancient site of power.

Suddenly, without opening her eyes, Reila could see the entire battlefield. The tableau unfolded from a point high above the witches' circle. At the same time, she could feel the firmness of the barrow marker stone beneath her. All of her senses, except sight, remained lodged in her body.

The witches extended their protective auras around their husbands. The Islander party was as ready as it would ever be.

The Hrogi wave crashed against a breakwater of Islander steel and armor.

Kelf hacked off the point of an extended spear and kicked out the knee of his assailant. He had no time to deliver a mortal stroke. A flurry of six Hrogi raiders crowded around him. His flanking allies, occupied with their own opponents, could not reach him.

An ax struck Kelf's side. The blade sheared skin and muscle away from his ribs. Fragments of chain mail punctured blood vessels. He staggered.

Reila accepted the pain. She cried out, as she always did on the first blow. Kelf, freed from the agony, drove the point of his blade through the ax wielder's hauberk and into the man's heart.

Reila funneled her suffering into the earth as fast as she could. It never seemed fast enough. In exchange, the goddess sent the forces of renewal. The energy struck Reila with a potent kiss. She shaped it and thrust it toward Kelf.

The bond-warrior's slashed muscles knit together. His body spit out the fragments of metal. His skin closed over the wound. The healing was nearly complete by the time Kelf started to withdraw his sword.

Kelf's steel hung up in the ax wielder's armor. The bond-warrior yanked it free, but the delay cost him. A mace grazed his helmet. Broadswords slammed against his upper arms.

Reila stopped the ringing in her husband's head. She neutralized the effect of the sword blows—the blades had not penetrated his armor, but without her intervention his limbs would have gone nerveless from the sharp impacts.

One of the Hrogi, expecting to take advantage of a stunned opponent, left himself open and died.

Reila drained off more agony. Perspiration soaked her hair and dripped from her nose. The goddess once again gave generously of her essence. Reila sent the gift toward her husband.

Though she concentrated on Kelf, she took in the overall struggle. The Hrogi pressed in on every edge of the circle. Several Islander soldiers lay dying amid grass, crumpled shrubs, and barrow cobbles. All five of the bond-warriors fought on, thwarting their foes' momentum. The circle grew tighter around the barrow knoll, but at a dear cost to the raiders.

As the Hrogi witnessed the bond-guardians surviving damage that would have sent ordinary men into shock or death, they concentrated their attack on the five. Reila could hardly make out Kelf amid the horde. So many men tried to attack at the same time that they interfered with each other. High Warrior Fonis, given so many convenient targets, laid waste with his battle ax.

Dazed from the pain, disoriented by the constant, horrendous amount of energy she was forced to channel, Reila's trance-induced gaze drifted past the battle.

A barrel-chested Hrogi warrior stood at the periphery.

He wore a horned helmet, inlaid with tiny rubies. One of his arms rested in a sling. He cradled a drawn but unsullied broadsword in the opposite gauntlet, waving it idly as if it were a willow switch, rather than a weapon designed for two strong hands.

Chieftain. Reila wished one of her party's fighting men would break free, and cleave that ornate helmet down the middle. That man had to be the spur behind the relentless Hrogi pursuit these past two days.

It was fortunate that Kelf could not hear her wish. Even without the weapons flailing in his face, he did not dare charge. Spilled blood—some his, but mostly that of his enemies—had turned the sod at his feet to muck. He could barely maintain his balance on the slick surface. He kept to his task, fighting Hrogi. He had found his rhythm. Each exchange left another enemy dead or gravely wounded.

The pain became a constant, hypnotic tide. Reila let the energies flow at their own pace along the path she had established. What little coherent thought remained she devoted to observing the enemy chieftain.

The man gazed straight at the bond-warriors. He slowly nodded his head. Then he stared even more intently at the bond-witches. He nodded more deeply, and his lips moved, as if counselling himself.

A scream from Sandel, the youngest of the bond-witches, brought Reila's attention back to the battle. The body of Sandel's bond-mate, Flin, lay nearly decapitated at the center of a knot of Hrogi warriors. A giant, thickly muscled raider brought a heavy battle ax down on Flin's abdomen, splitting through armor and internal organs to Flin's spine.

Sandel flopped to the ground, dead.

The death of the first pair of bond-guardians shifted the stream of energy flowing through the bond-witches. For the span of two heartbeats, the surge drove away every shred of Reila's pain.

In a moment of clarity, she saw the Hrogi chieftain, staring in fascination, not at the defeated bond-warrior, but at the lifeless bond-witch.

Then the energies stabilized, and the suffering resumed. Kelf had erred, letting himself be distracted by the defeat of his fellow guardian. He took deep wounds.

Reila grappled with the misery. She healed her partner. Kelf regained his equilibrium, and in a deft display of skill, slew four opponents almost at once. His victories totalled nearly twenty.

But she had been dealt too potent a blow. The brief interlude of comfort had erased her ability to cope with the severity of the anguish. She misdirected the shaping.

The owl of shadows took her consciousness away to its roost.

Reila woke to a tug at her neck, and to the caress of light rain, soft as fog, as her cheeks. The newly moistened heath shrubs cast up a fecund aroma, almost enough to quench the fetor of blood and intestines. If this were the afterworld, it felt and smelled too much like the one she had left.

She opened her eyes.

A filthy Hrogi warrior leaned over her, knife in one hand. He held her pewter-and-schorl pendant, the sigil of her cult, in the other palm. The severed ends of the leather loop tickled her exposed throat.

The warrior grunted in surprise as she stirred. He turned and spoke to someone behind her. She could not understand his harsh inflections, though the Hrogi and Islander languages had evolved from the same roots.

The chieftain came into view. Fresh blood stained the cloth that held his wounded arm. The battle had apparently reached him, though his stride indicated no loss of vitality. He waved his sword preemptorily. His warrior moved away from Reila.

"Alive? This is new."

The chieftain spoke with the clarity of a scholar, only the accent betraying that Island speech was not native to him. He gazed at her with fervent, almost sexual intensity, yet it was not physical lust she read in that glance.

"For years, over many raids, I have fought the *hrolf* warriors—the sons of your goddess. I have seen them kill so many of Hrog's best that we have run in terror back to our longships. Not until a month ago had I seen an entire cadre of *hrolf* defeated. Do you know what we found after that battle?"

He jabbed the High Witch's ribs with his boot. Reila winced, to see Maer's body tainted. "For every slain magical warrior, we found an equal number of women, lying in a tent. Dead, but unmarked, with no trace of poison on their lips."

He knelt down, and said softly, "Why do you still live?"

She did live. And as the shock of the battle and the confusion of reawakening faded, she realized what that meant.

As if the chieftain could read the widening of her eyes, he turned and swept his sword across the site of the battle. "Search the bodies. See if one of the *hrolf* is alive. Do *not* kill him."

Though the chieftain used Hrogi, the timbre and fine elocution of his voice allowed her to grasp his meaning. She moaned silently, deep in her throat. The chieftain verged on discovering the secret that had kept her people's small, low-lying homeland unconquered for two hundred years.

Struggling, Reila raised her upper body and perched unsteadily on her elbows. She watched as two Hrogi warriors abandoned their looting and began to systematically examine the dead. The one with her necklace joined them.

Three men. Four counting the chieftain. The only other surviving enemies lay on the bloodstained sod, making peace with their patron gods. Their wounds would kill them soon. The raiders had barely carried the day.

"You cost us more men than I could believe," said the chieftain. "More than I would have risked, had I foreseen. Yet, it may have been worth it after all."

He sheathed his blade. From the folds of his sling he removed the necklace of a bond-guardian. She recognized it as that of High Warrior Fonis, husband to Maer.

The Hrogi chieftain bent down and placed the pendant beside the one that rested on Maer's breast.

"I always find a match," the chieftain said. "The pattern of the gemstones differs from one *hrolf* talisman to the next, but for each there is another of the same pattern around the neck of one of you witches."

The bond-guardians should never have worn their sigils into battle, Reila thought bitterly. Yet how could any of them have surrendered the symbol of their covenant?

"I am Thros," the chieftain said as he stood up. "And you?"

She turned her face away, denying him not only her name, but the sound of her voice as well. She would not sully it on Hrogi ears.

The chieftain sniffed. "Perhaps we will have other chances to be introduced."

She knew by then that he meant her to survive. Not for rape, though that would probably be included. He wanted her for what she could tell him.

Thros. She knew that name. Nephew of the king of Hrog. Commander of the invasion. He had wanted to chase down their party very badly, then, to risk his own safety on a pursuit so deep inland.

Reila could understand now why this Hrogi invasion had been so overwhelming, far more so than that of a decade ago, and more threatening than any since the unification of the three kingdoms, and the creation of the bond-guardians.

The searchers called out suddenly. Thros turned. Reila opened her eyes.

The enemy soldiers had uncovered Kelf. Bloodied, chain mail and woolen garments yawning with gashes, he looked the part of a corpse, but Reila knew he must be alive. As did Thros.

"Bind him thoroughly, and bring him here," Thros ordered. His gaze had already shifted to Reila, and to the expression she could not banish from her face.

Tears cut through the mud on her cheeks. Her mate was so pale. The enemy warriors grunted under his limp weight as they brought him to the top of the barrow. They dropped him on top of Hara and Sandel's bodies.

He did not stir.

Thros ordered the man who had cut off her necklace to guard her closely, then the chieftain kneeled beside Kelf. He pulled cloth and mail away from wounds, held the flat of a small knife under Kelf's nostrils to see if breath would fog the burnished metal, and felt the neck for a pulse.

Hindered by his wounded arm, Thros clipped free Kelf's pendant. Taking Reila's from the guard, he compared them. He nodded.

"This man will die within the hour," Thros said. He dangled the matching talismans before her eyes. "But you can save him, can't you?"

She knew she should let him die. Then she would die as well, and Thros would learn nothing more than he had already deduced. Kelf would have argued so, had he been conscious.

But as she looked at Kelf's lacerated gauntlets, she saw the strong, manly hands that had lifted the cup of bonding to her, the day they began the seven-day rites required to become guardians. As she looked at his grimace-locked eyelids, she saw his eyes, pale gray and intent, as he pledged his devotion to her on the final day of the rites. And as she shifted her gaze to his bruised lips, she remembered their touch on her body the night the rites concluded—and their touch over the years since, and the fine children that had sprung from their passion.

If it had been her life alone at stake, she would have made the sacrifice with no hesitation. She could kill herself, but she could not kill him, not even through inaction.

The trance claimed her almost before she was aware of her decision. The earth stirred, as full of power as ever, but the vessel of her body could barely channel that strength. She reached out and found the flame still burning in Kelf's chest. She stoked the blaze as if with a bellows.

The vents in his organs sealed shut. New blood filled

drained channels. His bodily defenses rallied to attack the infections that had already taken hold in his abdomen and one of his legs.

Reila collapsed to the sod, head ringing, faintly aware of the gasps and murmurs of the Hrogi. Then even that sound vanished.

The clouds had broken, and the light from the setting sun was gleaming off of the droplets on the grass as Reila woke again. A tiny mason was inside her skull, chiseling at the bone from the inside. It hurt merely to hold her eyelids up.

Kelf, stripped of armor and bound more securely than ever, lay a few paces away, on top of a skirt obviously torn from Sandel's body. She was bound as well, though only with leather laces around her wrists and ankles.

Their glances met. Though scabbed, scarred, and still vividly bruised, Kelf had regained the alert demanor so characteristic of him. Color filled his formerly pallid countenance. She had not been able to restore him completely, but the injuries were now far from mortal. In some ways, he was in better condition than she.

A fen hawk caught a mouse and disappeared into the distance with it. Still the bond-mates stared at each other, saying nothing.

"Ah, awake at last," called a merrry voice.

Reila turned as Thros approached. He had donned a fresh sling. Behind the Hrogi chieftain the other three raiders clustered around a bed of coals. Two flatland hare sizzled on skewers, blessing the site with their aroma. Reila felt no hunger, but she thanked Mother Earth for another means to stifle the lingering stench of carnage.

"That was fascinating," Thros said, waving at Kelf's nearly-healed form. "Our magicians have speculated that it is possible to channel the power of the earth, or the sun, or the sea. Many have tried, and been killed or robbed of their minds by the forces they tried to focus. To think that what was needed was to use one adept as the conduit, and another as the recipient."

"The Hrogi have always been slow thinkers," Kelf said.

Thros scarcely glanced in the bond-warrior's direction. "Even if that were so," the chieftain said calmly, "we are good learners, once we are taught a thing."

"I will teach you nothing," Reila said.

"Ah, you have a voice," Thros said. "But it speaks nonsense."

Thros sauntered over to Kelf. Kneeling down, he seized a bit of earlobe between the thumb and middle finger of his mail gauntlet. And squeezed. Blood sprayed. Kelf flinched.

"You can imagine other ways I might have given him pain," Thros said. He stood. "I am not drawn to torture, but sooner or later you *will* cooperate, for your man's sake. You have already shown me that it is not in your nature to let him die. Surely you will not allow him to suffer, either."

She could not hide her emotions. Her expression told her enemy what he wanted to see.

"I thought not. I have only to keep you both bound, and see that your partner does not harm himself."

"It is a long way to Hrog," Kelf said.

"The swiftness of the journey will amaze you," Thros promised. He grunted in deep satisfaction. "When my people begin their next campaign in this land, we will be able to match your *hrolf* warriors with *hrolf* of our own. My lord had thought to abandon these costly raids. Now he will judge otherwise."

He caught Reila by the chin and tried to make her look him in the eyes, to see the triumph shining there, but she lowered her lids. He chuckled, flipped her head dismissively to one side, and moved off to enjoy his share of the victory meal.

Bile, bitter as heartwort soup, rose in Reila's throat. Of all the possible outcomes of the battle, few could have been worse.

Inevitably, she turned to Kelf. The newborn dusk had filled out his pupils. She saw into them as if they were windows, straight into his thoughts. He now agreed that she had been right not to let themselves die. The purpose of their survival was laid out for them.

They could only let themselves die now if they took Thros with them.

The Hrogi took no chances with Kelf. They checked the knots on his bonds and tied him securely to the bulky corpse of High Warrior Fonis. Kelf couldn't roll over, much less break free.

The captors paid less attention to Reila. Slight of build, thin, and obviously exhausted from channeling magic, she gave them no cause to feel threatened. They checked the bindings on her wrists and ankles, and tossed her on the opposite side of the sleeping area from Kelf. They knew the intricacy of their knots and the awkwardness of her position, hands behind back, would keep her from freeing herself. The distance would prevent her from aiding Kelf to untie his bonds.

The three soldiers did little to hide their lust for her. "Save your strength," Thros ordered. "We've a fast, hard march tomorrow." The men shrugged. Obviously weary from the battle and two days of constant pursuit, they didn't argue. But they continued to peer in her direction.

Thros himself carried bits of the cooked hare to the few of his wounded comrades who had not expired by sunset. He fed them, let them drink as many draughts of pungent Hrogi liquor as they could tolerate, and spoke soothingly to them. By the close of twilight, the poison in the liquor had done its work. The chieftain uttered a prayer, and turned away from the bodies.

The Hrogi retired early. Thros promised Reila they would all be underway toward his army's beachhead before dawn. Soon the only sound coming from the raiders were rhythmic, sleep-deepened breaths and the scuffing of the lone guard's feet as he paced, and even these drowned within frog croaks and cricket songs.

Early in his watch, the guard banked the fire. With the loss of the light from the coals, the night closed in, heavy with the reek of corpses and wet heath. A new mass of clouds slowly drew a curtain over the stars. The moon, waning through its final quarter, would not rise until after midnight.

Now, thought Reila, *while their sleep is deepest, while the night is darkest.*

Reila's exhaustion vanished. The power of the earth goddess came arcing into her from the far side of the camp. From Kelf.

The energies did not heal her bruises, nor the lacerations on her wrists. Kelf shaped the magic his way, according to his skills. She received it her way, as she had practiced in the hall of her sect.

She checked the position of the watchman. His silhouette told her he was looking the other way. As silently as possible she shifted over the ground to the body of an Island warrior. The Hrogi had taken away nearby weapons and thrown them in a pile, but before daylight had faded, she had memorized the location of a cutting edge they had missed.

Her bindings made her effort extremely awkward, but she managed to maneuver her wrists toward a sword shard that protruded a finger-length from the body of the warrior. She began sawing at the leather around her wrists.

The watchman turned. She stopped. Perhaps he had heard her. Even if he had not, he might decide to walk toward her. If he did, he would immediately realize she was not where she was supposed to be.

The Hrogi stretched, sighed, and turned to watch a pair of bats flitter past and disappear toward the fens.

The leather parted. Wrists bloodied from the task, Reila brought her hands to the front of her body. She cut through the cords around her ankles and waited for sensation to return fully to all her limbs.

She rose in a fluid, confident motion. Catlike, she padded rapidly to the source of the nearest weapons—those lying beside the Hrogi who had cut off her necklace. She could not see them in the murk, but she found them with the instinct of a warrior—a light sword and a small mace, well-matched to her limited upper-body strength. She grasped the handles of both.

The sleeping man woke to the rasp of his blade leaving its sheath. Abandoning silence, Reila brought the mace down, crushing the man's skull before he could rise.

The watchman turned, reaching for the pommel of his blade. Sprinting forward, Reila drove the point of her steel into his throat just as his weapon cleared the sheath. He gurgled, raised the sword as if to strike, and abruptly lost his balance.

Even in daylight, only the most expert of swordsmen could have placed a thrust as precisely as Reila had, in the narrow gap between the man's jaw and the collar of his hauberk. But for the moment, she was such an adept.

The watchman was still staggering when she reached the third Hrogi warrior. He had spun from his bedroll to his feet, and peered in her direction as if confused, in the dark, as to which of the combatants was his enemy. When she leapt foward, he raised his battle ax.

He fended off her sword thrust. Steel sparked against steel. He charged. Light-footed, unencumbered by armor, she stepped to the side and tripped him. As he went down, she slammed her mace against the back of his neck.

He sprawled onto the sod, arms wide, and stayed there. She couldn't tell if he were unconscious or dead, but with luck, she could make sure later.

She sensed, rather than heard, the hiss of a swinging broadsword. She ducked a stroke that would have decapitated her. She sprang forward and whirled.

Thros cursed her, and levelled his blade at her. They stood apart, he in his armor, one-handed but clearly strong, she in her simple woolen tunic and skirt, invigorated by the energies of the goddess, but lacking in physical brawn.

He waded in, slashing. She darted backward. Her blade licked out, hit chain mail. She danced away from his backhand slice.

She had mobility, but he had protection. Thros jabbed

again. She side-stepped, parried, thrust quickly while he recovered. Her sword point met only steel.

"I should have killed you this afternoon," Thros said.

"Yes, you should have," Reila taunted. She wanted him angry enough to lose his calm. Perhaps that would earn her an opening.

But the opposite happened. Fully awake now, given time by the stalemate to think, Thros found his strategy. "I should have killed one *or the other* of you."

She said nothing, but inside she shuddered. He had found her weak point.

He wasted no time taking advantage of it. Immediately he pressed in the direction where Kelf lay bound, stripped of armor, incapable of avoiding a deathstroke. Even a lesser blow would break her husband out of his trance. Once she lost her ability, the skirmish would end just as poorly.

Reila tried to hold her ground. She forced Thros to parry. His vicious slash drove her back. She dared a thrust at his face, but he blocked it. The sword penetrated the chain mail just enough to blood his forearm.

Not enough. The best she could do was slow him down for a few exchanges.

She couldn't give up. One way or another, the Hrogi must not win. She struggled against mounting desperation.

She knew that in the heat of battle, she could not find her own solutions. But she had Kelf, who sat apart from the fight, able to observe, able to counsel. No words could pass through the conduit of sorcery, but he guided her hands and feet.

She let his influence take root deep in her muscles, and refused to overlay her own concerns, her own judgments.

Thros pressed again. She retreated. Her riposte was thwarted.

She waited for her body to tense, to adopt some special tactic, but it merely continued to retreat. Thros advanced straight into her. She ducked, parried, and danced, but nothing more. The night wind blew over her sweat-drenched hair, and the chill raced down her spine.

Her heels bumped against a human leg. She read victory in the shadows below Thros's eyebrows.

She had to stand her ground. She couldn't leave Kelf unguarded. She would rather be cut down herself.

But her feet said jump. She trusted the message.

As she leapt clear, Thros seized the opportunity. He stabbed downward.

And skewered the lifeless body of an Islander warrior.

Kelf had altered her retreat slightly to one side. In the dark, neither Reila nor Thros had realized they were fighting over the wrong dark lump on the ground.

The dead warrior still wore armor. Thros had thrust with such force that he had penetrated it, but now his sword was lodged. Though expecting Reila's thrust, he could not avoid it. She drove her sword into his throat.

He let go of his weapon and sank until he was supine on the bloodied grass, not two paces from Kelf.

A small gap appeared in the clouds. A handful of bright stars peeked through. Their light, though scant, revealed the expression on Thros' face. Shock. Surprise. Disbelief.

With the threat gone, Reila allowed herself to pity her foe. Overconfidence had done him in. He had solved so many mysteries, he had been convinced there were none left.

The chieftain of the Hrogi sighed deeply. The sigh became a rattle. Reila turned from the body and cut her bond-mate loose.

OUT OF THE FRYING PAN
by Elisabeth Waters

Elisabeth Waters has appeared in several of these volumes; most recently, I think, with the beautiful "Shadowlands" in S&S VI. This adventure brings back a series character, Eirthe, who first appeared in Andre Norton's MAGIC IN ITHKAR. In addition to several fine short stories, Lisa has won the Gryphon Award; her award-winning novel CHANGING FATE began as the splendid story "A Woman's Privilege" in the third of these volumes and will appear from DAW Books. We're tickled pink that Lisa will soon appear as a novelist "in her own write."

Elisabeth Waters is in her late thirties; was born in Rhode Island and has a B.A. from Randolph-Macon College (in Ashland, VA, not to be confused with Randolph-Macon Women's College in Lynchburg, VA). She also has a Master's Degree in computer science from the University of New Haven. It comes in handy when my computer suddenly stops working—as it all too frequently does for no perceptible reason. I doubt if that's what she had in mind, though.

One of an editor's greatest pleasures is to see a younger writer whose first story she published become a well-known and independent writer on her own. That's happened to many writers in these pages; Diana L. Paxson and Mercedes Lackey come immediately to mind. To this company we can now add Elisabeth Waters.

Eirthe scowled at the invisible wall she had just walked into. "Now how do I get past *this*?" she demanded, shoving back the long black braid that had come unpinned at the impact and fallen forward over her right shoulder.

The salamander perched on her left shoulder leaned forward to sniff delicately at the barrier. *Hmmn. I'd say you need a magician.*

"A magician?" Eirthe looked about her in dismay. The cone of the volcano she was trying to reach loomed up ahead of her, and the ground underfoot was a gray-black flow of cooled hardened lava—though 'cooled' was a relative term. Eirthe could feel the heat even through the thick soles of her boots, though it was not quite hot enough to scorch the hems of her skirt and cloak. Alnath, of course, was impervious to heat; to a salamander even the heart of the volcano would be a pleasant environment. But neither the heat under her feet nor the small orange flames Alnath was putting out near her left ear could make Eirthe feel other than cold. "Really, Alnath, where do you expect me to find a magician around here?"

The question was rhetorical, but Alnath answered literally. *Try the village we passed at the bottom of the hill.*

Eirthe sighed and began to retrace her steps. It seemed unlikely to her that there would be a magician in a village that small, but Alnath frequently knew things she didn't.

When she walked into the common room of the village's one inn, with Alnath concealed discreetly on her wrist, under her cloak, she discovered that the salamander was right. She recognized the clear light tenor voice even before she saw the figure in the mage's robe sitting by the fire playing the lute and singing for the assembled company—and presumably also for supper. The mercenary-magician Lythande was an old acquaintance.

Eirthe chose a table in a quiet corner while everyone's attention was on Lythande and told the innkeeper who came to serve her that she'd like to buy the minstrel a

drink. She kenw that Lythande didn't eat or drink in
public, but she also knew how long the magician could
sit over a full tankard of ale, giving every impression of
enjoying it.

As she had anticipated, the offer was enough to bring
Lythande to her corner at the end of the set. "Ah, Eirthe," Lythande said, as if they had last met yesterday,
instead of nearly six years ago. "And Alnath," as Alnath
scrabbled along the bench to greet the magician, who
was one of the very few people she would agree to touch.
"Greetings, Essence of Fire." Lythande said, stroking
the salamander with a callused fingertip, while Alnath's
fire blazed cobalt blue with pleasure. "And how is Cadmon these days?"

"He's dead, Lythande," Eirthe replied.

"I see," said Lythande quietly. "A most grievous loss
for you indeed."

Eirthe nodded, blinking back sudden tears. It was a
relief to talk to someone who understood the problem
without requiring long difficult explanations. Say that
your business partner had died and your hearers would
murmur sympathetically "how sad" before pointing out
that there were other glassblowers in the world, if a candlemaker felt she had to team up with a glassblower.

What most people didn't realize was that Eirthe and
Cadmon had become partners because each of them was
under a curse, and their curses had canceled each other
out. Cadmon made wonderful glassware, but anything
put in it burned to vapor almost instantaneously. Eirthe
made beautiful elegant tapers, as well as sculpted candles
almost too real to burn, but the curse put on her was a
cold spell; her fire wouldn't burn and neither would her
candles—unless they were put in one of Cadmon's
glasses. Together their products made a very safe lamp;
if it was tipped over, the candle promptly went out. They
had met each other eight years ago at a major trade
fair, within hours of the time their respective curses were
imposed, and had been good friends and partners ever
since.

Now, with Cadmon gone, Eirthe was discovered for the first time just how bad the curse on her was.

"It isn't that I'm about to starve," she told Lythande. "Cadmon and I always knew that one of us might be alone some day, so we were very careful to save money. I don't need to work for the rest of my life as far as finances go, but what else am I to do? It's not in my nature to sit around being useless! Without Cadmon to make glasses for the candles, there's no point in my making candles, even when I can build a fire to melt the wax over. I can still get a fire to burn," she explained, "but only in the firepit Cadmon made me—which certainly isn't much help on a cold night on the trail. I don't even dare get too close to the fire here, for fear I'll put it out! I'm cold all the time now, and it's miserable!"

"I can certainly see that it would be," Lythande agreed. "So what brought you here?"

"It was Alnath's idea," Eirthe explained. At least Lythande wouldn't think her crazy to be taking advice from a salamander. "She said that going to Heart of Fire—the volcano here—would help me."

"Did she say how?" Lythande inquired.

"Well, no," Eirthe replied, "but who should know fire better than a fire elemental?"

"There is a certain logic to that view," the magician acknowledged. "You certainly have my sympathy, but I gather you require some more tangible assistance. What is it you want from me?"

"I want to hire you to get me to the volcano's cone. There's some sort of barrier part way up the side of the mountain; I bumped into it this afternoon."

The blue star between Lythande's brows furrowed with thought as the magician came to a decision. "There are many things to do while awaiting the final battle of Law and Chaos, and this may well be one of them. We'll go have a look at this barrier first thing in the morning."

So the next morning Eirthe stood again in front of the barrier, with Alnath perched on her shoulder, and watched Lythande run a hand over its surface, then poke a fingertip through it. "I can't say that I think much of this barrier, Eirthe," Lythande remarked; "it's the kind of thing I'd put up to keep sheep from wandering over a cliff."

"Thank you very much!" Eirthe retorted.

Lythande chuckled. "I'm not calling you a sheep; I'm just saying that whoever put up this barrier either wasn't much of a magician or wasn't putting much effort into it." Half the magician's body followed the finger through the barrier, while the other hand reached out and grabbed Eirthe's wrist. "Come along, Eirthe," Lythande said, pulling her through.

To Eirthe, the barrier felt a bit like the surface of the water when she went into the lake at home—no, more like coming out of the water, for the air was hotter and drier on this side of the barrier. The heat increased as they continued up the slope toward the cone, and the air became more sulphurous and more difficult to breathe. They were about ten feet from the edge of the crater when the lava started to bubble out.

Lythande jumped quickly aside from the channel the lava was flowing down, dragging Eirthe, whose reaction to heat had diminished greatly over the years. And a voice spoke from within the volcano. "You are well come," it said in pure soprano tones. "It's been a long time since anyone sacrificed a virgin to me."

Eirthe opened her mouth to protest, and promptly choked on the sulphur in the air. In the time it took her to stop coughing she had plenty of time to think. She knew she wasn't a virgin, and she knew that Alnath wasn't either—assuming that the volcano cared about the virginity or lack thereof of a salamander, which it might—who knew what a volcano thought about anything? Did this mean that Lythande, after living who knew how many ordinary lifespans, was still a virgin?

"What makes you think any of us is a virgin?" Eirthe asked, when she got her voice back. "Or that we came here to sacrifice one?"

"A sacrificial procession, including a virgin, is the only thing that can pass through the barrier I put up," the volcano explained patiently. "I should think you'd know that, but then, it has been a long time."

Eirthe heard Lythande mutter something that sounded like a curse, but decided not to ask for clarification of the words.

"You put up the barrier?" she asked the volcano. "Why?"

"I was tired of being the garbage dump for the entire district," the volcano replied. "Anything—or anybody—they didn't want down the hill they brought up here and threw into me. Diseased animals, unwanted babies, murder victims—and then they had that plague. The fools didn't seem to realize that plague victims can give a volcano heartburn!"

"I can see how that might happen," Lythande's voice said behind Eirthe. "So you put up a barrier—"

"And the only thing that can get through it is a virgin in the company of someone who wants something," the volcano finished the sentence. "So tell me," it asked Eirthe, "what is it you want?"

"Do I have to say right now?" Eirthe asked. "Can I have some time to think about it, and, uh, put my request into the proper words?"

"I should have thought you would have done that before you came here," the volcano said. "But no matter, take all the time you need. You have until sunset."

"What happens at sunset?" Lythande asked.

"If a virgin hasn't been sacrificed by then," the volcano said simply, "I erupt."

"Oh." Eirthe was aware that this was hardly an intelligent comment on their current situation, but she couldn't think of anything else to say. She and Lythande retreated a little way downhill and sat on a boulder to consider their options.

"I'm sorry to have dragged you into this mess, Lythande—"

"It isn't your fault," Lythande said fairly. "I should have checked the barrier spells more carefully."

"Then you are a virgin?" Eirthe fought a brief battle with her curiosity, and lost. "Do you have to be one for your magic to work, or is it just that while you're pretending to be a man it's hard to find an opportunity to change that condition?"

Lythande looked grim. "And how do you know I'm not a man?"

Eirthe shrugged. "I don't know how; I've just known ever since I first saw you that you were a woman. You didn't seem to want it known, so I kept quiet about it."

Lythande scowled. "Kindly continue to keep it quiet. In answer to your question, while virginity per se is not strictly necessary to my magic, the day any man finds out I'm a woman is the day I lose my power—so I remain a virgin."

"Well, that answers that question," Eirthe said. "Now for the next one: have you any ideas on how to get us out of here?"

"I gather," Lythande said, sounding slightly amused, "that you do not consider sacrificing me to the volcano to be a viable option?"

"Of course not!" Eirthe said indignantly. "I don't kill— I got the curse in the first place when I refused to make candles for a wizard who wanted to use them to kill people, and I'm certainly not going to kill you to get the curse lifted. I'd rather be accursed than a murderess."

Lythande regarded her from under raised eyebrows. "It's a refreshing change to see someone who is willing to suffer for her principles. I'd like to see you free of the curse, but I really have no intention of diving into a volcano to do it." She frowned thoughtfully. "I don't suppose the proximity to the volcano has weakened the curse any?"

Eirthe walked over to the lava flow, scooped up a handful, and began to mold it into a statuette as it cooled in her hands. "It doesn't look like it."

Lythande looked intently at the figure taking shape and said suddenly, "Tell me exactly what it was the wizard who cursed you wanted you to do."

Eirthe paused to collect her memories of the event into reasonable order. "He was called Garak, and he wanted me to make candles in the likenesses of all the rich merchants at the Fair—I was at an annual trade fair that spring; my father had died during the winter, and I was continuing with his business. But when Garak asked me, I remembered that Father had made a candle of one of the goldsmiths the previous year, which vanished after one of his drinking bouts with Garak, and then the goldsmith burned to death in his bed and they said the blankets weren't even charred—and Garek had a lot more money after that. . . ."

"The Law of Similarity," Lythande murmured. "Was he running a protection racket?"

"That's what I thought at the time," Eirthe said, "but I couldn't prove it. Anyway, I refused to have anything to do with him—and he wasn't that good a magician, so I was pretty sure he couldn't pull it off without me. Unfortunately, he had gotten caught up in the worship of one of the proscribed gods, which was where he got the power for the curse."

Lythande sat quietly for several minutes, apparently deep in thought. Eirthe continued to refine the statuette into the likeness of a young girl.

"So what you're saying is that your candles held enough magic to be Similar to the people they were modeled after."

"Yes, I guess so," Eirthe said uncertainly. "I never really thought of it in those terms. . . ." Her voice trailed off as she looked at the figure in her hands. "Lythande? Do you think the volcano would consider this to be a virgin?"

"Its substance certainly is," Lythande said promptly. "You can't get a substance much more virgin than lava newly poured from a volcano." She reached over and took the figure from Eirthe, handling it gingerly by the edges. "And there's quite a bit of life in it, both from its essence and from your work on it." She handed the figure back to Eirthe and shrugged. "It's worth a try, I suppose. Formulate your request into words, and do it carefully. While the volcano is probably not as difficult and malicious as the average demon, it's always best to be very precise with your words."

"Be careful what you pray for, because you might get it?" Eirthe said lightly.

"You will almost certainly get it," Lythande corrected her.

Eirthe nodded. "I'll be careful," she promised. "At least this is one virgin that won't give the volcano heartburn!"

Together they went back to stand at the volcano's edge, with Alnath still perched on Eirthe's shoulder. "Have you decided on your wish?" it asked.

"Yes," Eirthe said, choosing her words carefully. "I am a candlemaker under a curse so that I can't use fire and the candles I make will not burn. I want to be released from the curse, but not as if it had never been; I want the release to apply only from this moment forth and not to change the condition of any candles I have made in the past."

"Very well," the volcano said. "Give me the virgin and you shall have your will."

Eirthe dropped the lava figure she had fashioned into the volcano, closed her eyes, held her breath, and prayed somewhat incoherently to whatever god might be listening. But even so, she felt as if she had been suddenly cast into hell.

At first she thought the volcano had erupted after all; red light blasted at her closed eyelids, there was a roaring sound, punctuated by shrieks from Alnath, in her ears, and every inch of her body seemed on fire. It was several minutes before she noticed that she was being carried over the shoulder of someone running downhill. Then there was the sensation of being pulled through the barrier again, the light and the noise were gone, and her skin stopped hurting. The air was breathable again, too.

Lythande laid her gently on the ground and dropped to kneel beside her. "What happened?" she asked.

"I'm not sure," Eirthe said shakily. "The volcano didn't erupt, did it?" She cast a nervous glance uphill.

"No, it didn't," Lythande assured her. "It took the sacrifice and the lava subsided, but Alnath started screaming and you suddenly doubled over and collapsed. So I grabbed you and got out of there."

Eirthe shuddered. "It felt as if I'd been thrown in there instead of the sacrifice." She turned her head to look at Alnath, suddenly aware that she could feel the heat radiating from the salamander. "Alnath, are you all right?"

Yes, came the salamander's prompt reply, *but it really did feel as though we were in the volcano!*

Eirthe nodded. "Either there was too much of me in that figurine, or it was part of lifting the curse—I hope!" She struggled to sit up. "Where's my belt pouch—oh, here it is." She pulled out a flint and steel with shaking hands and struck them together. Sparks flew, landing on the edge of her cloak, and she hastily beat at them, then pulled her hand back with a cry. "Ouch!" She looked at the slight burn on her hand. "Well, it appears the curse is lifted—now I'll have to get used the handling fire again."

Lythande smiled. "Be careful what you pray for—"

Eirthe finished the sentence. "—for you will certainly get it."

EDYTH AMONG THE TROLLS
By Lois Tilton

One thing I never claimed is infallibility. When this story came in, it was titled "Edric Among the Trolls"—and I read it with so much fascination that I never noticed its absence of a female lead character. (I also failed to notice that it had been submitted to *Marion Zimmer Bradley's Fantasy Magazine,* not SWORD & SORCERESS. I put it in the wrong pile, and there it stayed.) I remembered how much I had liked Lois Tilton's previous story— "Hands"—which I printed in S&S V. When I reread it for printing, I was somewhat dismayed. Ms. Tilton, however, like the pro she is, kindly did a rewrite for me; and we're happy to present this story in its new form.

Lois Tilton has also written several short fiction pieces, including science fiction and horror as well as fantasy, and will have a novel, VAMPIRE WINTER, out well before this volume is in print. It's scheduled for December 1990. She also teaches the odd class in philosophy (if they're anything like the classes I taught, they're very odd indeed) and has "recently ventured into sf criticism." Well, better her than me.

She also has a husband, two kids, "known collectively as The Forces of Evil"—(well, anything is when you're trying to write—how well I remember)—"and some cats who aren't exactly forces of good." (Are any?)

Three figures on their haunches near the mouth of a dank, lightless cave: naked, filth-crusted bellies sagging over the dark red, wrinkled skin of their genitals. Massive jaws at work, they tore at a rotting carcass on the floor of the cave. One picked up a length of femur, a few shreds of muscle still adhering. It cracked the bone with a loud snap, then proceeded with relish to suck the putrescent marrow.

A fourth figure, smaller than the rest, crouched at a distance from the grisly feast. This one's belly was hollow, with sharp, protruding ribs beneath skin turned a dark blue-gray with cold. One hand clutched a thong around her neck: Edyth Egilsdottr among the trolls.

Boldly, a rat emerged from a fissure in the rock. Whiskers twitching, it crept slowly toward a gobbet of fat and gristle lying unnoticed on the floor of the cave. But the movement caught the attention of one of the feasting trolls, and a hugely knuckled hand struck just as the rat took hold of its prize. A sharp squeak, a slight snap of bone. The troll stared at the limp creature in its hand with a slightly puzzled frown creasing the low, bony ridge of its forehead. Its jaws ground slowly, its other hand still clutched a loop of reeking intestine. As it swallowed, it glanced from one hand to the next, from rat to carrion, then shrugging, tossed the smaller portion aside and crammed the length of gut into its mouth.

Edyth was on the rat in an instant. She tore at the throat with her teeth, sucking desperately at the warm, sticky blood. Even starving, she hadn't been able to make herself gag down the cold, half-decayed carrion the trolls so relished.

The one who caught the rat grunted as it watched her devour the warm carcass, all but the hide and hair, even crunching the small bones. The warmth in her belly was comfort, life. Edyth drew her knees up close as she huddled on the floor of the cave, wrapped her arms around herself. Outside, the days were growing shorter, and she longed for the touch of the pallid northern sun. In this place was no warmth, no fire, not even the heat of other bodies, for the flesh of the trolls was as cold as the frost-split rock from which their race once sprang. She was naked, as they were—necessary to maintain the illusion that was her only safety in this place, and there wasn't even a hide to wrap around herself, for the trolls devoured their carrion down to the hide and bone. Her hand stole up to the thong around her neck and again clutched the amulet hanging from it, her protection, the sole reminder of her humanity.

It had been weeks, she thought, but sometimes it seemed she had been among the trolls forever. Her knees and haunches were growing as callused as theirs, her hair as matted with filth. Her breasts were shrunken with starvation. She hadn't imagined it would be this way.

A memory haunted her, fading sometimes, as all her memories seemed to fade—the face of her Master the wizard Nemian, and his gnarled, time-spotted fingers holding out the amulet. *Here, my girl. So you can walk invisible among the trolls.* As indeed she did, but not as she had expected. The trolls saw her, but as one of their own kind, a sickly, barren female. They waited with indifference to see if she would live or die.

Now the feasting trolls raised their heads as a massive figure filled the cave entrance for a moment, then shambled inside. The newcomer sniffed sharply, and its eyes, fixed on Edyth, were flat green glowing discs. She clutched the amulet and prayed furiously to a whole pantheon of guardians. This one was the male she had come to think of as Stoneface, and it had taken an interest in her lately that was too horrifying to contemplate. Almost, it seemed that a suspicious thought might be flickering behind the bony ridge of its skull, but after a moment Stoneface snorted and crouched down next to the remains of the carcass.

Edyth shuddered in relief. The trolls were incredibly stupid, but there was nothing dull about their senses. *The amulet will disguise your scent,* Nemian had said, but nothing about being mistaken for a female troll in season.

The trolls were stirring nervously now as the sky to the east began to lighten. One by one, they abandoned the few remaining bones and retreated farther into the depths of their cave, where the sunlight could not follow. Stoneface turned its head toward Edyth and uttered a warning grunt. She groaned inwardly, reluctant to abandon this patch that held a little of her body warmth, but got stiffly to her feet and shambled troll-like after Stoneface, deeper into the cave.

Living like a troll, her eyes had adjusted to the darkness. The cave floor was littered everywhere with their refuse. She kicked aside a scrap of pelvic bone, willing it not to be human. Legend had it that trolls prefered man-flesh to other meat, but she had never seen them kill a human during all her time in the cave. Still, she could imagine them eating a man, a woman, wrenching off her limbs like a roasted fowl's, consuming her raw, down to the very bones.

Here, in this corner, was evidence—human remains. She crouched down to investigate, by touch as much as by sight. Amid damp, rotting tatters of cloth she found the metal buckle of a belt, a few coins, a knife. She tested the blade with her thumb, found it rusted. And at any rate, it was not what she sought.

Foggily, she remembered: *treasure, riches, reward.* It was in here somewhere. It had to be. She had to keep searching, remembering the reason. The wizard Nemian, her Master. . . .

Memory escaped again. The trolls ignored her as she sifted through the debris. A young one played with a couple of stones, a female regurgitated partly digested meat and scooped it into her infant's mouth. Edyth had been surprised to discover that the trolls didn't suckle their young, but then she had never before thought of them as having young at all. A few times she had seen them fornicate—momentary, passionless encounters, a few thrusts, a grunt of satisfaction, nothing more.

There was a brief commotion in the cave. The youngster clashed its two stones together, making a visible spark in the darkness. It dropped them, squealing in fright. The trolls were as terrified of fire as they were of sunlight.

Edyth emitted a short, harsh laugh, making a nearby troll lift its head, broad nostrils flaring in suspicion. She dropped her eyes back down to the pitiful relics she had been examining. Some traveler, perhaps, killed within the last year. No use to him any more. No use to Edyth, now.

Exhaustion made her tremble. She didn't know how much longer she could last in this place. Some day soon she would sink into a stupor from which she would never arouse, and then the trolls, who never scrupled to devour their own dead, would suck the marrow from her bones.

She wanted to live. She wanted to be warm, to be clean—to be human again. But she couldn't, not until she found it, the treasure, the . . .

A wave of dizziness blurred her memory. There were times when she almost had forgotten who she was. She took hold of her amulet, and it came back to her with a sudden shock—the ring, the arm-ring of King Elessen! Yes, yes, she remembered now! The arm-ring, and once she found it, rewards beyond her power to imagine!

She shuffled deeper back into the cave, into the corners where the darkness was near absolute, searching for more ancient leavings. According to legend, trolls had inhabited these caves for untold generations, amassing their treasures along with the remains of their victims. Her Master had told her so. Treasures . . . they must be hidden somewhere. . . .

Edyth woke as the trolls around her began to stir. It had to be sunset. There was a lethargy weighing her down, as heavy as lead. Cold and hunger were draining her life. A spasm twisted her gut. She must have food tonight, something more than the carcass of a rat.

Shivering, she stumbled toward the mouth of the cave, following the trolls. There was frost on the ground. The newly-risen moon made the crystals glitter like diamonds. The sharpness of the fresh air helped to clear her head.

Behind her in the cave there was a shrill squeal of pain, and Edyth turned around to see one of the females swatting the young troll that had gotten into trouble earlier. Its mother, she thought, as the youngster retreated sullenly. It was too young to leave the safety of the cave.

Most of the others had already gone into the night, their forms ahead of her disappearing into the darkness. Despite their clumsy gait, the creatures could move fast enough, Edyth thought, following in their tracks. The frost sent burning pain flaring into her legs, but numbness set in quickly. She ran bent over with hunger cramps, and soon she was limping.

Footsteps behind her—she slowed, gasping, and saw the young troll, less than her own size, trotting along her trail. There was a vacant, idiot grin on its lumpy face as it paused next to Edyth and grunted a greeting.

"Go away!" she whispered harshly, giving it a shove. "Go back to the cave! I'm not your mother!"

The youngster ignored her, panting happily. Edyth gathered her breath and stumbled after the others. The troll-cave was well up on the side of a mountain, where the few trees were twisted, stunted specimens, but the trail descended into the spruce forest, and soon even the voices of the trolls had faded away. In the distance, a wolf pack howled, voices raised one after the other, and Edyth supposed the trolls would be heading that way. Despite their formidable strength, they were more often scavengers than hunters. Edyth staggered from tree to tree as the slope dropped sharply. At least here it was a little less cold.

At the bottom of the hill, she turned around and stared back up the slope, gasping. Could she make it back all the way to the troll-cave? She pressed on through the brush, but in a little while exhaustion and despair brought her to her knees. It was no use, her strength just wasn't enough any more. Her mind whirled dizzily, and for a moment she couldn't even remember why she was out here. The amulet, it had something to do with the amulet around her neck—a treasure. . . .

She started in sudden terror at the sound of wolves howling, so much closer now! She stared around wildly, looking for some kind of weapon to hold them off. She had seen a pack once bring down a stag, darting, snap-

ping, dragging the guts from the living belly, glistening
and steaming, the blood in the snow. No use to run. . . .

No, wait! The sound came again, the baying of a pack
in pursuit—dogs, not wolves! Dogs—men! She was
saved!

In desperate relief, she cried out loud in a cracked
voice, "Here! Help!"

She ran, stumbling, heedless of the brush clawing her
bare legs, toward the voices of the dogs. Suddenly,
behind her, there was a great crashing of branches and
a figure burst through the trees, directly at her—a troll!

Then she recognized the youngster who had followed
her out of the cave. It ran to her, clutched her, whimpering in terror. Something flickered through the trees in
the distance. Torches! She could hear the dogs, closer
now, they had the troll-scent. They'd be closing in soon,
the pack, the torches, the hunters with their spears—
men, safety, warmth, food.

The young troll cried. It shouldn't ever have left the
cave, Edyth thought fleetingly. Too young to defend
itself against a pack of hunters and their dogs. She gave
the troll a rough shove. "Go on, move! Run!" She cursed
in despair as the creature still clung to her. The men
would kill it, the men with their warm clothes, warm
fires, warm food. Where were the other trolls? Where
was its own mother? Why hadn't she made sure it stayed
back in the cave where it belonged?

Sobbing in frustration, she grabbed hold of its paw,
larger already than her own hand, and pulled it after her.
"Come on, run!"

They stumbled for a while up the slope, fleeing the
dogs, back to the troll-cave, back to the hunger and the
cold. But the pack was almost as fast as the wolves they
were bred to hunt, and Edyth soon knew they were closing in. Too late. Desperately, she looked around—there!
A large tree up ahead, and she dragged the young troll
over to it, gave it a shove. "Get up there! Now! Hurry!"
She wondered too late, could trolls even climb? But the
youngster finally got the idea and started to pull itself
heavily up into the branches.

Edyth saw the first dog come breaking through into the clearing, and she climbed up into the tree after the troll, jerking up her legs out of reach as the hound leaped, snapping. In an instant she was surrounded by the pack, huge, shaggy-pelted hounds with lolling red tongues and gleaming teeth. They had the troll-scent. She—she had been among the trolls, had slept in their cave, absorbed their scent! They might tear her to pieces. In a panic, she cried out, "Help!"

A torch flared. A man came through the trees, a hunter. He hesitated at the sight before him, while Edyth, afraid to move, kept calling out, "Help! I'm human!"

More hunters were coming up now. They all were staring at her, and Edyth was suddenly and painfully conscious of her nakedness. She fumbled with her hands to cover herself, blinking in the torchlight. She heard them discussing her in low voices and grasped her amulet. Didn't they believe her? Had she really been transformed into a troll, after all? Desperately, she cried out, "Help me! In the name of the gods! Call them off!"

A hunter finally strode forward to the foot of the tree, beating the dogs to quiet them. "You say you're a human?"

"Yes! Don't you know trolls can't speak?"

The hunter grunted in dissatisfaction, but he gestured to the others, who finally started pulling the dogs away from the tree. Awkwardly, Edyth climbed down, still trying to shield her body from them.

The hunter gestured for someone to bring her a cloak. As she gratefully wrapped it around herself, he growled, "We took you for a troll. They raided our cattle tonight, took two head of oxen, carried them off." Accusation.

The hounds were still straining at the leash, trying to get at the tree, and one of the handlers wrinkled his nose at Edyth's odor. "Whew. Smells like a troll all right, that one does!"

They wanted answers. Edyth's head was spinning. She couldn't think of the words, couldn't remember what to say. But there was the young troll without its mother, still up in the tree, and the dogs had its scent. Lead them away. "I . . ." She shivered convulsively, teeth chattering. "T . . . troll-cave."

"You mean, *you* were in the troll-cave?"

"Y . . . yes. Hid in there."

Their faces showed stark, scornful disbelief. She groped in the fog of her memory for something to convince them, but she couldn't quite remember now—why had seen been in the cave, after all? "Lost," she finally stammered, "I was lost."

One of them spit on the ground. "That's horse dung! Trolls'd eat anyone they found in their cave. Rip your head right off your shoulders, like they did my best ox!"

"No," Edyth said, "I . . . took off my clothes. They took me for one of them, for a troll." Her hand closed around the amulet, her Master's gift.

The leader silenced the rest. "Never mind. The trolls—where'd they go?"

Edyth urgently tried not to think of the small troll just overhead in the tree. She urgently willed it to stay quiet. "I . . . don't know. I lost sight of them. I was trying to find a house, a village, someplace. . . ."

The leader scowled distrustfully, but a new voice said, "Wait. You. What's your name?"

She had to pause, to remember. "Edyth. Edyth Egilsdottr. From . . ." She couldn't remember the rest.

But the man nodded, satisfied. "That was the name, right. Fellow was through here, asking for you just a day or so past. Said he thought you must be lost in the woods. Name of Magni. Your husband, was he? You run away from your man?"

Magni. Edyth thought she ought to remember. Magni, and another name. Nemian. Yes, her Master. But, husband? Did she have a husband now? Confused, she shook her head, and the hunter snorted disdainfully. "Don't find that many naked women running around in the woods, in a troll-cave. This is the one, all right. Better get her back to the village."

"What about the trolls?"

"Too late. We'll never pick up the trail again now."

The leader glared again at Edyth, as if their failure was her fault. The dogs were still snarling at her suspiciously, but the men took Edyth back with them, and she didn't care if they did it grudgingly. The hut was rough, built from newly-hewn timbers, but the fire-pit was glowing, she was warm, warm at last. She was saved from the troll-cave.

She had washed away the stench of troll. She had clothes again, her stomach was full of human food.

The villagers crowded around, full of questions, repelled and fascinated at once by the woman who lived with trolls.

"You et man-flesh, did you?"

"No! They . . . the trolls . . . they ate mostly carrion—boar, deer, sometimes a goat or a pig."

"Or an ox," a voice grumbled.

"You saying they don't eat human flesh?" another one challenged.

"No—I mean, I never saw . . . But I wouldn't, I never . . ."

"What about the treasure?"

"That's right! They say there's a treasure in a troll-cave. Gold."

Edyth felt a sudden alarm. She grasped her amulet. "Treasure? No, no. Just bones, a few bits of rusted metal. Nothing else. No treasure."

But there was something in her memory, half-forgotten. *Treasure*. An arm-ring . . . King Elessen . . .

No. She resisted it desperately. She had searched, she could remember now. Searched for weeks through the heaps of decaying refuse littering the darkest corners of the cave. Nothing. Nothing.

Her hand still clutched the amulet. And yet . . .

Four days after her rescue, Edyth left the hall. Two men at work repairing the cattle barn saw her walk into the forest, called out. She made no answer. The scent of spruce in the air, fresh and alive, the dry brown needles underfoot. She came to a clearing that looked familiar, stood there, gazing through the trees, higher up the slope, the mountain, the cave.

Her resistance was weakening. She didn't want to go back. She didn't. The cold, the stinking carrion, the constant hunger. The brutish company of the trolls. She wanted to be human. . . .

But the treasure. The arm-ring. Power, riches, reward.

No. The cave was empty, she knew it was.

The treasure.

No! Only a buckle, a rusting knife!

The arm-ring. The reward.

She didn't want to go back. *Please, Master, I don't want to go!*

"Hey, you! Troll-woman!"

Edyth started, spun around. Behind her were two of the villagers. She could recognize them by now—Wilm, the chief, and Hanno, the one whose best ox was taken by the trolls. Both men were carrying spears.

"Just where were you going, troll-woman? Back to the cave, weren't you? Back to those he-trolls, is that it?"

"No! No, I'm not!"

"Back to get that treasure, I'll bet!" said Wilm.

"There isn't any treasure! I've told you that! It's all a lie!"

"Maybe," said Wilm. "Maybe not. But I think I'll just go see for myself. You'll show us the way, won't you?"

"No!" Edyth protested.

"Shut up!" growled Hanno. "Even if there isn't any treasure, we finally know where to find those gods-damned trolls! Burn them all out! Now, get moving!" He lifted his spear menacingly.

Edyth glanced upward, toward the peak of the mountain. Her mind was whirling with confusion again. Images of trolls, burned and slaughtered. Treasure, vast golden mounds of it, with King Elessen's legendary arm-ring gleaming on the top. A heap of half-rotted rags. An infant troll, whimpering for its dead mother. "No," she protested weakly.

"Hey!"

All three men turned toward the sound of the voice.
A man was running up the hill. "Edyth, is that you?"

The villagers lowered their spears. Edyth saw that the
stranger was young and well-dressed, carrying a sword.
He seemed somehow familiar. . . .

"Edyth?" The newcomer turned to the sullen villagers.
"Was she trying to wander away again? Thank you for
brining her back."

The men paused. "Your woman, is she?" Wilm
growled. "Keep her locked up this time, I would. If you
don't want little half-troll whelps out of her," he added
viciously.

The stranger frowned as they made their way down
the hill to the village. "I hate these backwoods louts!"
Then his voice grew concerned as he looked more closely
at Edyth. "You look terrible! I've been asking for you
in every flea-bitten village for leagues! We expected you
back over a tenday ago, at the latest. Where were you?
What went wrong?"

Edyth groped in the fog of her memory to retrieve this
face. Magni? Her husband? "Magni?" she asked aloud.

"That's right, it's me. Here, wait." He pulled open
Edyth's shirt, took hold of the amulet. Before she could
protest, he snapped the thong. "There."

A sudden cold rush of clarity dispersed Edyth's confusion, blowing away the fog that had clouded her memory.
She remembered it all now. Magni—*not* her husband,
but her fellow apprentice. And their master Nemian, the
thrice-damned amulet, the reason she had been sent to
the trolls. The treasure, King Elessen's arm-ring—none
of it had ever existed. It was all an illusion, she'd endured
it all for an illusion, the weeks freezing and starving in
that cave. . . .

"Are you all right now?" Magni was asking.

Edyth shuddered, inhaled slowly. "Yes," she breathed.
"All right now."

"Good. Like I said, we were worried. Winter's starting
to come on, and you weren't back yet from the trolls.
Even the Master was concerned. We thought maybe
they'd eaten you, after all!" His laugh was slightly forced.

She stared at him bleakly, suppressing a shudder.

"Well, never mind," he added quickly. "The Master is anxious to hear your report. I've got horses waiting down in the village and I've left silver to repay them for your clothes. Let's go."

They started down the hill, but suddenly Edyth put up a hand. "Wait. Just a minute. I want to check something."

It was the tallest tree in the clearing, she recognized it at once in the daylight, and peered up into the branches. Had the little troll escaped? Did it have enough sense to climb down before sunrise trapped it? Whatever had happened, there was no sign of it now. She sighed. Well, she'd never wanted to be the mother to a troll.

"What was that about?" Magni asked her.

"Nothing. It's all right. Let's go back."

The wizard Nemian frowned at the amulet he was holding in his gnarled, spotted hands. A minor malfunction, he decided finally. The spell that affected memory was out of adjustment. Not a major problem. The girl managed well enough, after all. Quite well, in fact. He put the amulet aside for the moment.

He was very pleased with the results of Edyth's investigations. Quills scratched rapidly on parchment as two scribes took notes while she recounted every detail of her time among the trolls. "Excellent!" the Master exclaimed at each new revelation concerning their diet, mating habits, the way they raised their young. "My girl, you've done well! As always."

Edyth accepted his praise wearily, along with a cup of hot spiced wine from the hand of a very junior apprentice. She'd been answering questions for hours without a break.

Now Nemian dismissed his scribes and rested his bony hand paternally on Edyth's shoulder. "Lass," he began, "I appreciate the . . . unexpected complications of this last task. I know you must be longing forward to a long rest, a winter in the warm scriptorium writing up your notes. But the fact is, you're the best field observer of all my apprentices. None of the others ever come back with the details that you do.

"Now—and I wouldn't do this if it weren't truly an urgent case—but I've just received word that a scoriated wyvern was sighted this fall on an island just off the Howling Coast. A species considered extinct for the last fifty years! I know how excited you must be!

"But we must act in haste! I know you understand. This kind of news will draw all sorts of low adventurers, treasure seekers, the worst kind of riffraff!" Edyth winced as the ancient fingers dug into her shoulder. The wizard paused. "So, you see, reluctant as I am to send you out so soon on another task, I'm afraid I must."

Edyth tried to protest. "But Master, please! The Howling Coast! In winter!"

Nemian frowned. "Now, my girl. You know I've always sent the most favorable reports on your progress to the Collegium. Up until now. And won't you be eligible for your journeyman examinations in another year or so, with a good recommendation? We wouldn't want anything to stand in your way.

"So." He picked up the amulet again, thoughtfully. "Of course, you'll have to enter the wyvern's lair unseen. . . ."

THE OPAL SKULL
by Cynthia Ward

Although Cynthia Ward lives in Silicon Valley, in Mountain View—a little town about thirty miles south of my Berkeley home, I've never met her; so I know only what little she's willing to reveal in the autobiographical sketch she sent me; which says this is her first professional sale. (She says she sold an idea to Marvel Comics in the winter of 79/80, but "doesn't think that counts." Well, no.) She's 29, has a B.A. in English and works as a word processor. She and her husband have a Maine coon cat, and it's a native of California while *they're* from Maine. A Maine coon cat is the largest feline I've ever seen outside a cage at the zoo.

She says that the basis of this story is that bone can be "opalized" as well as fossilized. Tell me—does that bit of scientific knowledge make this story science fiction? My feeling is that it doesn't read like science fiction, which is a compliment.

The flames roared forward, leaping and writhing as if animated by demonic purpose. Fleeing before them on a foundering horse, Nelerissa Hayseed found it difficult to believe they were not deliberately pursuing her.

The hot air tasted peculiarly flat as she drew breath to

call herself fifty sorts of fool for even thinking of crossing the Golden Wide in high summer. The vast plain's very name betrayed how short a time the grass was green before the sun toasted it shining gold, then baked it panther tawny, then burned it dull brown. The Wide got so tinder-dry that even the horse-barbarians kept to its edges in the depths of the dry season.

Nelerissa was here because the Blade had surely also heard of the opal skull. He'd have no qualms about daring the Golden Wide in summer. So she could not afford any. Her reputation was at stake.

When the caravan-master had ordered the caravan off the River Road to avoid the meandering loops of the ever-flowing Julukela, Nelerissa had recognized his order as preposterously foolish but, though dry straw-dust filled her nostrils, though yellow-brown smoke from distant fires hid the sun, she said not a word. For leaving the Road would put more distance between herself and the Blade, or put her ahead if he had somehow managed to leave Areherna first.

The caravan was only a three day ride from the Western Mountains when a foolish guard smoking bhang started a fire. Suddenly the grass was aflame and the wagons were catching. The merchants ordered the guards to save the wagons. Nelerissa did not join them in emptying water-barrels ineffectually on burning wood and canvas. She jumped on the best steed and kicked it into a run for the Great River.

At first the fire burned toward the south. Then the wind died down and the flames roared in every direction, or so it seemed to Nelerissa. Though the fire had started not fifteen minutes before, she felt as if she had been in flight for hours. She was reeling in the saddle, drenched with sweat, gasping for breath. The smoke was rising straight up to the sky, but fine ash drifted down to fill her throat and blur her eyes. Her arms were aching, cramping, from hugging her mount's neck; she did not trust her grip on the reins to keep her in the saddle. The horse was shaking under her as if after a long day's journey.

They were surrounded by animals running in the same direction as they, toward the Julukela. Most of the beasts were visible only as ripples in the waist-high grass, but Nelerissa glimpsed antelope beside wolf, bison beside panther. Even the horse seemed oblivious to the killers. She had heard of predator and prey fleeing together from fire, but she had never thought to see such a thing.

This close to the Western Mountains, the Golden Wide was not utterly treeless; the foothills stretched ragged fingers of pine and oak along the Great River as if seeking to hold back the water flowing off their flanks and away. The trees were only a few yards distant. But the plainsfire had swept ahead, a hundred yards to Nelerissa's right, and four or five pines were igniting like immense oil-soaked torches. In sun-baked grass a wildfire burns fast and erratic, in straw-dry wood it becomes even more dangerous.

The Western Mountains beckoned, looking almost as close as the trees, but Nelerissa, raised in the North Hills, was not fooled into making a run for the foothills. She knew they were impossibly distant.

In the dim light of the noon sun she brought the horse to an abrupt stop and leapt down, drawing her sharpest dagger. She slashed a wide strip of cloth from her cloak and tied the strip around the horse's head, covering its eyes as the caravan-master had instructed at journey's start. Then she drew up her sun-cowl for protection from a more immediate heat, took the reins, and led her mount into the stand of trees.

Ears twitching, the horse snorted its terror. Nelerissa, too, was afraid. The fire had disappeared from sight as they'd stepped among the trees, but she could hear, as clearly as the horse, the crackle and roar of flames devouring wood with tireless, voracious appetite.

She could not move as fast as she wanted, for she could barely see; the smoke and branches cut off the light of sun and fire. The ground, invisible, uneven, overgrown, was treacherous with fallen boughs and snaking roots. The pines and oaks stood close together, like ranks of soldiers; the branches and bushes clutched with inhuman fingers.

The wind picked up; the light strengthened, becoming eerie and wavering; the roar grew monstrous, but could not mask the explosions of burning pines. Glancing to her right, Nelerissa saw flames reaching around nearby boles. Looking up, she saw a rippling sheet of fire stretching across the treetops.

Firestorm!

Directly overhead, a burning pine burst loudly as a thunderclap, and sparks fell in a hot rain. Nelerissa ducked her head and covered it with cloak-wrapped arms. A coal struck the blindfolded horse's brow. It squealed piercingly and reared up, wrenching the reins out of Nelerissa's hand and almost taking her arm out of the socket. Then the horse ran right into the fire.

Nelerissa took a step toward the flames. They enfolded the horse in translucent orange sheets. The animal shrieked like a woman in the Imperial Interrogation Chambers. The flames reached for Nelerissa, touching her face with pain though they fell short by yards. The horse was lost. Nelerissa turned and ran.

She ran as if branches were not lashing her face, as if ashes were not abrading her throat, as if the air were not scalding her skin above the fold of cloak she held before her nose and mouth. The heat was greater than she had ever felt, though she had grown up at the edge of the Wide; she knew now how a clay pot must feel in the kiln.

She tripped over a root and sprawled on a waist-high pine. The springy sapling bent easily under her weight and the needlelike leaves effortlessly pierced cloth and skin. Then she felt a coal burrowing into her shoulder thorugh cloak and tunic. She jumped up brushing at her shoulder, to see flames flowing down the surrounding tree-trunks and racing through the undergrowth to enclose her in a deadly ring.

She leaped forward screaming, "Gods preserve me!"

Her head felt very hot. She smelled burning hair.

She landed on hard stone, and stumbled. But she

recovered; cobblestones ran under her bootheels as she staggered sobbing for breath across the River Road. The smoke and ash were thick as City fog. She could barely see her own feet.

She stepped on air, she had overrun roadside and riverbank, she was falling. She landed facedown in soft mud and inch-deep water. Without pause she was rolling over and over, trying to extinguish the flames in hair and clothing, not caring that the water was cold as snow-melt.

Finally Nelerissa raised her head, spitting to clear her mouth of silty, rotten-tasting muck. She found her cowl and hair were gone and the skin was exceedingly tender; her touch stung her scalp like flame.

In the wavering firelight she saw not brown grass but green reeds. Marsh stretched before her as far as she could see, about two feet in the smoke and ash. She had reached the Julukela.

She still had to get to deep water. That was the safest place, if any place could be safe in fire.

She scrambled forward. The bank dropped swiftly away. Crouching so the water was chin-deep, she drew a dagger from her baldric and slashed a reed. She cut off the tip and submerged completely, one end in her mouth.

She quickly came up gasping for air. Perhaps in the old heroic ballads one could hide in a river and breathe through a reed, but the Julukela reeds were segmented, divided into tiny, sealed chambers.

Pushing off from the bottom with violent force, Nelerissa struck out for open water. The current tugged her toward the east but she did not waste energy fighting it. She submerged frequently to find bottom, her boots pulling her feet down like lead sinkers. When she reached neck-deep water, she stopped swimming.

Even here she was surrounded by animals, deer and antelope and even a tawny panther. The latter nearly stopped her heart when it screamed, an eerie yowl, a fierce futile warning to the fire. The other animals did not react to its threat.

Nelerissa stayed submerged except when snatching a breath. She caught glimpses of the fire advancing into the marsh, a sheet of fluid light which dried the reeds and then devoured them. The air stank. The sky was black with smoke and ash. Sparks passed overhead like stars in flight.

A spark landed gently as a snowflake on Nelerissa's face, just below her eye. She sank rubbing her cheek violently. The sharp bright pain stopped piercing like a lance, but did not withdraw.

She did not want to surface again, but of course she had to. She straightened in an eruption of spray and sucked in a deep breath, tense as an overtuned harpstring as she anticipated another spark's bite.

The north bank, the far bank, had caught fire. Flames embraced the trees more intimately than a lover. The wind and sparks had done their hellish work. Thank Resdren Patron of Thieves that she was in water.

The water originated in the Western Mountains, and the combination of glacial cold and kiln heat soon had Nelerissa shivering violently. She knew this was dangerous; she was losing body heat but could not leave the water to warm up. So she brought herself into the shallows of the contemplative state taught by North Hills shamans. She did not lose awareness of where she was, what was happening, what she needed to do, but she became largely insensible to the cold, the heat, and her pain.

She did not want to think of anything. But she found herself remembering how she had come to be in this hell.

Hayseed and the Blade were the two best thieves in the City. She thought she was the best. He thought he was the best. On that point the residents of the Sink kept changing their minds, and betting odds. The Blade reigned supreme when he stole the coronet of the hostage princess of Leileth; Hayseed was the favorite when she lifted the enchanted ruby key and spirited the choicest gems from the Chief Merchant's treasure chamber. So when rumors came from the West telling of a human skull of pure opal, there was nothing for it but to go in pursuit. People were even daring to ask her in the taverns when she would be leaving the City! Everyone knew that whoever won such a prize would be the undisputed Emperor of Thieves in Areherna.

Few caravans crossed the Golden Wide in summer, but old Dogears brought her word of one assembling for depature and she went to the Western Gate. She saw no sign of the Blade; she hoped Dogears had been right when he'd sworn the Blade had not yet left the City. She presented herself to the caravan-master by a name that was not hers. The caravan-master had no problem with hiring a noncitizen when she had impressive skills with knife and sword. She did not tell him she possessed the half-mythical Northern skill of fighting without weapons. Only one other shared this secret. Anyone else who'd learned it had died of it.

Despite the danger of the season, the three month journey passed without incident until, three days' ride from the Western Mountains, a guard intoxicated on bhang set the world afire.

When Nelerissa emerged from the River the world was gray and black. The earth was burnt, the trees were sticks, the road was blanketed with ash, the sun was setting in a smoky sky. Nelerissa started west, aiming her steps toward the one spot of color, the great glaring bleeding orb of the sun.

The sun vanished and the stars did not appear, hidden as they were behind smoke and ash. Nelerissa stumbled onward through the black night, trusting to the sound of soggy leather boots on stone to keep her on the River Road.

Sunk in the trance that allowed her to ignore her pain and hunger and dizziness, she barely even noticed when she collapsed.

She was in the hands of barbarians, the violent horsemen of the Golden Wide. Three or four of the half-naked savages were picking her up. In the dawnlight she saw their brightly painted skins and brightly colored leathers, and their profusion of jewelry. Laden with gaudy brass bangles, fine gold rings, gem-crusted silver pectorals, and cheap copper-strung bracelets and neck-laces of cut glass, the horse-barbarians were a sight that hurt the thief's eyes. But she made not comment. They were savages. They were talking among themselves in a harsh, guttural language she didn't know. And she didn't have the strength to speak.

One of the barbarians thrust his painted face so close that she oculd smell the grease in his hair. "You are blessed by the Gods." He spoke the Imperial language in a surprisingly mild accent, and all the barbarians were handling her with surprising gentleness. "You passed through the Fire of Summerhell. The Gods have purified you for a great task. Strangers may not live among us, yet we must not hinder the will of the Gods. Our shaman will tend you before we bring you to your own people."

Nelerissa was puzzled. Her own people were all dead or scattered, fallen to the Empire of Areherna; the plains savages had remained unconquered because when hope-lessly surrounded they killed themslves and every mem-ber of their families—and every horse of their herds. Wiser heads in the Imperial bureaucracy had prevailed before there was no one left to trade with for the neut-ered culls that could outrun the finest race-horses bred in the Empire. So the horse-barbarians had become the only people to hold Preferred Ally status. But they were no less savage for that.

Nelerissa wondered if the barbarians meant to haul her all the way back across the Golden Wide. With their infamous horses and secret oases they might make a shorter journey of it than the caravan had, but the trip must still take a couple of months.

Nelerissa did not resolve the dilemma. She blacked out again.

She dreamed.
Shadows loomed and swayed as she fled south and east, south and east, down endless hilly coast, to the Imperial City. Out of the shadows of the slums stepped a slim swift man, a total stranger in an alien city, who

dispatched the last of four men who'd jumped her. Shadows danced with her and her rescuer as he honed her skills with sword and knife, and taught her the skills of purse-cutting and of breaking and entering. In the shadows of a long, ill-lit room she secretly practiced weaponless combat with another North Hills refugee she had chanced to encounter in a Sink tavern. Shadows lay like velvet over the room in which she found the Blade with another woman, proving the other reason for his name. In shadow she conducted her exploits as her former lover's rival for the title of Emperor of Thieves.

And in all the shadows that lay over her mind, a human skull all of matchless depthless opal yawned its fleshless gleaming jaws and laughed endlessly, telling her it could not be won.

On a bluff above the Great River, Nelerissa crouched bareheaded in the autumn sun, inaudibly humming a popular ballad. At least it had been popular when she'd left the City. In the five months since, that ballad had probably been supplanted a dozen times over by the tunes of other minstrels. How she'd loved living at the heart of the Empire, surging with its every pulsebeat. She'd loved hearing every popular song when it was fresh. She'd loved strolling through markets and shops containing the finest clothes and weapons and curios from every corner of the world. How she'd yearned to live in Areherna when she'd been young! When the Empire had massacred her people she had gone to its capital, not only because the mass of the City's fifty thousand citizens easily absorbed thousands of outlaws and refugees, but because Areherna was the center of the world. In the hustle and bustle of the City, in the struggle to survive and then the struggle to dominate her new profession, she had forgotten all that she had loved about her homeland.

Now, crouching on a cliff-edge in the warmth of the afternoon sun, watching peasants scythe barley as they sang an ancient harvest-tune, she felt as if she were above her own long-gone village. She liked the feeling. Though she surely didn't miss the field labor and innumerable other chores of a poor rural village, she missed the North Hills with sudden, powerful pain.

The tiny village below the bluff was Grathred, the home of the opal skull. She had learned its name and location when she'd awakened from a month of fever-dreams and spell-induced sleep to find herself in a foot-hill village, where she'd been left by the horse-barbarians with the warning that if she died the shaman would know it and they would be back with lances leveled and torches lit. The herbwoman would not let Nelerissa leave the village until she regained all her strength. The herb-woman also saw no reason not to give directions to Grathred when the stranger said she had come on a pilgrimage to see the sacred relic sent by the gods.

Knowing they were the chosen of the gods, the people of Grathred raised their voices in praise as they worked. The slow-melting snow and occasional rains made it possible for crops to be harvested later in the Western Mountains than anywhere else in the Empire, but even here beside the Julukela River this barley-harvest was unusually rich for so late in the season.

Nelerissa Hayseed the master thief knew why the barley crop was bountiful. It was the villagers' belief. Because they believed they had divine help, they were inspired to work all the harder. Seeing their fine crops as further evidence of the gods' favor, they did all they could to keep that blessing. All this made the gods' actual assistance unnecessary.

The villagers' joyful singing and purposeful activity made it clear the opal skull was still in their possession.

The sun's heat was beginning to hurt her scalp. So Nelerissa moved into the shade of a resin-fragrant pine and drew on the dun-colored cloak the herbwoman had given her. Then, hood raised against the sun, she returned to the cliff-edge, to watch the farmerfolk, and study their village, and wait for night.

A forest of beeswax candles formed a crescent behind the one other item on the altar. This object was, in size and shape, in every detail down to the rough tooth-edges, a human skull. Yet it consisted not of yellowed bone but of stone gleaming with gorgeous subtle colors, reds and blues and greens; it was indisputably an opal. An opal of such size and beauty that it could serve as an Emperor's ransom, or make a robber the undisputed Emperor of Thieves.

Nelerissa knelt before the altar examining that for which she had come far and suffered much. It was huge; it was fabulous; it was practically in her hand. It would allow her to retire in tremendous wealth, her reputation secure for all time. What did that count for?

Her searching eyes found no evidence of physical traps and snares, as they had found none at the entrance of the small wood church. But there were other dangers. For the second time in as many minutes, Nelerissa sank into the trance all North Hillfolk had been taught.

Nelerissa had an advantage most Hillfolk had not. In the deepest level of the trance she could see magic. Because of this she had been apprenticed to a shaman. She had learned little more than tricks for unbinding spells when the Empire had invaded. Pure luck had preserved her life and freedom; the ability to see and disarm spells had helped her become one of the greatest thieves in Areherna history.

The thief knew the skull-shaped opal of Grathred had not been sent by the Gods. The best opals in the world came from the slopes of the dead volcanos on the far side of the Western Mountains; the first Imperial Army to reach the eastern edge of the range had even found human bone turned not to plain gray stone, as in other places, but to opal. They had also found the ultimate source of the Julukela, in hot, evil-smelling mountain springs. For perhaps as long as centuries the opal skull had washed downriver, until it lodged on the bank at Grathred. It was a gorgeous, awe-inspiring, but mundane object.

Mundane, but surely not without magic. The village priest would have laid upon it the most powerful spells he knew. As she entered her trance, Nelerissa expected to find odd-hued flames which burned the opal without consuming, spells to ward off danger; the intricate lace-work of brilliantly colored threads, spells to hold the opal intangibly bound to the altar; the pulsing, bruise-colored radiance of lethal protective spells.

She found no spells.

Astonished, Nelerisssa widened the focus of her con-centration to the small door behind the altar, and all through the nave. She found nothing until she cast back as far as the main entrance and learned that the church was no longer empty save for her; in that doorway, swathed in colorful sheets of enchantment, shone the red flame of another soul. A soul she recognized.

She broke trance and, with the silence of an experi-enced thief or warrior, rose into a crouch facing the entrance and the newcomer. She ran her fingers rapidly down the hilts on her baldric, found what she sought, and laid the throwing-knife on the cloak spread beneath her, then loosened her sword and parrying dagger in their scabbards.

She watched the figure advance slowly along one wall, avoiding the aisle down the middle of the rows of benches. With every step the figure became more clearly defined by the golden candlelight. The heavily ringed hands came first into focus: one gripped the glemaing hilt of a long slim sword; the other held out an amulet dangling on a thong or string. For anyone without Neleris-sa's talent, an amulet was necessary to detect magic. The face came into focus, painfully familiar, more lined than when she'd seen it last but still youthful at thirty-five.

For all his slow-moving caution, the man quickly reached the front of the tiny nave. His expression changed from wariness to awe as his gaze fell upon the huge opal.

"So you're here at last!" Nelerissa cried as she rose up and threw the knife.

The knife stopped an inch from the man's breast and dropped to the floor. Nelerissa was not surprised. As always, the Blade wore magical protection. The beauti-fully wrought but crassly numerous rings on his fingers

were, in actuality, talismanic protection against spells.
The amulets she knew to be hidden in his tunic shielded
him from blades and spears and arrows. The Blade was
named for his ability with the long slender sword at his
side. He was a very good swordsman. But he was not
the best, and knew it, and worried constantly about it.
And he was no magician, with the ability to avoid or
disarm spells. Only Hayseed and the powerful sorcerer
whose services and silence the Blade bought knew that
he spent his ill-got wealth on charms and spells to protect
him from death mundane or magical.

Even when he'd tutored his apprentice thief in blade-
work he had not put aside his amulets and talismans.

As the throwing-knife clattered on the stone floor, the
Blade's right hand raised the sword to guard position
while his left hand deposited the amulet around his neck
without catching the thong on ear or norse and unsheathed
his parrying dagger.

Then, face dark with anger, the Blade advanced
silently on the one who had tried to kill him.

Nelerissa spoke again. "Leave now. I will not let you
take the opal."

"Hayseed, you tried to *kill* me! Has it come down to
this?"

He rushed her.

They crossed swords before the altar.

The Blade's eyes widened in the candlelight. "By
Resdren, Nel, what happened to your hair?"

Nelerissa pressed the attack, her sword flickering for
his throat. He parried automatically.

"Your head's all scarred!" Her scalp from brow to
neck was a mass of glassy white and rough pink flesh.
"Oh, gods, Nel—"

Her thrust was a feint; her swordpoint dropped toward
his crotch. His sword swept down to deflect hers, while
his dagger blocked her left-hand thrust. She altered the
angle of her dagger-blade to stab his left wrist while her
sword shot for his heart. Her dagger stopped on air as if
on stone, while her sword was wrenched from her grasp

by a quick twist of the Blade's wrist. The steel blade rang on the stone floor.

Though he'd sounded shocked and sorrowed by Nelerissa's burn-scars, the Blade did not stop when he had the advantage. He caught her dagger between his dagger's blade and quillon as he thrust his sword for her bare throat and said, "Only one of us may return to the City."

The sword reached its target to find the target gone.

The second the Blade's dagger had locked her own, Nelerissa had released the hilt and leapt sideways. From the Blade's right she kicked, twice, with all her strength. Her foot connected with swordarm, then jaw. Before the dislodged sword struck the floor, before even the crack of the neck's breaking faded, she had moved to another place, her arms up in guard position.

The Blade collapsed like a puppet whose strings had been severed.

The people of Areherna knew how to punch and kick, but they were brawlers; they had no art, they did not know how to use their bodies as weapons. But this knowledge had done Nelerissa's people little good against ten thousand Imperial infantrymen and a hundred Army wizards; they had been massacred. A few escaped and a few were enslaved; the latter all died or escaped within months of being brought to the City. The Empire decided North Hillfolk made poor slaves, and continued to believe that Northerners who fought without weapons were a myth, like the Southerners who were said to carry their heads in the hands, or to not have heads at all, wearing their faces on their bellies.

So the Blade had never seriously considered spending the remnants of his money on protection from unarmed attack. A swift sword was adequate defense against an unarmed foe.

The Blade stared up at Nelerissa from where he lay flat on his back. His head was jerking. His body was motionless. Blood stained his lips as he gasped, "You said . . . not true. . . ."

"Of course I told you it wasn't true," Nelerissa said. When he'd questioned her about the legends of weaponless combat she'd acted like she didn't know what he was talking about. And through grim discipline and iron will she had kept her body from betraying its training when they'd drilled with sword and dagger. "I was young and stupid when I came to the City, but not stupid enough to betray my people's ancient knowledge."

"Can't move," the Blade said. His voice was weak, wavering, barely audible. "Ah, gods. You broke my neck."

"Ven, I warned you to leave," Nelerissa said, and realized her voice was thick. She'd known she would probably have to kill him for this prize, and hadn't been grieved by the thought. So why was her throat filling and her eyes watering?

"Kill me, Nel," said the Blade, who so feared death that he gave a sorcerer all his fortunes to buy protection. "I can't live like this."

It would be a mercy, Nelerissa knew. But she just stood staring at her handiwork.

"Kill me!"

Nelerissa knelt and placed a hand on the Blade's cheek. "Farewell, Venetes," she said, leaning her face close to his, and with a single quick motion of her free hand she drew a stiletto and pierced his heart.

He died instantly. She closed his eyes with her fingers, then withdrew her stiletto from his heart and wiped the blade on the inside of her cloak. She sheathed the stiletto, and her sword and dagger. She drew in a shuddering breath.

She stepped up to the altar and raised the skull in her hand. She stared into the empty black sockets.

What was the worth of the opal? Was it the wealth of an Emperor? The value of a reputation? The life of a man? The faith of a village?

The small door behind the altar opened and a man rushed in, his priest's robes swirling around his ankles. He must have been awakened by the clash of arms or by the Blade's cry of death. He reached the altar before he saw Nelerissa and froze. His eyes kept shifting, looking up and down; his attention was torn between the sacred relic in her hand and the scarred tissue of her head.

She held out the opal skull. "You laid no spells over this! Do you think the gods sent it only to see it stolen?" She half-turned, pointing with her empty hand, and cried, "Look!"

Mindful of the blazing forest of candles, the priest did not lean over the altar but stepped around it. He gasped.

"This man came to steal the gift the gods gave to Grathred. But I stopped him. The gods have sent me to protect Their gift and watch over your village."

The priest staggered forward a step, then went to his knees, resting his brow on the floor. "All praise to the gods!"

He spoke a quick, passionate prayer, then straightened to look upon the woman.

She pointed again at the body. "Do you think this man is the only one who'll ever come to Grathred seeking to steal the gods' gift? I have come to teach your people how to stand against thieves and other rogues."

"But—but we have no weapons!" the priest stuttered. "We have only a few daggers and spears. Would you teach us to fight with sickles and mallets?"

"I shall teach you the secret art of fighting without weapons."

The priest bowed low again, but kept his head up, looking at Nelerissa. His experession was suffused with awe. "O servant of the Divine, you may stay in Grathred for as long as the gods allow!"

"I accept," said Nelerissa Hayseed, and so, once again, began a new life based on a deception, but a life of greater use than the one she'd found she had left in Areherna.

RETIREMENT PLAN
by Margaret Howes

One thing I always try to do is to end these anthologies
with something short and funny; and, as usual, it's by a
first-time writer. (Writers older in this business seem to
have their best ideas at 7500 words and up and I'm
always hurting for the shorter lengths; so much so that
I tell young writers that the best way to make a first sale
to me is with something *short and funny*.) I can't resist
something that's both short and funny; so little of Sword
and Sorcery is.

Margaret Howes says that "This is my first professional sale unless you want to count three stories in *The
Tolkien Scrapbook*." (Well, no, I don't). "As for biography, I am retired myself, and now I tell stories in the
Society for Creative Anachronism, take my granddaugh-
ter to events, and try to write, mostly science fiction.
However, I *have* wondered about the later lives of some
of those brawny heroes, female *or* male, if they survive
long enough to have the effects of their careers catch
up with them."

Me, too. I guess women's sword and sorcery has
come of age. We're catching up with the (iconoclastic)
male heroes; even John Wayne made a movie about an
aging gunfighter (THE SHOOTIST). And now the women
are starting. Well, we all get old—a process made tolera-
ble only by the unpleasantness of the alternative.

Yngilda woke, and suppressed a groan. After a very good meal they had given her the best bed at the inn, and it was much too comfortable to leave. Why did I ever get into this business, she wondered. My parents were ready to arrange a perfectly respectable marriage for me, and I might have raised a family of children to take care of me in my old age. She snuggled down for a few more moments, pulling the blankets over her shoulders, and sighed. No use putting it off. It was well before dawn, but the villagers could be gathering even now, waiting for a look at the hero who had come to slay the dragon.

She pushed away the blankets and sat up, stretching her left leg, easing the bad knee. Then she hung her head down, pulling on the sore spot in her lower back. She stood up and stretched all over, first with caution, then more smoothly as her joints and muscles loosened. Using cloth strips, she carefully bound her left knee and right elbow. Finally she splashed cold water from the basin on her face, rinsing her eyes well.

Arming was a slower process, too, than it had been years before. Boots, padding and leg harness, the thick gambeson and haubergeon. She wouldn't pull up the mail coif and don helm and gauntlets until she approached the dragon's territory, but the padded undercap conveniently hid her gray hair.

Sure enough when she left the inn, fully accoutered, most of the people were there raising a ragged cheer. She drew herself erect and lifted her head, responding to their cheers with a pose of conscious gallantry. They didn't need to know what an effort it took these days, or how precisely she set herself before swinging into the saddle on Briand, her black stallion. To them she was still Yngilda, the glorious dragon slayer.

Later, riding away from the village, she felt guilty about her slothful thoughts before rising. Clearly these people were desperately poor. All of them must have contributed to give her the best food and bedding they had left. The dragon had not killed a human within living memory, but it took a regular toll of their livestock. She had passed a field where one man dragged a plow, guided by another. They were slowly being starved out.

On the other hand, she asked herself, have I simply raised false hopes in these people? I don't know if I'll even be able to kill this dragon. I'm not what I used to be. Still fairly trim and hard muscled, St. Michael be praised, but reflexes slowing down, the bad knee and elbow, the scars that ache in cold weather, and I plain don't have the endurance any more. If I can do it on the first pass, maybe. If not, they'll just have to get themselves another dragon slayer.

Her last fight, more than a year ago, had been a near thing; and that was a young, inexperienced dragon. This one was said to be old, and extremely wise.

But now she had ridden long enough to work out the morning aches and pains. She straightened up, settling comfortably into the rhythm of Briand's powerful stride, knowing she could never have endured the stuffy life of castle or manor, dealing with family squabbles. This was what she loved, and nothing could ever replace it. Riding out on a fine crisp morning, with the sun just clearing the horizon, the birds singing, and the clean air of the open country in her nostrils. Clean? She sniffed, hard. Yes, now she could detect a faint sulphurous reek. She reined Briand in, and looked about her. From what they told her in the village, she should be nearing the dragon's lair. On each side were the stony outcrops they described, although there was more vegetation than she would have expected. Perhaps it was farther on? No use taking any risks, not at her age. She donned coif and helm, pulled on her gauntlets, loosened her sword in the scabbard, set lance and shield at ready, and rode on alertly.

Then the dragon came! It seemed to explode straight out of the rocky hillside, soaring in a tight circle, then stooping for the kill. She ducked under her shield and gripped her lance, but her elbow collapsed and the lance fell to the ground. Yngilda took a blast of heat and knew she was dead. A moment later, she knew she wasn't. Incredulously, she searched the air for the dragon, then discovered it down on the ground not far away. One wing was splayed out at an awkward angle. She felt a thrill of triumph. One more dragon! Now for a hard charge on Briand, with lance in rest, except that this time she couldn't do it. And the dragon would rise for another stoop . . . it didn't. There was something strange about the behavior of this dragon; why was it down? She looked it over carefully. The scales were dull; many were cracking. That great wing was torn at the edges. Half the claws of one foot were missing. She risked a glance into the dragon's eyes, that mistake every young would-be dragon slayer was warned against so strictly. They were misty, dim windows onto dying fires.

Now the dragon opened its terrible jaws, and gave forth a wave of heat, a cloud of dark smoke, and a few flickering flames. Yngilda's mouth quivered with the beginnings of laughter. It wasn't pity she felt. It was fellowship.

"Dragon!" she called.

No answer.

She spoke formally. "By St. George and St. Michael, I command you: answer me!"

The sound thrummed in the air, deep and weary. "I hear you."

"Dragon, your scales are dull. Your fires burn low. You have grown old."

"So have you." A tinge of amusement there. "You had better flee quickly, human. Soon I will be able to fly again, and I'll kill you yet."

"I don't intend to flee," Yngilda said tartly. "I should go back without even a singe and tell them I've given up? I'd live out my life as a laughing stock and a pauper to boot. I can still swing my sword left-handed and deal some hard blows. But why should we try to kill each other? Will you stop plaguing the poor villagers? Why do you do it? If you kill me and live, they will only send for a younger, stronger fighter."

The dragon rumbled.

"My wings aren't what they used to be, but when the wind is good I can still soar all day long. I want to live, and take the air. I haven't touched the humans in the village. The cattle and sheep are tastier, anyway."

Yngilda understood. She pondered for a little, then laughed out loud.

"Dragon, west of here is a mountain valley full of fat deer. On the outer slopes of the mountain are prosperous villages, many of them, with plenty of cattle and sheep. If I lead you there, will you leave this place? You can take as many deer as you like, and a few sheep and cattle now and then from each village in turn. There are caves in those mountains. You can easily find one for yourself, and I'll find another and set myself up—I don't care to stay in towns or villages either. Kill a deer for me, when I need it, or some other meat. I'll keep the villagers assured that you will never take more than they can spare. Then you can still soar, for as long as your life lasts, and I can live, too, and ride."

"Do you know how much *they* will think they can spare?"

"Surely you can be reasonable, and I'll tell them you are too terrible to attack. They'll believe *me*."

Silence for a while. The dragon cautiously flexed its wings. Yngilda tried her elbow, which was beginning to function again.

"I agree," said the dragon at last. "Human, I am called Raskharr."

"Raskharr, I am called Yngilda."

"I thought you might be." Again the note of amusement.

She dismounted with care, picked up her lance, managed to hang onto it while she mounted again, and set it in its socket. The dragon slowly spread both wings, and lumbered into the air.

Yngilda rode west, humming a tune, with the dragon flying overhead.

DAW

DAW PRESENTS THESE BESTSELLERS BY
MARION ZIMMER BRADLEY

NON-DARKOVER NOVELS

☐ **HUNTERS OF THE RED MOON**   (UE1968—$2.95)
☐ **WARRIOR WOMAN**   (UE2253—$3.50)

NON-DARKOVER ANTHOLOGIES

☐ **SWORD AND SORCERESS I**   (UE2359—$4.50)
☐ **SWORD AND SORCERESS II**   (UE2360—$3.95)
☐ **SWORD AND SORCERESS III**   (UE2302—$4.50)
☐ **SWORD AND SORCERESS IV**   (UE2412—$4.50)
☐ **SWORD AND SORCERESS V**   (UE2288—$3.50)
☐ **SWORD AND SORCERESS VI**   (UE2423—$3.95)
☐ **SWORD AND SORCERESS VII**   (UE2457—$4.50)
☐ **SWORD AND SORCERESS VIII**   (UE2486—$4.50)

COLLECTIONS

☐ **LYTHANDE** (with Vonda N. McIntyre)   (UE2291—$3.95)
☐ **THE BEST OF MARION ZIMMER BRADLEY** (edited
by Martin H. Greenberg)   (UE2268—$3.95)

DAW

BESTSELLERS BY MARION ZIMMER BRADLEY

THE DARKOVER NOVELS

The Founding

☐ DARKOVER LANDFALL UE2234—$3.95

The Ages of Chaos

☐ HAWKMISTRESS! UE2239—$3.95
☐ STORMQUEEN! UE2310—$4.50

The Hundred Kingdoms

☐ TWO TO CONQUER UE2174—$3.50
☐ THE HEIRS OF HAMMERFELL UE2451—$4.95
☐ THE HEIRS OF HAMMERFELL (hardcover) UE2395—$18.95

The Renunciates (Free Amazons)

☐ THE SHATTERED CHAIN UE2308—$3.95
☐ THENDARA HOUSE UE2240—$3.95
☐ CITY OF SORCERY UE2332—$4.50

Against the Terrans: The First Age

☐ THE SPELL SWORD UE2237—$3.95
☐ THE FORBIDDEN TOWER UE2373—$4.95

Against the Terrans: The Second Age

☐ THE HERITAGE OF HASTUR UE2413—$4.50
☐ SHARRA'S EXILE UE2309—$4.99

THE DARKOVER ANTHOLOGIES with The Friends of Darkover

☐ DOMAINS OF DARKOVER UE2407—$3.95
☐ FOUR MOONS OF DARKOVER UE2305—$3.95
☐ FREE AMAZONS OF DARKOVER UE2430—$3.95
☐ THE KEEPER'S PRICE UE2236—$3.95
☐ LERONI OF DARKOVER UE2494—$4.99
☐ THE OTHER SIDE OF THE MIRROR UE2185—$3.50
☐ RED SUN OF DARKOVER UE2230—$3.95
☐ RENUNCIATES OF DARKOVER UE2469—$4.50
☐ SWORD OF CHAOS UE2172—$3.50

A note concerning:

THE FRIENDS OF DARKOVER

So popular have been the novels of the planet Darkover that an organization of readers and fans has come into being, virtually spontaneously. Several meetings have been held at major science fiction conventions, and more recently specially organized around the various "councils" of the Friends of Darkover, as the organization is now known.

The Friends of Darkover is purely an amateur and voluntary group. It has no paid officers and has not established any formal membership dues. Although the members of the Thendara Council of the Friends no longer publish a newsletter or any other publications themselves, they serve as a central point for information on Darkover-oriented newsletters, fanzines, and councils and maintain a chronological list of Marion Zimmer Bradley's books.

Contact may be made by writing to the Friends of Darkover, Thendara Council, Box 72, Berkeley, CA 94701, and enclosing a SASE (Self-Addressed Stamped Envelope) for information.

MARION ZIMMER BRADLEY'S FANTASY MAGAZINE

Fans of Marion Zimmer Bradley will be pleased to hear that she is now publishing her own fantasy magazine. If you're interested in subscribing and/or would like to submit material to it, write her at:

P.O. Box 249
Berkeley, CA 94701

(If you're interested in writing for the magazine, please enclose a SASE for her free Writer's Guidelines.)

(These notices are inserted gratis as a service to readers. DAW Books is in no way connected with these organizations professionally or commercially.)